The fiery brill

on the cover is
tionary process
waves in diamon
inch. No print o
radiant glow of

So look for th[e] ... Heart whenever you buy a historical romance. It is a shimmering reflection of our guarantee that you'll find consistent quality between the covers!

BLUE FIRE

His eyes were terrible, like blue fire, and she could almost feel the scorching flames. She backed up another step and then another as he continued menacingly toward her. She hit the bed and went sprawling across it.

She realized how vulnerable she was and scrambled to her feet just as he reached her.

"Do you know I could have killed you?" he asked, grabbing her arms and hauling her against his chest.

"Are . . . are you going to hurt me?" she asked, ashamed of the way her voice quavered but unable to help it.

Her question startled him. He buried his face in her hair, inhaling the scent of sunshine and woman that was uniquely Angelica. Hurt her? How could she even think such a thing?

Suddenly finding her mouth was all that mattered, that and tasting her. . . .

Angelica clung to him, starved for the honey of his kiss. It felt so natural to be in his arms. This was where she belonged, and now he knew it, too. His hands were everywhere, stroking and caressing, robbing her of strength and will and even reason. When her legs would no longer hold her, she sank backward, carrying him with her onto the bed. . . .

ZEBRA BOOKS
KENSINGTON PUBLISHING CORP.

ZEBRA BOOKS

are published by

Kensington Publishing Corp.
475 Park Avenue South
New York, NY 10016

First printing: August, 1988

Printed in the United States of America

With gratitude to my superagent, Cherry Weiner,
who has more faith in me than I do in myself,
and
To Nira, Phyllis, and Susan for being there.

Prologue

"Throw down your guns and come out before you fry! We won't shoot!" a voice called from outside the shack.

"Like hell you won't," Kid Collins muttered furiously, shoving the last three cartridges into his Colt Peacemaker and blinking rapidly to clear his vision. The smoke inside the cabin was getting thick. They'd set the roof on fire to drive him out. He glanced up and judged that he only had a few more minutes before the entire thing collapsed on him.

A bullet thunked into the windowsill above his head, but he did not bother to return the fire. With only three bullets left, he would have to be sparing. He pulled the silk scarf that he wore around his neck up over his nose and mouth to help filter the air so he could breathe.

The Kid knew he had only one chance and that one was slim at best. If Midnight, the horse he had ridden to town that morning, had not been frightened too far away by the sound of gunfire, then he might yet get out of this alive. And he *had* to get out of this alive. He couldn't let these men get away with murder.

The Kid glanced over to where the two bodies lay. Pete was sprawled on the floor exactly where he had fallen when the stray bullet had penetrated his brain. His homely face bore a look of eternal surprise as he stared unseeing at the burning ceiling. Rose was on the bed where the Kid had laid her after carrying her inside.

Less than an hour ago she had stood in the doorway of the cabin, smiling and waving a greeting to him as he returned from his trip to town. For one awful moment, the Kid relived that scene, Rose smiling, the sound of a gunshot, her body crumpling as blood stained the front of her dress scarlet. He had vaulted from his horse, running and firing at the unseen assailant as he went. Pete had come racing from the barn, but they were too late.

"My baby!" Rose had cried in despair, cradling the small mound of her pregnancy even as her life's blood poured from her. By the time the Kid laid her on the bed, she was dead.

He hated to leave them like this, knowing what would happen when the roof collapsed. Rose was his sister, the only family he had had left, and it seemed a sacrilege to let her burn.

"Hey, Ace, maybe they're all dead," a voice outside theorized.

"Why don't you go in there and find out," Ace replied sarcastically.

"Yeah, come right on in," the Kid whispered, pulling his lips back in a feral grin. "Give me a target. Just one target . . ."

But no one seemed willing to test the theory, and no target appeared. The Kid heard an ominous creaking from above. He would have to make his move soon.

Reaching up under the scarf that covered his face, he stuck two fingers in his mouth, drew a deep breath and whistled shrilly. "Come on, Midnight," he urged, squinting through the smoke for sight of the horse he had trained so carefully over the years.

"They don't sound dead to me," one of the ambushers called, and another volley of shots struck the house.

The Kid ducked, not daring to waste any of his precious ammunition, and listened, his ears straining for the sound of running hooves. At first he thought he was imagining it, but then he heard the shout of surprise from the ambushers as Midnight raced into the clearing in front of the house.

With one last look at his sister and her husband, he whispered, "Good-bye, Rose," and charged out the door. Operating on instinct, he snapped off two of his remaining shots at his attackers to cover himself as he gathered Midnight's reins and leaped into the saddle. Vaguely, he felt something strike him in the side, but he spurred the gelding viciously just as the cabin's roof collapsed with a roar.

Too late, he realized he was heading in the wrong direction, away from town and any help he might find there. He tried to recall what lay in this direction, where he might go to escape his pursuers, but his brain seemed suddenly sluggish and unable to function. For a moment his vision blurred, and he shook his head frantically to clear it.

What was wrong? Why couldn't he think? And then he felt the pain, hot and searing, low on his left side. Damn, he'd been hit. How badly, he could not tell, but he could feel warm blood running down to soak his jeans.

Just stay in the saddle, he told himself over and over. Midnight's thundering hooves pounded the prairie as they raced along, sending waves of agony washing over him. He stuffed his Colt into its holster so he could use both hands to hold on to the saddle.

Behind him he heard the attackers gaining on him. Already Midnight was straining. The horse would not be able to keep up this pace much longer. Once again the Kid's vision blurred, and once again he shook his head to clear it.

Not like this, he thought wildly, not after all he'd been through. Not gunned down by strangers, men who didn't even know who he was, who killed him only because he had chosen to help some poor squatters. And he couldn't die without avenging Rose's death.

But it was too late. His vision blurred yet again and when he cleared it, he saw the Comanches up ahead. They had come for him, and now they sat their horses, still and silent, waiting till he reached them. Unable to stop himself, he rode on and on, straight toward the savage phantoms.

He knew they were phantoms. Comanches no longer roamed the Texas plains. They had been penned up on reservations years ago. He stared at the specters. Was his father with them? Was he sitting there among the stony-faced Indians, grinning at the thought of taking his son back with him to hell? The Kid squinted, but he couldn't see his father. No matter. If he went to hell, he would see the old man soon enough.

Shouts. Someone behind him was shouting a warning. Could they see the Indians, too? Were ghosts visible even to living men, or were his pursuers justly going to join him in perdition? The thought made him jubilant. Drawing a painful breath, he risked letting go of the saddle horn for one quick second to brush the scarf away from his face and let wail a Comanche war cry.

Chapter One

Angelica cradled the shotgun carefully as she watched the Indians riding into the ranch yard. Fear sparked along her nerve ends, a reaction as natural as breathing to a person who had lived most of her nineteen years in fear of a Comanche raid. But reason whispered another, saner message, and so she stood her ground at the front door of her Spanish-style home—a home that had been built like a fortress to withstand Indian assaults—instead of running for cover as she would once have done.

"What do they want? Why are they off the Reservation?" a disgruntled voice inquired from inside the partially open front door.

"I haven't the faintest idea, Mamacita," Angelica replied impatiently. "Just keep that rifle ready in case they try anything." Meanwhile, her mind was racing. How long had it been since she had even seen a Comanche? How long since the sight of a full moon—a raiding moon—had filled her heart with dread? A long time, but apparently not long enough, she realized. It would take more than the passing of years to cure her of her inbred wariness of these strange and dangerous people.

She shifted the shotgun to cover one of the men, who had separated from the group and was riding forward.

He lifted a bronzed hand and said, "Greetings, Burns-like-embers."

Angelica blinked in surprise at the Indian name that had been given her so many years ago. No one had ever called her that to her face except the little Indian girl she had played with on the reservation during the few times she had gone there with her father to deliver beef. That little Indian girl was long since dead, a victim of one of the "civilized" diseases. No one else even knew the name except . . . Angelica stared at the Indian, and slowly recognition dawned. "Black Bear, is that you?"

The man nodded, his long black hair stirring gently in the spring breeze. Angelica somehow managed to choke back the gasp that rose in her throat. What had happened to the fierce young warrior who had chastened his younger sister for playing with a white girl? The haunted scarecrow before her bore little resemblance to the young man she remembered. He would be no more than ten years older than she, but he looked much older, and she realized that the years of suffering when he and a handful of other renegades had dodged the soldiers across the barren Staked Plains had taken their toll.

She let her gaze run over the rest of the group. Obviously a hunting party, the men were dressed in a ragged combination of traditional Comanche garb and reservation-issued clothing. The weapons they carried appeared to be either castoffs or treasured souvenirs of a better time. Even their horses were scrubs. Black Bear, who might once have owned hundreds of prize mounts, now rode a scruffy bangtail.

But she knew better than to express her pity to a proud Comanche warrior. The fact that she and her people had conquered him was enough. She would not gloat. Instead she managed a small smile. "What brings you here, so far from your new home?"

Black Bear did not return the smile. In fact, his somber

expression grew almost angry, and Angelica realized she had accidentally implied that Black Bear was playing the renegade once again. "We are hunting," he said, almost defensively, and then added, as if reluctant to admit such a thing was necessary, "The army gave us permission to leave the reservation and hunt buffalo."

"Buffalo!" Angelica was aghast. There were no buffalo! The hide hunters had exterminated them years ago. How long since she had seen even a single one of the shaggy beasts? Longer even than since she had seen a Comanche. "The buffalo are gone," she told him, wondering how she could explain the unexplainable. But he had said the army had given permission for this hunt. Surely, they knew how fruitless it would be. Surely, the Indian agents knew. Surely . . .

"We will find them," Black Bear said with impatient certainty. "Where is your father, Burns-like-embers?" he asked, dismissing the topic of buffalo. "I would speak with him."

Angelica waited for the pain that always came with mention of her father and was relieved to note that this time it was only a dull ache. After a second, she was able to explain, "He died last fall."

Black Bear nodded his understanding. "He was a brave man," the Indian said, granting his old enemy the greatest praise he knew.

Angelica smiled slightly, recalling the time this man had spared her father's life in a battle because her father had often delivered beef to the reservation.

Before she could mention it, however, Black Bear spoke again. "I would speak with your husband, then."

Angelica hesitated a moment and then gave a mental shrug. If Black Bear and his friends had meant them harm, they would have ridden up shooting. There was no reason to hide the truth from them. "I have no husband, Black Bear," she admitted finally, wondering how the Indian would accept the news that a female of marriageable age not only lived alone but operated a large ranch by herself. In the Comanche culture, an unmarried woman would starve if she had no male to care for her.

Black Bear was shocked, but he covered it well, and for the first time his weathered face showed some hint of amusement as he looked her over from head to toe. He was, she knew, looking for some indication of why no man had found her suitable as a wife, and she waited uncomfortably, wondering what flaw he would decide had prevented her from finding a husband. Undoubtedly, he would think her unusual hair a drawback, but he would probably consider her excessive height an advantage. A tall, strong woman would be capable of much work. The wind whipped a lock of her red-gold hair across her eyes, the hair that had inspired her Indian name, and she brushed it aside, lowering the shotgun as she did so.

"It is too bad that no white man has chosen you, Burns-like-embers," Black Bear decided at last, still looking slightly amused. "I would offer you a place in my lodge, but I already have two wives, and they fight all the time. I have no wish to hear another woman screaming."

Angelica felt a stirring of wrath at his teasing, but he did not pause for her response.

"It is not good for a woman to be alone, so I have brought you a man, Burns-like-embers," he announced with what could only be called a smirk. He made a swift gesture with his hand, and one of the braves kicked his pony into motion. For a second, Angelica had the awful feeling that he had instructed one of his men to kidnap her. How humiliating to be captured by the Comanche at this late date, when she had spent the better part of her nineteen years eluding them. But then she saw that the Indian was leading another horse, an animal of far higher quality than any the Indians were riding, an animal carrying a white man's saddle and drawing a travois.

As the horse drew up parallel to the house, she saw that the travois carried a man. A white man. "Good heavens!" she exclaimed as she took in his pale face and his bloodstained clothing. Forgetting any thought of danger to herself, she deposited the shotgun on the ground and hurried to the travois. "Mama!" she called over her shoulder. "Mamacita!"

But there was no need to call. Maria was at her side in an instant. "Who is he? Do you know him?" the Mexican woman asked.

Angelica shook her head as she smoothed golden hair off the man's forehead to test his temperature. His skin was clammy, though not cold, but he did not respond to her touch. He was probably in shock, but at least he was alive. Maria was less gentle. She nudged Angelica aside and lifted the man's eyelid.

"He is alive," she decreed while Angelica noted that she had never seen an eye quite so blue.

Angelica turned to Black Bear. "Who . . . What . . . Did you . . . ?" She could not decide on a way to frame her question that would not offend the Indian.

He seemed to understand her dilemma and stiffened proudly. "No, we did not shoot him," he told her with disdain. "We are hunting, and we hear them coming. This man," he gestured toward the travois, "and six others chasing him. He rides to us and the others run away."

Angelica closed her eyes for a moment, overcome by a sudden weariness at this news. Trouble and more trouble. Were Snyder's men shooting people down in broad daylight now? Where would it all end? She forced herself to remember where she was, however, and opened her eyes once again. "It was good of you to bring him here," she said.

But her intended compliment offended Black Bear. He bristled angrily. "It was not goodness!" he told her bitterly. "The army follows us around, watching so we do not steal any horses or cattle. What would they think if they found a dead white man?"

Angelica knew a pang of sadness for this proud man who had been brought so low. He was right, of course. If a white man were found dead, the Indians were bound to be blamed and summarily hung by the settlers who had spent most of the last two decades in fear of their lives from the Comanche. How sad that Black Bear was moved to an act of compassion only by fear of his own life. "If the army, or anyone else, asks you any questions, just send them here to me. I'll explain everything."

Black Bear nodded grimly. "I know we can trust your father. That is why we come here."

"You can trust me, too," Angelica assured him. He nodded once more and then abruptly turned his horse, kicking it into motion. In another instant the yard was empty of Indians, only the echo of their ponies' hooves indicating they had ever been there.

Angelica glanced down at the man on the travois. Thank heaven Robbie wasn't here to see the poor fellow like this. Her brother was far too young to have witnessed as much suffering as he already had. Seeing both his parents die had been unavoidable. At least he would be spared this.

Maria sighed, loud and long, and Angelica knew the sigh was a combination of relief that the Indians were gone and despair over the man they had left. "Handsome devil, isn't he?" Angelica observed to her foster mother with some irony. And he would be, too, under better circumstances. If his golden hair were combed, and he had a little color in his cheeks, he would be positively beautiful. Even in his present dilapidated condition, he was the best-looking man Angelica could ever remember seeing.

Maria grunted. "What do we do with him now?"

Angelica considered this as she met her foster mother's dark gaze. "I guess we could put him in Papa's room for the time being." Maria's reaction was disapproving, judging from the way she planted her hands belligerently on her ample hips, but Angelica pointed to the man's long legs. "He'll dangle off any of the other beds," she said reasonably, and at last, Maria agreed.

Angelica made a remark about how ungentlemanly the Indians were not to have offered to carry their "gift" into the house, but Maria replied that she did not want any filthy savages in the house anyway. After a brief discussion of the problems presented by the very tall stranger, the two women decided to let the horse carry him at least as far as the interior courtyard of the house. Although Maria had some prejudices about Comanches in her house, she would tolerate an animal, at least for a brief time.

The ranch house was built in the mission style, a large rectangle with thick adobe walls and narrow windows on the outside for protection. Inside was a courtyard onto which all the rooms opened. It was to this courtyard that the women led the horse and its burden.

Maria was as strong as her well-padded figure indicated, and Angelica was equally capable, but they still had their hands full getting their visitor into what had once been Angelica's father's bedroom. Using the travois as a stretcher, they finally managed to get him into the bedroom, where they laid him on the floor. While Angelica went after hot water and bandages, Maria undressed him.

When Angelica returned, Maria sent her away again, reminding her how improper it was for an unmarried girl to see a man undressed. Knowing a small sense of disappointment, Angelica contented herself with tending to his horse, which she took back outside and turned loose in one of the corrals after she had unsaddled it and rubbed it down.

By then she had begun to wonder anew who the stranger might be, so she took the liberty of looking through his saddlebags for some clue. She found the bags surprisingly empty of the type of supplies a traveler would be carrying, like spare clothes and food. Instead she found only a letter. She glanced at the name on the envelope, and without hesitation, since the envelope had already been opened, she pulled out the letter.

"Dear Kid," it read in an elaborately female handwriting. "I hope this letter finds you well and happy." So much for that, Angelica thought with an ironic smile, picturing the unconscious man the Indians had delivered. "We all miss you very much, especially Colleen, who cries for you every day. You know she expects you to marry her when you return. We all hope that will be soon." Of course, Angelica thought. A man that handsome would certainly leave a trail of broken hearts behind him. "Cole and Miles send their regards. We all pray this trouble with your sister can be settled quickly, but Cole says to remind you that if you need help, you must send for him and the men.

"It almost broke my heart to cut your beautiful hair before you left, but I saved it all and have woven it into a wreath. Cole was angry when I told him it was a 'mourning' wreath, but I explained that a true mourning wreath is made from hair of the deceased's friends. In this case, we are only mourning because we miss you and long for your return."

The letter went on with news of happenings around the ranch, including the information that baby Sean, whoever that might be, had started to talk. Then she read the last paragraph. "Please let us know if we can be of any help to you. Our prayers are with you. I remain, your devoted friend, Rachel McKinsey Elliot."

Elliot, Elliot, now where had she heard that name? Long blond hair. Miles and Cole. Cole Elliot? "Dear Kid?" Yes, of course! Angelica glanced at the name on the front of the envelope again, and all the pieces of the puzzle fell into place. The man in her father's bedroom was Kid Collins! "Oh, thank you! Thank you!" she murmured prayerfully as she raced back into the house.

Grateful that there was no one around to see her unladylike dash, Angelica slid to a halt on the smooth tiles outside her father's old bedroom and threw open the door. "Mama! Do you know . . . ?"

Her words strangled in her throat at the sight of the first naked man she had ever seen. Still stretched out in repose on the floor, he was magnificent. Tall and straight and firmly muscled, his body was liberally sprinkled with the same golden hair she had admired on his head. The hair was thicker on his chest, and she let her fascinated gaze drift down to where it thinned and then thickened yet again.

"Oh, my," she murmured in the instant before Maria threw a towel over his loins.

"Madre de Dios! I told you to stay out of here!" Maria exclaimed furiously, struggling to her feet so she could shoo the girl back out the door.

But Angelica was still staring at the beautiful stranger, noticing that the white bandage Maria had wound around his waist was whiter than the towel that covered his . . . "Oh, Mama, are they all . . ." she made an ineffectual gesture with her hand, "like that?"

Maria muttered something profane. "I do not know," she snapped. "I have not seen them *all.*"

Maria's sarcastic tone instantly drew Angelica's wayward attention and reminded her how improperly she was behaving. She felt her cheeks burning with chagrin. How easily she slipped out of her carefully practiced role as lady of the house. It had begun with simply running like a child through the courtyard and ended with gaping at a naked man. She would have to be careful not to run like that anymore, she told herself sternly. There was no telling where such intemperance might lead! She tried to look repentant. "Sorry," she ventured, failing miserably.

"Out with you," Maria commanded in her no-nonsense-tolerated voice.

And that reminded Angelica that she had a very good reason for being there. "Do you know who he is?" she demanded, pointing toward the man on the floor but discreetly refraining from looking at him again.

Maria made an impatient noise, but Angelica ignored it. "He's Kid Collins!"

Maria was unimpressed.

"Kid Collins, the gunfighter! Oh, Mama, don't you see? He's the answer to our prayers!" Angelica sobered respectfully. "The Virgin sent him to us," she said, crossing herself.

Maria scowled in disapproval. "I think you forget you are a Methodist, *Angelita,* and besides, I do not think the Virgin knows any gunfighters."

Angelica found this argument impossible to counter, so she changed the subject. "He can help us, Mamacita. I know he can."

Maria glanced over her shoulder at the still form on the floor, "If he lives," she cautioned.

A shiver of dread danced down Angelica's spine. "How badly is he hurt?"

Maria shrugged. "The bullet passed through just above his hip. I do not think it hit anything important, but I cannot be sure. And then there is the possibility of infection. If the fever gets too bad . . ."

Angelica nodded. She knew how dangerous a bullet wound could be. Even a minor one could fester and kill. "Well, we'd better get him up on the bed before he catches pneumonia lying on the floor," she said practically. She took a step toward him, but Maria grabbed her arm.

"First you will go outside, and I will put some clothes on him. *Then* we will put him in the bed," she said, drawing the girl toward the door.

Angelica managed to cast one last look at the stranger over Maria's shoulder before being hustled out. "You never did answer my question," she wickedly reminded her former nurse before Maria could close the door in her face.

Angelica saw Maria start to chasten her again but then

change her mind. The Mexican woman's dark eyes narrowed, and she smiled mysteriously. "The answer is no, they are not all . . . *like that.* And you better hope this one," she gestured toward the man on the floor, "never gets you or you will be crying for your *mamacita,* for sure!"

When the door slammed, Angelica stood staring at it for quite a while, wondering if her Mamacita was right.

Kid Collins lay very still for a long time, listening to the silence. When he was certain that he was alone, he opened his eyes. Just a crack at first, so he could verify that he was, indeed, lying in a bed.

It was a big four-poster bed, so big that for the first time in his life he could stretch out full-length and not hang off over the edge. Surprise widened his eyes, and then he saw the rest of the room. The furniture was, like the bed, oversized and purely masculine, the wood dark and polished to a brilliant shine. Heavy velvet drapes hung at the windows, letting in just a trace of late afternoon sunlight. How was that possible? The last he remembered, the sun had been directly overhead. Could so many hours have passed without his knowledge?

Or perhaps there was no more time for him. In a searing flash he recalled everything—Rose and Pete, the gunfight, the burning cabin, his race for freedom, the blood pouring down his side, the Indians, his father . . . Had he really seen his father, or had that been a dream? If he really had seen his father, then he must truly be in hell.

He glanced around again, vaguely amazed that hell should be furnished so elegantly. And except for the burning in his side, there was no evidence of fire. Then the door opened, and he knew he was not in hell at all. Only heaven hasdangels.

"Oh! You're awake!" the angel said and smiled. She seemed delighted. She moved gracefully across the room, pausing at the window to draw back the drapes. Late afternoon sunlight spilled in, turning her hair the color of glowing coals. "How are you feeling? Do you have any pain?" she inquired as she drew closer to the bed. Her slender white hand reached out and touched his face. "You don't seem to have a fever," she decided as her cool fingers softly caressed his cheek.

The Kid stared, not daring even to blink. If this was part of the dream, he didn't want to know it, not right away. He'd never realized that eyes could be so green or that a face could be so lovely it would hurt his heart just to look at it. But the angel's smile began to fade as she watched him, and slowly, she withdrew her hand from his face. "Mr. Collins, are you all right? Can you hear me?" she asked, her growing alarm all too obvious.

He hadn't meant to cause her any trouble. "Yes," he croaked. His voice was rusty from disuse, so he cleared his throat and tried again. "Yes, I'm fine," he said, There, if this *was* a dream, that should wake him up for sure.

The angel smiled again. "How does your side feel? Is it hurting much?"

The Kid considered. It hurt like blazes, now that he noticed. Maybe his theory about hell and angels was wrong. There wasn't any pain in heaven. His mother had told him all about it. She had been dead for almost twenty years, but he remembered that quite clearly. "Yeah, it hurts," he admitted.

"Mama has something that will make you feel better," the angel promised. "You're very lucky, though. The wound doesn't show any signs of getting infected and . . . What's wrong?" She frowned down at him.

He frowned back up at her. What was going on? And why was it taking him so long to figure it out? Maybe he'd been shot in the head, too. He blinked to clear away the last remnants of his fog and glanced around the room again. This was a room, in a house. A very nice house, to be sure, but still a real, honest-to-god house. He looked at her again. She was wearing a calico dress and an apron. The apron had some spots on it, stains that had not washed out. Angels did not wear stained aprons.

"Where am I?" he asked, feeling very suddenly like a total idiot.

The angel's worried frown lightened instantly into a relieved grin. "I'm sorry, I should have told you right away. No wonder you're so confused. You're at my ranch, the Diamond R. The Indians brought you. Do you remember that?"

The Kid nodded slowly. He remembered, all right, relieved to know that the Comanches had been real and not the demons he had thought them. "But what the hell . . . I mean . . ." He faltered, suddenly recalling to whom he was speaking. She might not be an angel, but she was still a lady. Rachel had taught him how to treat ladies, and he knew perfectly well not to swear in front of one. But she seemed undisturbed by his slip.

"I know, you're wondering what they were doing off the reservation. They told me they're on a special pass to hunt buffalo, of all things." She must have seen his surprise, because she explained. "I tried to tell them that there aren't any buffalo anymore, but they either didn't believe me or didn't want to believe me. I just can't believe the army would allow this," she murmured thoughtfully.

The whole story was a little hard for him to accept, especially the part she hadn't mentioned. "Why did they bring me here?" he asked. From what he knew about Comanches, which was plenty, he knew the act could not have been motivated by kindness.

The girl shook her head, making her red-gold hair shimmer. "That's the strangest part. The army is following them around and making sure they don't misbehave. They were afraid that if someone found your body, they'd get the blame, so they brought you here. They trusted my father, so . . ." she shrugged eloquently.

Her father? The Kid searched his memory. She had said this was the Diamond R Ranch. "Your father is Cameron Ross," he determined.

She smiled, obviously pleased that he had figured that out, but then her smile faded again. "My father *was* Cameron Ross," she corrected. "He passed away several months ago."

"I'm sorry," he said, trying to remember everything he knew about Cameron Ross. The man must have been a tough old bird. With the Comanche finally penned up for good on the reservation, settlers were just starting to come to this part of Texas. Cameron Ross had lived here twenty years and was well known all over the state, even as far away as the Circle M Ranch. The Kid had heard tales of him most of his life.

And this girl had lived here for almost twenty years, too, the Kid realized with surprise. He took another long look at her. She was really something special. In spite of the simple calico dress and the stained apron, she carried herself like a queen. When she spoke, her voice was soft and sweet, and her slender hands moved gracefully to accentuate her words. As she looked down at him, her emerald eyes glittered expressively. Even her hair, which was tied carelessly back with a ribbon, proclaimed her different from all other women. In the direct sunlight, it seemed to glow like the embers he had thought of before. Here in the shadow by the bed, it simply gleamed, warm and inviting, as if a man could bury his face in it and find comfort.

He gave himself a mental shake. What on earth was wrong with him to be thinking such fanciful thoughts? Maybe he really had been shot in the head. He lifted a hand to search for telltale bandages.

"Oh, dear," Angelica murmured in dismay when she saw the gesture. The poor man was probably in pain, and here she was babbling on about Indians. "I'll get Mama right away. She can give you something for the pain. And are you hungry?"

As he thought this over, Angelica admired the way his brow crinkled. He really was quite handsome, his features finely molded into near perfection, and he really did have the bluest eyes she had ever seen. She'd noticed that the instant she opened the door. She tried valiantly not to remember how he had looked the other time she had opened the door to this room.

"Yeah, I guess I could eat something," he allowed.

"Good," she said, curling her hand into a fist as she resisted the urge to smooth the golden hair his fingers had mussed. She had touched him several times now, and she found the urge to do so again alarmingly strong, especially when she remembered the texture of his hair and the delicious prickle of his unshaven cheek. For an instant the image of the rest of him flashed into her mind, and she ruthlessly forced it away. In self-defense, she turned with a swish of her skirts. "I'll tell Mama to hurry."

"Miss Ross?"

The sound of her name on his lips startled her. Slowly, she turned back to face him. "Yes?" she asked warily.

"I . . . uh, thanks for taking me in and taking care of me," he said, obviously unaccustomed to speaking his gratitude. Or, she suspected, to being in the position of needing the kind of help she and Mama had given him.

She was about to reassure him that it had been no trouble at all when she saw him glance down and for the first time notice what he was wearing. The blue eyes narrowed and his long fingers plucked suspiciously at the nightshirt that had once belonged to her father. She could almost see his thought process as he imagined someone removing his clothes—all of them—and dressing him in this garment.

Perhaps she found this so easy to do because her own thoughts kept straying in that direction. Once again she pictured him lying naked on the floor. Heat flooded her face just as he lifted his suspicious gaze to her. "Oh, no!" she quickly denied. "I didn't take care of you! It was Mama, she's the one who—" Angelica groped frantically for the proper phrase—"who bandaged your wound and . . . and everything . . ."

She saw something flicker in those bright blue eyes that might have been relief but that might also have been something else entirely. He was, after all, a gunfighter, a man who had lived a very rough life, if the stories she had heard were even half-true. Perhaps he would find the thought of a young woman undressing him very pleasant. The warning her *mamacita* had given her earlier echoed in her ears, and the boldness she had felt when he was unconscious evaporated. Angelica tried to swallow but found her mouth had gone dry. "Well, I . . . I'll get Mama," she said, backing toward the door.

When it slammed behind her, the Kid let out a long, weary sigh. He hadn't been lying; he was in pain, but for a minute there, that had seemed the least of his worries. The thought that this beautiful young woman had been fussing over him while he was unconscious and helpless and yes, dammit, buck naked, bothered the hell out of him. The prospect of being naked with this girl under other circumstances held a very definite appeal, but only if he were awake to enjoy it. For reasons he did not care to examine, he was very grateful that her mother was the one who had undressed him.

Angelica paused outside the door to place her hands on her burning cheeks. She had to cool her blushes before facing Mama, who would demand to know what had happened.

But by the time she finally felt calm enough to face the woman who had raised her, there was no need to go searching. Maria was approaching with a laden tray.

"He's awake," Angelica said, suspecting that Maria was already privy to that information.

"*Sí,* I hear you talking. I bring him some soup." Maria made a nodding motion with her head indicating that Angelica should open the bedroom door for her. The girl glanced down at the tray, which bore a bowl of rich broth heavily laced with tiny strips of beef, a dish of stewed apples, and a pot of coffee. With a small smile, she wondered what Kid Collins would think of such meager fare. Then she opened the door and stepped back to allow Maria to enter the room.

Maria greeted their guest in Spanish, and he responded in the same language. That wasn't too amazing since most people in Texas spoke enough "Mexican" to get by. But to Angelica's surprise, he continued to converse in fluent Spanish after Maria had identified herself, thanking her for taking him in and bandaging his wound.

Angelica pulled the door closed, but something in his voice made her stop, leaving the door slightly ajar so she could still hear them speaking. She got the strangest feeling that he wasn't so much thanking Maria as verifying that it had indeed been the Mexican woman who was responsible for his care.

Maria made a slightly suggestive remark about how she had not minded the task, and Angelica gasped aloud. In her whole life, Angelica had never heard her *mamacita* say anything even remotely suggestive to a man. In the next second, Angelica found all her preconceived notions about the woman who had been like a mother to her dashed beyond repair. Maria was actually teasing him about what a beautiful body he had, and from his replies, he didn't mind a bit!

With growing outrage, Angelica realized that Maria was *flirting* with the man. How scandalous! Why, she was old enough to be his mother! Not to mention the fact that Maria would skin Angelica alive if she ever even *thought* the things Maria was saying out loud in there. And then he asked Maria for a chamber pot.

That was the last straw. Angelica closed the door with a snap and stalked righteously away, her face scalding. So much for eavesdropping. From now on she would conduct herself like a proper lady. A *very* proper lady. Whatever insanity had come over her since the arrival of Mr. Kid Collins was now cured. She went outside to await the arrival of her hired hands, who had taken Robbie out with them to work that day.

The Kid sank back wearily against the pillows as Maria removed the tray. He'd never been very partial to soup, but that had tasted mighty good, and truth to tell, he doubted his stomach could have handled anything more substantial. God, how he hated being laid up. At least his side had stopped throbbing. Whatever Maria had put on it had worked a small miracle. "Thanks," he said, giving her a grin. "That was great."

"Later I will make you something good, something that will bring your strength back," she promised, returning his grin, and then her expression turned speculative. "So, what do you think of my Angel?" she inquired.

The Kid stared at her incredulously. Not angels again. "Your *what?*" he asked, almost afraid to hear the answer. He was starting to feel strange, as if he were slipping back into the dream once more. He had lost a lot of blood. That could explain it.

"My Angel," she repeated, "My Angelica." When the name still did not bring a response, she added, "The girl who was here before, with the red hair and the green eyes. You do remember her, don't you?"

"Oh, Miss Ross," he realized with some relief. "Her name is 'Angel'?" he asked, unwilling to believe such a coincidence. He was right. This whole thing was getting stranger by the minute.

"Sí, Angelica, that is her name," Maria clarified, oblivious to the undercurrents. "She is pretty, no?"

There was nothing strange about that statement. "She is

pretty, yes," he concurred.

"She owns this whole ranch, too, she and her brother. Her mama and her papa are gone." Maria sighed with regret. "It is a heavy burden for a woman, and her brother is just a child." Maria sighed again and shook her head. "She should have a man to help her."

The Kid agreed. When his former boss, Rachel McKinsey, had found herself in the same predicament, she had proposed marriage to her foreman, his good friend Cole Elliot. Maybe Angelica Ross should do the same thing, depending on who her foreman was, of course. The Kid was just about to suggest it when he noticed the speculative gleam in Maria's dark eyes.

Before he had time to react, however, it was gone, and Maria was smiling guilelessly down at him. "You will rest now. Later I will check on you and see if you need anything."

She glided silently from the room, leaving him to wonder how he could have imagined even for a moment that Maria would consider a gunfighter like Kid Collins a suitable match for Cameron Ross's daughter.

Angelica waved a greeting to the riders as they came into the yard, but she could not quite manage a smile. Two men and a boy, all that was left of the dozen men who had worked the Diamond R six months ago. What was she going to do?

Thoughts of Kid Collins teased at her, and she wondered if a man like that could be convinced to help. Recalling the letter she had found in his saddlebags and the information that he had been helping his sister gave her some hope in that direction. But then Robbie was off his horse, distracting her.

"Angel! There was a fire today!" he shouted as he ran across the ranch yard toward her, his short legs pumping furiously to cover the ground.

"A fire? Where" she asked in alarm as she caught his sturdy body. She knelt in front of him and held him by the shoulders.

"Far away from here," he explained breathlessly, and she could see he was disappointed to have missed out on the excitement. "We saw some men from Mr. Snyder's ranch, and they told us about it, though. It was those settlers over on South Creek. Their cabin burned clean down."

Angelica's heart froze as her imagination played out the scene in her mind. If Snyder's men knew about the fire, then she was certain it was no accident. "Did they say what happened to the settlers?" she asked, managing to sound calm and hoping that Robbie would not sense her fears.

Robbie shrugged with the kind of unconcern only a ten-year-old can affect. "They'll move away now. They'll have to, won't they, since they don't have a house?" he asked reasonably.

"Yes, I suppose so," Angelica said, forcing a smile and silently praying that the poor settlers had been given that option. What was happening to this country? When they had finally driven out the Comanche so they could live in peace, along came a white man even more ruthless.

That thought reminded her of the news she had for Robbie, and gratefully, she changed the subject. "We had some visitors today," she told him, rising and leading him into the house. "Indians."

His hazel eyes glowed greener until they were almost the color of her own. "Indians!" he repeated, delighted.

She playfully pulled off his battered hat and ruffled his carrot-colored curls. "Yes, Comanche," she explained, giving him a loving smile. As she told him the story, she could not help thinking how much she adored him. He was more like her child than her brother, even though only nine years separated them. She had never cared much for her stepmother, but in producing Robbie, Inge had covered a multitude of sins.

By marrying the stern German woman, Cameron Ross had sought to provide a stabilizing influence for the daughter who was growing up wild on the plains of West Texas. Inge had achieved some measure of success in that area during her short reign at the Diamond R, but her greatest contribution to Angelica's life had been Robbie.

Being fairly certain about how babies were made, Angelica often had a difficult time believing that the dour Scot and the stiff German could have accomplished such a thing. But Robbie's existence proved that they had managed, at least once. Regardless of who Robbie's parents were, however, Angelica considered him her baby. Since the day Robbie was born, Angelica lavished on him the affection neither of his parents seemed capable of giving. Then, during the worst of the Comanche uprisings, both children had been sent to the convent in New Orleans where Angelica's mother had been raised. That time of exile when they had had only each other to depend on had strengthened the bond between them.

Mamacita attributed Angelica's passionate nature to the French mother neither of them had ever known. Having seen the faded daguerreotype of Mignon Ross, Angelica knew she had inherited little else from the petite blond woman who had died giving her life, but that capacity for love was enough. Angelica would give every drop of her volatile French blood and even her stubborn Scottish blood to protect Robbie.

"Is the man still here?" Robbie asked when she had finished her tale.

"Yes, he's sleeping in Papa's room," Angelica told him. "And you'll never guess who he is."

"Who?" Robbie asked, his eyes huge in his elfin face.

"Kid Collins," she replied importantly.

Robbie hooted joyously. "Can I see him? Right now?" he begged, pulling on her skirt.

Somehow Angelica managed to restrain him, explaining that their guest was sick and needed to rest. By the time supper was over, and Maria verified that Mr. Collins was up to having a visitor, poor Robbie was almost frantic.

That was why Angelica was surprised at Robbie's reluctance to enter the bedroom when the moment finally arrived. She had hoped Robbie's enthusiasm would cover her own hesitancy. The thought of entering that bedroom again conjured disturbing visions she had been unable to suppress all afternoon. Of course, she knew she was being silly. After all, he had no idea she had seen him in the altogether. Any awkwardness was in her own mind. All she had to do was act naturally.

Pinning on a pleasant little smile, she rapped on the bedroom door and pushed it open before she could lose her nerve. "Mr. Collins, there's someone here who wants to meet you," she said, drawing her brother into the room. He didn't exactly drag his heels, but she had to use more strength than she had expected to get him inside. "This is my brother, Robbie Ross. Robbie, this is Mr. Collins." She gave the boy a little push toward the bed, but he didn't budge.

She glanced up at Collins, wondering what it was about him that had intimidated her brother, and to her amazement, the man was smiling. Her breath lodged in her chest for a second.

"Pleased to meet you, Rob," the Kid said, extending his hand.

Robbie blinked at this new form of his name, considered it a moment, and decided he liked it. He grinned. "Pleased to meet you, too," he said, crossing the room with his version of a manly swagger and taking the offered hand.

"Maria tells me that you're the man of the family now," the Kid said, sobering with difficulty. The boy's awed expression was quite humorous, but he didn't want Robbie to think he was mocking him. "I guess you're the one I need to thank. Your womenfolk have been taking mighty good care of me."

Robbie sobered, too. "Angel said you were hurt bad."

The Kid glanced up at the girl, who still hovered by the door. She was even lovelier than he remembered, but her expression was wary, as if she were prepared to jump in and rescue the boy if the Kid said or did anything untoward. He gave her what he hoped was a reassuring smile and turned back to the boy. "I got shot," he explained. "But I'll be up and around in a few days."

"Who shot you?" Robbie asked solemnly.

That, the Kid thought, was a very good question, one to which he would find the answer as soon as he was able to leave this bed. "I don't know," he admitted reluctantly. "Some men didn't want me around here, and they tried to get rid of me."

Robbie nodded. "Some men got rid of most of our hands, too," he explained. "My Papa always said this country was getting too crowded. I guess other people think so, too."

The boy's guileless statement told the Kid a multitude of things about the Diamond R, and another glance at the girl's troubled expression confirmed every one of them.

"Robbie, I think we should let Mr. Collins rest now. We want him to make a quick recovery," she said with a strained smile.

"I don't," Robbie contradicted ingenuously. "I want him to stay here for a long time."

Angelica watched Collins's reaction to this, and seeing his warm amusement, she decided this was the perfect opening. "Well, then, why don't you leave the two of us alone for a few minutes and maybe I can talk Mr. Collins into doing just that."

Nothing else could have so easily convinced Robbie to leave the room. With a delighted whoop, he raced for the door, remembering his manners only at the last second. He came to a sliding halt, reminding Angelica of her own mad dash earlier in the day. "I really didn't mean that about you not getting well," he confessed sheepishly. "I just want you to stay."

"I know," Collins said. "That's all right."

Satisfied, Robbie cast his sister a hopeful look and ducked out the door. Angelica closed it with elaborate care while gathering her wits to face the man lying in the bed. When she did, she found him suddenly wary, all the warmth he had exhibited for the boy gone.

She forced a small, unconcerned smile to her lips. "Robbie admires you very much, Mr. Collins."

The sound of his name brought to mind something he had been wondering about all afternoon. "How did you know who I was?" He had been so careful about concealing his identity for this trip that he had cut off his trademark, shoulder-length hair, and left all his normal clothes, which might have identified him, behind at the Circle M.

Angelica winced inwardly at having to confess her invasion of his privacy. "I . . . well, I found the letter in your saddlebags and . . ." She made an apologetic gesture. "A woman alone can't be too careful who she takes into her home, Mr. Collins. I had to know who you were."

He nodded, not pleased but understanding. For a difficult moment he tried to remember what Rachel had said in the letter. He had picked it up in town that morning and read it hastily in his rush to get back to Rose and Pete. When he thought of what had happened later, all memory of the letter fled. In an effort to block out those thoughts, he concentrated on what the girl was saying.

"Were you telling Robbie the truth? Do you not have any idea who shot you?" Angelica watched the way his blue eyes blazed at her question.

"I don't know their names, if that's what you mean, but I know enough about them to start hunting."

His fury was a palpable presence in the room, but as

much as it disturbed her, Angelica knew it would work in her favor. "What do you know about them?"

The Kid drew a deep breath and let it out slowly as he fought for control of the rage that threatened to explode inside of him. How he hated feeling so impotent, hated lying here helpless when he should be out there finding Rose's killers. "I know that they didn't want my sister and her husband to settle around here. They'd been giving Rose and Pete some trouble, so she asked me to come and help. I got here a couple of weeks ago, and everything was pretty quiet until this morning." He paused, visualizing that terrible moment when Rose had been shot, and then hurried on. "Some of them attacked the house. They killed Rose and Pete and burned the place. . . ."

"The fire!" Angelica exclaimed, lifting her fingers to her lips.

The Kid's eyes narrowed suspiciously. "You knew about it?"

Angelica shook her head vigorously. "Robbie and my men heard about it today from some cowboys. I was wondering what happened to the settlers. . . . But you got away?" Her eyes asked a question.

"Just barely," he admitted. "If I hadn't run into the Indians, I'd be dead now."

Angelica studied his face, shuddering slightly at the bitterness she saw reflected there. How well she understood his feelings. Instinctively, she moved closer to the bed. "Mr. Collins, I'll send my men out at first light to find the bod—to find your sister and her husband," she corrected. "Would it be all right if they brought them back here? We have a cemetery where my parents are buried. It's even been blessed by a priest, so it's hallowed ground," she added, in case that made a difference to him.

She watched him once again fight for control of the rage she understood perfectly. At last he said, "Yes, that would be fine. Thank you." But he looked away, silently telling her how he hated to be beholden to a stranger for something he should be doing himself.

But this was not the end of the conversation. Angelica still had a proposition for him, and now that she knew his story, she knew he could not turn her down. "Mr. Collins, your sister wasn't the only person around here having problems."

Instantly, his blue eyes were on her again, but now they were shuttered. He was not inviting her confidence, but she plunged ahead anyway.

"I told you that my father passed away last fall. Well, ever since then, some mysterious things have been happening around here, and one by one all my cowboys quit. I have only two left now, and they only stayed because they've been here for years and are too old to find work anywhere else. I need help, Mr. Collins."

His eyes were still shuttered, telling her nothing. "Hire some more men," he suggested flatly.

"That's just it. No one will work for me. Word is out, you see. A lot of men won't work for a woman, and those who will don't want to get mixed up in a fight. I'm between a rock and a hard place, Mr. Collins." Angelica tried a small smile but it failed to move him.

"You must have some relatives somewhere, then," he offered.

Angelica stiffened. "And what if I do? Are you suggesting that I give up and move away, take Robbie someplace safe back East?"

"It makes sense . . ." he began, but she was having none of it.

"The Diamond R is my home. I was born here, and I plan to die here," she informed him. "But it's more than that. This is Robbie's home, too. Our father spent twenty years building this place for us. He trusted me to keep it safe, and I intend to do just that."

The Kid looked up at her, admiring the way anger only

enhanced her beauty. With her green eyes flashing and her cheeks flushed, she looked like some ancient warrior-princess ready to do battle. Seeing her like this, he almost believed that she could beat whoever was her enemy, and he did wish he could help her.

"Look, Miss Ross, I understand your problem, but . . ."

"I'd like to hire you, Mr. Collins. I can pay you well . . ."

"Now wait a minute . . ."

"And there'll be a bonus when the job is done . . ."

"I said wait a minute . . ."

"And you can hire as many men as you need . . ."

"I SAID WAIT A MINUTE!"

Angelica jumped, startled to discover that he was grasping her arm in a way that was bound to leave bruises. He seemed to realize it at the same instant and released her immediately.

"Miss Ross," he said with deliberate calmness. "I understand your problems, and I understand that you want to keep this place, but I have some problems of my own. Somebody murdered my sister, and I intend to find out who they were and make them pay."

He was right, of course, but Angelica couldn't let him go off on some mission of revenge. She needed him too badly. Desperately, she tried a different ploy. "And what about your obligation to me, Mr. Collins?" Angelica asked. "Don't you owe me something for saving your life? What if I hadn't been willing to take you in? Do you think the Indians would have carried you to the next ranch? No, I don't think so either," she said, reading his answer in his eyes. "If it wasn't for me, you'd probably be dead right now."

Instantly, Angelica knew she had made a tactical error in demanding gratitude from a man unaccustomed to giving it. The blue eyes hardened until they glittered like broken glass. But she had one more card up her sleeve. "And besides, I'll make you a little bet that the man who killed your sister—at least the man behind it—is the same one who's responsible for my problems, too."

"What makes you so sure?" he demanded, and Angelica noted with relief that his eyes had softened somewhat. He was at least intrigued by her theory.

"It's only common sense. Harlan Snyder moved here a little over a year ago. He brought in some cattle with brands that didn't stand close inspection, spread some money around, and made a lot of influential friends. Whenever some little squatter came along and staked a claim near his own, Snyder would buy him out. Occasionally, the squatter wouldn't sell, and something bad would happen, like what happened to your sister. Did she tell you that someone had tried to buy her out?"

The Kid shook his head. He thought for a long moment. "I guess Snyder decided that running them off was cheaper." Then his gaze grew speculative. "Did he try to buy you out?"

Angelica hesitated. "Not exactly," she hedged.

The Kid's gaze hardened again, but this time she knew his anger was directed against the absent Snyder. "What *exactly* did he do?"

"Well, he . . ." Angelica shifted uneasily under his steady gaze, loath to admit the truth. "Well, first he came courting."

"Courting!" The Kid stared at her. "Is he a young man?"

"I'd guess he's in his thirties," she replied.

An awkward silence fell as the Kid considered and discarded several other inappropriate questions, such as what, precisely, did she mean by "courting"?

Angelica decided to play her advantage since he was now, obviously, concerned with her predicament. "I have a contract to supply beef to Camp Hope, one of the Indian reservations up north. All I need are some men to round up the cattle and drive them up there. If we can do that, I'll be in a position to run the ranch for several years even without selling any more cattle for a while. But if we can't . . ." She paused, reluctant to even speak the words. "We'll lose the ranch."

He didn't reply, didn't even bat an eye, and for a moment Angelica was afraid she had not convinced him. "Please, Mr. Collins," she begged, reaching out to him. "Please help us!"

Her hand clutched at his shoulder. The solid feel of him beneath the thin fabric of the nightshirt startled her. Suddenly, all thoughts of her problems vanished. She was uniquely aware of the fact that she was alone with a man who was lying in bed wearing nothing but a nightshirt, a man who was far from the invalid he had seemed when she had taken him in.

The Kid looked up at her, unbearably conscious of her hand on his shoulder and of the nearness of her slender female body. He remembered the way she had felt when he grabbed her arm, soft and delicate, the way only a woman could feel. Her hair shimmered in the lamplight, as if it had a life of its own, and he knew a compelling urge to reach up and touch it, to pull it loose and let it spill around him. He knew exactly how she would feel pressed up against him and exactly how she would taste when her mouth opened under his. How long since he had known a woman like that?

Not since Lettie died . . .

Angelica saw the strange expression flicker in his eyes, and she jerked her hand away as if he'd burned her. "I . . . I'm sorry," she stammered, backing toward the door, some sixth sense screaming a silent warning that she had overstepped an invisible boundary into very dangerous territory. "Just, please, consider my offer. You . . . you must be tired. I'll let you get some rest now."

Without waiting for a reply, she ducked out the door, closing it behind her with more force than necessary. She had an unladylike urge to run to someplace safe, but she squelched it instantly. Running like a child had gotten her into trouble once already today, and she wasn't going to take any more chances. Besides, she asked herself sternly, what did she think she needed to be safe from?

Certainly not from some shot-up gunfighter who hadn't done a single thing to justify the way her heart was hammering against her ribs. The poor man probably thought she was touched in the head, the way she'd rushed out of there like a scalded cat. She'd probably only imagined that expression in his eyes. Why would a man that handsome find awkward Angelica Ross an object of desire?

Self-consciously, she lifted a hand to her hair and wondered for the first time all day what condition it was in. The ribbon holding it back from her face was drooping, and the red-gold locks could certainly use a good brushing. And her dress, she thought with disgust, was certainly nothing to write home about. A calico Mother Hubbard, it served her well for household chores, but the worn and faded garment certainly did nothing to enhance her position as a successful lady rancher.

No wonder the man had reacted in such a peculiar way to her offer. He probably wouldn't want to work for someone who looked more like a hoyden than a lady. She stalked across the courtyard to her bedroom, where her meager wardrobe hung. Surely, she must own something that would impress him. The next time he saw her, he would see a different Angelica Ross, she vowed. Then he would understand exactly who and what she was.

She was no angel, the Kid decided, lifting a hand to rub the shoulder she had grasped. More likely she was a demon sent to torment him. And she must have sensed his reaction to her touch, judging from the way she'd hightailed it out of here.

He hadn't felt like that in almost four years, not since

Lettie's death. He'd loved Lettie like he'd never loved another woman, and a part of him had died with her, the part of him that looked on women with desire. Not that he'd been exactly celibate all that time. On the few rare occasions when the need had become unbearable, he had paid to have it eased. But never, not once since that awful day he had put Lettie's broken body in the ground, had he truly wanted anyone else.

He hadn't even wanted Rachel, he realized with amazement. All his worries had been for nothing! For the past few months, he had found himself growing increasingly restless, and part of that restlessness had revolved around his liking for Rachel Elliot's company. He had often visited the Circle M ranch house, where his best friend Cole Elliot lived with his wife and their children. And it had surprised him how much he had enjoyed seeing Rachel, admiring the way she sat serenely by the hearth, watching her hands working a needle through cloth to make something pretty, observing how she tenderly guided her baby through his first steps.

When Rose's request for help came, his immediate response was only partly caused by a duty to help his last living relative. The other reason was a decision to get away from Rachel before he tried something he'd always regret.

Now, of course, he realized that what he had enjoyed was the peace being in Rachel and Cole's home had brought him. Desire, the kind of desire he had felt just moments ago for this girl he hardly knew, played no part at all in his feelings for his best friend's wife.

The Kid closed his eyes, suddenly feeling unutterably weary. Angelica Ross had asked him for help, had *begged* him for help. And she was right, he owed her that much and more for saving his life. Ordinarily, he would have no trouble making the decision to accept her offer of a job.

But there was nothing ordinary in the way he had reacted to her touch just now. If he took the job she had offered, if he stayed around here, he would see her every day. Would he be able to withstand the torment of working with her that closely?

And what if he couldn't?

Chapter Two

Angelica waited nervously by the fountain in the courtyard of her fortresslike home. The drip of the water ordinarily would have comforted her. Her father had placed the fountain here as a source of water in the event of an Indian attack. More than once, the precious liquid had saved their lives, but today she simply found the endless trickling an irritant to her impatience.

At long last Maria came out of Collins's bedroom, and Angelica jumped to her feet. With great difficulty, she moderated her steps and managed to stroll casually over to her Mamacita.

"How is he this morning?" she asked.

Maria did not reply right away. Instead, she took a minute to look Angelica over from head to toe while Angelica tried not to squirm under the scrutiny. Even though Angelica towered over the Mexican woman by a good five inches, she suddenly felt as if she were ten years old again and wishing she had scrubbed behind her ears. Surely, Mama would have something witty to say about Angelica's unusual appearance.

But to her surprise, Maria did not mention it. "He is much better. The wound is not infected."

"Do you think . . . I mean, I'd like to speak with him for a moment. Is he still awake?" Angelica squared her shoulders, reminding herself that she was still the lady of the house, no matter how amused Maria's dark eyes were.

"*Sí*, I am sure he will be glad to see you, especially when he sees how you have dressed up for him," Maria conjectured with a smirk.

"I did not!" Angelica hotly denied, but her outrage was wasted. Maria had already turned her back and was heading toward the kitchen, her shoulders shaking with silent laughter.

When her Mamacita was out of sight, Angelica walked over to the bedroom door and paused outside, taking a moment to smooth the fabric of her skirt. The dress was left over from her convent days, and it fit more snugly now than it had then. But it wasn't fancy, no matter what Mama had said about her being dressed up.

However, the dress *was* pretty, Angelica admitted reluctantly. The forest green calico with a sprinkling of yellow roses was a good color for her. Not that she'd chosen it for that reason, of course. She had no wish to look attractive for a gunfighter. She only wanted to appear neat and capable, the way one would expect a lady rancher to look.

She touched a tentative hand to her hair. Earlier that morning she had spent a good deal of time twisting the heavy, red-gold mass into an intricate knot at the back of her neck instead of allowing it to fall free or simply braiding it as she usually did. Satisfied that none of the pins had come loose, she quickly lowered her hand. No use tempting fate.

Drawing a deep breath and forcing her mouth into a pleasant good-morning smile, Angelica knocked on the bedroom door.

"Maria! Get in here quick!" his voice called urgently.

Alarmed, Angelica threw open the door, but to her surprise, the bed was empty. Her gaze swept over the room, and she found him standing halfway between the bed and the large armchair that sat over by the window. He was leaning against the wall, his face ashen.

"What on earth are you doing out of bed!" Angelica cried, rushing to him.

That, the Kid thought, was an excellent question. And where in the hell was Maria? The last thing he needed right now was to tangle with this girl in his weakened condition.

Angelica's good Samaritan impulse faltered when she reached him. Even slumped against the wall, he loomed huge and imposingly masculine above her five feet, seven inches, making her feel oddly small and vulnerable. And he was wearing only her father's nightshirt, which hung loosely on his large frame and ended just at his knees. Below that, his long, hairy legs stuck out. "Can I help you?" she asked.

The Kid almost groaned aloud. Help from her was the last thing he wanted just now, but he didn't see that he had much choice, not unless he wanted to faint in a heap at her feet. "Yeah, I, uh, think I'd better get back in bed," he admitted reluctantly.

Angelica considered all the options within the space of one swift second and decided she had no other choice. "Here, lean on me," she said, offering him her left shoulder so she would avoid bumping his injured left side.

She slipped her arm around him, being careful to grasp him well above the bandage. "Lean on me," she urged again. "I'm strong." Yes, she thought, as strong as a horse and as big as one, too, or at least she had always felt that way. Ever since she had shot up to her present height at the age of thirteen, she had been taller than all the women and many of the men she knew. But now, as she conducted this blond giant toward her father's bed, she felt petite for the first time in many, many years.

The Kid looked down at the top of her head so near his own chin. "You're taller than I thought," he muttered aloud.

Angelica felt her face burning at this remark. Of course,

like most men, he preferred a woman who was tiny and helpless. Well, Mr. Kid Collins, she thought angrily, a tiny, helpless woman wouldn't be much use to you right now.

Keeping her head down so he would not see her scarlet face, she concentrated on matching her steps to his shuffling gate and trying to ignore the feel of him pressed against her. Were all men's bodies so hard? And did they all smell so good? No, to both questions, she realized with chagrin. Although she had never been quite this close to any other man except her father, who hardly counted, she knew instinctively that no other male body would feel exactly the same as the one currently pressed against hers from shoulder to hip.

But he only smelled good because Maria had given him a bed bath this morning. Angelica told herself that he probably smelled just as disgusting as any other man when he was dirty. Or did he? He had been very dirty when he'd first come. Had she found him disgusting then? Before she could decide, he stumbled slightly, making her stagger as his full weight descended on her for the first time.

"Sorry," he muttered, sorrier than she could know. It was bad enough needing her help like this without adding everything else into the pot. In spite of the fact that his side felt like it had been lanced with a red-hot poker and he was as weak as if a giant leech had sucked out every drop of his blood, one or two parts of him were functioning with above-average efficiency. He was acutely aware of every square inch where her body touched his, and as they approached the bed, he knew an insane urge to pull her down onto it with him and cover her until every bit of him touched every bit of her. At the thought, an involuntary groan escaped his lips.

Hearing the groan, Angelica knew a moment's panic. "Just a little farther," she said breathlessly.

Steadfastly, she stared at his bare feet, counting each step. How beautiful he was. He even had beautiful feet.

They were long and slender, like his hands, and sprinkled with that same wonderful golden hair that adorned every other part of him. When she thought of the places on his body where it grew in profusion, her face burned scarlet once again. With more relief than she had ever known, she caught sight of the edge of the bed.

"Careful, or you'll tear open your wound," she cautioned as she eased him down into a sitting position.

He blamed his weakened condition. Under other circumstances he would never have behaved so abominably, or so he told himself. In any event, as he sank down on the bed, he leaned more heavily on the girl than was absolutely necessary and allowed one hand to brush against her breast.

He felt her stiffen instinctively at the touch, heard her small gasp of surprise, but then he realized the main reason why this impulse had been a terrible mistake: her nipple was pebble hard beneath the green calico of her dress. Dear God, he thought in dismay, she feels this attraction, too. That's *all* I need.

He sank down on the bed, letting his hands fall from her in what he hoped was a perfectly natural gesture. Maybe she would think his touch had been an accident. He winced as desire sluiced through him, holding his breath until the hot tide receded.

Angelica jumped away the instant he released her, fighting an overwhelming urge to cover the breast his hand had accidentally brushed. How shocking that such a casual contact could startle her so. She had been repelled, of course, and yet some primitive part of her had responded, sparking every nerve in her body to tingling awareness.

But then she saw the agonized expression on his face, the obvious evidence of his suffering, and she was instantly ashamed. The poor man was in pain. "I'll help you lie down," she offered in contrition.

"Don't touch me," the Kid growled through gritted teeth,

not even daring to open his eyes for fear the sight of her would snap the tenuous hold he still had on himself.

Well! Angelica jumped back again, stung by his harsh rejection. Of all the ungrateful . . . ! If it hadn't been for her touching him, he'd be lying in a heap on the floor right about now! What if she'd refused to help him? What if she'd pointed out how improper it was for a single girl to let a man drape himself all over her, especially when he was practically naked! She was furious, at him for being so rude and at herself for being so attracted to him.

"What did you think you were doing, anyway, getting up out of bed like that?" she demanded, planting her hands belligerently on her hips.

The Kid's eyes popped open. He could not help noticing once again how perfectly lovely she was with her hair the color of living flame and her eyes glittering like precious jewels and every inch of her willowy figure tautened in outrage. Her breasts thrust forward until he could see the buds of her nipples straining against the green calico. Her breasts weren't overly large, but they weren't small, either. Just the right size to fill a man's hand . . . He snapped his eyes shut and groaned again. He had to stop this, right now.

Carefully, favoring his wound, he began to work himself around to a prone position.

Oh, dear! Angelica thought, he really was in pain. Once again she moved closer, obeying her instinct to help him.

"Don't help me, dammit!" he snapped, swinging his long legs up onto the bed with obvious difficulty and throwing the covers over them. This accomplished, he slumped back against the pillows.

Turning on her heel, every drop of her French and Scottish blood boiling in her veins, she stalked toward the door. So much for her plan to impress him. So much for her plan to convince him to stay and help them. It would be a cold day in hell when she needed a man like that for anyth—

"Miss Ross?"

Angelica halted. She turned back to face him. "What?"

The Kid managed an apologetic grin. "I'm sorry I yelled at you," he began, feeling his way. She looked as if she might bolt if he so much as looked at her cross-eyed, and although he knew he was only asking for trouble, the last thing he wanted was for her to leave. "It's just that, well, I'm not used to being laid up, and my side hurts and . . ."

He tried the smile that he knew from experience women loved, hoping to melt her understandable resistance. Now that he was safely in bed, where he would no longer have to endure her touch and where any embarrassing manifestations of his desire would be hidden, he wanted her to stay. "Could I have a drink of water?" he asked in a stroke of brilliance that surprised even him.

Angelica hesitated only a moment before responding to his request. After all, he had apologized, and he did have a good excuse for acting the way he had. If she were in his place, she would probably be testy, too.

Keeping a careful distance from the bed, Angelica poured a glass of water from the pitcher Maria had left on the bedside table. She handed it to him in such a way that their fingers did not even brush. If he didn't want her to touch him, that was fine with her, too!

The Kid accepted the glass and drained it. "Thanks," he said, smiling again and handing it back to her.

Angelica was a little surprised. For a moment she had thought his request was just a ploy of some sort, part of a mysterious game he was playing with her that she did not understand. Now she remembered that loss of blood made a person very thirsty, and she felt a little silly for her suspicions. "More?" she asked.

"No, that's fine," he said, watching her. The dress was pretty, very pretty, and the stained apron was gone. And her hair. She'd spent a lot of time putting it up like that. He'd pulled a strand loose during their little wrestling match, and it hung down beside her cheek. She seemed unaware of it.

He thought of Rachel Elliot, whom he'd never seen looking less than perfect. She would know immediately if her hair was coming loose, but this girl didn't. He pictured Angelica the way she had looked yesterday, delightfully mussed and earthy, and he knew instinctively that the neat dress and the carefully combed hair were not her normal style. She had dressed especially for him.

"I pulled your hair loose," he said.

Self-consciously, Angelica reached up and found the wayward strand. So much for trying to look like a proper lady.

She forced a smile and changed the subject. "What *were* you doing out of bed? You could have hurt yourself, you know," she chastened gently.

He returned her smile with a rueful one of his own. "I had a wild idea that I'd feel better if I could just get out of this bed for a while." He cast a look of comic dismay toward the chair by the window. "That chair looked a lot closer before than it does now."

Angelica shook her head. "Next time, ask someone to bring it over by the bed," she suggested. She straightened her shoulders and folded her hands primly in front of her in a creditable imitation of a proper lady.

"Mr. Collins, I know you haven't had much chance to think about the offer I made you yesterday, but . . ."

"Yes, I have," he contradicted her. His smile vanished, and Angelica was certain he had decided not to help her. To her surprise, he said, "Tell me everything you know about Harlan Snyder."

"I don't know much more than I told you yesterday," she replied. "There were a few settlers who moved here during the last few years, ever since the Comanche have been under control. My father figured that there'll be a lot more in the years to come, but apparently Harlan Snyder decided differently. The settlers who didn't sell out met with unfortunate accidents. Nobody ever traced them to Snyder, but he was the only one who profited from the settlers' leaving." Angelica shrugged. "He only bothered the ones who settled on choice spots, too, like near reliable water."

"Like my sister," the Kid murmured bitterly.

Angelica nodded and fell silent.

"Tell me about Snyder himself," the Kid prodded. "What's he like?"

Angelica had to think about this a moment. How would one describe him? "He's a big man, not tall but big, and he smiles a lot, but it's not a friendly smile. At least I don't think so. He acts like a respectable rancher and pays his bills on time, so everyone treats him well. Since there's no evidence that he's involved in the trouble, people tend to believe the best about him, I guess, especially because he's got some money."

The Kid listened closely, his blue eyes narrowed speculatively. "You said Snyder courted you," he prompted.

Angelica shifted uneasily. This was not a subject she wanted to discuss. She found the whole thing rather humiliating. "Well, yes," she admitted reluctantly. "He started calling on me. I never gave him much encouragement, but that didn't seem to bother him. He never really proposed or anything, although he hinted about marriage several times, but I know what he was really after," she added. She didn't want him to think her completely naive.

"You do?" he asked, astounded.

"Of course! He wanted this ranch, and he figured marrying me would be the easiest way to get it," Angelica explained defensively.

The Kid stared at her incredulously. She actually believed that Snyder only wanted the ranch. Could anyone be that innocent? Could any woman so beautiful really be that ignorant of her own appeal? Dear God, she was in even more danger than he had guessed. If Snyder was the kind of man who could cold-bloodedly murder total strangers and burn their home down around them, what might he do to a girl like this?

"Can you send some telegrams for me? Today?" he asked.

Angelica blinked in surprise at the abrupt change in subject. "Why?"

"You said I could hire some men. I want to send for them," the Kid explained, anxious to get on with it. By the time they arrived he would be back on his feet. They could do the roundup in a few weeks, and then drive the cattle north to the reservation. . . .

"You're going to help me?" Angelica asked.

The Kid's gaze snapped back to her. "Yes," he said, silently calling himself seven kinds of a fool. He was letting himself in for all sorts of torture by taking this job. "Do you have some paper handy? I'll make up the messages."

"Yes, I think there's some right here," she said, hurrying over to her father's bureau and rummaging in a drawer until she found an old tally book and a stub of a pencil.

When she returned to the bed, she offered them to him, but he shook his head. "You wouldn't be able to read my writing. I'll tell you what to put down and who to send them to. Miles Blackmon at the Circle M Ranch," he began, mentally dismissing his friend Cole Elliot. Rachel was pregnant with their third child, and Cole didn't need to be involved in anything dangerous. But Cole could spare a few good men and would be happy to do so. The other telegram would go to Stumpy Smith and his partner, One-Eyed Jack. Between Miles and Stumpy and the men they brought with them, the Kid could make up a roundup crew no one would dare tangle with.

When he had finished dictating, Angelica read everything back to him to make certain she had gotten it all right. She considered simply handing it to him to look over himself, but suspected that perhaps an inability to read and write lay behind his reluctance to compose the messages. She knew from having lived around illiterate cowboys all her life that men tended to be touchy about admitting such a thing.

"Sounds like you got it all," he told her when she had finished. He made an adjustment in the arrangement of the bedclothes, giving Angelica the definite impression she was being dismissed. For some unexplainable reason, she felt disappointed.

She straightened from where she had been leaning over the bedside table to write. "I'll have one of my men go into town and send these as soon as they get back," she said and then remembered where her men were. "I sent them over to your sister's place this morning. . . ." She let her voice trail off when she saw how his expression grew bleak at the reminder of his loss. She didn't want to intrude on his privacy, but she did need to know what arrangements to make. "I can send for the preacher or a priest to speak over them if you like."

But he shook his head. "No, no preacher," he decided, although it pained him to lay Pete and Rose to rest without any ceremony. "I don't want Snyder to find out you had any connection with what happened there at all. With luck, nobody will figure out that I was the one who got away. I don't think they actually saw my face," he said, recalling how he had tied on the bandana during the fire. Unless someone had seen him in town and made the connection, which he doubted, he might be able to conceal his participation in the gunfight at South Creek.

He was glad now that he had taken such pains to disguise his identity for this visit. His intention had been to avoid drawing the kind of attention to Rose and Pete that his reputation would bring. Now, of course, having his identity known would be a benefit to Angelica Ross. Within five minutes of when those telegrams were sent, the whole town would know he was here and for whom he was working.

Within a day, Harlan Snyder would know it, too. The Kid was counting on that to protect her, at least for a while.

Angelica watched his face as he made his decision about his sister and brother-in-law, knowing how difficult it was for him and grateful that he had taken her welfare into consideration. "I'm sorry," she said. "We'll have a private service, though, with just the Diamond R crew."

That seemed to please him, if she could judge by the slight flicker in his azure eyes. "Thanks," was all he said.

Their gazes held for a long moment.

"I . . . Thank you for helping us, Mr. Collins," she said, impulsively offering him her hand.

Something else flickered in those blue eyes, and for an instant Angelica feared that he would refuse to shake with her. But at last he lifted his own hand from where it rested on the coverlet and closed his fingers around hers with elaborate care. His hand was surprisingly smooth for a man who worked cattle for a living.

"If you're feeling up to it later, Robbie would like to visit you again," she said, taking a step toward the door. He nodded, and then she was gone.

Angelica still felt slightly breathless by the time she found Maria in the kitchen. The Mexican woman was preparing the noon meal for their small crew. "He's going to help us, Mama," Angelica announced triumphantly.

Maria did not seem the least bit surprised. "That is good," she remarked blandly, barely glancing up from rolling out biscuits.

"He's sending for some of his friends to work the roundup, too," Angelica elaborated in an attempt to get a reaction.

Maria only nodded and said, "We can use some extra men."

Sighing in frustration at Maria's nonchalant attitude,

Angelica pulled out a chair at the table where Maria was rolling her dough and sat down. "Where's Robbie?" she asked after a moment, drawing circles in the flour that dusted the table top.

Maria gave a little chuckle. "He is out in the barn playing gunfighter."

Angelica winced. Having her impressionable brother romanticizing the trouble they were in was the last thing she needed. Unfortunately, in view of what had happened to Collins's family, she and Maria had decided that it was no longer safe to allow Robbie to go out with their men to work the cattle. As a result, the boy would have a lot of time for hanging around the house and making a hero out of Kid Collins. Angelica briefly considered using this time to tutor the boy a bit and take his mind off their visitor, but since she enjoyed the task even less than Robbie did, she found the thought decidedly unappealing.

"Mr. Collins is handsome, no?" Maria remarked.

The comment was harmless enough on the surface, but Angelica had known Maria too long not to suspect an ulterior motive. Maria *never* noticed whether a man was handsome or not, or at least, if she did, she never mentioned it to Angelica. Angelica decided not to spring at the obvious bait. "*You* certainly seemed to think so," she accused her foster mother with only the barest hint of jealousy. "You were actually flirting with him yesterday."

At last Maria looked up from her biscuits, lifting her eyebrows in feigned amazement. "How do you know?" she inquired.

Angelica felt her face growing warm. She had caught herself in her own trap with that one. Rather than go into an explanation of how she had happened to overhear the conversation in question, she decided to stay on the offensive. "Really, Mama, he's young enough to be your . . ."

The accusation died on her lips as she realized that Mr. Collins probably wasn't anywhere near young enough to be

Maria's son. She frowned as she took a good hard look at the other woman's amused face in an attempt to judge what had never seemed important before.

"My what?" Maria prompted, laughter dancing in her dark eyes.

"I don't know," the girl admitted, still frowning. "How old are you anyway?" Odd that she had never given this matter any thought. Maria had always been just her Mamacita, ageless and with no past or even any future beyond what happened day to day on the Diamond R Ranch. Angelica had always simply taken her for granted, and Maria had encouraged that attitude by never referring to her past life in any way.

"I'm old enough," Maria demurred, going back to rolling the dough.

Angelica stared at the work-roughened hands maneuvering the rolling pin. What, really, did she know about this person who had been more than a mother to her?

To her surprise, Angelica realized that she knew precious little. When Angelica's mother had died giving her life, Maria had come to nurse the child and stayed to raise her. To Angelica's knowledge, Maria had no friends and certainly no life beyond caring for Angelica and, later, Robbie.

But suddenly, a very startling fact occurred to Angelica, one with which she was so familiar that she had never really thought about its implications: Maria had been her wet nurse! That meant . . . Angelica's head spun with possibilities, none of which were very pleasant to contemplate. What a self-centered, selfish brat she must be never to have considered them before, especially when she loved Maria as she had never loved another human being!

Maria looked at her curiously, and Angelica realized that she had made a startled noise as the painful thoughts filtered through her brain. "What is wrong?" Maria asked in concern.

Angelica knew the expression on her face must match the

turmoil in her heart, and she did not bother trying to hide her feelings. "Oh, Mama, I just realized . . ." She hesitated, reaching a tentative hand to touch Maria's arm. "What happened to *your* baby all those years ago?"

Maria's dark eyes widened for just a second, reflecting an agony Angelica could hardly bear to look upon. "He died," Maria said flatly, resuming her rolling with a brutal force which Angelica knew would make tonight's biscuits awfully tough.

But that was the least of Angelica's worries. Long ago, Maria had had a baby, a boy, and that baby boy had died. This was much more information than she had ever possessed about Maria's past, but far less than would satisfy her sudden need to understand everything about her foster mother.

"And your husband, Mama, what happened to him?" If there had been a baby, then there must have been a husband. Had some great tragedy taken them both?

Maria froze, her hands poised above the dough, clutching the rolling pin in a white-knuckled grip. "I was never married," she said in a voice so strained Angelica hardly recognized it.

"No! That can't be true!" Angelica insisted, jumping to her feet. The Mamacita who had raised her, who had drilled into her the difference between right and wrong and the importance of doing right, could never have done a thing like that! Why would Mama lie to her?

But she wasn't lying. "It is true, *Angelita,*" Maria said, lifting tortured eyes to the girl. "For nineteen years I have dreaded this moment when I would have to tell you. Sometimes I even think that maybe it will not happen, that maybe you will never have to know the truth about your Mamacita, but even then, I know I am fooling myself." She shook her head sadly, releasing the rolling pin and wiping her hands absently on the apron that covered her plain gray work dress.

Angelica's mind was whirling, trying to make sense of the unthinkable. There simply had to be a reasonable explanation. "You were raped, weren't you? Some horrible man forced himself on you and . . ." But Maria was shaking her head slowly and determinedly. "Then you were in love with a wonderful man, and he died before he could marry you. . . ." That wasn't true either, and Maria's eyes glittered with unshed tears as she continued to shake her head.

Now Angelica did not want to know. The look in Maria's eyes told of a pain too awful to contemplate, but Angelica could not stop the words Maria had kept secret for so long. "It is worse than you can even imagine, my angel," Maria said in that strange voice. "I was a whore."

"NO!" Angelica cried, throwing her arms around Maria as if she could smother any more confessions. "No! You couldn't have been! Not you!"

Frantically, Angelica tried to remember a time when Maria had even looked at a man in a way that might be considered improper. She failed. The woman she clung to had always been the epitome of propriety. In fact, Angelica had often chided her for her prudish ways. How could the mama she knew ever have done such a thing?

Maria gently disengaged herself from Angelica's protective grasp. "Sit down, *Angelita*, and I will tell you the whole story. It is time you knew anyway."

Numbly, Angelica obeyed, although she was terrified of what she might learn. Maria pulled out a chair for herself and turned it so she would be facing the girl. "I was a whore," she repeated in that same, horrible voice that did not seem to belong to her at all. "I lived in a shack not far from here, and the vaqueros would come . . ." She stopped at Angelica's agonized cry and picked up the thread of her story at a later time. "I had a baby. When I found out that I carried the child, I prayed to the Virgin. I promise that if she gives me a healthy little girl, I will change. I promise that I will raise her to be a good Catholic and that I will never do any other bad thing as long as I live."

Maria's dark eyes glowed with a strange light as she recalled those promises. "My baby was a boy, and he was very sick. He only lived a month, not even that, and when he died, I wrapped him in a blanket and buried him myself. I did not tell anyone. I thought the Virgin had not heard my prayers. I thought a person who had been so bad could not expect to be heard. I wanted to kill myself, but I was too sad and tired to do it, so I just sat in my house all alone for three days, and then your father came."

"My father?" Angelica repeated incredulously. Now she knew that something was terribly wrong. Her father was the most straitlaced person she had ever known. Never in a thousand years would he associate with a woman such as Maria described, and he would certainly never let her within a mile of his precious daughter.

"Your mother died when you were born. They tried giving you milk from a cow, but it made you very sick. The midwife said that if he did not find a nurse for you, you would die."

"But he would never . . ."

"No, he would never," Maria agreed, her lips curving in a small, sad smile, "unless it meant that you would die. I was the only woman with milk that he could find. He told me I could come and live at the ranch, but only if I would promise not to see men anymore." She laughed mirthlessly. "He said he would kill me with his own hand if I did, and he thought that his threats kept me good. He never knew that I would have killed *myself* before I ever went with another man."

Maria's black eyes grew soft as she looked at Angelica again. "I will never forget the first time I took you to my breast, *Angelita*. You were so small and weak, you could not even suck. I had to let the milk drip into your mouth at first. But after that taste, you wanted more. You were very greedy, little one," she said with a warm, reminiscent smile that brought tears to Angelica's eyes. "The minute I saw you, I knew you were the little girl I had prayed for. The Virgin *had* heard my prayers and answered them."

But Angelica still could not accept the story, not knowing the woman Maria had become. "You're the best person I know, Mama. How could you ever have been a . . . what you said you were?"

Maria took Angelica's hands in her callused grip. "People can change, Angelica, if they want to, if they *need* to. Always remember that."

"But my father never changed," she pointed out stubbornly, reminding Maria of how rigid Cameron Ross had always been, imposing his standards on everyone and everything around him. "I can't believe he let you stay all these years. I haven't needed nursing for a long time."

Maria frowned, releasing Angelica's fingers. "He did not let me stay. When you were weaned, he sent me away. He did not want a woman like me around his daughter a minute longer than necessary. I died inside that day I left you. It was even worse than when I buried my own son. But," she added, her lips quirking into an ironic smile, "he did not know how stubborn you were." Her smile broadened as she recalled that distant time. "You cried and cried for me. You would not eat, and you would not let anyone else comfort you. The woman he had hired to take care of you could not stand it. She warned him that you would starve if he did not bring me back. After a week, he sent for me again."

Angelica shook her head in disbelief.

"It is true," Maria said. "You know how much he must have hated that, asking me to come back. He was a proud man, but your life meant more to him than his pride."

Angelica understood her father's pride only too well, and marveled at how much her father must have loved her. If only she had known while he was still alive, maybe she could have behaved differently. She wouldn't have defied him so often or gotten into so much trouble. She might even have tried to be the lady he wanted her to be.

But it was too late to make it up to him. The best that she could do was to take care of his son and keep the ranch together as she'd promised. Which reminded her of one other question. "Why didn't he get rid of you when he married Inge? His whole purpose in doing that was to give me a good example in how to be a lady, and I was old enough to understand things by then. I wouldn't have starved myself."

Maria shrugged eloquently. "I do not know. Maybe by then he was used to me. When he brought her home, he called me into his office. I thought he would tell me I had to leave, but he said he wanted me to help Mrs. Ross. He said he had not told her about my past and that I was not to mention it either." Maria sighed. "That is the last time anyone ever spoke of it until today."

"I'm so sorry, Mama," Angelica said, reaching out to hug her again. "I never meant to bring up all these bad memories for you."

"And I am sorry to make you so sad, but I am glad, too," she added, pulling out of the hug so she could see Angelica's face. "All these years, I was afraid you would hate me if you knew."

"Hate you!" Angelica repeated in genuine amazement. "How could you think that?"

Maria shook her head sadly and gently stroked the girl's flame-colored tresses. "When you love someone, it hurts to find out they are different than you thought. Sometimes you do not love them anymore."

"But I'm not like that," Angelica protested. "You know I'll always love you."

Maria's smile returned slowly. "No, you are not like that. You are loyal, maybe too loyal sometimes, and I love you, too."

Angelica hugged her *mamacita* again, but before she could say more, she heard the sound of horses and a wagon out in the yard. "The men are back," she said, pulling reluctantly out of Maria's arms. The two women shared a long look as they both considered the grim burden that wagon carried and the unpleasant task before them.

Maria rose reluctantly. "I will go and tell Mr. Collins," she offered. Angelica gratefully nodded her agreement.

"Miss Angelica, we got everything set up just like you wanted," the gangly cowboy told her. He hovered in the doorway to her father's office as if reluctant to give her the news.

Angelica looked up from where she sat at the large desk flipping through the worn Ross Family Bible for scripture passages suitable for a funeral. "Thanks, Hank. Did I tell you what a good job you and Curly did on the coffins?" she asked, managing a friendly smile for this man who had served the Diamond R faithfully for a decade.

"Yes, ma'am, you did," he replied, shuffling his overlarge feet and tugging self-consciously on his gray-streaked beard.

"I know Mr. Collins will be pleased," she added in an attempt to make him feel better. She knew he had been shaken by horrible job of recovering the bodies from the charred remains of their home and bringing them back here. Angelica was upset herself, and she'd only had a glimpse of the canvas-wrapped bundles before her men had put them into the hastily constructed coffins.

"It's the least I could do after you told me how he's going to help us, miss," Hank said. His weathered face creased into a frown. "When I think of all those no-good rannies who ran out on you, I could just . . ."

But Angelica waved away his outrage. "Then don't think about them, Hank. I don't blame them for leaving, anyway.

I couldn't pay them enough to make it worthwhile for them to risk getting shot at."

Hank made a disgusted noise. "There's such a thing as loyalty to the brand," he muttered.

Angelica smiled her understanding. They'd had this conversation before, and Hank simply would not be reconciled to the fact that not all the Diamond R cowhands had been as loyal as he and Curly. Sometimes Angelica was tempted to tease Hank by suggesting that maybe it was stupidity and not loyalty that had kept them here. But Hank had never exhibited much of a sense of humor, and she doubted he would get the joke. "If you'll get Curly, I'll get everyone else together and tell them it's time for the service."

A man of few words, Hank nodded and left. Angelica stared at the empty doorway for a long moment, reflecting on how fortunate she was to have men like Hank and Curly. In the last few weeks they had done the work of ten men and even humored Robbie into thinking he was helping, too.

She sighed, dwelling for a moment on troubles past and speculating on what new ones lay ahead. But she couldn't just sit there feeling sorry for herself, she finally decided, rising from the desk chair. She had a funeral to organize.

The late afternoon sun had painted the courtyard a rich golden hue, she noted with approval as she crossed it to reach Mr. Collins's bedroom. Was it appropriate to hold a funeral at suppertime? she wondered, glancing at the two rough coffins which had been placed side by side beside the gurgling fountain. She shuddered slightly at the thought of what the boxes held and all the shattered dreams they represented.

All around, in a dozen flowerbeds, bright spring flowers turned their faces to the sun in cheerful defiance of the mournful occasion. Impulsively, Angelica set down the large Bible she carried, plucked a handful of blossoms from the bunch nearest her and carried them over to the plain wooden boxes. With great care, she spread some on each coffin in an effort to relieve the starkness of the bare planks. There, she thought, stepping back to view her handiwork. Not good, but better at least.

That done, she turned back toward her original destination. She paused outside the bedroom door, listening for the sound of voices. Robbie and Maria had gone to help Mr. Collins prepare for the funeral. He had insisted on getting up and dressed, in spite of his weakened condition. They had compromised with his stubbornness by agreeing to hold the service here in the courtyard instead of at the graveside up on the hill.

Hearing only a quiet murmur from within the room, Angelica lifted her hand and knocked. "Come in," Collins's voice said.

She was halfway through the doorway when she saw him. It was the shock of seeing him in her father's clothes that did it, she told herself even as she closed her gaping mouth with a snap and forced her lungs to function normally again. The fact that her father had never done quite so much for that black broadcloth suit had nothing whatsoever to do with her breathless reaction.

Collins was sitting in the chair he had been trying to reach that morning, and as she came into the room, he rose carefully to his feet. His face was pale, but he seemed much steadier than he had earlier. "Maria said it was all right to wear the suit," he said apologetically, obviously misinterpreting her surprise as disapproval. "My own clothes are too stained."

"Oh, yes, that's fine," she quickly assured him. "I'm glad to see someone getting some use out of it. Do you think you can walk all the way out into the courtyard?"

He nodded, determined to make it to Rose's funeral even if he had to crawl. Maria had explained how they had decided to have the service right outside his room. He'd caught a glimpse of the flowers decorating the courtyard and knew that he could not have chosen a prettier spot himself. "Are you ready to start?"

"Yes," she said, and he watched her hand fidget briefly with her skirt. She was wearing black for the occasion, and although the color didn't do much for her, it provided a nice contrast to her brilliant hair and eyes. Her beauty was a balm to his inner torment.

"Let's go, then," he said, glancing around to find Robbie.

The boy instantly scampered to his side. "You can lean on me," Robbie offered eagerly.

The Kid gave him a grateful grin and placed a perfunctory hand on his small shoulder. "Thanks, partner," he said, and they started for the door.

Angelica stepped aside, watching apprehensively until she was certain that Collins would not fall. She followed in their wake, and Maria came along behind her.

There were several benches in the courtyard, the Kid noticed, and someone had moved one over near the coffins. He sat down on it and motioned for the boy to sit beside him. Only then did he allow himself to look at the plain wooden boxes that held the remains of the last of his family. Pain and anger washed over him as he thought of the injustice of it all. Pete and Rose had only been trying to build a life for themselves. They had never made any trouble for anyone. Someone was going to pay for this and pay dearly.

Maria had come up to stand behind the bench where he and Robbie sat, and two cowboys moved in closer from where they had been waiting at a discreet distance, clutching their battered hats in their work-worn hands.

"Mr. Collins, these are my men, Hank and Curly," Angelica said.

The Kid offered his hand and the men took it, each in turn. He recognized their type immediately. They were good, dependable workers who would serve Angelica faithfully, but they were not fighters. The taller one, Hank, was obviously the leader. The shorter, bald-headed man called Curly was a follower. He would do as he was told, but no more. Still, they were both old enough to be steady, and they would be a big help during the roundup.

"I'm pleased to meet you, boys," he said, even though both men were considerably older than he. "I'd like to thank you for what you did for Rose and Pete."

They muttered their replies, uncomfortable at accepting his gratitude. Then Hank said, "We're real sorry about your family, Mr. Collins, but we're glad you've decided to help Miss Angelica."

"It's the least I can do," the Kid said simply.

An awkward silence fell as no one could quite think of anything else to say. Angelica cleared her throat. "Are we ready to begin?" she asked.

Curly and Hank stepped back to a respectful distance, and Collins nodded. "Yes, go ahead," he said.

Angelica retrieved the Bible from where she had left it earlier and opened the large, heavy book to the passage she had marked. Conscious that all eyes were on her, she straightened her shoulders and read in a loud, clear voice, " 'Behold, I shew you a mystery; We shall not all sleep, but we shall all be changed, In a moment, in the twinkling of an eye, at the last trump: for the trumpet shall sound, and the dead shall be raised incorruptible, and we shall all be changed. . . .' "

She read on, lingering over the promises that "death is swallowed up in victory," and wondering how she could convince the solemn man seated nearby of that. At the moment he looked inconsolable, his blue eyes clouded with the same unspeakable agonies she had seen earlier in Maria's. A simple hug had erased Maria's pain, but how could she reach this man?

When she had finished reading the passage promising eternal life, she closed the Bible, and said, "We did not know Pete and Rose Hastings, but we do know that they were good people who wanted to live in peace. Their only mistake was choosing to live on land someone else wanted. We know that they were innocent, and the Lord must know it, too. Surely, He will welcome them into His kingdom with open arms."

Angelica hugged the Bible to her chest and allowed her gaze to rest for a moment on the two flower-strewn coffins. Then she lifted her eyes and looked at Collins, who was staring at her. He had such an odd expression on his face that for a moment she knew a vague unease over what violent thoughts might lurk behind those intense blue eyes. He certainly had every right to feel violent after what had happened to him, but to her surprise, his voice was calm when he said, "Thank you. That was very nice."

Shaking off her feelings of alarm, she gave a little nod of acknowledgment. "Would you like to say something?" she asked.

The Kid considered. There were many things he wanted to say, many promises he wanted to make Rose and Pete, but not in front of strangers. He would make those promises in his heart and keep them there, too. "No, you said everything important," he replied.

Angelica cast around in her mind for something else to do. These people deserved more than just this brief tribute from someone who didn't even know them. She tried to recall what words had been spoken at her father's graveside, and remembered the perfect closing.

" 'The Lord is my shepherd, I shall not want . . .' " she began, catching Robbie's eye. The boy quickly joined her in reciting the words to the familiar Psalm.

" 'He maketh me to lie down in green pastures . . .' " Maria's voice blended in, and Angelica heard a murmur from Hank and Curly, who must have been drawing on childhood memories for the words.

" 'Yea, though I walk through the valley of the shadow

of death . . .' " To Angelica's surprise, Collins's strong baritone voice rose above the others, repeating the phrases with the confidence of long familiarity. Her startled gaze found him, but he didn't notice her stare. He was looking at the coffins, that strange expression marring his handsome face again. With difficulty, she resisted the impulse to go to him and offer some sort of comfort. What could she possibly do or say to ease the pain of his loss?

" '. . . and I will dwell in the house of the Lord forever.' "

For a long moment, no one moved. Then Hank came forward a step. "We've dug some graves for them up on the hill with Mr. Ross and his wives," he said. "It's real nice up there."

The Kid nodded, suddenly unutterably weary. "Thanks," he said, rising carefully to his feet and surprised to discover that his wound burned fiercely. If he didn't get back to bed soon, he'd have to be carried there. Robbie was still beside him, on his feet also. The Kid reached out a hand to steady himself on Robbie's head and sent the boy staggering. Angelica was there in an instant.

"Here, take the Bible," she told her brother, thrusting the large book into his hands.

"I want to help Mr. Collins," Robbie protested, but Maria shushed him, pulling him to safety when Angelica's frantic motions almost knocked him down. Hank and Curly moved to assist Angelica, but Maria signaled them to stop, suspecting that the girl did not need or want their help.

Much as she had earlier that day, Angelica got Collins's arm over her shoulders and headed him back toward his room. This time he did not hesitate to give her some of his weight, and Angelica realized how much his determination to see his family laid properly to rest had cost him.

"Just a few more steps," she told him as they approached the bed.

Behind them, from the doorway, Robbie's voice piped,

"I'm going to help Hank and Curly. They told me I could."

Angelica couldn't repress the smile that curved her lips. Robbie was determined to impress his idol somehow. "That's good, honey," she called over her shoulder as she eased Collins down to sit on the bed. "I know Mr. Collins appreciates it."

"Yes, I do," Collins confirmed, although his voice was strained and far weaker than it should have been.

"Come now," Maria's voice said from behind Robbie. "We will let Mr. Collins rest."

Angelica heard Robbie's obligatory protest, and then the door closed, muffling his voice and Maria's. Meanwhile, she had her hands full. "I'll help you take the jacket off before you lie down," she offered.

He made a feeble attempt to assist her, and soon he was free of the constraining garment. Angelica tossed it over the bedpost. "Do you need some help with your shoes?" she asked, making a gesture with her hand.

He caught that hand with more strength than she thought him capable of and studied her fingers with great interest. "You picked the flowers, didn't you?" he asked after a moment, lifting his azure eyes to her face.

Angelica glanced down in dismay at the green stains on her fingers. "Yes," she admitted, tugging in an attempt to get him to release her hand and allow her to hide it behind her back. Why hadn't she taken an extra minute to wash up after her impulsive action?

But his grip only tightened, and she looked back at him in surprise. His eyes glittered with what could only be unshed tears, and once more her heart ached for his grief. When he spoke, his voice was hoarse with it. "Those things you said were real nice. Rose would have liked that. She would have liked the flowers, too. . . ." His voice cracked, just slightly but enough to hint at the depth of the emotions he was attempting to conceal.

No longer able to resist, she reached out for him, drawing his head to the comfort of her breast. She had no words to make things right again, but she knew from her own bitter experience the solace another human could offer. At first he stiffened in surprise, but she drew him closer, and he surrendered to the embrace with an agonized sigh.

He knew it was wrong to hold her like this, to use his grief as an excuse to bury his face in her softness and breathe in her womanly scent. But the grief was there and it was very real. He needed her, needed to hold someone warm and living as reassurance that he, too, was still alive. Telling himself that was excuse enough, he lifted his arms and embraced her with gentle strength so she could not get away.

Wrapped in the circle of his arms, Angelica touched his hair. Tentatively at first and then with increasing confidence, her fingers stroked the golden strands that glittered in the fading sunlight. In an ancient gesture of comfort, she allowed her fingers to caress his nape and lowered her cheek to rest on the top of his head. Her eyes closed as she inhaled the maleness of him, and a strange warmth seeped into her bones, creating an even stranger euphoria. His arms tightened, pulling her into the cradle of his thighs, and she went willingly.

Closer, he had to have her closer. Longing to draw her into his very soul, he tightened his arms into a bone-crushing grip and sank backward onto the bed until she was touching him everywhere, as he had fantasized that morning. He felt her surprise and even her instinctive resistance, but right and wrong didn't matter just now, not when he needed her so much.

Angelica stiffened for an instant, every bit of her common sense warning her to resist this intimacy, but a more primitive part of her understood his desperation. His body spoke to her more eloquently than words ever could have, convincing her of his need. His mouth sought hers as if her lips were a balm for the agony he felt. Without conscious thought, she surrendered to the kiss, allowing him to drink deeply of the cure. His hands began to move over her, tracing the contours of her body, molding her to him desperately, as if the touch of her could absorb his anguish.

For one tortured moment, they were one. Angelica took his pain, dispelling the torment with a feminine prowess as old as time itself. Glorying in this power she had never dreamed she possessed, she clung to the man who had made her feel like a woman for thc first time in her life.

She shifted slightly to accommodate herself to his length, but her movement jarred him. She felt as much as heard the grunt of pain that told her she had struck his wound. Horrified, she pulled her mouth from his and stared down into his startled face.

"I . . . I'm sorry," she whispered breathlessly, breaking the spell that had held them. Suddenly she was acutely aware that she was literally draped on top of him and that he was lying on a bed and that she had been *kissing* him, for heaven's sake. How could this have happened? What on earth had she been thinking? But she hadn't been thinking at all, of course; that was the whole problem. "Did I hurt you?" she gasped, feeling her face flame and somehow managing to scramble free of his embrace and stagger to her feet without injuring him again.

"No, I'm fine," he lied, as breathless as she and unable even to move from where he lay sprawled on the bed. What on earth had he done? How could he have lost control like that? How could he have taken advantage of her innocent gesture?

Suddenly, his side was throbbing like hell, and he was too weak even to offer an explanation. The sudden burst of passion had drained his last reserves. "I'm sorry," he managed feebly. "That shouldn't have happened."

Angelica placed a hand over her clamoring heart and drew a shaky breath. Why was he sorry and for what? The kiss had been terribly improper, of course, but she didn't think she wanted him to be sorry he had done it, at least not until she decided how she felt about it herself. "I . . . that's all right," she said inanely. "I didn't mind."

Oh, Lord! What a thing to say! Her already burning face heated up considerably, and she lifted trembling hands to cover the cheeks she knew were scarlet. "I mean . . . you weren't yourself and . . ." You're making it worse, she told herself, backing away in self-defense.

If he'd had the energy, the Kid would have cursed. He had frightened her half to death. He would be lucky if she or one of her men didn't put another hole in him, one that did more damage than the bullet that had brought him here in the first place. He tried to call her back so he could make things right, but his lips didn't seem to want to cooperate. He noticed that they still tasted of her, but they wouldn't form her name.

She was moving farther away, or at least he thought she was. Her voice sounded as if it came from a great distance. "Is something wrong?" she asked.

"No," he replied, or thought he did, just as the room grew dark.

Angelica blinked. He was asleep. Could someone fall asleep right in the middle of a conversation like that, especially just after he'd been kissing someone the way he'd been kissing her? "Mr. Collins?" she called hesitantly.

No response.

Suddenly, a new fear assailed her. What if he wasn't asleep at all? What if . . . ? She rushed back to him, touching his face with anxious hands. Her hasty move jarred him again, and he groaned involuntarily. His eyelids flickered but did not open.

Thank heaven, she breathed. He really was only sleeping. He looked awfully uncomfortable, though, and she knew she should call Mama to help her put him properly to bed. And she would, in just a moment. But for one blissful second, she allowed her fingers to stroke his face, across his forehead and down his cheeks where the faint stubble of his beard scraped deliciously against her fingertips.

He was so very beautiful, and he had kissed her. Oh, she had no romantic illusions about that kiss. She knew it had only happened because of his grief. Still, for a few magical moments, he had needed her, needed her the way a man needs a woman. But he had said it should never have happened. What did he mean by that?

It would be a while before she could ask him, and until then she would just have to wait, although patience had never been one of her virtues. Until then . . . For the second time that day, she responded to an impulse. This time, she bent down and touched her lips to his again. It was, she decided when she pulled away, much better when he kissed back. She would have to remember that.

Chapter Three

Angelica looked down at the mounds of earth that marked the graves of Pete and Rose Hastings. Hank and Curly had done a neat job of laying these two strangers to rest. She sighed, wondering if that made any difference at all to the Hastings. At least knowing the bodies had been properly buried would be a comfort to Mr. Collins.

At the thought of him, she frowned slightly. Reaching up, she touched her lips as she remembered how he had kissed her yesterday. She hadn't seen him since because exhaustion had made him sleep the rest of the day and all through the night. Maria hadn't even let her help put him to bed, but today would be different. As soon as Maria finished giving him his breakfast and his bed bath, Angelica was going to pay him a visit.

Anticipation tingled through her. What would happen? Would he treat her differently? And how should she treat him? She had never kissed a man that way before and wasn't quite sure how much such a kiss would change their relationship. Most certainly, her feelings for him had altered dramatically although she wasn't exactly certain what her new feelings were. Had the kiss been equally important to him?

Shaking off these disturbing thoughts, she began to divide the flowers that she had carried up the hillside, placing a small bunch on each of the graves there. The cemetery was getting crowded, she noticed sadly, laying some blooms by the headstone of the mother whom she had never known, the stepmother whom she had never liked, and the father whom she still missed dreadfully. Who would be next? she wondered, unconsciously picturing Collin's face. For one horrible moment yesterday, she had thought he, too, had slipped away from her. Why she should have been so panicked by the thought, she had no idea. He was, after all, a virtual stranger, or at least she had tried to convince herself of that fact all through last evening and the night that followed.

But he wasn't really a stranger, she had finally been forced to admit. Although she knew very little about him, she knew him well. She had shared his grief, and they had touched in a way that transcended the physical. She understood instinctively that their kiss had only been a symbol of what had passed between them in that moment, a communion that surpassed what words or even long acquaintance could create.

Angelica shivered slightly at the implications of her thoughts and brushed the last clinging remnants of the flowers from her hands. She wondered if the encounter with Collins had affected him in the same way, and what his reaction would be when next they met. A part of her feared learning the answers to her questions, but the rest of her turned eagerly back toward the house. By the time she reached the bottom of the hill, she was fairly running.

The Kid lay in his bed, staring blindly up at the ceiling of the large room as he mentally replayed the moment when he had kissed Angelica Ross. Of all the dumb things he had done in his life—and there had been a few—that had been by far the dumbest. He had made a commitment to help her run her roundup, to be her employee for the next two months or more. Nothing in their agreement included pulling her down on the bed and attacking her. Thank God, he'd been exhausted and in pain, or heaven only knew what else might have happened.

He'd known from the very beginning that she was an uncommonly attractive girl and that he would have to be very careful not to respond to that attraction. Still, he had somehow managed to ruin everything before he'd even been here forty-eight hours. Now she would either be mad as a wet hen or she would be all sweet and lovely, convinced that the kiss had meant far more than it had.

He wanted her to be mad, no question about it. He could deal with that. She'd already shown him a few flashes of the temper that went with her red hair, and he knew he could defuse her anger with a humble apology and a promise to behave himself in the future.

What he didn't know was what he would do if she came in here all happy and smiling, believing that the kiss signified the beginning of something romantic between them. The thought caused a curious ache in his chest that felt suspiciously like longing, but it was a longing he couldn't allow himself to feel. Angelica Ross was a woman he had no right to want, and her life was already complicated enough without her getting tangled up with a gunfighter. And God knew, this gunfighter never wanted to get tangled up with another woman, not after Lettie.

No, if she showed any signs of the interest in him that her willing response to him had indicated, he would have to squelch it quickly, although how he could do that without ruining any chance they had of working together, he had no idea. He actually winced when he heard the knock on his bedroom door. By now he knew her knock. "Come in," he called.

The door opened and there she was. Smiling. God, her smile could light up a room, he thought, fighting the urge to groan aloud as he saw all his hopes for her anger going up in smoke.

"Good morning," Angelica said, placing a hand over the fluttering in her stomach. He got better-looking every time she saw him. His sky blue gaze met hers across the room for a heart-stopping instant, but then skittered away. How odd, he looked almost guilty. She could feel her smile slipping as she considered this. Why should he feel guilty?

The answer was obvious, of course. He probably felt he had taken advantage of her after the funeral yesterday. She had told him that she didn't mind, but perhaps he didn't remember. Or perhaps he thought she was only being polite. He might even expect her to be angry at the liberties he had taken. Could he have forgotten that she had reached for him first? She knew an overwhelming urge to reassure him, but could not quite decide on how to bring up the subject. She settled for, "How are you feeling today?"

"Tired," he said, bringing his gaze back to touch her again. She was even more beautiful than he remembered, and for an awful moment he could recall exactly how she had felt in his arms, soft and warm and luscious. Curling his fists into the bedclothes with the effort of banishing that memory, he steeled himself against her determined smile.

"Yesterday was a strain on you, I know," she said, moving closer to the bed. He seemed to tense as she approached, but maybe that was only her imagination. He watched her unblinkingly, although she could not quite read his expression. Her smile began to feel uncomfortable, so she let it slip a bit more.

He watched her sunny expression flicker and die. Good, she had sensed his wariness. Now it would be a simple matter to wipe yesterday out of existence. "The funeral seems like a bad dream," he began, choosing his words carefully. "I remember you said some nice things about Rose and her husband. Did I ever thank you for that?"

Had he thanked her? Angelica's eyes widened in astonishment, but she managed to say, "Yes, you did." If he had forgotten that, what else had he forgotten?

"Good," he said, maintaining his detached pose. "I also remember I had a little trouble getting back here. Did one of your men help me?"

This time her mouth dropped open, but she caught herself and closed it instantly. *One of her men?* Was it really possible that he did not recall what had happened? She felt her cheeks growing hot with embarrassment as she explained, "N—no, I helped you."

"You?" he said with a creditable imitation of amazement. "*You* put me to bed?" He did not have to feign any emotion for that statement. He'd spent most of the morning struggling with uncomfortable images of her undressing him, and he'd hesitated to ask Maria about it for fear she'd guess his concern involved more than modesty.

"Oh, no!" Angelica assured him, her face scalding now. "Maria did that . . . that part. I just helped you get back here and . . ." *And held you and kissed you and don't you remember?* But he didn't. His eyes revealed no hint of recollection. She wanted to demand to know how he could have forgotten what was to her a momentous event, but she had no experience with such things. What was proper etiquette for reminding a man he had kissed her the day before?

"I appreciate that, Miss Ross," he was saying, his blue eyes solemn and innocent. "You've done an awful lot for me."

More than you know, she wanted to say, but of course, she didn't. "I expect you'll pay me back when you can," she said instead, forcing herself to smile in spite of her disappointment.

That sad smile tore at his heart, but he kept his expression blank. "I intend to do just that," he replied, with more sincerity that she would have guessed.

Angelica stared down at him, resisting with difficulty the urge to reach out and brush an errant lock of golden hair off his forehead. Vainly, she cast about for something to say, something that would justify her continued presence here. She had entered the room hoping to be greeted warmly by a man with whom she had shared a tender moment. Instead, she faced a formal stranger who treated her only with the deference due his employer.

Well, she *was* his employer, when all was said and done. No matter what might have happened before or what he remembered, he was still working for her, or at least he would be as soon as he got better. Even as the thought flitted across her mind, she saw his blue eye close in weariness.

"Oh, I'm sorry. You must be tired," she stammered, remembering that he had said that very thing only a few minutes ago and feeling more a fool with every passing second.

The Kid reluctantly lifted his eyelids. He'd closed them so he would no longer have to see the hurt in her eyes, and he was glad to see she had managed to conceal it again. The kiss had obviously been something more than just a comforting gesture on her part, but he was determined to maintain his distance from her. "Was there something you wanted to talk to me about?" he asked, grateful that he still sounded like a conscientious employee and nothing more.

Yes, there was plenty she wanted to talk to him about, but nothing she felt bold enough to mention at the moment. "No, nothing that can't wait until you're feeling better," she said, surrendering at last to the urge to reach out to him.

His breath caught as he saw her hand coming closer. If she touched him . . . But she didn't, not really. She simply straightened the coverlet, and then, as if she suddenly realized what she was doing, she snatched her hand away.

"I . . . I'll be going now," she said, startled at her own reaction. The cover had been warm from his body, stirring memories of how it felt to be pressed against that warmth. More than anything, she wanted to draw close to him again, to touch his face and smooth away the troubled look that clouded his eyes. But such a thing would be shockingly improper, and whatever would he think if she did? If only he remembered yesterday, then things would be different. She could slip her arms around him again and . . . But of course, he didn't remember.

She began to back toward the door, unwilling to turn and lose sight of him before absolutely necessary. "I'll be nearby," she promised. "Just call if you need anything."

He nodded. His eyes watched hungrily as she retreated, her slender body moving with a natural grace in spite of the fact that she was obviously flustered. Just as he had hoped, she was much too well-bred to remind him of what had passed between them. She would keep up her end of the charade. As long as he was careful never to slip again, things would be just fine.

After what seemed an eternity, she disappeared out the door. He breathed a long sigh of relief, and closed his eyes in genuine weariness.

Outside the door, Angelica paused to gain control of her skittering emotions. Embarrassment warred with disappointment, but anger finally flooded them both out, although who the object of her fury was, she wasn't sure. She had behaved like a lovesick fool over an incident that he couldn't even remember. Really, when she looked back, she realized how unimportant the whole thing had been and wondered how she could have blown it all out of proportion that way.

She should have known he was practically delirious. Hadn't he fallen asleep almost instantly? And from the way he had treated her on every other occasion, she was fairly certain that under ordinary circumstances, he wasn't the type of man who grabbed respectable young ladies and pulled them down onto his bed, either. She should be grateful he did not recall the incident. Such a recollection would only embarrass them both.

Except that she did not feel grateful at all. She was hurt, more than hurt. For some unexplainable reason, she felt cold and empty and aching inside, as if a part of her heart had been torn from her breast. Pushing away from the door, she strode across the courtyard to her own room, rubbing angrily at the unfamiliar sting of tears.

"Good afternoon, Miss Ross." Collins nodded politely as Angelica approached him in the courtyard. He was sitting by the fountain on the same bench where he had sat for the funeral a week ago. She tried to tell herself that the reason he did not smile was because he was thinking about his family, but deep down, she knew that wasn't the real reason.

He *never* smiled at her, Angelica admitted with annoyance as she returned his greeting, matching his distant tone. Was this the same man who had kissed her so passionately, who had revealed the starkness of his need to her just a short seven days ago? She could hardly believe that he was. Since their meeting the morning after the kiss, when he denied all memory of that disturbing encounter, he had continued to treat her with the same stiff courtesy he had used that day. Uncertain how to break through his wall of icy reserve and unable to think of a socially acceptable reason for even doing so, she simply imitated it.

"I'm glad to see you up and around," she said, giving him her cool, Lady Rancher smile. "You must be feeling much better today."

"Yes, ma'am, I am," he replied, rising as she drew closer. He was wearing a set of her father's range clothes, and he looked every bit as good in them as he did in her father's suit, she noticed reluctantly. "I've been wanting to get a feel for the place. I thought I'd take a walk around outside now," he added.

"Fine," she said, wondering whether she should offer to go with him and show him around, and whether he would appreciate such an offer.

Before she could decide, he said, "See you later." With a tip of his hat, he was gone without so much as a backward glance.

"Damn!" Angelica swore, fighting an urge to kick something. What was wrong with the man?

She'd given a lot of thought to that question since their first meeting after the infamous kiss. As hard as she had tried to forget the kiss ever happened, she had failed miserably. Memories of his mouth on hers had haunted her dreams, both waking and sleeping, every day since. Sometimes she even deluded herself into believing he must remember it, too, regardless of what he said.

She made a point of visiting him each day at least once, usually taking Robbie with her as a buffer. During those visits, she filled him in on the history of the ranch and every detail about running it that he could possibly need to know. Although their discussions were almost always strictly business, occasionally she would glance up and catch a strange expression in his sky blue eyes, an expression that hinted of things unspoken. But the expression would instantly disappear, and she would be left wondering if it were only a product of her overactive imagination.

"*Buenas tardes,* little one," Maria called as she entered the courtyard from the kitchen door carrying an armload of bed linens. "Come and take some of these."

With a frown, Angelica hurried to help her foster mother. *Little one.* How she'd hated that nickname ever since she'd turned into a carrot-topped bean pole. Somehow Mama had never seemed to notice how her "little one" towered over her, though, and she continued to use it.

"Where is Mr. Collins?" Maria asked, looking around in confusion as Angelica relieved her of half her load. "He was here just a minute ago."

"I know," Angelica replied as they strolled over to the nearest bedroom, where Maria deposited some of the linens in a trunk. "He went for a walk." She did not add the other thought that tortured her, namely that he had selected the flimsiest excuse he could think of to leave the instant she showed up.

"Is something wrong, *Angelita?*" Maria asked, straightening from her task. "You do not look yourself."

"I'm fine," Angelica assured her hastily, forcing a more pleasant expression to her face. "And isn't it nice that Mr. Collins is up and around?"

Maria still eyed her a little suspiciously, but she said, "Yes, he is young and strong. He is almost completely recovered now. Yesterday, he walked up the hill to see the graves."

"I didn't know that!" Angelica said, unaccountably angry that no one had told her.

Maria shrugged off the girl's outrage. "I did not know you wished to be told of his every move," she said, a sly twinkle in her eye.

Realizing that her anger was ridiculous, Angelica quelled it, managing to resume her nonchalant pose. "I don't," she denied. "I was just surprised, that's all." She forced herself not to squirm under Maria's knowing grin, certain that next her *mamacita* was probably going to start teasing her about her dress the way she had every day since Collins's arrival.

Just because Angelica had decided to start dressing the part of Lady Rancher, Mama had decided she had some ulterior motive in the selection of her gowns and speculated often on how Mr. Collins would like her choice. The green-barred muslin she was wearing today was another of her convent dresses and hardly qualified as a "gown" at all. Still, it was certainly different from the patched and faded gingham she usually preferred. Angelica wondered wickedly that Mama would say if she knew that underneath her neatly groomed exterior, she still refused to wear the proper undergarments.

But Maria neither teased nor goaded. She only shook

her head and said, "He seems very sad. Maybe you could visit with him more and try to cheer him up."

Angelica gave her foster mother a baleful glare. "I don't think my visits cheer him up," she said, achingly aware of how very true that was. What was it about her that had repelled him? She knew she was no raving beauty, not with her awkward height and her flaming hair. Still, she wasn't ugly either, and the mere fact she was a female in this land where women were scarce usually drew a certain amount of attention from men, although it was often the kind of attention that embarrassed her. At this point, however, she wouldn't have minded even that type of attention from him.

"If your visits do not cheer him up, then you are not trying very hard," Maria chastened. "He is your guest, and he has agreed to help you. The least you can do is be friendly to him."

Angelica almost sputtered. It was on the tip of her tongue to say that she had been a lot more than friendly and look what it had gotten her, but she somehow restrained herself from blurting out the humiliating truth. Instead, she thrust her armload of linens back at Maria. "All right, Mamacita, I'll go be friendly," she said crossly. Ignoring Maria's startled expression, she stormed out of the courtyard, through the house and into the bright afternoon sunshine.

The Kid squinted through the smoke of his cigarette as he stared up at the small hill where the Diamond R cemetery lay. When he'd been up there yesterday, he'd discovered fresh flowers on the graves, and he'd known without asking who had placed them there. The more he learned about Angelica Ross, the worse things got. Now he knew that she was as beautiful inside as she was outside, and that she kissed like the angel he had once thought her.

Taking one last drag on the cigarette, he tossed it to the ground and crushed it viciously with his foot, taking out his frustration on the harmless butt. Muttering a curse, he stalked across the ranch yard toward the barn. Once he got to the far side of the large building, he would be unable to see either the house where she lived or the cemetery where she left flowers on strangers' graves.

Wasn't it bad enough that he'd had to bury his sister, the sister he hadn't even seen in ten years before her urgent summons? Losing Rose and her husband and taking a bullet in a running gun battle was plenty of suffering for anyone to have to endure at one time. Why had fate seen fit to add in the sweet torment of Angelica Ross? Being so close to her day after day but being unable to touch her or even acknowledge the desire that churned inside of him was the kind of exquisite torture the Comanches might have dreamed up.

He paused, having reached the rear of the barn and the solitude it offered. The back door of the building stood partly ajar, and he could smell the familiar scent of horses and leather from within. In the adjoining corral, his own horse, Midnight, ran loose, looking eager for some more challenging activity. The Kid was equally eager, but that would have to wait, at least for a while. Until he knew he was completely back to normal, he wouldn't dare go riding out any place where he might encounter someone who could recognize him. He wouldn't be of any use to Angelica Ross if he were dead.

At that thought, his hand went automatically to the gun he had strapped on when he had gotten dressed earlier. The feel of the smooth wooden grip beneath his hand and the weight of the weapon resting on his hip were strangely comforting. Responding to a habit born of years of practicing, he drew the gun in one lightning-quick motion.

Not bad, he judged, considering he'd just spent a week lazing around in bed. But not good enough, not by a long shot, especially when he realized he had flinched involuntarily at the way the rapid movement pulled against his wound. A flinch like that could cost a man his life, as he knew only too well.

Jamming the pistol back into the holster, he turned, facing away from the barn and the corrals and the other ranch buildings. Choosing a lone cottonwood tree as his adversary, he drew on it in earnest. Again he flinched, marring the smooth motion of the draw. Cursing softly, he shoved the gun away and tried again. And again. And again.

Angelica crept silently through the musty stillness of the barn. She had almost given herself away when she had come storming around the corner of the building and discovered him practicing his quick draw. Luckily, he had been too engrossed in his task to notice her approach, and she was able to steal away unseen.

But her curiosity was too fierce to keep her away for long, and she had sneaked back, this time choosing to approach through the barn so she could stand at the back door and observe him secretly. She had often heard stories about men who made a science of pulling their guns out faster than anyone else, but she had never thought to see one in action.

Carefully, her heart beating frantically against her ribs in apprehension at the possibility of being caught spying on him, she eased her way to the partially open door and peered around. There he was, just as she had first seen him. For a moment he stood perfectly still, like a statue carved in granite; then his hand blurred, and the next instant he stood holding a gun on some invisible opponent.

Had she blinked and missed the movement? Next time she would see it for sure, she vowed, watching him replace the gun and pose himself again. She waited long seconds, holding her eyes open until they began to water, and then it happened again. Before she knew it, he was holding the gun once more, but in spite of the fact that she hadn't blinked, she hadn't seen him draw that time either.

What phrase had Robbie used to describe this kind of draw? "Fast as chain lightning," that was it, and how accurate the description was, she would never have guessed. Forgetting her fears of being caught, she continued to watch as time and time gain his hand brought the gun up and then shoved it home again.

Now her heart was pounding for a different reason. She had never seen him like this, standing tall and strong and powerful, a man in complete control of his destiny. All traces of the unconscious victim who had been carried to her door were gone, and in his place stood the legendary Kid Collins. "Kid Collins, Gunfighter *Extraordinaire*" she characterized him, her convent French providing the only proper word to describe him.

Her lip curled in disgust at her own whimsy. A fine man she'd picked to squander her girlish fantasies on. His heart was probably harder than that six-gun he seemed so fond of. Making a fist, she lifted her hand and banged it silently on the wall beside her to vent her frustrations, but instead of smooth wood, her hand encountered the rough surface of a rawhide lariat hanging beside the door.

Glancing at the rope, she entertained a brief but satisfying picture of tightening it around a certain fickle gunfighter's neck. First she would build a loop, just like her father's Mexican vaqueros had taught her in the old days when she'd been allowed to run wild. Then she would twirl it in the quick, silent spin called a hoolihan catch, and the rope would settle over him. . . . As the picture formed in her mind, a slow, wicked grin spread over her face. It would serve him right, she thought, but could she still do it? Many years had passed since she had thrown a rope.

Without conscious thought, she plucked the lariat from its place on the wall. She only wanted to see if her skill had deserted her, she told herself as she threaded the end through the honda to make a loop.

The Kid slid the Colt back into its holster yet again and allowed himself a small smile of satisfaction. The stiffness in his side was gone now, and he could pull the gun without anticipating the pain of stretching his still sore wound. A few more days and he would be completely back to normal. He reached for the gun again just as he heard the faint whizzing sound.

Angelica watched in complete surprise as the rope did exactly what she had intended it to do and settled neatly over his shoulders. Instinctively, she yanked it tight as she had been taught to do those long years ago. The pull would bring a horse or a cow to heel, but this was no dumb animal she had captured. Her quarry went down with amazing speed, twisting and turning and coming up again on one knee as the lariat and his Stetson went flying free. Angelica stood staring into the dark barrel of a forty-five, the click of its cocking hammer echoing in her ears.

Staring at the gun in growing horror, she swallowed against the sudden dryness in her throat and instinctively raised her hands, dropping her end of the lariat into the dust.

"I . . . I . . . Don't shoot me!" she stammered, humiliated to find her voice was trembling along with the rest of her. No one had ever pointed a gun at her before, and she discovered that looking down the wrong end of the barrel was an utterly terrifying experience.

The Kid stared at her incredulously for a long moment, replaying what had just happened in his mind and unable to reconcile the facts. Angelica Ross had thrown a rope over him, with amazing accuracy and for no apparent reason. And by God, now he was holding a gun on her!

Shocked to discover the truth of that last thought, he swiftly released the cocked hammer and stuffed the pistol back in his holster. "What in the hell did you think you were doing?" he demanded, lunging furiously to his feet.

"I was . . . It was a joke," she tried, relieved that the gun was gone but hardly reassured by his livid expression. Still trembling, she backed up a step toward the questionable safety of the barn. "My father's vaqueros taught me how to rope when I was little, and I just wanted to see if I still could do it or if that convent school had ruined me and I . . ."

She knew she was babbling and forced herself to stop, swallowing the senseless explanations. He didn't look a bit mollified.

Unconsciously, the Kid advanced on her. "Do you know I could have killed you?" he asked through gritted teeth, the thought chilling him to the marrow even as his blood began to boil in fury. What a stupid, idiotic trick to pull! Didn't she have any idea how dangerous it was to attack an armed man? What if he had fired without thinking as he had trained himself to do? What if his bullet even now were lodged in her heart, her life's blood draining out? The vision filled him with a horror so overwhelming, he could no longer even think straight.

Angelica cringed, knowing only too well how close he had come to pulling the trigger. She had no doubt that if he had, she would be lying dead on the ground at this very moment. "I . . . I'm sorry," she said, trying to swallow the metallic taste of fear. "I didn't think . . ."

His eyes were terrible, like blue fire, and she could almost feel the scorching flames. She backed up another step and then another as he continued menacingly toward her, his huge body taut with emotions she could only guess at. Some distant voice of reason argued that he would hardly do her bodily harm to punish her for almost getting herself killed, but the physical evidence seemed to indicate otherwise.

She took another backward step and bumped into the barn door, which pushed inward just as his hands reached out for her. Responding to her primal instinct for survival, she did the only sensible thing: she turned and ran.

Through the barn and out into the yard she went, and still she heard his pounding footsteps behind her. She grabbed up two handfuls of her skirt to free her long legs. Into the front door of the house, through the entryway, out again into the courtyard. Was he still following? She did not know, could not tell if the sound was his boots on tile or her own heart pounding in her ears.

But safety lay ahead, the safety of her room. He would never dare follow her there. The heavy wooden door beckoned, the knob turned easily under her hand, and she was inside. Frantically, she pushed the door closed behind her, but before the latch caught, a counter weight struck the other side, flinging it open again and sending her flying across the room until she hit the bed and went sprawling across it.

He was there, filling the doorway, and he kept coming. The door bounced violently against the wall and rebounded, slamming shut with a crash that made the furniture shake, but neither of them even noticed.

In the room's comparative dimness, Angelica could not make out his expression, but his mood didn't seem to have improved noticeably. Suddenly, she realized how vulnerable she was sprawled on the bed, and she scrambled to her feet just as he reached her.

"Do you know I could have killed you?" he asked again, grabbing her arms and hauling her against his chest. The words sounded tortured, as if they caused him agony to utter, or perhaps that was only an illusion because of the way his breath rasped in his throat.

Her own breath came in labored gasps as she searched his face to judge his true emotions. Now that her eyes were growing accustomed to the interior light, she could clearly read the anger that had driven him to chase her. "I'm sorry," she whispered. "I never meant . . ."

He did not seem to hear her words. His eyes bored into

hers as if searching for something, something hidden deep inside of her. Her body trembled uncontrollably as she hung limp and defenseless in his grip. "Are . . . are you going to hurt me?" she asked, ashamed of the way her voice quavered but unable to help it.

Her question startled him and broke through the anger that had made him so strange. He blinked in surprise. "Hurt you?" he repeated in amazement. Then, as if suddenly realizing the way he was holding her, his grip gentled, and his hands moved soothingly, as if to massage away the discomfort he had caused. "I could never . . ." he began, but his voice caught and his hands slid around her, crushing her to him. He muttered something incomprehensible, and she realized that he, too, was trembling. Her own arms went around him, clinging to the comfort he offered.

The Kid buried his face in her hair, inhaling the scent of sunshine and woman that was uniquely Angelica. Hurt her? How could she even think such a thing? He would die before causing her a moment's pain. That's why he was shaking like a newborn foal. That's why he'd felt compelled to frighten her until she understood how closely she had courted disaster.

Her body was warm and soft and infinitely precious. His hands worshiped her, paying tribute to every inch of her back and shoulders and then tangling in the heavy mass of her flame-colored hair. He was vaguely aware that her hands were busy, too, touching and caressing in return, but he could not stop to analyze that fact. Finding her mouth was all that mattered, that and tasting her again.

She was sweeter than he remembered and more eager, so much a woman that she made him even more a man. Wants and needs surged and blended within him until they were indistinguishable. He felt strong enough to move a mountain and yet too weak to stand upright a moment longer.

Angelica clung to him, starved for the honey of his kiss. So natural did it feel to be in his arms that the past week of indifference might never have happened. This was where she belonged, and now he knew it, too. His hands were everywhere, stroking and caressing, robbing her of strength and will and even reason. When her legs would no longer hold her, she sank backward, carrying him with her onto the bed.

His weight was a magnificent burden that she bore gladly. It pressed into her, imprinting his image on her soul. Now his hands explored new territory, discovering the swell of her breasts and the swollen tips that throbbed for his touch. His lips left hers, trailing a fiery path down her throat as his fingers loosened the buttons of her dress to clear a path for his maruading kisses.

Following his lead and responding to a need equally great, her own fingers went to work, releasing his shirt until she could touch the golden hair that furred his chest. As she did, his breath strangled in his throat, and she could feel his heart thundering beneath her palm.

With an agonized moan, he reached down and tore open her chemise. Buttons flew everywhere, but no one paid them any heed. He captured her breasts, cupping them like two rare fruits, and then lowered himself until the curling hairs of his chest teased the tender buds of her nipples.

Angelica cried out at the unspeakable sensations that coursed through her, and she arched her back, craving closer contact. But he denied her, holding himself aloof, tormenting her with gentle strokes and feather-light kisses until she writhed beneath him. At last she could stand it no longer. With all her strength, she pulled him to her, mouth to mouth and breast to chest.

She started when a heavy weight struck her hip, but by the time she realized it was his gun, he had released the holster and let it thump to the floor. Now his body pressed intimately to hers, telling her of his desire, and her body responded, rocking against him in the ancient rhythm.

His hands grasped her hips as if to still them, but the grip soon became a caress while their mouths continued to mate in imitation of the ultimate union. Angelica caught his leg with hers, and in the tangle, her skirt rose above her knee. His hand found the bare skin and traced it higher and higher still, his fingers sending flames of desire to lick against her thighs until they ignited her very core.

Her mouth captured his surprised gasp when he encountered no barrier to her womanhood. His mouth captured her amazed gasp when he found her most sensitive spot. He stroked and teased, sending waves of ecstasy flooding through her until she begged him in senseless phrases for the fulfillment she craved.

His hand left her for a moment while he fumbled with is own clothing, but she knew enough to understand his actions and waited impatiently until he was free to join himself to her. She helped him, sliding her hands inside his jeans to clasp his lean flanks and draw him close.

She opened to him, offering everything she had to give, and he took it, or at least he tried. And tried again. His whole body jerked in surprise.

"My God!" he said hoarsely, as if he had just come to his senses. "What am I doing?"

He began to pull away, but she would not let him, could not let him. "No, please!" she pleaded, wrapping her legs around his. It couldn't end like this. She wanted him more than she had ever wanted anything; she wanted him in a way she had never known possible. Her mouth sought his again, and for a moment he resisted. But only a moment.

Angelica cried out when he took her, although the pain was slight compared to the glorious pleasure that accompanied it. Her eyes flew open, and in that instant she stared into his very soul. He whispered her name as he slowly filled her, easing past her broken innocence to claim what she surrendered so willingly.

His eyes mirrored the amazement she felt, and she wondered if he found the experience as overwhelming as she.

This was what she had waited for all her life, this moment with this man, her passage into womanhood.

He mumbled some endearment as he lowered his mouth to caress her throat, and she closed her eyes again against the sensation of his body moving within hers. His hands instructed her, and soon they moved together, her pleasure mounting with each thrust.

Could anyone feel like this and live? she wondered wildly. No mortal body could bear this intensity. Surely, she would die in just another moment. And then she did die, but it was a blissful passing into a golden netherworld where the two of them melded into one being.

It seemed a long time before their breaths slowed to normal and they slipped back into reality. Gradually, Angelica began to notice how burdensome his weight was becoming. As if sensing her discomfort, he stirred and then raised himself up on his elbows.

Their gazes met for a long moment that seemed to stretch on into infinity. Angelica easily read the emotions that played across his face, beginning with fogged passion and ending with a sort of stunned amazement. She wondered vaguely if her own expressions were similar. Her emotions certainly were. What on earth had she just done?

The actions that had seemed so right, so *inevitable,* just minutes ago in the heat of passion now seemed foolish and insane. She had given herself, given the precious gift of her virginity, to man she hardly knew, a man she wasn't even sure she liked! The body he had recently kindled to desire went cold with apprehension. What would happen now?

The Kid looked down at her in horror, both at his own actions and at hers. He had never in his entire life lost control like that, never been so violently compelled to possess a woman as he had just now. In fact, for the past four years, he had barely known desire at all, which made the events of the last few minutes even more astonishing.

And what had come over *her?* For a while there, he had

wanted to believe she was a wanton. Why else would she have responded to him like that? Why else would she have pulled him down on the bed and begged him to love her? He couldn't begin to guess at her real reasons, but he did know he had misjudged her. In spite of her response, she had been innocent, and knowing that, he had taken her anyway. Now she was staring up at him with terrified eyes, eyes his guilt could no longer allow him to meet.

With a groan, he rolled away from her, carefully lowering her skirt as he did so. He did not want to see any traces of her blood, proof of what he had stolen from her. Lying beside her, he adjusted his own clothes while he desperately tried to think of a way to make all this right again.

Woodenly, Angelica fastened her dress over the ruined chemise. She felt as if she had shattered into a million pieces and then come back together again, except that nothing was in quite the same place anymore. Everything about her had changed in the space of a few frenzied minutes. Frantically, she tried to make sense of it all.

What thoughts were going through his mind right now? Was he congratulating himself for having bedded her so easily? Did he think she was now his mistress or, even worse, that she would allow him to share her bed while she paid him for his services with his gun? Should she send him away to preserve what was left of her virtue or should she keep him here because she needed his help in preserving her home?

The thought of sending him away left her feeling strangely empty, although she knew that was probably the safest thing to do for her own peace of mind. But even if she did decide to send him away, how could she force him to go if he simply refused? Uncharacteristic tears stung her eyes, reminding her how much she had altered in so brief a time. He cleared his throat, and she braced herself for what he would say to her now.

"This . . . this was a mistake," he said slowly, cautiously

feeling his way to subject he could discuss with a little more confidence. He turned his head to look at her rigid profile and thought he caught the glimmer of tears in her eyes before she clamped them shut. He cleared his throat again. "It never should have happened, what with me working for you and all. But what's done is done, and there's no going back now," he continued, his voice growing firmer as he broached the plan he knew was the right one.

Angelica winced under his words. Here it came, his proposition, the proposition she might well be powerless to resist. She braced herself, prepared for anything except what he said.

"I think we should get married right away. . . ."

"*Married!*" she cried. Her eyes flew open, her tears gone in an instant as she frantically tried to analyze his statement. Why did he want to marry her? He couldn't love her, she was certain of that. After all, they hardly knew each other. He hadn't needed a wedding ring to get her in bed, either. What then would marriage give him that he didn't already have? The answer that occurred to her sent rage boiling through her.

"You're no better than Snyder!" she hissed, scrambling away from him in disgust. On legs that still trembled in the aftermath of passion, she bolted up from the bed and stared down at him with contempt.

"Snyder?" the Kid echoed, pushing up to a sitting position and wondering where he'd lost track of the conversation. "What does he have to do with this?"

"He wanted to marry me, too, or have you forgotten? Ever since I inherited this ranch, I've become awfully popular," she sneered, ignoring the ache in her heart that the knowledge caused. "Was that what this was all about? You thought if we . . ." She made a helpless gesture with her hand, and finished, "Then I'd *have* to marry you, and you'd be set for life?"

"Hell no!" he bellowed in outrage, throwing his legs over

the side of the bed and lunging to his feet. Where had she gotten an idea like that? In truth, he hadn't even considered what would happen after the wedding or how he would benefit. "I thought I'd do right by you, that's all."

"*Right!*" she echoed in mock amazement, the urge to hurt him as she had been hurt goading her. "What does a man like you know about what's right?"

Her words did hurt, scraping at old wounds he'd thought long since healed, and for a moment he saw only the red glow of his own rage. All he'd wanted to do was make up for what he'd done to her. He'd tried to put himself in her place and think what she would want, what any decent woman who had just been bedded for the first time would want. He had failed to consider her very obvious contempt for him, however. "Do you think just because a man hires out his gun, he doesn't know the difference between right and wrong?" he asked through stiff lips, his rage cold as ice now. "You don't know me very well, Angelica."

The sound of her name on his lips sent a quiver along her still sensitive nerve endings, recalling as it did the first time he had uttered it in the throes of passion, but she fought hard to cover her reaction. Lifting her chin in defiance of the tender feelings that stirred unbidden in her heart, she managed a haughty glare. "That's just it, I don't know you at all. You can't expect me to marry a man I've only just met, no matter what the circumstances, Mr. Collins."

He curled his hands into fists as he resisted the urge to shake that prissy expression off her face. "Oh, I think we 'know' each other pretty well now," he said sarcastically, glancing significantly at the rumpled bed.

The reminder send a scalding heat to her cheeks, but she refused to reply to his taunt. "I won't give my hand or my ranch to a perfect stranger," she informed him instead.

Bristling at her scorn, he closed the distance between them in one swift stride and grabbed her arms in a punishing grip. "I've had more than your 'hand,' Angelica, and don't you forget it."

As if she ever could, she thought wildly, but when she spoke, she somehow kept her voice calm. "You're hurting me, Mr. Collins."

He thrust her away as if she'd burned him. "Damn it, at least call me by my name," he raged, frustrated by his inability to break through her icy hauteur. At this moment he could hardly recognize her as the passionate woman he had held in his arms a short time ago.

"What am I supposed to call you?" she taunted. " 'Kid' or 'Christian'?"

Christian? "Where in the hell did you hear that?" he demanded, hating the heat that he felt crawling up his neck at the sound of the name he never used, the name his fanatical mother had given him, the name his heathen father had refused ever to utter, calling his only son Kid instead.

Seeing she had scored a hit, she smiled triumphantly. "It was on the letter I found in your saddlebag." She saw him wince and gloated for a moment, gathering the tattered remnants of her pride around her. "I'd like you to leave now, *Christian,"* she said, driving home another barb, but it cost her dearly. Her hard-won control was starting to slip, and she had to cross her arms over the churning in her stomach. Praying he wouldn't see she was beginning to tremble from reaction to all that had happened, she pulled herself up to her full height and waited for him to leave.

The kid straightened, too. Leave? What exactly did she mean by that? "You want me to leave the ranch?" he asked hollowly, amazed at the dread he experienced waiting for her answer.

"Leave the ranch?" she repeated, stunned at the way her dramatic gesture had been misinterpreted. She had only wanted him out of the room so she could fall apart in privacy. The thought that he might actually vanish from her life shook her to her marrow, but how could she admit that? "I . . . no, I don't want you to leave the ranch," she managed to say in a feeble imitation of outrage. "I hired you to do a job, and it's not done yet, is it?"

He stared into her shining emerald eyes, trying in vain to read her true emotions. Something violent glittered there, but what it was, he could not discern. "No, the job's not done yet," he said slowly.

He waited to see if she would say anything else, but the silence stretched out between them for several seconds. Her cheeks were flushed, and her slender body trembled like a willow in the wind. Instead of putting his arms around her, he forced himself to walk to the door, open it, and go out without even glancing back.

Angelica stared blindly at the door as her eyes filled and overflowed with the tears she had been fighting so hard. No longer able to stand upright, she sank weakly to the floor, clasping her knees for comfort. Newly tender places on her body protested the movements, reminding her of all that had taken place in this room. She was no longer an innocent girl, but a woman. Would the change show? Would Maria and Robbie be able to see the difference in her? And if they did, how would she explain when she could not even understand what had happened herself.?

The tears she had hoped would bring relief only increased her misery, and she scrubbed them from her face in irritation until she was able to stop them altogether. There was no use sitting here on the floor crying as if her heart had been broken, she told herself over and over until she made herself believe it. After all, she did not love the man, so why should she be disappointed to discover that he was after her ranch just like the man she'd hired him to fight? It was pride, that was all, she told herself, and a woman in her position could not afford to indulge herself in luxuries like pride.

She needed Mr. Christian "Kid" Collins, and she would keep him here for as long as she did, but not a moment longer. When everything was settled, she would pay him off and send him on his way. Ignoring the twinge that thought caused her, she rose resolutely to her feet.

Looking around the room, she was surprised to discover that nothing had changed. She might be irrevocably altered, but her world was still the same. The heavy cherrywood chest, washstand and wardrobe that matched her ornate four-posted bed still sat in silent splendor against the immaculate whitewashed walls. The ridiculously romantic woodland scene framed in worn gold leaf still hung on the wall. Only the wrinkled coverlet on the bed gave any indication that a cataclysmic event had occurred here.

She could have smoothed that away with a few swipes of her hand, but for some mysterious reason, she could not bring herself to go near that bed, at least not yet. Turning away in disgust at her own weakness, she instead began to strip off her clothes, anxious to rid herself of all outward reminders of what had happened to her.

When she had washed away every trace of his touch with the tepid water in the pitcher on her washstand, she dressed again in completely new garments, leaving the discarded ones in a heap on the floor. This time, she even put on the pantalettes she hated so much, although she did not allow herself to analyze her reasons for doing so.

Then she hesitated, wondering what to do next. She could not hide in her room, although she knew a strong desire to do so when she considered the prospect of coming face-to-face with Collins again so soon. The room held too many memories.

Cautiously, after first making certain that the courtyard was empty, Angelica slipped out the door and stole across to the door of her father's office. She found refuge in this room that was seldom used. The book-lined walls gave the place an air of solidity and safety, both of which she needed in order to get control of her thoughts and emotions again.

Work, that's what she needed, something to blot out the memories and make her feel normal again. With an enthusiasm she had never before experienced for the task, she hoisted the large ledger book that contained the financial records of the ranch onto her father's huge desk. Usually the sight of the long rows of figures made her cringe with dread, but today she attacked them eagerly. Today she would make them balance or die trying.

How long she sat there, laboriously adding and subtracting, she had no idea, but sometime later the door flew open, startling her into dropping her pencil.

"*Dios!*" Maria exclaimed. "It is worse than I thought."

"Mama!" Angelica chastened, laying a hand over her racing heart. "You scared me to death!"

Ignoring the rebuke, Maria closed the door behind her and crossed the room in quick, anxious strides. "What does this mean?" she demanded, holding out the bundle of white material she was carrying.

Angelica stared at it in momentary confusion, and then she saw the bloodstains and realized the garment was the petticoat she had been wearing earlier. She stared at the evidence of her lost innocence in sudden panic, not daring to meet Maria's searching gaze. How could she tell Maria what had happened? How could she admit her weakness and her sin to the person whose good opinion mattered most to her? "It . . . it's my time of the month . . ." She improvised, but Maria cut her off with a harsh exclamation.

"No, it is not. You forget I do your laundry, *Angelita,* and your time is passed. This blood is from . . ." Maria's voice broke, and Angelica looked up to find tears sparkling in her foster mother's eyes. Her own eyes filled as she read Maria's pain and disappointment.

"Oh, Mama, I'm so sorry!" she cried, wishing she could somehow erase that awful expression from Maria's eyes.

Seeing the girl's distress, Maria reached for her, dropping

the soiled petticoat and enfolding Angelica in an embrace meant to comfort them both. Maria's gesture broke what was left of Angelica's fragile composure, and she wept into Maria's consoling softness.

"Did he hurt you, little one?" Maria asked softly when Angelica's tears had slowed to a trickle.

Angelica shook her head. Even though she was ashamed for Maria to know the truth, she could not lie.

Maria muttered something in rapid Spanish, her voice vicious, and Angelica undertsood enough to know it was a curse on Collins. "If your father was alive, he would kill that son of a . . ."

"No!" Angelica said, pulling free of Maria's arms. "He didn't rape me, if that's what you're thinking." As much as she hated for Maria to know how wantonly she herself had behaved, she could not let her foster mother think her an innocent victim either.

Maria narrowed her dark eyes suspiciously. "Are you saying that you were willing?" she asked, plainly not wanting to believe it.

Angelica forced herself to hold Maria's accusing gaze. Although the word "willing" hardly covered the eager way she had responded to Collins, Angelica gratefully accepted it as a compromise between Maria's ugly fantasy and the shameful reality. "Yes, I was willing," she admitted through stiff lips.

"*Madre de Dios!*" Maria exclaimed. "Do you know what you have lost? Do you know what you have given to this man, this *stranger?*"

"I think so," she whispered, but Maria did not seem to hear.

"Do you love this man, little one?" she demanded.

Angelica blinked at the suddenness of the question. "I . . . I don't know," she answered quite truthfully. "I hardly know him."

"Well, I know him," Maria declared bitterly. "I have

known a hundred like him. He takes his pleasure from a woman and never thinks of her again."

"He isn't like that," Angelica protested automatically, although how she could be so certain of his character, she had no idea.

"How can you be sure? You said yourself you hardly know him. What has he done to make you think he is any different from other men?" Maria challenged. "When he was finished with you did he speak to you of marriage?"

"Yes, he did!" Angelica replied indignantly.

Maria made a derisive noise. "Do not lie to me, Angelica. If you were planning marriage, I would have found the two of you together, like lovers. Instead he is locked in his room alone, and you are in here doing something you hate," she said, making a deprecating gesture toward the ledger book.

"But he did propose to me," Angelica insisted, only then realizing how idiotic her refusal was going to seem to Maria. Still, she could not let Maria think she had been seduced and abandoned, like some brainless creature in a dime novel. "He said we should get married right away because of . . . because of what happened. But I refused."

Maria stared at Angelica in utter astonishment as she felt her outrage taking a new turn. Where before she had held Collins responsible for ruining her *Angelita,* it now appeared that the girl had been a more than willing participant. To make matters more confusing, he had even offered to make things right, and Angelica had been the one to mess things up. "You *refused* him?" she asked incredulously.

"How do I know he wanted me and not just this ranch and an easy life?" Angelica countered in an effort to justify what Maria obviously considered her irrational behavior. "How do I know he didn't seduce me just so I'd *have* to marry him? He'd practically a stranger, and he's a gunfighter, too. Men like that can't be trusted!"

"You trusted him enough to hire him and to take him to your bed," Maria pointed out with ruthless logic.

"That's not the same as marrying him," Angelica replied stubbornly, even though her cheeks were scalding with shame at Maria's blunt reminder of her folly.

"And what if he gave you a child, *Angelita?* What will you do then?" Maria demanded relentlessy, unwilling to allow Angelica the illusion that she had been right to refuse Collins's offer.

A child? Angelica stared at Maria in horror. She hadn't even considered this possibility, although life on the ranch had long ago taught her the results of mating. "I . . . I don't know," she stammered as the awful reality of her situation began to sink in. "I suppose I'd have to marry him then."

"If he is still around," Maria warned, but then she noticed Angelica's obvious distress and the new tears shimmering in her eyes. Almost against her will, Maria recalled her own hand in all of this. From the first, she had thought that Collins would make a fine husband for her Angelica and had taken every opportunity to throw them together. Unfortunately, she had not expected her careful matchmaking efforts to have such immediate and explosive results.

On the other hand, she was almost certain that Collins genuinely cared for the girl. Until a few minutes ago, she had also been convinced he was an honorable man, and from Angelica's account, he had even done the honorable thing after his momentary lapse. Perhaps there was still hope for this situation, and whether there was or not, Maria simply could not stand to see her little one hurting like this. "But maybe nothing will happen," she soothed, softening her voice. "And you are right, a woman should not marry with a man she hardly knows."

Maria kept talking, taking Angelica's hands in her own and offering words of comfort, but Angelica hardly heard them. All she could think of was the possibility of bearing Christian Collins's child. Oddly enough, the idea was not at all unpleasant unless she considered the additional possibility that he might not be there with her to help raise it. Slowly, she began to realize that she wanted him there with her whether she had a child or not. That desire frightened her because she did not know what it meant. Could she be in love with him after all? Or were these strange longings only a result of thcir physical intimacy? At last Maria's words began to register with her consciousness.

"He has promised to help you, and if he is a man of his word, he will be around here for a long tine," Maria explained in an attempt to both comfort and encourage. "You will soon find out whether it is you or the ranch he wants, and then you can decide what *you* want. You see, *Angelita,* things are not quite as bad as you thought."

Angelica knew Maria well enough to recognize this speech as an attempt to soothe her battered emotions. Unfortunately, her emotions needed soothing so much she was more than willing to take whatever comfort she could get. "Yes, you're right, Mama," she agreed, forcing a smile that she hoped looked brave. "He will be around for a while."

"And you will not allow him back in your bed?" Maria cautioned, deciding that little detail should be settled immediately.

"Oh, no!" Angelica replied, appalled at the very suggestion that she would ever be that weak or foolish again.

"*Bueno,*" Maria said with a decisive nod of her head. "Now, put that dusty book away and come help me with supper." Seeing Angelica's hesitation, she added, "He said he would like his supper on a tray tonight. I do not think he will come out of his room this evening."

More relieved than she wanted Maria to know at the assurance that she would not have to face Collins again so soon, Angelica eagerly accepted Maria's invitation. Angelica wasn't much help with the actual cooking, a job she loathed, but she busied herself with the other tasks of getting the meal on the table.

It wasn't until later, when the family had gathered in the parlor and she no longer had anything to occupy her, that Angelica realized her relief had changed into an annoying impatience. As much as she dreaded seeing Collins again, she also missed his presence. The thought was very disturbing.

As was his custom, Robbie went to visit Collins after the evening meal. In the past, Angelica had often accompanied him, but tonight she refused his invitation. Maria's sharp look might have conveyed approval at such circumspect behavior, but Angelica had to admit that it was only her reluctance to face Collins with Robbie as a witness that kept her from going. When Robbie had gone on alone, Angelica excused herself to her room, even though it was much too early for bed. She did not want to endure Maria's concerned glances another moment, and she felt a strong desire to be alone with her thoughts.

To Angelica's relief, Maria had removed the pile of clothing from the corner and straightened the bedclothes, effectively erasing all physical traces of what had happened there earlier. As she undressed, however, she experienced a strange self-consciousness, as if Collins's presence still hovered unseen with the room. Calling herself an idiot, she swiftly slipped on her nightdress, ignoring the shivers of awareness that prickled over her.

Putting out the light, she got into bed, even though she did not feel the least bit sleepy. Staring up into the darkness, she tired to fight the memories, tried to deny the way her body still tingled, tried to ignore the yearning to be held that left her feeling weak with longing.

But as the hours passed, she grew weary from the struggle. Even recalling Maria's dire warnings of an unwanted pregnancy could no longer defend her mind from the onslaught of images. The memories overwhelmed her, and she relived every vibrant moment of her time with Christian Collins. Desire flickered to life again, and she found herself wishing that he would burst into her room once more and take her in his arms again.

She tried to tell herself that she was being wicked and wanton, that she was crazy to want him like that when she could not yet trust him and when she knew the dire consequences having him could cause. The consequences she might already have to face, she realized, placing a hand over her flat belly and trying not to picture a child growing there as a result of her indiscretion.

But another voice whispered to her in the darkness, suggesting that perhaps she—and Maria, too—had been a bit too hasty in judging Christian Collins. Perhaps his offer of marriage really had been a sincere effort to make amends for what he had done and nothing more. Had she ruined everything with her quick temper and even quicker assumptions?

No! That couldn't be true, she wouldn't let it be true! Like Maria said, he would be here for the next several months. During that time, she would see him and work closely with him every day. If this strange longing she felt did not fade, if he proved to be the man she hoped he was, there would be plenty of time to renew their relationship.

Time, that was all she needed. Time would settle everything. On that thought, she finally fell asleep.

The sun was already high in the sky when Angelica awoke the next morning. After she had hastily washed and dressed, she did not hesitate a bit as she walked out of her room. Her gaze went immediately to the room across the way, where he would be. Today, she would not be afraid to face him. It would be awkward at first, she knew, but she would get over that quickly enough. Then they could get on with the business of learning about each other, a task Angelica was eager go begin.

All traces of breakfast had been removed from the dining

room, and Angelica braced herself for Maria's chiding as she entered the kitchen. Maria was sitting at the kitchen table with Robbie, and they both glanced up when she came in. Maria gave her a concerned look but limited herself to a guarded "Good morning." When Angelica returned the greeting with a smile, Maria seemed oddly surprised and not at all relieved. She resumed her task of deftly picking pebbles from the dried beans. Robbie was slouched in his chair, his freckled face a mask of despair.

"You look like you lost your best friend," Angelica teased her brother in an attempt to cheer him out of his uncharacteristic grump.

Robbie lifted his hazel eyes to meet her gaze and sighed dramatically. "Mr. Collins went to town, but he wouldn't take me along," he complained.

A strange apprehension shivered up her spine. "He . . . he went to town?" she asked, looking to Maria for confirmation.

"*Sí,*" Maria said, her voice carefully expressionless. "He says he is getting restless just sitting around here. He says he will see what rumors he can pick up." She wanted to believe the story but was afraid to give Angelica too much confidence in it.

Angelica nodded numbly, well aware of the suspicions behind Maria's innocuous explanation. They both knew there was no reason for Collins to go to town. Her men could pick up rumors. And what if he ran into trouble? As awful as that thought was, it paled in comparison to the one that followed: What if he had simply lied about the trip to town? What if he were gone for good?

Chapter Four

The Kid forced himself not to look back as he rode out of the ranch yard. Instead, he concentrated on how good it was to feel the sun and the wind in his face as Midnight carried him on his way. He reveled in the sense of freedom after all those long days and nights of confinement. His side was still a little sore, but his strength seemed to increase with every yard the horse traveled.

His searching gaze took in the lay of the land, noting the primitive beauty of the grassy plains, dotted now with the colorful wildflowers that marked the coming of spring. Above the plains stretched the soaring sky, where a lone hawk circled lazily in search of prey. He hadn't been in this country for years, not since he'd crossed it with his father looking for the hidden encampments of Comanche. In all that time, he had forgotten how much he loved the wildness of the place.

Some men felt dwarfed by the incredible distances and endless expanse of heavens hanging above. Only a select few would feel at home in this untamed land, and he was one of them. He looked upon the immensity as a challenge rather than an obstacle.

With sadness, he wondered if his brother-in-law had felt this way, too, if that was the reason he had stayed to fight rather than running when someone denied his right to live here.

The Kid knew instinctively that Rose had shared his love of this wild land. But now she and Pete had joined the many others who had paid dearly to settle this part of Texas. As always, that thought filled him with rage over the injustice that had been done to them just because they dared to settle on land someone else wanted. With the Comanche gone, nothing would prevent more evil men from moving in now and taking over. Nothing, that is, except men like Kid Collins.

Telling himself he was being a sentimental fool, the Kid reined up on a rise and turned Midnight so he could cast one last look at the Diamond R Ranch buildings. From this distance, even the sprawling house looked small and vulnerable, and he resisted the urge to ride on back, reminding himself sternly that the danger to the Diamond R was certainly not imminent. And it wasn't like he was leaving for good, either, although that would probably be the smart thing to do if he wanted to be sure he kept his hands off Angelica Ross from now on.

With a disgusted sigh, he nudged Midnight into motion again and resumed his trip to town. "Why is it," he asked the horse, "that everything always comes back to her?"

As usual, Midnight kept his thoughts to himself while the Kid struggled with his memories of Angelica once more. He still couldn't quite believe what had happened between them. He'd spent his life keeping a tight rein on his emotions, never allowing them to slip beyond his control. And he always made a point of treating ladies with every bit of the respect due them. A man like him got to meet precious few of those rare creatures in his lifetime. The idea of tumbling one—especially one to whom he owed his life and to whom he had promised his allegiance—was unthinkable.

But unthinkable or not, it had happened. Why had he been unable to resist the compulsion to make love to her? As much as he hated to admit it, the answer to that question was surprisingly simple: even with Lettie, the only woman he'd ever really loved, he had never in his life experienced the uncontrollable desire Angelica Ross aroused in him.

The memory of how he had taken Angelica, forcing her innocent body to yield to his invasion, appalled him. And when he thought about the frightened look in her eyes afterward, he actually groaned aloud.

Disturbed by the sound, Midnight lifted his head, and the Kid absently patted the horse's neck in reassurance. "Sorry, boy. It's just that I can't figure out what else I could have done to make things right. Dammit, I asked her to marry me!"

The memory of her rejection still galled him, although looking back, he could see her side of it a little more clearly than he'd been able to at the time. Like she'd said, she didn't really know him very well. Nobody wanted to marry a total stranger, and reluctantly, he admitted that even what little she did know about him was bad.

He'd shown up on her doorstep half-dead from a bullet wound. Then she discovered that he was a notorious gunman. When she asked him for help, he gave her an argument about it, and she couldn't know his initial refusal stemmed only from his concern that his attraction to her would lead to trouble. He'd been right to be concerned, too, although he had grossly underestimated how much trouble that attraction could cause in so brief a time.

"She's got me between a rock and a hard place," the Kid complained to his companion. Midnight flicked his ears in what might have been a sympathetic gesture, but the Kid hardly noticed as he considered his dilemma. He had given his word to help her, help she desperately needed. He had sent for men to assist him, men who would be arriving any day now and whom she expected him to lead. He could not shirk his responsibilities, so he could not possibly leave her.

On the other hand, if he stayed around her, how was he going to control the mysterious forces that had brought them together yesterday? Of course, after what had happened, she was bound to be wary, and that would help. She wasn't likely to ever respond to him like that again, and if she had any sense at all, she'd never even be alone with him. He was certain she had more than enough good sense, so maybe he didn't have to worry too much. If they both made a conscious effort to avoid each other . . .

Yes, that's how it would be, they would avoid each other the way they had done last evening. He had stayed in his room until he thought he'd go stark raving mad, and Maria had told him about finding Angelica hiding away in her father's office. This trip to town would keep them apart today. When the other men arrived, they'd start the roundup. Once they did, he'd be out on the range all the time and would see very little of Angelica. Then they'd drive the cattle to the reservation, and he would be completely separated from her for the next few weeks. As soon as the job was done and he knew Angelica was secure, he could leave for good and never have to see her again.

" 'Out of sight, out of mind,' isn't that what they say, boy?" he asked the horse, who shook his head in what might have been agreement. "And who wants to be tied down to a redheaded woman with a temper to match? A woman like that could make a man's life hell!"

Or heaven, a small voice whispered in his head. Unwanted memories tormented him, of the way she had smelled and tasted, the way she had moved beneath him and the way she had felt wrapped around him. Fighting those thoughts, he forced himself to remember how she had scorned him afterward, refusing his proposal and ordering him out of her room. Sure, they'd been good together, at least for those few mindless moments when nothing else had mattered except meeting their physical needs. But good sex wasn't everything. He had to remember who he was and who she was, and how a man who made his living with a gun didn't have any right to even think about a woman like Angelica Ross.

With a curse that brought Midnight's ears up again, the Kid kicked the horse into a ground-eating gallop. A little hard riding would drive her from his mind. Or so he hoped.

By the time he reached the little town of Marsden's Corners, the Kid had managed to suppress all thoughts of Angelica and concentrate instead on the problems she—and consequently he—faced. He rode warily into the town, expecting trouble to appear at any moment. Since the telegrams had been sent to his friends under his more widely known name instead of under the given name he had instructed Rachel and Cole to use when writing to him, the townsfolk would surely have figured out who he was by now. Snyder would have heard, too, and might well have someone on the lookout for him.

But even the Kid's naturally suspicious nature had a hard time imagining any danger in Marsden's Corners. The place wasn't so much sleepy as dead. He didn't see a single person stirring on the broad main street, and only a few horses stood hipshot in front of the saloon, their tails lazily swishing at flies.

He reined up in front of the only store, Marsden's Mercantile, and swung down, tying Midnight to the hitching rail out front. The thump of his boots on the wooden sidewalk sounded unnaturally loud in a quiet street as he crossed to the store's doorway. Pausing a moment to allow his eyes to accustom themselves to the dimness within, he inhaled the mingled smells of leather, new cloth, pickles and the myriad other items the building contained.

"Morning, mister, or is it afternoon yet? I reckon I've lost track of the time." A small, plump woman climbed down from the ladder where she had been standing, dusting merchandise on a high shelf. He remembered her from his last and only trip to town.

"It's still morning, Miz Marsden, but it's getting close to noon, or my stomach's lying to me," he said with a perfunctory smile.

The woman smiled back and moved a little closer, peering at him carefully, as if she could not quite make out his face as he stood silhouetted in the doorway. "Oh, it's you. Mr. Collins, isn't it?" she asked, but he could tell there was no real question in her mind. He nodded, prepared to see the recognition and the wariness that would follow as she realized his identity.

Instead she simply continued to smile. "If your stomach's complaining, there's a free lunch over at the saloon, although I'd bet a growing boy like you needs more than stale crackers and moldy cheese," she guessed.

The Kid's grin became genuine at her teasing. He hadn't been called a growing boy in a long time, and the remark was especially humorous because, in spite of her widow's weeds, Mrs. Marsden was probably no more than a year or two older than his own twenty-seven years. "Maybe you'd like to volunteer to feed me," he teased back.

She swatted at him with her dustcloth. "A boy doesn't get *that* big without a lot of food," she judged, measuring his height with a critical eye. He easily stood a foot or more taller than she. "I'm afraid I'm not up to a task like that."

She turned away, heading for the front counter and moving with a restless energy that belied her words. She looked like the type of woman who could meet and tackle any task, head-on. He admired that quality in a woman, and he caught himself thinking of how Angelica Ross was like that, too. He resolutely shook off the thought and followed Mrs. Marsden to the counter.

"I don't remember there being any mail for you, Mr. Collins, but I'll check," Mrs. Marsden was saying.

While her back was turned, the Kid frowned, reminded that she had not seemed to recognize him as who he really was. She only remembered him as the stranger who had visited the store a week earlier. Surely, the gossip would have reached the town's single store first.

"No, no mail," she confirmed, turning back to catch his frown. "But don't look so sad. She'll probably write again real soon." He knew she was assuming that the other letter he had received addressed in a feminine hand had been from a sweetheart. Her cheerfully sympathetic expression transformed a face that would otherwise have been considered plain into one that was almost beautiful. Her dark brown eyes twinkled up at him, and for a moment he wondered how Angelica's green eyes would look filled with laughter like that. Now he would probably never find out. Again he mentally shook himself and forced a smile.

"I really wasn't expecting another letter so soon anyway," he said. "I just needed a little tobacco and some clothes." He was getting tired of living off Angelica's charity by using her father's things.

"I reckon we got something back there that'll fit you," she said, motioning toward the rear of the store. "I'll get you some Bull Durham. Do you need papers?"

He told her that he did and then went to find some shirts and jeans to replenish his lost wardrobe. A few minutes later, he carried his selections to the front of the store, where she had laid out a sack of Bull Durham tobacco and a package of cigarette papers.

"I'll be needing a razor and a comb, too," he said,

recalling just how dependent he had become on Cameron Ross's possessions.

"A whole new outfit, eh?" she said, reaching back to fetch the requested items. "You must have found a job."

"Yeah," he said, deciding to try for the reaction he had failed to get before. "I'm working for the Diamond R now."

"Oh, I'm so glad!" she said, surprising him by showing only relief and no recognition. "That poor girl has been so shorthanded lately, I was afraid she wouldn't be able to meet her army contract."

The Kid mumbled some sort of reply, but his mind was racing. There could be no doubt about it. Mrs. Marsden had no idea that he was Kid Collins, the gunfighter who had just been hired by Angelica Ross. What could have happened? Was it possible that his telegrams had never been sent? Were Angelica's men in on the conspiracy, too?

He paid for his purchases from the small store of gold eagles he had been carrying on his person when his sister's cabin had been attacked. As Mrs. Marsden wrapped his things, he mulled over the possible explanations for the fact that his identity was still a secret. None of them pleased him. He would have to ask some pretty pointed questions as soon as he got back to the ranch.

"You tell your new boss I said 'hello and don't be such a stranger,' " Mrs. Marsden said, handing him his package.

"I'll do that," the Kid promised, still unable to shake the feeling that something was very wrong. He had only intended to stay in town long enough to make these purchases and maybe grab a bite to eat before starting the long ride back to the ranch. As much as he'd needed the time away from Angelica to cool things off a bit, he also didn't like the thought of being away from her very long, another feeling he didn't dare analyze too closely.

But on the other hand, he also needed to get a feel for what was going on in the world outside of the Diamond R ranch house. Maybe he would take advantage of the free lunch at the saloon and see if anyone else in town knew who he was. Maybe Mrs. Marsden was the only one who hadn't heard the news.

In anticipation of a long afternoon, he took his horse and his package to the livery stable and left them there before strolling down the wooden sidewalk to the Dirty Dog Saloon. The establishment wasn't the best of its kind he'd ever seen, but it wasn't the worst, either. The room was large and square, the plank floor stained by mud and tobacco juice. A long bar ran along the far wall, but there was no mirror to reflect the patrons and not even any lewd paintings to relieve the barrenness of the walls. A few tables with mismatched chairs were scattered about, but only one was occupied. Two men were playing a desultory game of poker while a girl in a tawdry blue dress watched with little interest.

All of them looked up when he entered. He nodded politely and made his way slowly to the bar, aware of their silent stares. He ordered a beer from the rotund bartender, who had watched his approach through eyes narrowed in speculation. Perhaps here someone would guess his identity.

"You're new around here, aren't you?" the bartender asked, setting the beer before him.

"Yeah, that's right," the Kid said, picking up the glass. He blew off the head and took a long swallow.

"If you're looking for a job and you know how to use that gun, Mr. Snyder over there is looking for men."

The Kid was glad he'd already swallowed the beer. It was pure luck to encounter Snyder like this, although he wasn't certain whether the luck was good or bad. Wiping his mouth with the back of his hand, he turned slowly to get a better look at his new enemy.

"That's right," one of the poker players said, eyeing the Kid over his cards. "I am looking for some men. There's been trouble around here lately. Maybe you've heard?"

Snyder was just as Angelica had described him, broad-shouldered and thick of body, although no one would ever call him fat. The Kid judged his age to be early thirties, but Snyder had obviously accepted the responsibilities of adulthood early to have attained the air of confidence and command he now possessed. His black hair and mustache were carefully groomed, and his custom-made suit marked him as a prosperous rancher. Sitting down, he seemed of average height, and he had the kind of smile that could curdle milk right in the cow.

The thought of Angelica facing this man alone made the Kid's blood run cold, but he kept his face expressionless. "You paying fighting wages?" he asked with carefully calculated interest.

"To fighting men," Snyder allowed, his chilling smile still firmly in place.

"I'll think about it. I haven't made up my mind about staying yet," the Kid said, turning back to the bar. The free lunch wasn't quite as unappetizing as Mrs. Marsden had predicted, so the Kid shooed away a few flies and fixed himself a snack.

Behind him he heard Snyder's voice rumble to one of his companions, but he could not make out the words. Then he heard light footsteps that could only belong to the girl. Her cheap perfume announced her arrival long before she sidled up beside him.

"Buy a lady a drink?" she asked.

The Kid glanced down at her. She was small, almost as short as Mrs. Marsden but much thinner. Her frailty made her look even younger than she was, which the Kid guessed to be around Angelica's age. She wasn't pretty, and wouldn't be pretty even if she'd had the advantage of wealth and ease. As it was, late hours and hard living had already robbed her of the bloom that a girl her age should have, the bloom Angelica possessed in abundance. The thought of Angelica and the pang it caused caught him off-guard for a moment, but only for a moment. He quickly suppressed it and gave the girl a smile.

"Sure, I never turn down a chance to drink with a pretty gal. Give her whatever she wants," he told the bartender.

Without asking her preference, the fat man reached under the bar and brought up a glass and a bottle. He poured a shot for the girl and started to put the bottle away again.

"Pour me a shot of that, too," the Kid said, keeping his voice pleasant.

The bartender froze, his piglike eyes rising to study the Kid for a moment. "I'll give you some of the good stuff," he offered.

"Whatever's good enough for the lady is good enough for me," he said, putting that unmistakable tone in his voice that warned the bartender he couldn't push this cowboy too far. The man responded to it and instantly changed his tactics, turning his porcine gaze on the girl in a silent message.

She, too, responded immediately. "You don't want this rotgut," she said quickly, one of her hands reaching out to clutch the Kid's arm. "Let Otis give you something good."

The Kid looked down at her, easily reading the fear in her eyes. He knew if he pressed, he would discover that the amber liquid in the girl's glass was tea. It was a common scam, one practiced wherever a saloon was lucky enough to have girls shilling drinks. He also knew from the expression on her face that the girl would be the one to suffer if he exposed the deception. Her haunted eyes reminded him too much of another girl, the girl who had died in his arms four years ago. He wouldn't push the issue.

In a compromise, he grinned slyly. "Well, then, Otis, why don't you give us both some of the good stuff?"

Otis's round face mottled with suppressed rage, but he reached below the bar again, producing a different bottle and two new glasses. With a finesse that impressed the Kid, he swept away the first glass, disposing of its contents into the slop bucket beneath the bar. "On the house," he said with a chilly smile that revealed crooked, yellowed teeth.

The Kid returned the smile with one equally cold. "To pretty girls," he said, raising the glass to the girl beside him. He drank the shot in one gulp, and noticed with regret that the girl did, too. He knew she probably didn't get the real thing very often, but she must get it often enough to have developed a taste for it. The thought disturbed him more than it should have.

"What's your name?" he asked, concentrating on her big blue eyes. They were her best feature. With her slender, almost skinny frame and her faded blond hair, she really looked nothing at all like Lettie. Why, then, did she remind him so much of the woman he had loved long ago?

"I'm Sunny Day," she informed him with a trace of pride, giving him a name she had obviously made up to suit her image of herself as a saloon girl. The Kid blinked in surprise, thinking with some irony how little the name suited this poor, drab creature.

"Well, Sunny, would you like another drink?" he asked, deciding to play along with the flirtation. A lonely stranger should be more than grateful for the attention of a young girl, and since no one seemed to know who he really was, he wanted to continue his masquerade.

The girl cast an apprehensive glance at the bartender

before making her decision. Plainly, he did not want her to have another drink. "No, thanks. I've had my limit." She turned her gaze back to the Kid. "Are you planning to stay around here long?"

"Haven't decided yet," he replied, taking a sip of his beer. It was just as he'd suspected. Snyder had sent the girl over to find out who he was and what he was doing in town.

"Where are you from?" she asked a little too quickly. She wasn't trained for this sort of thing, and she was botching it. He pretended not to notice.

"Here and there," he said genially, feigning an interest in the curve of her small breasts.

"Say, stranger, maybe you'd like to sit in for a couple hands," Snyder said, impatience tinging his invitation. He was getting tired of waiting for his information.

The Kid turned back to face the table, quickly calculating how much cash he had on him. There was no better way of getting to know a man than by playing cards with him, but the Kid was afraid he didn't have enough money to make the plan feasible. "What are the stakes?"

"Jake and I were playing for matches, but since you're obviously a man of means, we'll raise it to a dollar. How's that sound?" Snyder said, proving that the Kid had underestimated the man's determination to learn his identity.

"Sounds fine," the Kid readily agreed. "Come on, Sunny," he said, picking up his beer with one hand and sliding his other around the girl's waist. A lonely stranger would want the girl close. "You'll bring me luck."

They took two chairs side by side. That put Snyder on his right, Sunny on his left and Jake on her left. Another empty chair separated Snyder and Jake.

"I'm Harlan Snyder," he said with that creepy smile. "I own a ranch south of here, the Bar S. This is Jake

Evans, my foreman."

Jake Evans was a mean-looking hombre with a hatchet face and close-set eyes. He nodded with ill-concealed indifference at the introduction.

"Pleased to meet you," the Kid said in a mockery of courtesy.

Snyder's bushy eyebrows rose when the Kid failed to complete the introduction by stating his own name, but the rancher made no comment. It was considered extremely rude and possibly even dangerous to ask a man his name if he didn't volunteer it. "Why don't you deal?" Snyder offered, placing the worn deck in front of the Kid.

When the three men had anted, the Kid deftly shuffled and then allowed Sunny to cut the cards before he dealt them. As he did so, he blessed his good friend Miles, who had finally taken pity on him and taught him the finer points of poker. In his younger days, he had been a miserable failure at the game, never quite grasping the necessity for bluffing and keeping a poker face.

The men examined their cards. Snyder opened by betting a dollar, and the Kid called him, as did Jake.

"Cards?" the Kid inquired. Jake took two, Snyder only one. The Kid dealt himself three.

The Kid squinted at what he held, which was absolutely nothing. He would fold when his turn came. Yes, he mused, he'd learned a lot about the game since he had played cards with the other Circle K cowhands that time for the chore of milking the cow when Rachel was too sick to nurse her baby. Of course, in losing all those games, he had won Cole and Rachel's undying gratitude for saving their baby's life.

"Oh, hell, I'm out," Jake grumbled.

"So am I, I'm afraid," Snyder announced, his grim smile turning curious. "Tell me, stranger, what did you have in that hand that made you so happy?"

The Kid pursed his lips, only then aware that his pleasant memories had been reflected on his face. His companions had misinterpreted his grin, to his advantage that time. Next time he might not be so lucky. He'd have to watch his step and stop being so damn sentimental. "A pair of aces," he lied, shoving his cards back into the deck before anyone tried to see them.

The other men exchanged glances as the Kid wondered at his own behavior. He didn't usually have a problem keeping his mind on the business at hand, and never did he find himself distracted by memories when he had a job to do. Since coming in here, he'd thought of Lettie and of Cole and Rachel. And he'd even thought of Angelica. What had made him go soft so suddenly?

Not daring to answer that question, he simply decided he wouldn't let himself think about any of them again. That was much too dangerous, especially considering who was sitting beside him.

He settled down to some serious card playing. The afternoon dragged by, but the Kid was barely aware of the passage of time. Snyder seemed more intent on drawing him out than on winning his money, and Jake was only there to assist Snyder in whatever his plans were. The Kid's stack of winnings grew and shrunk during the next few hours, but since he won as often as he lost, he finished the afternoon with about the same amount of money he had started with. To Snyder's disgust, he gave up precious little information about himself in the process.

What he learned about Snyder was that the man was not easily bluffed and that he wasn't afraid to stick with a hand he believed in. Although the Kid saw Jake dealing from the bottom a time or two, Snyder himself did not appear to be cheating. The Kid caught himself wondering if Harlan Snyder could possibly be the man who had ordered Pete and Rose killed. But maybe Snyder only cheated when winning was important to him.

Snyder had just sent Sunny for a new bottle of whiskey. He was idly shuffling the cards and looked up with what appeared to be unconcern. "Have you thought over my offer of a job yet?"

The Kid shrugged. "The pay sounds right, but I'm a peaceable man. I was hoping to get away from trouble. That's why I came way out here."

"There's no law out here, if that's the kind of trouble you're worried about," Snyder assured him.

The Kid felt his hackles rise at the suggestion that he might be on the run, but he kept outwardly calm. "That's a comfort," he said noncommittally. "I'd like to look around a day or two before I make up my mind about staying." There was, he decided, no use in announcing to the other side that he already had a job working for Angelica. Better to keep them guessing. Snyder would find out the truth soon enough, and maybe by then the Kid would have learned some useful information.

Snyder's smile was confident. "When you decide, just ride on out to my place. Jake here will put you to work."

Jake said nothing, but the Kid knew he would do whatever Snyder told him.

When Snyder offered to refill the Kid's glass from his bottle, the Kid declined. "I think I'd better go hunt up some supper before I put away any more red-eye," he said, rising from the table. "I don't think I've won enough to make you gents sore at me for leaving the game, so I reckon I'll pack it in now."

Snyder murmured his consent while the Kid tucked his winnings into his pocket.

"Will I be seeing you again?" the girl asked hopefully.

The Kid looked down at her, struck once more by her fragile vulnerability. "Sure, honey," he promised, unable to disappoint her.

A smile transformed her face, making her almost pretty, but it vanished the instant she noticed Snyder's scowling disapproval.

"I guess I'll be seeing you later, stranger," Snyder said, a note of warning in his voice.

Could Snyder possibly care whether the Kid spent time with Sunny? The rancher had hardly glanced at the girl all afternoon except when giving her an order to fetch something, and yet the implication was clear. He wanted the Kid to leave her alone. Could Snyder be the kind of man who didn't want something unless someone else did? That would certainly explain a lot, especially if he were indeed the man behind Pete and Rose's killings.

Without another word, the Kid left the stuffy saloon, which had grown crowded in the last hour, and wandered out onto the sidewalk, inhaling deeply of the warm, fresh air. The street was more lively than it had been earlier. Several dozen horses were hitched along the rails now, and men in range clothes came and went at the mercantile, the livery stable, and the restaurant. The telegraph office appeared to be closed. The only other buildings on the street were private homes which he assumed belonged to the town merchants.

His stomach rumbled, interrupting his thoughts, and he turned his footsteps toward the town's only eating establishment, a nondescript building boasting a sign that simply said Eats.

One common table dominated the restaurant, lined on either side with benches for the diners. Several other men were already seated there, a mixture of townsfolk and cowboys who were engaged in a spirited political discussion. Since the Kid did not know any of the local candidates, he cheerfully declined an invitation to express his views.

A harried-looking man brought him a plate of food and a cup of coffee. The fare was beef and beans, a predictable offering, and he ate it hungrily, remembering his skimpy nooning.

"Are you looking for a job, stranger?" one of the cowboys asked when the political talk had died down a bit.

"Haven't decided if I'm going to stay around yet," he hedged, wondering for whom the cowboy was asking. The man didn't look like a hardcase, which would rule out Snyder, but it wasn't always easy to tell. Some folks had told the Kid he didn't look like a hardcase either.

"We're hiring out at the Rocking W," he said. "We're about two days due east of here, if you get the itch to travel."

"Thanks," the Kid said, surreptitiously eyeing the other men around the table for their reaction. "I heard that they're hiring up at the Diamond R."

To his amazement, the other men seemed surprised by the news. "You must've heard wrong, stranger," one of them said. "That's Cameron Ross's old place. He passed on last winter, and I heard tell his daughter is going back East real soon. She's let almost all her men go already."

The Kid studied the others for signs of duplicity, but they betrayed none as they nodded agreement with this assessment of the situation. Plainly, they all sincerely believed that Angelica was ready to pack it in. No wonder she had been unable to attract any hired hands. She'd told him the word was out, and now he knew what the word was. If people had thought she was in danger, someone would have come to her aid, but they only thought she was giving up, so no aid would be necessary. Whoever was behind this plot was even more clever than he had guessed.

Dropping some coins on the table, the Kid nodded his good-byes to the others and left the restaurant, having decided that he needed a little time alone to digest this information along with his supper. As was his habit when in a new place, he took a walk around the town to acquaint himself with the rear entrances and hidey-holes of the various buildings, in the event that he might someday need them.

To his surprise, the sun was setting as he made his final turn down behind the saloon. The poker game had lasted much longer than he had thought. Now he'd have to return to the ranch after dark, a prospect he did not relish. No sooner had he come to that realization than he heard a woman's voice pleading, louder and closer than the noise coming from the saloon.

"No, please! Don't do that! It hurts, it hurts!"

It was coming from a shack out behind the saloon. The sound of a slap and the woman's cry of pain echoed clearly through the evening air.

A man's voice rumbled threateningly, and again the Kid heard the sound of flesh striking flesh. The girl's voice rose in a sob. "No, please!" she begged again.

"Lettie," the Kid whispered, anguished memories of her beaten, broken body flashing across his mind's eye. Without conscious thought, he was running toward the house.

The Kid threw open the door. "Lettie?" he called, quickly scanning the small room.

The place reeked of sex and cheap perfume. The only movement came from the two naked figures on the bed. The man straddled the girl, his large fist raised to strike her yet again as she sobbed in terror, but at the sound of the Kid's intrusion, the man's head jerked around in surprise. "What the hell?"

Snyder couldn't believe his eyes. It was the stranger from the saloon, the one who couldn't seem to make up his mind about anything. Except that now he didn't look quite so uncertain. "What the hell do you want?" he demanded, furious at being interrupted.

The Kid watched as Snyder slowly lowered his raised

fist, the fist he had used to strike the girl. But the girl was not Lettie. It was Sunny. Somehow the knowledge only increased his sense of outrage. "I heard somebody call for help," he said with forced calmness, noting grimly that Snyder was no longer smiling. In fact, he looked positively irritated.

"Nobody in here needs any help," Snyder snapped, suddenly realizing the indignity of his position. Hastily, he twisted free of the girl, sat down on the bed beside her, and jerked up the sheet to cover himself.

The Kid shifted his gaze to the girl. Robbed of the sheet, she lay huddled in a ball in a vain attempt to conceal her nakedness, her pale body quaking with terror. "How about you, Sunny? Did you need any help?" he asked.

Plainly too frightened to speak, she turned pleading eyes to the Kid. He'd seen that whipped expression before. There was no way he would leave the girl to Snyder's mercy.

"She's fine," Snyder answered for her. "Tell him," he ordered, giving her a nudge with one large foot, but to his disgust, she only whimpered. "She just carries on like that so I'll pay her more," he explained, managing a semblance of his usual poise. Damn, he didn't appreciate this fellow barging in like this. He'd have Jake Evans or one of the boys take care of him first thing in the morning. For now, he'd just get rid of him the easiest way. Forcing a conspiratorial grin, he said, "Look, stranger, this is none of your business. You're a real hero, busting in like that, but now you see how things are, you can leave with a clear conscience. And I'll tell you what, you ride on out to my place and tell Jake I said to give you a job and a twenty-dollar bonus just for signing on."

But the Kid was barely listening. He was only aware of the way Sunny cringed from the man next to her and the way his own blood roared at the thought of Snyder striking her. "Thanks all the same, but I've decided not to work for you, Snyder," he said coldly. "Now, I think you've about worn out your welcome here. Maybe you'd better put on your pants and get out before Sunny tells me what you did that hurt her so bad."

Snyder made a strangled noise as his fury raged out of control again. Of all the nerve! Who did this saddle tramp think he was talking to? He would break him in two with his bare hands!

Snyder was half off the bed before he noticed something that froze him in place. The stranger's eyes, which had looked so mild and vague before, now glittered like cold steel. His handsome face with its winsome grin had hardened into an expression Snyder knew only too well. Instinctively, Snyder's gaze dropped to the stranger's gun hand, and in that instant he knew the man for what he was. "Who are you?" he demanded.

The Kid watched Snyder's face grow scarlet with rage as he realized his predicament and sank back onto the bed. Ignoring the question he had no intention of answering, the Kid pulled his lips back into a parody of a grin. "I'm not a patient man, Snyder. I already asked you real nice to leave. Now don't make me forget my manners in front of the lady."

For a long moment, the two men engaged in a silent battle of wills. Finally, the Kid flexed the fingers of his right hand ever so slightly, just enough to attract Snyder's attention. Snyder flinched, and then his eyes narrowed in hate as he lost the battle with his pride.

With a vicious curse, Snyder lumbered from the bed, still clutching the sheet. "You'll be sorry for this, stranger. You don't know who you're dealing with. I'm a bad enemy, and you're going to find out just how bad." He stalked over to the chair where his suit was neatly draped and snatched up his trousers. "I'll make you wish you were never born," he threatened, stepping into them and letting the sheet fall to the floor.

"Do you do your own dirty work or do you hire it out?" the Kid asked with what sounded like idle curiosity. "Just so I know who to watch for," he explained.

"From now on, you'd better watch everybody and sleep with one eye open," Snyder warned, putting on the rest of his clothes with angry jerks. At last he reached for the holster that hung over the back of the chair.

"Just leave it, Snyder," the Kid commanded.

Snyder's hand paused over the leather as he calculated his chances of getting his gun out first. At that moment he would have sold his soul for the chance to put a bullet through the stranger's grinning face.

The Kid understood his desire, and his grin widened. "I've done this before," he cautioned. "I could get six shots into you before you cleared leather."

Snyder clenched his fist and drew it back, seething with an anger so great he could scarcely contain it. The stranger would pay for this with his life. But it wouldn't be a quick death, he decided. No, he wanted to be there to witness his revenge. Planning the details would give him more pleasure than that stupid girl on the bed ever had. The thought calmed him just enough so he was able to restrain his fury.

In an elaborately casual gesture, he straightened his vest and stepped away from the gun. "That's all right. I'll just come back after you've gone and get it from Sunny," he said, giving the girl a look that made her whimper.

"It won't be here," the Kid informed him. "I'll leave it for you at the livery stable. We'll let them guess how I got it from you."

Once more the rage welled up in Snyder, threatening to erupt in the violence his pride demanded. But through the years he had learned the importance of waiting for the proper time. At this particular moment, the stranger had the upper hand. Only a fool would challenge him, and Snyder prided himself on being a wise man. As such, he would wait for a better opportunity.

The Kid watched him carefully, ready to respond to any threatening motion, but Snyder made none. Although the rancher's dark eyes glittered with hate, he turned abruptly and strode to the door. He paused for just a moment before opening it, looking back over his shoulder at the Kid. "Remember what I said, stranger," he said, indulging himself in one last threat. "Keep one eye open."

As soon as the door closed, the Kid moved. Catlike, he stole to the window, drawing his gun as he went. He peered carefully out while keeping his body away from the glass, but Snyder did not stop. The rancher kept walking, down the alley and around the side of the saloon until he was out of sight. The Kid had half expected him to pull out a hidden weapon from someplace and sneak back to take a potshot. How easy that would have made things. A quick, neat shootout and everything would be settled.

Breathing a sigh of disappointment, he forced his tensed muscles to relax and drew a few deep breaths to calm the surge of excitement his encounter with Snyder had caused. Then he stuffed his gun back into the holster, reminding himself that he still wasn't certain Snyder was the one responsible for Rose's death. If they had shot it out, the only thing that would have been settled was that Snyder would never be able to hurt another woman.

"Is he gone?" a trembling voice asked from the bed.

The Kid turned to face the girl. She was sitting up, her arms crossed to cover her breasts and her legs drawn up modestly. Her face was wet with tears, and she was shaking like a leaf. Now that he had the leisure to notice, her arms and legs were covered with marks that would most certainly become bruises by morning.

"He's gone for now," the Kid said, going to retrieve the sheet from where Snyder had dropped it on the floor. "What in the hell was he doing to you?" he asked as he spread the covering over her.

She grasped the fabric, clutching it to her breasts with trembling hands, and lowered her eyes, as if she were ashamed to meet his gaze. "He . . . he likes to do strange things. He likes to hurt people." As she spoke, she wiped the moisture from her cheeks with the edge of the sheet. As he listened, the Kid actually felt bile crawling up his throat at the disgusting images her words suggested.

He swore savagely, making the girl jump, and when her startled gaze lifted to him, he saw again the expression that had reminded him so much of Lettie. For a moment, he felt the pain of Lettie's loss all over again, and the feelings somehow spilled over to include the girl on the bed.

"Are you hurt?" he asked gently.

"I don't know," she said, reaching up to touch her face tentatively. He noticed that she wasn't shaking as badly anymore. "Do you think my eye is going to be black?"

The Kid bleakly remembered the sounds of the blows he had heard from outside and leaned over to get a better look at her face. The twilight shadows made it difficult to see. "I can't tell. Do you have a lamp around here?"

"On the table," she said, pointing toward the opposite wall. He found and lighted it from a box of matches lying on the table. Carrying the lamp back to the bed, he set it on a wooden crate that served as a nightstand and took another look at her face.

"It looks all right, but you won't be able to tell for sure until tomorrow," he judged.

She nodded solemnly, gazing up at him for a long minute, and then her expression changed. A small smile teased around her lips, and the wariness slowly faded from her eyes. "You *are* a real hero, you know?" she said, her admiration plain.

He stiffened slightly at the title Snyder had given him. The last thing he'd intended to be was somebody's hero. Right was right, and wrong was wrong. A man had to do the former and fight the latter. It was as simple as that, at least for him. Snyder, he was certain, had another viewpoint altogether, but the Kid would not dwell on that now. Uncomfortable under her praise, he backed up a step. "Well, then, if you don't need anything else, I'll be going," he said.

"No, wait!" she cried in alarm, grabbing at his sleeve to hold him there. "You can't leave yet! What if he comes back?"

That was a definite possibility, one that Sunny obviously dreaded. But it was already getting dark, and the long ride back to the ranch lay before him. If he was going to have to watch his backtrail on the way, he wanted every advantage. Still, he couldn't leave the girl here alone. Then he realized he probably wouldn't have to stay long. "Don't you have to get back to work?" he asked.

She shook her head. "Mr. Snyder paid Otis for the whole night."

"But he'll go back to the saloon now and . . ."

Her head was still shaking, her smile growing conspiratorial. "He won't go back there. How would he explain why he wasn't with me? He's too proud to admit he got run off." Her pale blue eyes glittered with mischief. For the first time he looked at her and really saw her, not as a reminder of things past but as a person in her own right. His own lips quirked into a grin.

"I reckon you're right," he agreed. "No man wants to admit something like that, least of all a man like Snyder."

Her smile flickered uncertainly and her fingers tightened almost desperately on his sleeve. "That means . . . that means you can stay here with me . . . all night. . . ."

Her meaning was clear: she was offering herself. He wasn't surprised. She was grateful, and giving her body was probably the only way she knew to repay him and to ensure that he would stay with her. But he could also see that she was forcing herself to make the offer. After what had just happened, the last thing she could want was to go to bed with another man.

He laid his hand over where her icy fingers rested on his arm. "I'll stay, but you don't have to do anything," he assured her.

Her eyes widened in surprise for a moment. "Are you sure? I mean . . ."

"I'm sure," he said, patting her fingers and gently prying them loose from his sleeve. Glancing around, he found a faded robe hanging on a peg beside the bed. He plucked it down and handed it to her. "Here," he said, turning away to grant her some measure of privacy. "Do you have any coffee? I could use some."

"There's a pot on the stove, but it's pretty old," she said.

He picked up the coffee pot that rested on the small stove. It was nearly empty, and when he looked inside, he found only dregs. He could hear the girl getting up out of the bed and the rustling sounds of her putting on the robe.

"I'll do that," she said, coming up behind him and taking the pot from his hands. She was still shivering a little from her ordeal, but when her gaze met his, he saw that the shadows were gone from her eyes. She gave him a tentative smile, which he returned.

He stepped back, allowing her room to work, and watched with admiration as her small hands efficiently emptied the dregs and prepared a fresh pot of coffee. She really was a nice girl, he thought to himself. Under other circumstances, he would probably find her appealing in a very practical way. And he should definitely be looking for someone who could take his mind off Angelica Ross.

Except that poor little Sunny Day could never hold a candle to Angelica Ross. He swallowed a disgusted sigh as he considered the possibility that no other woman ever could either. But maybe it was just too soon, he reasoned. Surely, this premonition that he might never find another woman who stirred him like Angelica did would fade in time. Stepping away, he toed out a chair from the table that obviously served as her dining room and sat down.

"Where are you from, Sunny?" he asked, watching as she set the pot on the stove.

She went still for a moment and then turned to face him, her eyes wary and watchful again, as if she wanted to gauge his sincerity before replying. She studied him for several seconds and then said, "Tennessee, or at least that's where I was born. But me and Otis left there a long time ago. We've been a lot of places between here and there."

"You and Otis?" the Kid repeated in surprise. Somehow the idea of the fat bartender and the skinny girl as a couple seemed incongruous, although he knew that girls who made their living the way Sunny did needed protectors. Sometimes the "protector" even turned out to be the girl's husband, who lived off her earnings.

Before he could do more than form that disturbing thought, Sunny surprised him even more by saying, "Otis is my brother. He's been taking care of me ever since I was a little kid."

Taking care of her? By turning her out to whore? The very idea appalled him, but he was careful not to let Sunny see his reaction. There was no point in making her feel bad. "How long have you been in Marsden's Corners?" he asked to change the subject.

"Almost a year now," she said. The wariness was gone from her eyes, and she took the other chair at the battered table.

He studied her face. In the warm lamplight, she no longer looked sallow and worn out. He noticed again how young she was. "Snyder said there's been some trouble around here. What did he mean?"

She shrugged inside the robe, and the front gaped to reveal her breast, where an ugly bruise was rapidly forming. He hastily looked back at her face, but he could see from her shamed expression that she had caught him looking. She quickly closed the robe. "Somebody's been running off anybody who tries to squat on the unclaimed land around here. That's all I know," she said.

"Has anyone been hurt?" he asked, wanting to know what rumors were circulating. He kept his tone impersonal. He'd be a fool to reveal his avid interest in the subject.

"A couple folks turned up dead, but most of them just hightailed it out of here." She ran her fingers through her tangled hair in a self-conscious gesture, and she clutched the robe more tightly around her.

"Somebody told me there was a fire a few days ago," he prompted, steeling himself against the ugly memories.

She seemed unconcerned about the tragedy. "A cabin burned down over on South Creek." Her tone said that cabins burned down all the time, which of course they did. When every meal was cooked over an open fire, a single incident of carelessness could cause a disaster. Except that this fire had not been caused by carelessness.

"What happened to the folks who owned it?" he persisted.

"Nobody knows. They must've just moved on." But Sunny was getting bored with this conversation. "Say, have you ever been to New Orleans?"

He blinked at the sudden change in subject. "Once, a long time ago," he admitted.

"I'd sure like to go there someday," she said wistfully. "What's it like?"

He struggled to remember something that might interest her. In truth, he had found the place much too tawdry and crowded for his tastes. As he described some of the more appealing aspects of the city, his mind was replaying what she had said about the fire. No one professed to know what had become of Pete and Rose. When their bodies had disappeared, Snyder's men must have been puzzled, but they could not make any inquiries without arousing suspicion. One good thing he had learned was that no one except the men who had chased him seemed to know about the third person in the fire, the one who had escaped.

While he described some of his adventures in New Orleans, Sunny got up and poured them each a cup of coffee. They sipped and talked as the evening darkened into night. Her expression softened and her blue eyes grew dreamy with visions of faraway places and exciting adventures. When she smiled, her whole face changed. He couldn't help thinking that if he'd been drinking whiskey instead of coffee, she would look beautiful to him by now. He almost wished she did. How easy things would be if he could turn to her and forget the torment of Angelica Ross.

Sunny laughed appreciatively at his anecdotes and touched his arm from time to time. "You're awfully nice," she said once, making her meaning clear. If he wanted to take her to bed, he was more than welcome.

He could not help feeling gratified, especially when he compared Sunny's adoring manner with the way Angelica had haughtily ordered him out of her house yesterday, as if he were no better than the dust she wiped off her shoes. He thought back to Lettie, to the way she had made him feel in the old days. Being with Sunny was like that. He was a fool to be thinking about Angelica Ross when he had a woman who wanted him right here.

Unfortunately, he couldn't seem to work up any enthusiasm in return. "Why don't you go on to bed," he suggested when he had run out of stories.

Her blue eyes studied him for a moment. "You can come too, if you want to . . ." she said, curiously embarrassed. He thought he caught a faint blush on her cheeks.

Gently, he reached up and touched one of those cheeks. "Not tonight," he said. "You've been through enough already. Maybe next time I'm in town," he lied.

She continued to study him with disconcerting directness. "You really are nice," she concluded at last, her wonder obvious. With a disbelieving shrug, she rose from the table and started toward the bed, but she paused halfway and turned back quickly to face him.

"You won't leave, will you?" she asked anxiously.

"No, I'll wait right here until daylight," he promised.

She considered this and then shrugged again. "There's no use in you sitting up in a chair then. You can share the bed, if you want."

The Kid glanced over at the bed and thought about the many hours ahead. His wound was already reminding him of the long day he had put in, and he had a hard ride ahead of him in the morning. "That's mighty nice of you, Sunny," he said gratefully.

Angelica stared up at the stars and pulled the paisley shawl more closely around her to ward off a chill that had nothing to do with the evening breeze. Kid Collins was gone. The certainty that she would never see him again caused a painful ache deep in her chest, and she wondered vaguely if her heart might actually be breaking.

She had told herself that she only wanted to check on the horses in the corral, that that was why she had come outside so late. Except usually she never bothered to check on the horses. That was Hank's job. The truth was she wanted to see if one certain horse had, by any chance, been returned to the enclosure.

She had been hoping against hope that maybe he had returned late and decided to sleep in the bunkhouse tonight rather than disturb anyone in the house. Now she had to admit the truth: the black gelding that Robbie had informed her was named Midnight was not there.

Fighting the crushing disappointment, she turned back to the house. She walked slowly, as if by postponing the inevitable moment when she would have to pass his bedroom door, she could somehow deny his absence. All afternoon, she had tried to pretend her apprehension was only caused by her concern over how she would deal with Snyder without Collins's help. By evening, she had no longer been able to deny that her feelings went much deeper than that.

Was it only because he had made love to her? She had tried to convince herself it was. After all, she hardly knew the man, as she had so vehemently pointed out to him. She couldn't possibly be in love with him or anything. The feelings churning within her must simply be lust.

Those feelings were definitely churning, though, whatever they were. All she could think about was seeing him again and having one more opportunity to say the things she should have said yesterday instead of ordering him out of the house. No wonder he had chosen to leave.

Since she'd talked things over with Maria, she was beginning to believe that his proposal had been a sincere effort to make an honest woman out of her. He had certainly seemed surprised to discover she interpreted his offer of marriage as something entirely different. While it was true that she did not know him well, she had probably made a serious mistake in assuming the worst, she mused as she entered the house and passed through the entryway.

The moonlight made eerie shadows in the inner courtyard. Her heels clicked forlornly on the tiles as she carefully avoided glancing over at the room that had been his. She jumped when she heard the rasp of a door opening, and her gaze darted hopefully to that room, even though she knew the sound had come from the other side of the courtyard.

"Is he back yet, Angel?"

Robbie's small figure materialized out of the shadows, his white nightshirt flapping around his skinny legs as he ran to her.

"Robbie, you should be asleep. It's late," she chastened gently, unwilling to respond to his question. Lovingly, she touched his orange curls, frowning when he brushed her hand away in annoyance. He was getting too old for such things.

"I was practicing sleeping light, like Mr. Collins taught me," he explained. "The Injuns do that so nobody can sneak up on them. I heard you walking out here and thought it might be him coming home."

"No, it's just me," she said, trying to smile away his concerns. Robbie had spent a lot of time with Collins during the past week. Obviously, they had covered a lot of ground. She wondered what else Collins had taught her brother. Nothing compared to what Collins had taught her, she guessed bitterly.

"Why isn't he home yet?" Robbie asked. "He was just going to town."

Angelica felt that ache in her chest again but steadfastly ignored it. "Maybe he decided to stay overnight," she suggested, loath to tell him that the man he idolized would most probably never return at all.

"Why would he do that?" Robbie insisted.

"I . . . I don't know," she said, unable to think of a legitimate-sounding excuse. She certainly couldn't tell him the truth.

Robbie frowned up at her. "You're lying, Angel. I can always tell," he accused with childish candor. "You think something happened to him, but you don't want to scare me. . . ."

"No!" she cried, instinctively gathering him to her. She had been too wrapped up in her own misery to even consider this possibility. A brand new fear uncurled inside of her, but she couldn't let Robbie see it. "I'm sure he's just fine," she said with feigned confidence.

Robbie wiggled free of her comforting embrace and glared up at her defiantly. "But what if those men who shot him came back?"

"No!" she protested again, unwilling to admit such a thing was possible. This was worse, much worse than having him desert her. "He . . . I know he's all right," she said, as much to convince herself as to convince her brother. "Did he . . . did he say how long he'd be gone?"

Robbie's forehead wrinkled in concentration. "No," he finally decided. "He just said he was going to town."

"There," she said, as if that scrap of information proved her point. "He was probably having fun and lost track of the time. He didn't want to ride back after dark because he doesn't know the area very well and might get lost." The argument sounded feeble to her own ears, but Robbie wanted to be convinced. She could see the worry clearing from his freckled face. She wanted to assure him that Collins would return with the morning light, but she hesitated to make a promise she had no power of keeping. The boy would only be doubly disappointed in the morning when it didn't come true.

"He should've taken me with him," Robbie lamented.

"I know the way back. I'll bet I could find it in the dark with no trouble at all."

"I'm sure you could," Angelica said, taking the opportunity to turn him toward his bedroom and begin marching him back where he belonged. "Now you need to get some sleep. I'll tuck you in."

"Tuck me in!" he cried in disdain. "I'm too big for that!"

"Oh, I'm sorry," she said with a genuine smile. "I forgot there for a minute."

He made a disgusted noise and darted across the courtyard to his room. He disappeared inside but instantly reappeared. "Angel, if Mr. Collins comes back tonight, you'll wake me up and tell me, won't you?"

"Yes, darling, I will," she said. That was one promise she could keep. Unfortunately, she didn't think she would have the opportunity.

Carrying this new burden of anguish, Angelica made her way to her own room, but once again she failed to find a refuge. Collins's presence was still too strong here. After she lighted the lamp, she glanced around for something to distract her thoughts, and instead caught sight of her large, four-poster bed. Nothing could have been a more poignant reminder of what she might have lost. A shaft of longing tore through her at the sight of it.

"Oh, Christian," she whispered, hugging herself against the pain as the memories assailed her. His lovemaking had not been particularly gentle, but it had been wonderful nevertheless. She remembered the way his hands and lips had moved over her body, urging her to respond and giving her more pleasure than she ever dreamed a mortal could know.

Looking back, she wished things could have ended differently. What would have happened if she had accepted his proposal? Would he have held her and kissed her and made love to her again? She knew the answer was yes, and that if she had agreed to marry him, he would be with her right now, safe and sound. Perhaps they would be cuddling together somewhere, making plans for the future.

In spite of her earlier insistence that she did not love the man and could not possibly want to marry him, she now found the idea far more appealing than the alternative. Tears stung her eyes at the thought, but she scrubbed them away, frantically forcing herself to think clearly, to analyze the situation. Perhaps there was another reason for his failure to return other than his death. Even the desertion she had earlier feared would be preferable.

But when Angelica thought back to yesterday, she remembered making it perfectly clear she intended for him to stay on at the ranch. If he had been looking for an excuse to leave, he would never have questioned her order to go, never have sought clarification of her wishes. And she remembered his apparent relief at her reply, as if he wanted to stay. He wasn't the sort of man to sneak away, either. If he was going, he would say so with no phony stories about a trip to town. She had been an idiot to waste the entire day worrying that he had left her when the truth was far worse. Why hadn't she figured it out sooner?

She wanted desperately to do something to help, to jump on a horse and go find him, to do anything that would end this horrible waiting. But of course it was foolish to go looking for him in the dead of night. She might ride right by and never even see . . .

Blinking away tears again, Angelica knew she could never stand the wait unless she took some action. Restlessly, she began to pace. Her hands twisted in front of her, and she wished for something to occupy them. That was when the idea came to her. She walked straight for the chest of drawers on the other side of the room. In the top drawer she found the velvet box that contained her rosary. The crystal beads felt strange in her hands, and she tried to remember how long it had been since she had handled them.

Although she had been baptized by a priest as one of her Catholic mother's dying requests, Angelica had not been raised in the church. On the rare occasions when there was a minister in the area, her Protestant father had taken her to services with him, usually at the Methodist church. During the years she and Robbie were exiled to the convent, the nuns had tried to make up for her lack of religious training, but she found the rituals too rigid for her taste. Now, for the first time, she realized that rituals might sometimes be comforting. Kneeling beside the chest of drawers, she fingered the beads for a moment until she found the beginning.

"Our Father . . ." she began, reciting the words slowly at first until they came to her with easy familiarity. At that moment she could not have said exactly what she was praying for. Did she only want his physical safety? Did she only—and selfishly—want him back? And if she did, was it because she needed him or because she wanted him or both?

As the beads slid through her fingers, the answers to those questions became unimportant. After a while, all she could think of was his face, the way it had looked in that magic moment when he had joined his body to hers. He couldn't be gone from her life forever. "Please, God," she prayed.

Chapter Five

The Kid's eyes flew open, but he lay perfectly still in the predawn darkness, listening for the slight noise that had awakened him. There it was again, the scraping sound of someone brushing up against the side of Sunny's house. Beside him, Sunny lay still, her regular breathing telling him she was still asleep.

Carefully, he reached for his pistol and drew it from the holster that hung on the bedpost at his head. The scraping noise was closer to the door now. Stealthily, he slid from under the thin cover without disturbing the girl. At least he'd had the foresight to keep his clothes on, he thought grimly. His idea had been to prevent Sunny from seeing his bandage and asking too many questions. Now, of course, he was glad he wouldn't be caught with his pants down.

On tiptoe, he stole to the door and flattened himself against the wall beside it, his gun ready. Whoever was sneaking up the front stoop had never spent any time with the Indians, the Kid decided. He made too damn much noise. The fellow might as well have fired off a cannon to announce his arrival.

The knob turned and the door slowly swung open. The Kid held his breath, waiting, waiting. A shadowy figure hovered in the doorway for a moment, straining to get the layout of the room and locate his quarry. The Kid saw the silhouette of a gun in the man's right hand. After what seemed like an eternity, the intruder finally moved, entering the room with a caution that was wasted because his heavy boots thumped noisily in spite of his care. The Kid resisted the urge to reprimand him for his clumsiness and instead simply raised the barrel of his gun and brought it down across the back of the man's neck. He fell with a grunt and lay perfectly still.

"Wh . . . what?" Sunny stirred and pushed up on one elbow. "Who's there?"

"I don't rightly know," the Kid informed her, dragging the intruder completely inside and closing the door so their voices wouldn't carry to anyone else who happened to be lurking out in the alley. "Seems we had a late visitor, but he fainted before I could get his name."

The girl muttered something unintelligible, and he heard her climb out of bed and fumble for the light. In the next second a match flared to life and then ignited the lamp. He glanced up as she came toward him, the ragged nightdress she had put on earlier flapping around her ankles.

"Do you know him?" the Kid asked, tucking his Colt into the waistband of his pants for the time being.

Rubbing the sleep from her eyes in a curiously child-like gesture, Sunny blearily studied the man's face for a minute and the shook her head. "Never saw him before, but Snyder's hiring men all the time. He might be new. Is he dead?"

He lifted his eyebrows at her apparent unconcern. "No, just unconscious. Do you have anything I can tie him up with?"

She stared at him blankly, and he realized she was not yet fully awake. Sighing in resignation, he took a closer look at the man and decided the fellow's belt and bandana would do the trick. In a matter of minutes the Kid had tied and gagged the intruder.

He couldn't leave the fellow in Sunny's house, that much he knew. Then he remembered a rain barrel over behind the saloon. It would serve his purpose well. The intruder groaned softly when the Kid hoisted him up over his shoulder, a groan the Kid echoed when he felt the strain on his newly healed side. He waited a minute until the sharp stab of pain receded and he was able to continue his chore. Cursing softly as his stockinged feet came in contact with the rough ground outside, he made his way across the alley.

The fellow still had not regained consciousness when the Kid had finished stuffing him butt-first into the empty barrel. As an afterthought, the Kid went back and retrieved Snyder's gun belt. When he had wrapped it around the man's neck with the holster hanging down his back, the Kid stepped away and admired his handywork before returning to Sunny's room. His side still ached, but not much. With satisfaction, he realized he had survived Snyder's first attempt on his life and was none the worse for wear because of it.

Sunny was sitting down with both elbows braced on the table, her chin resting on her hands. "You're a lot of trouble, stranger," she remarked with a small smile as he closed the door behind him and went over to where his boots were standing beside the bed.

"I'm right sorry about that, ma'am," he replied, returning her smile. He slipped his feet into the boots and stamped them on. "I reckon I've worn out my welcome around here, so I'll be on my way before you get any more uninvited guests."

Her smile faded. "Mr. Snyder really meant what he said, you know. This," she said, making a gesture toward where the intruder now resided outside, "was only the beginning. Now he'll be twice as mad. If you're smart, you'll make tracks out of here as far and as fast as you can."

"Nobody ever accused me of being smart," he informed her with a grin as he plucked his hat down from the peg where he had hung it the night before and adjusted it on his head.

Her startled gaze touched him again, and he saw genuine concern in her eyes. "You aren't going to hang around here, are you? That's crazy!" She rose anxiously from the table and came toward him, taking hold of his arms as if she would shake some sense into him. "Snyder will kill you. Don't you understand . . ." Then suddenly her expression brightened. "Hey, I know! We can go away together. Somewhere far, like New Orleans. Snyder will never find us there."

The Kid shook his head. "I don't run away from fights, Sunny."

"You wouldn't be running away," she argued. "You've got no quarrel with Snyder, not really. He's nothing to you."

But the Kid was becoming more certain with each passing minute that Snyder was very important to him indeed. Each new thing he learned about the man convinced him that Snyder was the one responsible for all the evil going on in this area. "I'm not leaving, Sunny," he said, gently removing her restraining hands from his arms and squeezing her fingers reassuringly. "Don't worry about me. I learned how to take care of myself a long time ago."

Her small face crumpled in disappointment, and she stepped back, crossing her arms over her middle in a defensive gesture. "I should've known. You men are all alike. All you ever think about is fussing and fighting."

He tried another smile and chucked her lightly under the chin. "That's not *all* I think about," he teased.

Her expression brightened again, and once more she reached for him. "We could go to bed now, if you want," she offered, slipping her arms around his waist and pressing her body urgently against his. "I'm not scared anymore or tired or anything."

The Kid looked down into her eager face and wondered what on earth was wrong with him. Why couldn't he feel even the slightest stirring of desire for a woman who was so obviously willing to satisfy him? If nothing else, he should take her to bed just to salve her pride. But the vision of a redheaded beauty shimmered before his mind's eye, and he knew it wouldn't be fair to Sunny to use her when he could never feel anything for her.

Instead, he lifted his hands to Sunny's face, bent down, and placed a very chaste kiss on her forehead. "I better not take the time right now," he said, pulling away from her. "It's almost dawn, and I want to get away from town before anyone discovers our friend out there." He couldn't take the chance that one of Snyder's men might follow him to Angelica's ranch and put her in danger. "I'll be back, and don't worry, I don't think anybody will bother you once I'm gone. It's me they're after, not you."

She frowned in frustration, but she nodded. "And you be careful."

"I'm always careful," he assured her, reaching into his pocket and pulling out a gold coin. "Here, buy yourself something pretty," he said, pressing it into her hand.

His generous gift had the opposite effect from the one he had intended. Her face screwed up in outrage. "Don't pay me!" she cried, trying to thrust the coin back at him.

"I'm not paying you," he hastened to explain, tenderly closing her fingers around the coin again. "You didn't do anything to get paid for, remember? This is just to make up for all the trouble I've caused."

That seemed to mollify her a bit, although she still

looked uncertain until he kissed her cheek and promised once more to return. By the time he left, she looked resigned and even a little hopeful. He felt lower than a snake's belly for leading her on and making her think he cared about her when all he felt was a sense of obligation because he had put her in a bad spot with Snyder. But brushing her off completely would be even more cruel, especially when he knew she might well need his protection in the future.

Getting out of town was much easier than the Kid had thought it would be. No one was around at the livery stable, and since he had paid in advance, he simply saddled Midnight and left. Apparently the intruder who had broken into Sunny's house had been alone. The Kid thought grimly that if Snyder had chosen such a clumsy performer for so delicate a task, solving Angelica's problems might not be as difficult as he had imagined. Unfortunately, he could not entertain that thought very long. Snyder was too smart to underestimate the Kid again. The next time he met one of Snyder's henchmen, he knew he would not get off so easily.

Dawn was barely breaking when Angelica stormed into the kitchen looking for something to eat. She had spent a restless night and was not in the mood for polite conversation. Consequently, she was annoyed to find that her *mamacita* was already up and busily making breakfast.

Maria's heavy eyebrows rose several notches as she looked Angelica up and down, taking in the girl's forest green riding dress with a skeptical glance. "It is early for a ride, is it not?" she asked.

Angelica tried to intimidate her with a glare, but failed. "Mr. Collins didn't come back last night," she said, looking away so she would not see Maria's expression and the pity that might be reflected in her eyes. "I think something might have happened to him, and I'm going out to look for him." She had spent most of the night agonizing over this decision, so she was certain it was the correct one. Whether it was or not and whether Maria agreed with her or not, she no longer cared. The only important thing now was finding out if he was safe.

Maria frowned, still skeptical. "Maybe he is gone for good," she suggested gently.

"No!" Angelica insisted. "He wouldn't just sneak away like that, without a word to anyone. He's not that kind of man."

Maria considered this as she wrestled with her own doubts. Two days ago, she would have agreed with Angelica's assessment of his character. Since then, he had betrayed her trust by seducing Angelica, but did that mean that her original opinion of him had been wrong? Perhaps she was letting Angelica's need to believe in Collins sway her, but she wanted to believe in him, too. "Do you think he is in some danger?" she asked, willing to be convinced.

Angelica could feel the fear rising up in her chest at that thought, but she pushed it back, refusing to let it get the better of her. She managed a careless shrug. "He's still recovering from his wound. Maybe he got weak and . . ." She made a helpless gesture with her hand, unwilling to elaborate on her suspicions.

"*Sí,* that is true," Maria agreed thoughtfully. "But I think it is too early to go looking for him just yet. Maybe he just stayed the night in town. We will give him time to get back, and then we will send the men out. . . ."

"No," Angelica insisted stubbornly. "I'm going, and I'm not waiting. If he's hurt . . ."

Maria shook her head, knowing she had to restrain Angelica's impulse if only to save the girl's pride in the event they were both wrong about Collins. "One thing I have learned about men is that the bad things women imagine hardly ever happen to them. Even if he is hurt, he will not like to be rescued by you. And how could you help him? Can you lift him onto a horse?"

Angelica had already opened her mouth to protest before she realized that Maria was right, as usual. What did she think she was going to do, throw Collins over her shoulder and cart him back to the ranch? She had a pretty good idea that both Hank and Curly together would have trouble with that one.

"All right, I'll take the men with me, but I'm not waiting long. We'll leave as soon as they have their breakfast," Angelica decreed.

Too restless to stay indoors, she stalked outside, hoping to hurry her cowboys along. It was a frustrating task. The men did not share her sense of urgency and refused to be rushed. By the time they had finished eating and gone back outside, Angelica was fit to be tied.

"I'm not waiting another minute," she declared, striding toward the kitchen door.

"At least give the men a chance to get the horses saddled," Maria suggested. "They haven't even had time to get out to the corral yet."

"I still don't understand why you won't let me go along," Robbie complained from where he sat at the kitchen table, glaring balefully at his sister. "I bet I could find him quicker than anybody."

Angelica stopped at his plaintive tone. Turning to face him, she forced her face into a reassuring smile. "I'm sure you could, sweetheart, but who'll take care of Mamacita if we all go running off after Mr. Collins?" she asked, hoping the excuse would sound reasonable to the boy.

Although he gave no indication that it did, at least he didn't raise any more arguments. Angelica was beginning to think she would jump right out of her skin if she didn't get away from the ranch soon. With each passing second she became more and more concerned for Collins's safety. All she needed was an argument with Robbie to push her completely over the edge.

"I have packed you some sandwiches in case you are gone a long time," Maria said, handing Angelica a neatly wrapped bundle.

"Aw, gee, they're gonna have a picnic, too," Robbie complained.

Angelica went over and gave him a small hug before he had time to dodge her. "I promise it won't be a picnic," she told him with a sad smile. "But if . . . I mean, *when* Mr. Collins comes back, maybe we'll all go on a real picnic. Will that make you feel any better?"

The boy nodded grudgingly, assuaging her guilt somewhat. Quickly, before he could duck away again, she bent and kissed his cheek.

"Angel!" he chastened her in outrage as she hurried out to find her man.

It was good to be home, the Kid reflected as he rode toward the Diamond R ranch buildings. Then he caught himself. *Home?* Now where had that thought come from? He'd only been at the ranch a week now, and he certainly didn't expect to stay here more than two or three months at the most. Why then did the sight of those buildings give him the feeling that he had finally arrived at a destination toward which he had been traveling his entire life?

Instinctively, he knew the answer to that question

somehow involved Angelica Ross. That was only logical, considering the answer to every one of his questions lately seemed to involve Angelica Ross. Frowning at the thought, he rode into the ranch yard, where Hank and Curly stood as if they had been awaiting his arrival.

"We was just coming to look for you," Hank informed the Kid as he swung down from Midnight.

"Look for me?" the Kid echoed in surprise. "Did you think I got lost?"

Hank grinned, showing the gap where one of his front teeth had been removed by an angry cow. "Miss Angelica thought maybe you got hurt or something. She's been in a foaming tizzy all morning over it. She was even gonna go with us to find you," he added with a wink.

The Kid stared at Hank in stunned amazement. Angelica? Angelica was worried about him? Angelica was going to go looking for him? He got the oddest sensation, as if something in his chest, something he had been holding very tightly, suddenly broke loose and filled him with a wondrous warmth. Responding to that warmth, he knew he must find her, must see her with his own eyes and discover the truth of Hank's insinuations.

"Could you take care of Midnight for me?" he asked, handing the reins to Hank without even waiting for his reply.

The Kid was halfway to the house when she came out the front door and paused. She held a package under one arm and was slapping a quirt impatiently against her tall riding boot with her other hand. She wasn't looking in his direction. Instead, she gazed off toward the road he had just come in on, as if she were searching the horizon for some sign of his return. He stopped where he was, just watching her for a long minute. She was a feast for the eyes with her slender body clothed all in green and with her flame-colored hair spread over her shoulders to glitter in the morning sunlight.

Without meaning to, he called, "Angelica."

Her head snapped around, and he watched transfixed as her expression changed from grim to joyous in one magical instant. "Christian!" she cried.

Angelica dropped the package of sandwiches and ran to him. He was here, he was safe, and nothing else mattered, nothing except holding him close for one final proof. Did he run to meet her, too? She could not be sure, but that wasn't important. The only important thing was feeling her arms around him and hearing the pounding of his heart against her ear.

It was such a reassuring sound, even though his heartbeat thundered crazily. His arms closed around her, crushing her to him as if he would draw her into himself. She held on tightly, only too willing to be drawn. For long minutes they clung, and Angelica reveled in the solid evidence that drove away all her phantom terrors. He was really here. He was really safe. He had returned to her.

The Kid nudged aside her flat-crowned hat so he could bury his face in the fragrant cloud of her hair and inhale the scent that was hers alone. Memory was a feeble thing, he thought wildly. The reality of her swamped his senses until he could barely think, until his conscious mind closed down around one single, glorious thought: right or wrong, he loved her.

And, by God, she must have feelings for him, too, or why would she have thrown herself into his arms like this? No sooner did he think it than he felt her beloved body go rigid.

Angelica inhaled again. No! It couldn't be! And yet it was. There was no mistaking that smell, the cloying scent of cheap perfume. Appalled, she jerked away from him, breaking with difficulty the hold he had on her.

"Wh . . . where were you last night?" she stammered in an attempt to cover her mortification. "We were worried about you."

The Kid looked down at her in confusion, not quite able to comprehend her rapid change of mood. The joy had vanished from her face, and in its place was an expression he could not read. "I went to town. Didn't Maria tell you?"

"I know you went to town," she snapped, taking a step backward to put some much needed distance between them. She didn't want to feel the heat from his body, which was tempting her to come close again. She could not surrender to that temptation until he explained away that awful perfume. "When you didn't come back last night, I . . . we imagined all sorts of things."

The words were an accusation, and he could tell from the way her emerald eyes glittered that she was angry about something, angry and hurt. She had been concerned for his safety. Was she only mad because she had worried needlessly, or was it something else, something for which he should feel guilty?

He felt the heat crawling up his neck and mentally cursed himself for that reaction. After all, she couldn't possible know he had spent the night in another woman's bed. And even if she did, the whole thing had been completely innocent. He needn't feel guilty, especially when he considered the way she'd scorned him two days ago. In light of that, he didn't even owe her an explanation.

"I got into a late poker game, so I stayed in town overnight," he explained anyway, rcsponding to some innate urge to pacify her so she would come back into his arms.

His words had exactly the opposite effect. "That's obvious," she said bitterly, noting he had not mentioned where he had slept. She felt the sting of tears and hated herself for that weakness. Blinking them away, she watched the crimson flush rise to his face. It was true! Exactly what she had thought was true, or why else would he be *blushing,* for heaven's sake? There could be no doubt he had been with a woman.

She was a fool! A complete idiot! She had sat up all night worrying and fretting and *praying* for a man who was out whoring! Rage and humiliation flooded her, filling her until she thought she might explode. She hated him, hated him with every fiber of her being, and she never wanted to see him again. With an agonized cry, she turned and ran.

The Kid stared after her in open-mouthed astonishment. What had come over her? "Angelica, come back here!" he called, but she did not stop her headlong flight back to the sanctuary of the house.

Well, she had tried to run from him once before without success, and she wouldn't get away from him this time, either, he vowed. He did not even hurry as he pursued her, oblivious to the fascinated stares of the two cowboys who had witnessed the whole scene.

As he entered the house, the Kid could hear her footsteps clattering across the courtyard outside, and he wondered if she would head for her bedroom again. It wasn't the safest room in which to have a conversation with Angelica, although he was pretty certain he would be able to restrain himself this time, at least until he'd said what needed to be said. In any case, he would find her wherever she chose to hide. Resolutely, he started toward the courtyard, but a childish voice caught him before he reached it.

"Mr. Collins!" Robbie cried, every bit as glad to see him as Angelica had been at first. The boy ran to him from the dining room, and the Kid had no choice except to scoop him up in his arms. "Where have you been? Angel was just going to look for you."

The Kid fought hard to keep his expression blank at this reminder. "I spent the night in town, that's all. No reason to get in such a lather," he told the boy with a reassuring smile.

"I was afraid you got shot again. Angel said that couldn't happen, but I could tell she was scared, too," Robbie informed him. "She'll be happy when she finds out you're back."

The Kid managed not to wince. "I better go find her then, Squirt. Do you know where she is?" he asked, setting the boy back on his feet again.

Robbie considered. "I think she was going outside to get her horse."

"I didn't see her out there," the Kid improvised, knowing he had to get rid of the boy if wanted to talk to Angelica alone. "Why don't you go look for her. If you see her, send her inside to find me, and then you can help Hank take care of Midnight for me."

"All right!" Robbie agreed enthusiastically. In an instant, he was gone.

The courtyard was deserted when the Kid got there. He went immediately to Angelica's bedroom and found the door ajar. He called her name, and when he got no response, he pushed the door open. The room was empty. Quickly, he considered the other possible places she might be. She could have gone to the kitchen, where Maria would serve as a chaperone should he follow her, but somehow he doubted she would seek Maria's company. Angelica had been visibly upset, and Maria was bound to ask a lot of questions Angelica would not want to answer.

No, he concluded, she would be hiding in some private place where no one would be likely to stumble across her.

Not bothering to ask himself how he could be so certain of her behavior, he crosses the courtyard to the room he had learned was the ranch office. This was the room in which Maria had found her before.

"Angelica?" he called, rapping sharply on the tightly closed door.

"Go away," Angelica said and then instantly covered her mouth in disgust of her own stupidity. Now that he knew for sure she was in here, he would never go away. Just as she had expected, the door flew open.

He stepped inside and shut the door behind him with a decisive click. Now they were alone, just as they had been alone two days ago. Something fluttered in her stomach, but she ignored it. She had been a stupid, weak fool then. Today things would be different. Resolutely, she stiffened her spine, lifted her chin, and gave him her fiercest glare, the one that usually sent Robbie scrambling for cover. Collins didn't even blink.

The Kid simply stared at her for a long moment. Now that he was here with her, he wasn't sure just what he wanted to say. He couldn't exactly tell her how he had suddenly realized that he adored her. No, that was the last thing he should admit, especially now that some of his sanity had returned and he was beginning to remember all the reasons why he shouldn't have fallen in love with her in the first place and the reasons why she could never love him in return.

Still, if she already did . . .

"What was all that about?" he demanded, jerking his thumb over his shoulder to indicate the earlier scene in the ranch yard.

Angelica was wondering that very thing. Whatever had possessed her to fling herself at him? If only she hadn't been so worried and so frightened for him, it never would have happened. Now, of course, it was much too late to think about how she should have behaved. Knowing she had no other choice, she decided to bluff her way through this. She would die before letting him know how her heart was aching. How could she have allowed herself to care for such a faithless man? "I was concerned for your safety," she informed him haughtily.

"Concerned?" He pounced on the word. It wasn't much, but it was a start. "How concerned?"

Pain was a heavy lump her her chest, but she did not flinch. "As concerned as I would be for any of my men who was missing," she lied.

Hope flickered inside of him. She was lying. He knew she was. "And is that the way you normally greet your men?" he prodded, stepping closer. A thrill went through him at her obvious response to his nearness.

Angelica felt a surge of panic as his physical presence threatened to overwhelm her fragile defenses. She retreated a step to maintain the distance she needed to continue thinking rationally. "You're very important to me, Mr. Collins. Naturally, I was worried about you," she allowed, proud to note that her voice was still steady in spite of the difficulty she was having getting her breath.

This was it, he knew. She was going to tell him the truth about how she felt. He lifted a hand to touch the fiery curl that rested on her shoulder as he whispered, "How important am I, Angelica?"

The true answer stabbed through her like a rapier even as the scent of cheap perfume drifted from his clothes to clog her senses. He was important, all right, so important that he had caused her more pain in the last two days than she ever wanted to experience again. But she would never let him know it. Holding herself completely still beneath his touch even though her every nerve screamed in protest, she said, "You are valuable to me because I need your gun to save my ranch. These men you sent for must have someone to lead them, someone who owes me his loyalty and . . ."

"Damn you, Angelica!" He grabbed her shoulders, pulling her close and resisting with difficulty the urge to shake that disdainful expression from her face. "It's more than that!" How could he make her admit it?

His hands seemed to burn right through the cloth of her riding jacket to scorch the sensitive skin beneath, but she couldn't let him know his effect on her. Drawing on reserves of strength she had never suspected she possessed, she did not blink in the face of his fury. Instead she took a deep breath, inhaling the offensive reminder of his treachery. That gave her the strength she needed to remain rigid under his hands.

Unconsciously, he tightened his grip on her, as if he could wring the words he wanted to hear out of her by brute force, and still she did not speak. Her eyes glittered like green glass, the expression in them even more disdainful than before. He swore again, wanting nothing so much as to haul her into his arms and press his mouth to hers until she melted into the woman he had known two days ago. But some instinct warned him she would not melt, not for him, not now. In an agony of frustration, he thrust her away, no longer certain the warm and willing woman he had made love to had ever even existed. "Damn you," he whispered fiercely, and then he turned on his heel and stalked out.

I will not cry, she told herself as the door slammed behind him with enough force to make the books on the shelves jump. He was not worth her tears; he was lower than the dirt under her feet. *I will not cry and I will not grieve and I will not love him, not for another minute!*

That was when she realized that she really did love him. "No!" she whispered in fierce denial, but it was no use. Suddenly, all the confusing emotions that had driven her nearly to distraction settled into place, and all her irrational thoughts made sense. Now she understood her compulsion to be near him. Now she understood her frantic concern when he failed to return to the ranch. Now, at last, she understood why she had surrendered so willingly, so eagerly, to his lovemaking.

She loved him, but the knowledge only brought her new pain because she had wasted her love on a man who was faithless and thoughtless and even cruel, a man who could go directly from her bed to another woman without a backward glance. And what else could she expect? Kid Collins was a killer. She had known that from the beginning. Never mind that he had been kind to Robbie. Never mind that he had been her lover.

Her lover. The words seemed to echo in her mind, taunting her with the reminder of how she had given herself to a man unworthy of the gift. How could he have made love to her so sweetly and then gone off to another woman's bed the very next day? And who was this woman? Judging from her scent, she could only be a cheap floozy, someone who sold her favors to any man who came along.

Is that how he saw her, too, as just a convenient female body on which to ease his lust? Angelica hugged herself against the agony of that thought, her eyes wide at the humiliation of it. No, she would not cry, not for a man like that, but as she stared at the door through which he had gone, her eyes dry and burning, she fervently wished she could.

"I win again!" Robbie crowed delightedly, sweeping the few remaining checkers from the board. "You take red this time. Maybe your luck'll change," he offered generously.

The Kid could not help but smile. "Checkers is not a game of luck. It's a game of skill, and I'm just letting you win so you'll like me better."

"Sure," Robbie said with a smug grin as he swiftly set up a new game. It was late evening, and they were sitting in the huge parlor of the ranch house, a room that reflected a curious mix of frontier and Eastern influences. Paintings of sylvan scenes in ornate frames hung beside wrought-iron sconces and animal skins. An intricately carved velvet-covered sofa dominated the room, and the table on which the checkerboard rested was mahogany inlaid with marble, but the chairs that he and Robbie had pulled up to it were made of cowhorn and rawhide.

The room was, the Kid suddenly realized, a lot like Angelica herself: half-civilized and half-untamed.

"Your move," Robbie prompted.

The Kid jerked his attention back to the game and made an ill-considered play that got his checker jumped by a gleeful Robbie. The Kid had lied when he said he was letting Robbie win. The truth was, he simply could not keep his mind on the game for thinking about Angelica and trying to make some sense of what had happened this morning.

For a minute there, he'd been certain she was happy to see him, far happier than a woman who only cared about his prowess with a gun should have been. She had hugged him, too, and that was proof positive her feelings ran far deeper than she wanted him to believe. And he knew now why she had pulled away.

Hank had solved that mystery a little later. "Whooeee," he had said, wrinkling his large nose when they met in the ranch yard. "You smell mighty pretty. I heard tell that girl at the Dirty Dog is persnickety about the way her customers smell, but you should've washed off in the creek on your way home."

So that was it! Sunny's perfume was what Angelica had reacted to and how she had known where he spent the night. The Kid remembered noticing the strong odor of perfume when he had first entered Sunny's house, but apparently he had quickly gotten used to it. The Kid knew from living with the Comanches that you could get used to just about any smell if you were around it long enough. Sunny's bed must have been saturated with the scent, since she probably applied it liberally to those of her customers who neglected to bathe before visiting her.

He had slept in that bed, picking up the scent, and that had made Angelica furious. Now the accusing tone of her voice when she had asked him where he had been made sense. He could have sworn the emotion behind those words was jealousy, but maybe that was only because he wanted her to be jealous. Her later behavior certainly didn't support the theory. He knew the way women acted when they were jealous. There was no better way to start a knock-down, drag-out fight than to bring a gift to one of the girls—and only one of the girls—at a cathouse. He'd seen it happen more than once.

Angelica hadn't acted that way. Instead she had become cold and distant, so distant he could not reach her at all.

"Who's winning?"

The Kid felt his whole body come alive at the sound of her voice. Very slowly, he lifted his head. She was moving across the wide room toward them with the easy grace that haunted his dreams. Her face was carefully cheerful, and her eyes held a guarded expression, as if she were hiding something.

"I am," Robbie announced proudly. "Mr. Collins

claims he's only letting me win, but he's let me win six times now."

She smiled fondly down at the boy. "Maybe you ought to let him win once, just so he'll keep playing," she suggested. The Kid noticed she only looked at the boy and studiously avoided meeting his own gaze.

He tried to decide what her reasons might be for doing so. Was she still so angry that she could not stand the sight of him? She certainly didn't look angry. Was she afraid she might betray something to him if she met his gaze? But what?

Still puzzled, he watched her move away and take a seat on the sofa with elaborate care. That was when he noticed the way she was done up. She looked like something out of a picture book. Her dress was gold, with all sorts of braid and doodads on it. Her hair was pinned up high on her head in an elaborate arrangement of curls. In contrast to her finery, he felt suddenly inferior, even in his new range clothes, and irritated because he was certain that was exactly the way she intended him to feel.

Angelica made one small adjustment to the way her skirt lay on the sofa and then decided she was completely satisfied with the picture she made. Such airs were normally foreign to her, but she found she possessed just enough female vanity to carry it off. This outfit was a costume, and this evening she was playing a part, the part of the Lady of the Manor to his lowly Hired Gun. If Kid Collins thought he could put her in the same category as his soiled doves, he was in for a surprise.

She folded her hands in her lap and gave Robbie a smile. Collins was watching her, she could feel his eyes on her, but she would not look at him, not just yet. Not until her heart settled down a bit, and she was sure her eyes would not reveal any hint of longing.

Besides, she already knew what he looked like. She had stolen a moment before entering the room to feast her eyes on the sight of him, and she reminded herself that he was, after all, only a man. When she looked up, she would see broad shoulders hunched over the small table, powerful arms braced on either side of the checkerboard, and a golden head bent in concentration. No, she wouldn't look at him until she was certain she would not meet his piercing gaze, the gaze that seemed capable of reading her inner thoughts and seeing into her very soul. If he could read her thoughts, he might see her memories of his powerful arms wrapped around her and his golden head pressed to her bosom. There were secrets she must keep from him, and so she waited until she was sure she could keep them to herself.

"I win again!" Robbie cried.

"You're too good for me, Squirt," the Kid said. "I think I'd better quit for tonight."

"Aw, just one more game," Robbie insisted.

"Robbie," Angelica reprimanded him. "Seven games is quite enough." At last she trusted herself to meet Collins's gaze and found him watching her with a peculiar intensity. What was he thinking? And what did he see when he looked at her like that? Did he see only her proud exterior, or could he discern the girl beneath the gold taffeta, the girl who tended to tremble each time she remembered his touch?

"And besides, it is bedtime," Maria decreed from the doorway, startling all three occupants of the room. Robbie might feel free to argue with a visitor about another game of checkers, but he knew better than to argue with Maria over bedtime. He gave a token groan but rose obediently at her summons.

Angelica knew a sudden sense of panic at the situation she had gotten herself into. What had she done by coming in here now? She must have realized deep down that Robbie would soon be summoned to bed, thus leaving her alone with Collins. Had she responded to some sort of unconscious desire to be with him? But how was that possible when she had spent the entire day avoiding him?

She fought the frantic urge to beg Maria to let Robbie stay up just a little longer, and somehow managed to wish Robbie a good night without betraying her inner turmoil. As soon as he and Maria were gone, she tried desperately to think of an excuse to leave, too, until she realized she was being ridiculous. If she wanted to leave, she could just go. Except that she didn't want to leave, not really. Once she finally admitted that to herself, she felt the panic subside.

Cautiously, she let her gaze drift over to where Collins still sat. He had propped one elbow on the table and now rested his chin on his hand as he studied her from across the room. His other hand idly toyed with the checkers scattered in front of him. As always, the sight of him did strange things to her body, making her lungs strain for each breath and sending her heart into palpitations. At least, she assumed it was palpitations, having never before experienced any.

Nervously, she cast about for something to say to break the strained silence. "You must have done some shopping in town," she said, choosing the first thing that came to mind. "Those are new clothes, aren't they?"

The Kid glanced down at his shirt, a little surprised at her observation. "Yes, I did," he said, remembering something else. "Mrs. Marsden at the store said to tell you 'hello and don't be a such a stranger.' "

"Oh, that's nice," she replied inanely, unaccountably jealous to learn he had conversed with Kate Marsden. Then she remembered what else she was jealous about concerning his trip to town. The anger welled up in her, and before she could stop it, she blurted, "You were awfully busy in Marsden's Corners, weren't you?"

The Kid's eyes widened at the bitterness in her tone and the color that had suddenly come to her cheeks. She was angry, spitting mad if the truth were told, although up until now she'd done a fair-to-middling job of hiding it behind that fancy dress and that prim little pose. Could he have been wrong? Could she really be jealous because she thought he'd spent the night with another woman?

It was on the tip of his tongue to ask, but of course, a man didn't ask a lady such a thing, not if he was any kind of a gentleman at all. The Kid figured he'd already stretched the bounds of propriety with Angelica to the outer limits. Maybe he could test her feelings for him some other way. "I ran into Snyder while I was there," he tried.

"Snyder! When? Where? What happened?" Her alarm gratified him somewhat.

"I saw him at the saloon." Then he recalled another useful piece of information that might get a rise out of her. "He offered me a job. Said he was paying fighting wages." For a moment, the Kid savored her look of worried astonishment. Could she actually believe he would leave her for Snyder? "Come to think of it, we never have discussed what *you're* paying me," he said, testing his theory.

Angelica felt her face going scarlet as she considered informing him that after what he had taken from her, he should serve her for free. But of course, she could never say such a thing, so instead she said, "I told you I'd pay you fighting wages and a bonus, too."

"A bonus?" he asked, just the slightest hint of innuendo in his voice. She looked so lovely when she blushed.

"What did you tell Snyder?" she asked, ignoring his barb.

"I told him I'd think about it," he replied, hoping that would disturb her.

Angelica made a small, choking sound as she swallowed the fury building inside of her. "And *are* you going to think about it?" she asked tightly.

"Of course not," he hastily assured her, instantly aware that he had gone too far. He only wanted to get a rise out of her, not make her distrust him. "In fact, by the time we parted company, we'd had a little falling-out. I had to leave town before dawn this morning to be sure none of Snyder's men followed me back here."

"How inconvenient," she said acidly, involuntarily picturing him slipping out of some woman's bed in the wee hours of the morning.

His eyes narrowed as he tried to read the real meaning of her words. What was going on behind those beautiful green eyes? Try as he might, he could make no sense out of her reactions. Obviously, the idea that he might change his allegiance disturbed her, but that was only natural under the circumstances and did not really prove she cared about him on a deeper level.

Still, he kept getting the impression that she was jealous about Sunny. If so, then she must care about him, maybe not as much as he cared for her, but a little, at least. If only she would accuse him outright of being with another woman, he could explain everything, how he'd rescued Sunny and how he'd slept in her bed and nothing had happened . . . But no, it even sounded false to him, and he knew it was all true. Angelica would certainly never believe him. Not to mention the fact that she hadn't asked for any explanation and didn't seem likely to. Which reminded him of something else, something he had intended to ask her first thing this morning.

"Snyder didn't know who I was or that I was working for you, and nobody else in town did, either," he told her.

Surprised at the sudden shift in subject, Angelica frowned at the hint of outrage in his voice. "Why should they?"

"Because I signed my name to those telegrams, that's why," he explained impatiently. "Everybody in town should have the word by now that Kid Collins is on your payroll."

But Angelica was shaking her head, confused over his annoyance. "When Hank sent the telegrams, he told Sam Grimes—he's the telegraph operator—not to breathe a word to anybody. Sam was a good friend of my father's, so I'm sure he kept quiet. Is something wrong?"

The Kid scowled. Well, that explained a lot. Now he had a new problem. "I was hoping that when Snyder found out you'd hired a gunfighter, he'd crawl back in his hole for a while, maybe long enough for us to get the roundup finished without any trouble."

Angelica made an unladylike noise. "You have a high opinion of yourself, don't you, Mr. Collins?" she asked, finally succeeding at getting in a barb of her own. "While it's true that I wanted to hire you for your reputation, Snyder isn't likely to be all that impressed. He's got known men in his crew, too, and he's also got the advantage of numbers."

The Kid stared at her in astonishment. She was right, of course. What in God's name had he been thinking? At first, he'd classified Snyder as a two-bit crook, someone who could be easily intimidated and summarily dealt with. Having met the man should have changed his opinion, *if* the Kid had been thinking straight. The problem was, he'd spent most of his time lately thinking in circles and about another subject entirely. Underestimating his opponent was the worst mistake a man could make in a business like this. If he didn't get back on track, he'd find himself dead.

"If we can't outgun him, then we'll have to give Snyder another good reason for leaving us alone," he murmured, thinking aloud.

Angelica watched him as he considered the possibilities. A lump of dread began to form in her stomach as she considered them, too. What had he said about having a falling-out with Snyder? She'd been so angry at him, she hadn't paid much attention. What did he mean by "falling-out"? And why would one of Snyder's men have followed him back here if not to do him harm? Visions of him being ambushed, shot down in a flurry of gunfire, shimmered before her.

The lump of dread grew larger until she felt her breath being squeezed from her chest. As horribly as he had treated her, she could not seem to convince herself not to care about what happened to him. And besides, she rationalized, it was in her own best interest to keep both him and the rest of the men safe, wasn't it? Yes, of course it was. But how?

Judging from his perplexed expression, he wasn't having much luck thinking of a way to keep Snyder at bay. Surely, there was something *she* could do, some way she could convince Snyder that he didn't have to use force to get what he wanted from her. . . .

Slowly, the idea took form in her mind. At first she resisted, knowing how unpleasant her part in it would be, but the more she thought about it, the more convinced she became that it was the only sensible solution. No one would be in danger, no shots would be fired, and the roundup could proceed without incident. Christian Collins would be safe.

"I'll tell Snyder that he can court me again," Angelica

announced.

Collins looked at her as if she'd dropped a hammer on his foot. "What?!" he demanded incredulously.

Feeling a little less sure of herself, she repeated her statement. "It's the perfect plan," she insisted. "If he thinks I'm going to marry him and he's going to get the ranch anyway, he won't have to stop the roundup or hurt the men or . . ." She let her voice trail off as he rose slowly and menacingly from his chair.

"No. Absolutely not." The Kid could hardly contain the emotions roiling within him, the chief among them being cold, naked fear at the thought of Angelica leading Snyder on. What might Snyder do to her if he thought she was willing to marry him? Visions of Sunny's bruised and abused body teased obscenely at his memory. Would Snyder expect such submission from his future wife? The Kid couldn't allow Angelica to put herself in that kind of danger for *any* reason, least of all to protect him and his men. "You are to stay as far away from Snyder as possible. Do you understand?" he asked, pointing a threatening finger at her as he advanced.

Angelica fought the instinct that told her to cringe from him and responded to a more civilized, feminine desire for combat. "Why?" she demanded, rising regally to her feet.

Why? The Kid stopped for a moment as he considered the answer to that question. He swiftly discarded the possibility of telling her the truth. That wasn't something he could explain to a lady. "Snyder's a dangerous man," he improvised. "If you were alone with him, he might do something . . ."

"That's ridiculous!" Angelica informed him furiously, irritated beyond reason that he of all people should be concerned about her virtue. "Snyder has always treated me with perfect respect! You shouldn't judge other men by your own standards."

Her barb struck a sore spot, a spot which he himself had flayed raw with guilt, and he reacted to the pain. "Snyder's standards aren't any better than mine, and if you didn't like what I did to you, you sure as hell won't like it when Snyder does it."

"You bastard!" she cried outrage as her hand swung up to slap his insolent face, but he caught her arm and twisted it behind her back. She struggled wildly, but he captured her other arm, too, pinning her helplessly against the unyielding strength of his body.

"And don't try slapping Snyder's face, either," he warned. "He'll slap you back just before he does this." The Kid clamped his mouth over hers in a cruel and punishing demonstration meant to hurt and frighten her, but he had not counted on how her touch would affect him. The taste and feel of her engulfed him. Startled, he relaxed his hold for one brief instant, but that instant was long enough for Angelica.

Through the haze of her fury, she felt his grip slacken and with a violent twist, broke free of his mouth. "Don't!" she gasped, fighting vainly against his hold.

She glared up at him only to discover that he looked as shocked as she felt. The dangerous stranger who had grabbed her was gone, and in his place stood the gentle, sensitive man who had won her love. His azure eyes glittered with a myriad of emotions, among them regret and confusion and a strange vulnerability.

"I . . . I'm sorry," he said, his voice husky and warm against her face. Angelica felt the fear and anger drain out of her as his hold on her gentled apologetically. "I didn't mean to hurt you."

"Yes, you did," she contradicted, but her voice was soft, tinged with love and forgiveness.

He closed his eyes and drew a ragged breath. She felt a

tiny shudder go through him as he struggled for control. When his eyes opened again, she saw only warmth and need and a reflection of her own desire. "I didn't want to hurt you, but you make me crazy, Angelica."

She smiled, lifting her freed hands to touch his face. "You make me crazy, too," she said. He turned his head to bury a kiss in her palm, a gesture that spoke of quiet desperation. Understanding that desperation, she turned his face toward hers. Lightly, she touched her lips to his, once and then again.

His arms enfolded her carefully, and she could feel him tremble with the strain of holding back. But she didn't want him to hold back, not anymore. She slipped her hands around his head, burying her fingers in his hair and pulling him closer. He needed no further encouragement.

This time she gloried in his strength, clinging to it with an almost desperate longing. Her mind still whirled with a thousand questions, but none of them seemed important at the moment. The only thing that mattered was being close to him again, feeling his mouth on hers, being cherished in his embrace.

And cherish her he did. With hands and arms and lips, he worshipped her, cradling her to him with a care that bordered on reverence. His mouth explored her eyes and cheeks and ears and throat, only to return once more to taste her essence.

He was right, she thought, they were both insane, out of control, the same way she had felt before, when he had made love to her. The mindlessness was seductive, soothing away all the hurts, tempting her to forget the betrayals. Nothing else mattered when he was kissing her like this.

The Kid moaned in frustration as his hands sought in vain to find her softness beneath the crisp fabric and rigid corsets that imprisoned her. He could sense her response, the need that was as great as his. When he held her like this, he no longer questioned whether she cared for him. Her body spoke to his on a primitive level where words were unnecessary. Words, in fact, only seemed to complicate and confuse what should have been something very simple. What *was* very simple. If they could only go someplace, someplace private, then everything would be fine. "Angelica . . ."

Her name flowed from his lips like warm honey, infinitely sweet. She would do anything he asked when he said her name like that. Anything at all, she decided, as her very bones seemed to dissolve along with her willpower.

"Angel!"

The cry jarred her, shocking her out of the haze of passion that was clouding her brain. Her name again, but not from his lips.

"Angel!"

Robbie's voice! They jerked apart just as the boy rounded the doorway. "Angel, have you seen my . . ."

He slid to a halt, his hazel eyes widening at what he thought he had seen.

"Hey, were you two kissing?" he demanded, obviously fascinated by the very idea.

Angelica frantically tried to calm her clamoring emotions. She felt as if she had been thrown from a cliff and then snatched to safety at the very last second. Every nerve in her body quivered in reaction, and her breath came in labored gasps. "No, of course not, silly," she told her brother in a voice that sounded little like her own.

Robbie was not convinced. He turned his frank stare on Collins, but saw only his back. The Kid had more to compose than Angelica. "Mr. Collins, were you kissing my sister?"

The Kid drew a shaky breath and managed a semblance of a grin as he turned to face the boy. "She said no, didn't she?" he hedged. "Sometimes it's better to mind your own business, Squirt."

The boy scowled, his earnest gaze going from one to the other of them and back again in confusion. Angelica tried desperately to think of something to say that would send him on his way, but her brain was barely functioning. All she could manage was to berate herself for getting herself into this predicament in the first place. Then she saw Robbie's expression lighten with understanding, and she knew real panic.

"Ooooh," he said with every ounce of his ten-year-old's wisdom. "I know what's going on. Are you two gonna get married?"

Angelica could not help the gasp his innocent question caused, and she did not dare even glance at Collins. What on earth was he thinking? Was he remembering how he had proposed to her and how she had scorned him? And would such memories cause him hurt or would they make him angry? Unwilling to find out, she kept her eyes on the boy and made a valiant effort to defuse the situation. "Of course we're not getting married, Robbie. Where did you ever get an idea like that?" she scolded, moving toward him because to do so was to move away from Collins.

The Kid watched her through narrowed eyes, her words echoing in his ears. *Of course we're not getting married.* He should have known. No matter how she might respond to him, how fervently she might return his kisses, Kid Collins still wasn't good enough for Angelica Ross.

And she could certainly never care for a man like him. What had ever put that foolish hope in his mind? She was talking to the boy now, asking him what he'd wanted. She wouldn't even look at her hired gunfighter, as if he'd ceased to exist. Bitterly, he told himself that as far as she was concerned, he probably had.

Angelica couldn't bear to look at him for fear of what she would see. Would it be contempt or fury, or would his eyes still glow with passion? At the moment, she would find any of those equally difficult to face. "What was it you wanted, honey?" she asked her brother, glad to hear her voice sounding more normal.

"Aw, I forget now," the boy complained. "It was real important, too."

"I'm sure it was. Maybe you'll think of it on the way back to your room. I'll go with you," she offered, anxious for a few minutes in which to compose herself. By the time she got Robbie settled, she would be ready to face Collins again. Then they could do some serious talking.

The Kid swore softly and at length when they were gone, calling himself every kind of a fool for having fallen under her spell again. How many times did she have to hit him over the head with it before he realized she just couldn't love him? In spite of the physical attraction she obviously felt as strongly as he did, she would never consider him good enough for her.

As soon as the sound of Robbie's and Angelica's voices died away, he stalked out of the room and out of the house. A hard ride was exactly what he needed to get Angelica Ross out of his system. With a grim smile, he wondered how far he would have to go to accomplish such a feat.

The next day, Angelica glanced down the dining room table to where Collins was sitting on the other side of her brother. He was eating his noon meal with a singleness of purpose far out of proportion to what the food deserved. She tried to convince herself that he might only be hungry from having spent the morning out working with Hank. After all, it was the first real work he had done since being wounded. But even that would not account for the way he had studiously avoided meeting her eye all day.

Last night when she had returned to the parlor, ready to confront him, she had found the room empty. Before she could even begin to wonder where he might have gone, she had heard the sound of hoofbeats in the yard. Rushing to the window, she had caught a glimpse of a black horse galloping down the road toward town.

Damn him, she thought now, not for the first time. Stabbing her fork viciously into a bean she did not intend to eat, Angelica fought off the visions of Collins rushing back to the arms of some unknown woman, visions that had haunted her all night. Not even the sound of his return a brief hour later had been sufficient to drive away her suspicious. He might not have been gone long enough to visit anyone else, but he had certainly left Angelica quickly enough.

She was certain that the kisses they had shared could not have meant as much to him as they did to her. If they did, he could never have left her. His behavior today only reinforced her theory. He had been leaving the dining room this morning as she entered, and although her traitorous heart leaped at the sight of him, she had somehow managed to appear calm as she greeted him. Not that it made any difference, of course. He hardly spared her a glance as he mumbled "Good morning" on his way out of the house.

His indifference had been the last straw in influencing her decision. He might have strong opinions on the best way to handle the situation with Snyder, but that didn't mean he was correct. She was still the boss of the Diamond R, and she must do what she felt was right. That was why she had sent Curly on an errand immediately after breakfast. Before long, he would return with a message, and Mr. Kid Collins would find out once and for all exactly who was in charge around here.

The sound of footsteps in the hall brought her head up. Curly came into the room and nodded a greeting to everyone assembled around the table for the dinner hour, but he came straight toward Angelica, extending a piece of paper, which she anxiously snatched from his fingers.

"Thank you, Curly. I really appreciate this," she said, giving him a warm smile that made him blush and shuffle his feet.

"No trouble, miss," he averred, beating a hasty retreat.

As he moved to the sideboard and began to fill himself a plate, Angelica tore open the sealed note. The writing was bold and distinctly masculine. She smiled at the message.

"Mama," Angelica said with calculated nonchalance, "I'll be having a guest for supper tonight. Do you think you can make something special?"

Maria looked up from where she sat at Angelica's right, across from Robbie. "Who is coming?" she asked, completely innocent of the forces she was unleashing.

"Harlan Snyder," Angelica replied. Then, turning with sudden alarm, she said, "Why, Mr. Collins, are you all right?"

The Kid grabbed his coffee and gulped it down in an attempt to stop his choking. After a few minutes, during which Robbie thumped him on the back and Angelica grinned at him with fiendish delight, he managed to regain his ability to speak. "You invited Snyder here for supper?" he asked through gritted teeth. "After what I told you last night?"

At the reference to last night, Angelica felt her face grow warm, but she stood her ground. "You didn't tell me anything last night that convinced me it wasn't a good idea," she maintained. Then she noticed that Hank, Curly, Maria and Robbie were listening in bewilderment, and she realized some explanation was in order.

"As soon as the men Mr. Collins sent for arrive, we'll start the roundup. Mr. Collins and I agreed that we should take some steps to protect you men while you work the cattle. Since we are fairly certain that Mr. Snyder is the one causing all the trouble, I decided that the easiest way to keep him from bothering us is to let him think I'm considering marrying him." Angelica ignored the outraged gasps from her listeners, and continued doggedly. "If he thinks he will get the ranch by marriage, he certainly won't be bothering my roundup crew."

Maria muttered something in Spanish, something Angelica knew she didn't want to translate. Curly and Hank stared at her with worried frowns, and Robbie was simply confused. At last she forced herself to meet Collins's gaze.

His murderous expression sent a jolt of fear through her. He looked as if he might cheerfully strangle her, and the way his large hands were clenched on the tabletop indicated he was restraining himself with great difficulty.

"I . . . I can't understand why you're all so upset," she stammered, turning to Maria for some much needed support.

Maria's round face creased in worry. "I do not know if this is such a good idea, *Angelita.* If Snyder is such a dangerous man . . ."

"He's hardly going to shoot me if we're courting," Angelica pointed out in exasperation. She looked to Hank and Curly for support, but they only shifted uncomfortably in their chairs and refused to look up.

"You aren't really going to marry him, are you, Angel?" Robbie asked.

"No, of course not!" she hastily assured him, and then realized in alarm that those were the exact words she had used last night when denying her intention to marry Collins. A hasty glance verified her fear that Collins recalled the incident as clearly as she did. His blue eyes glittered and his lips curled in contempt.

"Don't be so sure, Angelica," the Kid warned, rising slowly from his chair. "Snyder is the kind of man who gets what he wants, and he's not too particular about who he hurts in the process."

"I'm not going to be foolish," she insisted, hating the knot of fear forming in her stomach as the truth of his statement sank in. "I'll only see him here at the house, and we'll never be alone. . . ."

"I'll be your duenna," Maria said, laying a reassuring hand on Angelica's arm. "And one of the men will always be close by." Maria's dark gaze sought out Collins in silent challenge.

His lips tightened, as if he would refuse to comment, but after a moment, he gave up the struggle. "Yes," he said, and Angelica thought he sounded as if the words were being dragged out of him. "One of the men will always be close by."

Chapter Six

"Maria? Can I talk to you a minute?" the Kid asked, finding her alone in the kitchen as she finished up the dinner dishes.

Maria hesitated before replying, drying her hands on her apron and studying his face carefully. "What about?" she asked cautiously. He looked perfectly sincere and even a little unsure of himself, but she had known many men who could feign those emotions when the occasion demanded.

"About Angelica," he said, which was what she had expected. She gave him no encouragement.

The Kid watched her dark eyes narrow warily, and for the first time he was certain that she knew what had happened between him and Angelica. He should have guessed earlier, since her attitude toward him had changed from friendly to cold literally overnight, but he hadn't wanted her to know, so he hadn't let himself accept it. Now he had no choice. "Somebody has to warn her about Snyder," he said, doggedly ignoring hcr frosty stare and the hostility behind it.

"I have warned her and so have you," Maria reminded him.

"No. there's something else, something she needs to

know," he insisted. "There's this girl in town. She works in the saloon . . ."

Maria's eyes glinted at the mention of the girl. "The one who smells like lily of the valley?" she inquired sarcastically, recalling how the clothes he had worn to town still reeked of the scent when he had given them to her to launder this morning.

The Kid winced at the reminder, but he could not let Maria's disdain stop him from telling his story. "Yes," he continued. "She lives in a shack behind the saloon. I was just getting ready to leave town the other day when I heard her screaming. Someone was beating her, and when I went in to help her, I found out it was Snyder. It wasn't the first time he'd done it either. She said he likes to hurt people. Maria," he said, gripping her shoulder with emphasis, "he likes to hurt *women*."

"Men usually do," she replied, shaking off his hand.

"What does that mean?" he demanded, frustrated at her apparent refusal to take his warning seriously.

"I am wondering why you should care if she gets hurt when you have hurt her so much yourself," Maria said in challenge.

"Hurt her? I never hurt her," the Kid insisted, wondering what she could be talking about. Then a small suspicion teased at him. "What did she tell you?" he asked.

Maria searched his eyes, looking for some trace of duplicity. She saw only anger and a mysterious hurt. "She told me that you lay with her, and then you left her . . ."

"Did she tell you how she threw me out?" he asked, no longer bothering to disguise his feelings. "Did she tell you how she threw my proposal right back in my face?"

Maria's eyes widened in understanding. The hurt she had glimpsed before was now naked pain. His pride was wounded, of course, as any man's would be, but it was more than that with him: he loved Angelica! He had suffered at her hands, but still he cared for her, enough to want to protect her from Snyder. It was just as she had hoped. Only one last question remained.

"So when Angelica rejected you, you went straight to this other woman," she suggested, still wary.

He made an exasperated noise. "I told you, I only went in Sunny's house to save her from Snyder."

"Are you going to deny that you slept in this Sunny's bed that night? She must have been grateful, so of course you accepted her offer to . . ."

"No!" he snapped, but seeing her skepticism, he felt compelled to explain. "All right, I did sleep with her, but that's *all*. She offered to let me share her bed. She was afraid to be left alone, and I was glad for a chance to lay down, but I didn't do anything . . . Oh, hell," he swore in renewed frustration, certain from Maria's icy gaze that she did not believe him. Not that he could expect her to, of course. He hardly believed it himself. "Just warn Angelica, that's all I ask," he said, anxious to end this infuriating conversation.

To his infinite surprise, she smiled, a slow, satisfied smile. "I will warn her," Maria promised, patting his arm reassuringly. "And I will tell her how concerned you are about her safety."

Unable to make sense of her sudden change in mood or to think of an appropriate reply, he gaped at her in amazement for a long moment before muttering, "Thanks." Women, who can understand them? he wondered as he made a hasty escape from the kitchen.

When he had gone, Maria stared thoughtfully at the closed door for a long time. She had been wrong to judge him by the standards she used for most men. There were a few men—a precious few, she knew from experience—who could be trusted. Unless she was very much mistaken, Kid Collins was one of these. Imagine, he had spent the night with that saloon girl without sex. She was certain that he was telling the truth, although she had no reason other than her own intuition to believe him.

She trusted her intuition, though. Hadn't she already decided he might well be the man for Angelica even before the two of them had sensed the attraction themselves? The fact that their attraction had led them to bed already proved how strong it was. Of course, she could not condone such behavior, much as she might understand it, and she would watch them closely to make sure it didn't happen again, at least until the matter of marriage between them had been settled.

Maria was the first to admit that settling that matter might be a bit difficult, given the present circumstances, but as she well knew, nothing was impossible. The trick would be to keep them from doing any more damage to their relationship before it had a chance to heal on its own.

"Are you sure you are doing the right thing?" Maria asked as she helped Angelica into her gold gown later that afternoon. Maria had spent the last half hour arranging the girl's hair into an elaborate coiffure, so she lowered the gold taffeta carefully over her masterpiece.

"Of course I'm doing the right thing," Angelica insisted, her voice muffled by the material passing in front of her face. "I don't understand what everyone's so worried about," she said when Maria had settled the dress over her shoulders. "I won't be alone with the man for a single minute. What can he possibly do?"

Maria frowned, wondering if she should tell Angelica what Mr. Collins had told her about Snyder. Unfortunately, she knew Angelica better than Collins did and knew that the girl would take the information about Snyder's cruelty as a challenge rather than as a warning. No, Maria decided, it was better just to chaperone her and eliminate any possible opportunity for Snyder to harm her. Maria was confident that even if she failed, Mr. Collins would be hovering someplace very close by to ensure that Angelica was well protected. Maria's frown twitched into a small smile at the thought.

"What are you grinning at?" Angelica wanted to know. Suspecting that Maria might have found something amusing in her appearance, the girl adjusted the mirror over the washstand in her bedroom and peered closely at her own reflection. "This hair is ridiculous," she decided with a disgusted sigh.

"No, it is lovely," Maria contradicted. "You look like a fine lady. Mr. Snyder will certainly want you for his wife when he sees you tonight," she added sarcastically, giving Angelica a look that showed her disapproval of the plan.

Angelica made a rude noise. "That really *should* make me feel better," she replied with frown and lifted a hand to make an adjustment to her hairdo.

"Do not touch it!" Maria cried in some alarm, rushing to stop her. "It is perfect, and the dress is perfect and you are perfect." She paused, considering the wisdom of it, before adding, "Any man who sees you will want you."

Angelica's head snapped around and her eyes narrowed suspiciously. "I don't want any man to want me," she said.

Maria's dark eyes widened in mock amazement. "Then why did you invite Mr. Snyder here tonight? That is the plan, no?"

Angelica glared at her. "You weren't talking about Snyder, and we both know it." She turned back to face her reflection once more. "Mr. Collins doesn't want me, and I don't want him," she insisted.

Maria's eyebrows expressed her skepticism. "Then why were you so jealous yesterday when he . . ."

"I was not jealous!" Angelica cried, whirling on her foster mother. "Where did you get an idea like that?"

Maria's face remained impassive. "From Hank. He told he how you ran up and threw your arms around Señor Collins and then how you pushed him away and ran into the house. When Mr. Collins gave me his clothes to wash, I smelled the perfume and figured out what made you so angry," she explained blandly.

Angelica flushed at the memory. "Of course I was angry. I don't like my hired hands to go out carousing . . ."

"You never cared about any of the others doing it," Maria pointed out.

"Of course I did!" Angelica insisted, but her fervor faded under Maria's knowing gaze. "Well, I wasn't jealous," she maintained.

Maria shrugged. "Then you should have been. After all, he made love to you and then went to another woman. If you care about him, it is only natural to be jealous." Maria experienced a small pang when she saw the way Angelica hugged herself against the hurt that reminder caused. The girl's green eyes glistened suspiciously, but Maria resisted the urge to comfort her, even though she knew just what to say to accomplish that feat. The information that Collins had innocently shared the saloon girl's bed would certainly wipe the injured expression from Angelica's face, but would accomplish little toward bringing her and Collins together again.

Angelica was entirely too proud to admit her jealousy if she knew there was no reason for it. Far better to let her stew for a while. In fact, Maria decided, she ought to stir things up even more. "You cannot blame him for going to another woman when you tell him you will not marry with him."

Angelica almost gasped at hearing her own thoughts verbalized, but she still didn't want to admit the truth of that observation. "It's a good thing I refused him. I don't want to be married to a man like that!"

Maria pretended to be puzzled. "A man like what? When I spoke against him before, you defended him. I thought you said he could be trusted . . ."

"Mama!" Angelica cried in frustration. "That was before he . . . he . . ." She made a vague gesture with her hand.

"Before he was unfaithful to you?" she suggested helpfully. Once again, Maria knew a pang of guilt over the way Angelica's eyes clouded with pain, but she steeled herself against it. "As I said, he is not your betrothed. He is free to do as he wants."

"I can't believe you're taking his side in this," Angelica huffed. "Anyone would think you *wanted* us to get married."

Maria only smiled, infuriating Angelica even more.

"Don't get that smug look on your face," Angelica warned. "I told you, the man is a killer and not to be trusted. A woman would be a fool to get stuck with someone like that."

"Turn around so I can fasten your dress, little one," Maria said, still smiling as if she had not heard.

With an exasperated sigh, Angelica did as Maria bade her. What had gotten into her foster mother, anyway? For some mysterious reason, Maria had once again changed her attitude toward Collins. What about all those warnings her *mamacita* had given her? Angelica could think of no reason for Maria to have changed her mind so suddenly and so completely about Collins unless she was convinced that marriage between them was the only way to right the wrong that had been done. Not wanting to explore that subject any further, Angelica was content to let it drop. As soon as Maria finished fastening her dress, she went out to the parlor to await Snyder's arrival.

Snyder was prompt, a quality Angelica remembered from their previous acquaintance. He was also impeccably dressed, overwhelmingly charming and positively delighted with her invitation.

"You're looking even more lovely than usual this evening, Miss Angelica," he said, smiling his strange smile, the one that made her feel so uneasy.

"Why, thank you, Mr. Snyder," she replied, hoping her uneasiness did not show. She gave him her hand, and he clasped it warmly in both of his. "I'm so glad you were able to come on such short notice."

"You must know your invitation would always take precedence with me. And I thought I had long ago asked you to call me Harlan."

"Now that you mention it, I believe you did," she said, extracting her hand from his with some difficulty. "Please, Harlan, won't you come into the parlor and have a little sherry before supper?"

"I'd love to . . ." he began, but Angelica was still talking.

"You remember my brother, Robbie, don't you?" she asked blithely as she swept into the parlor where the boy was sitting on the sofa looking profoundly bored.

Maria had scrubbed him up and dressed him in his best suit for the occasion. Collins had given him his instructions, instructions that included never leaving Angelica alone with Snyder for a moment. The boy did not perfectly understand the reasons why he must not do so, but he was willing to accept his idol's instructions no matter how odious it might be to carry them out.

"Good evening, Mr. Snyder," Robbie said, rising to his feet with as much dignity as he could muster and extending his hand for the other man to shake.

"Good evening, uh, Robbie," Snyder said, casting Angelica a puzzled glance.

"Robbie was most eager to join us for supper tonight. He's the man of the family now, you know," she explained, as she poured a small glass of sherry for her guest.

"Yes, of course, Snyder agreed, although he was still a little flustered. Obviously, he could think of nothing to say to the boy and gratefully accepted the glass that Angelica handed to him.

Robbie, of course, had nothing to say to him either, so the two males simply stared at each other for a long moment before Angelica came to their rescue.

"Tell me, Harlan, what news do you hear from town?" she asked, seating herself on the sofa beside where Robbie had been sitting. The boy flopped down next to her again, leaving Snyder no choice but to take a chair across from them.

"Well, let's see now," he began, and soon he regained his poise and was telling her all the latest gossip. Angelica listened attentively, laughing at all the right moments even as she braced herself for any reference to Kid Collins and the run-in the two men had had.

Of course, Snyder made no reference to it, as common sense told her he wouldn't; nevertheless, by the time Maria summoned them to supper, her nerves were beginning to fray.

Kid Collins cursed softly as the small dinner party moved beyond hearing range. He had posted himself outside the parlor window that opened into the courtyard so he would be nearby in case he was needed. He should have known he wouldn't be needed, he thought acidly. That little vixen was putting on quite a show, and she already had Snyder eating out of her hand. The thought of Angelica using her considerable charm on a worm like Snyder enraged him, but what enraged him even more was the way she so obviously enjoyed doing it. Hadn't Maria warned her about how dangerous Snyder could be?

Grinding his teeth in frustration, he moved swiftly inside, thanking whoever had designed the Ross house for making it such a maze of corridors and entrances. In a matter of seconds he was in the kitchen, where he could hear everything happening around the huge table in the adjoining room He, Hank and Curly had eaten their evening meal earlier, so Angelica would have the dining room all to herself for her guest. At least she had taken his advice about keeping Robbie with her.

Ignoring the knowing look Maria gave him as she walked by carrying the first course of the meal, he jerked a chair from the kitchen table and straddled it. When Maria pushed open the door to the dining room, the sound of Angelica's laughter wafted through it, and he ground his teeth again.

Angelica wondered how long she could keep up this charade. Her face actually hurt from maintaining her cheerful pose all evening, and poor Robbie was not even bothering to cover his yawns anymore.

"This meal was absolutely delicious," Snyder said as he finished off his third helping of apple-raisin pie. "You aren't going to tell me that you baked this pie, are you?" he asked, plainly hoping to hear that she had.

"Oh no," she assured him. "Maria made everything. I'm afraid I'm not very good in the kitchen."

"I'll bet you're just being modest," Snyder accused good-naturedly. "Robbie, your sister is a good cook, isn't she?"

Robbie'e hazel eyes widened at such an outlandish thought. "Angel?" he said incredulously. He started to make another remark, but Angelica's glare stopped him.

"Angel, I'm finished," he said instead, giving her his most beguiling smile. "Can I be excused?" By prior agreement, his term of guard duty ended with the meal.

Swallowing her irritation, she returned his smile. "Yes, after you say good night to Mr. Snyder."

"Good night, sir," Robbie said perfunctorily and raced from the room without waiting for a reply.

Snyder was too relieved to be offended. "He's quite a boy," he remarked, but Angelica did not care to delve into what hidden meanings such a judgment might have.

"Yes, he is," she agreed noncommittally. "Shall we go into the parlor? I'm sure you'd like some brandy."

"Yes, I would," he said, hastening to pull out her chair. He offered his arm, and although Angelica would have preferred to walk without his assistance, she had no other choice except to take it.

"I've been looking forward to being alone with you because . . ." he was saying as they entered the parlor, but he stopped when he saw Maria ensconced on the sofa with a yard of knitting trailing down from her rapidly clicking needles.

Angelica bit back a smile at the expression on his face. Even she was surprised at how quickly Maria had crossed the distance between the kitchen and the parlor to precede them into the room. "Maria is the one you must compliment on the meal," she said, using the excuse of getting his brandy to free herself from his arm.

Since the sofa was the only piece of furniture in the room capable of holding two people and Maria was already sitting on it, Angelica would be spared the ordeal of sharing it with Snyder. He waited until she had handed him his glass of brandy and joined Maria on the sofa before sitting down in the chair he had occupied earlier in the evening.

"Please smoke if you want to," Angelica said, in a much more pleasant mood now that Maria was by her side.

Snyder murmured his thanks and pulled out a cigar. When it was lit, he complimented Maria on her cooking skills.

"Gracias, señor," she said without looking up from her knitting. Angelica had to bite back another smile at his disgruntled look. Plainly, he was not used to women who were impervious to his charm.

A few moments of awkward silence dragged by as Angelica waited for Snyder to finish telling her what he had begun as they entered the room, but she soon realized he had no intention of continuing his speech in front of Maria. She was forced to make small talk.

An hour later, when she had long since run out of things to say, Snyder finally—and grudgingly—said he thought he should be on his way. He was not at all pleased by Angelica's chaperone and had evidently given up hope of outlasting her. With her first genuine smile of the evening, Angelica escorted her guest out through the entry hall to the front door.

As soon as they were out of Maria's sight, Snyder took her arm and drew her to a shadowed corner of the large hall. Instantly wary, she tried to pull away, but his grip was unbreakable. Angelica knew a moment of panic until she realized he only wanted to have a bit of private conversation with her.

"What are your plans, now Angelica?" he asked in a conspiratorial tone.

"My plans?" she echoed, not certain what he meant.

"Yes, I know you aren't going to be able to meet your

army contract, and . . ."

"I *am* going to meet my contract," she contradicted, startling him somewhat.

He recovered quickly and gave her a condescending smile. "You can't hold a roundup with only two cowboys, my dear," he reminded her.

Angelica batted her eyes in a parody of innocence. "I know that," she said sweetly. "That's why I've hired a new crew. They'll be here any day now."

"A new crew? But where . . .?" Plainly he wanted to ask her more, but caught himself just in time. "How fortunate for you," he said instead, trying to look pleased at the news.

"Yes, I thought so." Angelica said, deciding she had better distract him before he started trying to find out where her crew was coming from. "I wanted the ranch to be on a sound financial basis so that when I marry . . ." She paused and covered her lips and tried to look embarrassed, as if she had just revealed a secret.

Snyder took the bait. He gazed down at her and grinned so smugly she wanted to slap his face, but she somehow managed to restrain herself.

"Oh, Angelica," he whispered, and before she could guess his intention, he swooped down and kissed her.

His lips touched hers for only an instant before she jerked away, but it was long enough to repulse her completely. Fighting the urge to scrub the taste of him off her mouth with the back of her had, she glared up at him in outrage. "Harlan!" she cried.

"I'm so sorry, my dear, but I couldn't restrain myself another moment," he said in a placating tone that had exactly the opposite effect on her.

"Well, you'd better learn to restrain yourself," she informed him hotly. "I may be alone in the world, but I have no intention of allowing you to take advantage of me."

Her fury seemed to surprise him, and he was instantly contrite. "Please believe me, I have no intention of taking advantage of your position, Angelica."

Angelica didn't believe him for a minute, but she pretended to be somewhat mollified and allowed him to take his leave with the impression that he had been forgiven.

No sooner had the door closed behind him than Angelica hiked up her billowing skirts and made for the door at the opposite end of the entryway with unseemly haste.

"What the hell?" Collins's voice asked as she raced past where he was standing in the shadows just outside in the courtyard. She did not stop to reply.

She was almost at the fountain when a strong hand pulled her up short. "What's the matter? What happened?" Collins demanded.

"That snake kissed me," she snapped, breaking free of his grasp.

"Kissed you?" he echoed, sounding murderous, but Angelica was too busy splashing the cool water over her mouth to pay much attention to his tone.

"I thought I told you not to be alone with him," she heard Collins snarl when she finally felt cleansed of all trace of the dastardly Mr. Snyder.

She straightened to face him. "I had to walk him to the door," she replied, annoyed that Collins would dare take her to task for something she had found so disgusting.

"And did you have to flirt with him, too?" he asked, sarcasm thick in his voice.

"I did not flirt with him!" she insisted.

Collins gave a derisive bark of laughter. "I'll bet Snyder thought different."

Angelica felt her face burn at his accusation and was

glad the darkness of the night hid her humiliation. "I had to make him think I was interested in him," she argued, loath to admit there was more than a little truth in Collins's statement.

"She is right," Maria's voice proclaimed from across the courtyard. They both turned toward her as she appeared out of the shadows. "Angelica had to lead him on. How else could she protect you?"

Her reminder stung him. It was, in fact, the real reason behind his anger. As furious as he was that Snyder had kissed Angelica, he was even more furious at himself for allowing her to place herself in such a position on his behalf. He was supposed to be helping her to repay her for saving his life. Instead, he was standing by while she played up to Snyder in order to save his life again. No wonder he felt so frustrated.

He started when someone laid a comforting hand on his arm, but to his disappointment, it was Maria's hand that sought to soothe his anger. "We will not let anything happen to her," Maria said reassuringly. Knowing he was the one who needed reassurance most, the Kid didn't let himself think which one of them her words were for.

"No, we won't," he agreed, looking down at Angelica's defiant face. She was so lovely standing there in the moonlight with droplets of water still glinting on her lips. With great difficulty, he resisted the urge to kiss them away. Instead he reached into his pocket and drew out a bandana. "Here," he said, handing it to her. "Dry your mouth."

A little surprised, Angelica took the bandana, but before she could use it, he said, "I reckon my job is over for the night. I'll see you ladies in the morning." With a curt nod, he left them.

Angelica watched him go, and continued to watch even when his tall figure became an indistinct blur in the far shadows and finally disappeared behind his bedroom door. Without conscious thought, she lifted the bandana to blot her lips and inhaled the masculine scent that clung to the cloth, a scent that brought back poignant and painful memories. Maria cleared her throat after a minute, making Angelica aware that she had been lost in those memories for quite a while. Guiltily, Angelica jerked the bandana away from her face.

"He is only jealous, little one," Maria said.

"Jealous!" Angelica could hardly credit the idea. "What does he have to be jealous about?"

Maria gave an eloquent shrug. "You kissed another man tonight."

"I did *not* kiss another may. *He* kissed *me* and I didn't like it one bit!" the girl said in one last effort to get someone to sympathize with her.

"I know you did not," Maria assured her, "and so does Mr. Collins, but he still does not like the idea."

"I don't know why it should matter to him one way or the other," Angelica insisted. "He's made it perfectly clear he doesn't want to kiss me himself."

"Has he?" Maria asked skeptically, but before Angelica could answer, she added, "Come, I will help you get out of that dress."

Deciding it was futile to argue the subject any longer, Angelica allowed Maria to lead her to her bedroom and help her undress. When at last Maria had gone, Angelica lay in her bed staring up at the darkness and wondering if Christian Collins really could be jealous, He had certainly been angry over that kiss, even more angry than she had been herself. Of course, he might just be worried about her because she was his employer.

That possibility disturbed her more than she wanted to acknowledge. No matter how much she might deny it to Maria, the truth was that she wanted Christian Collins to be insanely jealous, as jealous as she had been over the thought of him with another woman.

Of course, the situation was slightly different in that Collins knew she didn't care a fig for Harlan Snyder, while she knew nothing of the kind about Collins's lady love, whoever she might be. Still, Angelica wanted to get a little of her own back, no matter how unreasonable such a desire might be.

Hating herself for her weakness, she reached over to where his bandana lay on her bedside table. The cloth was cool, no longer holding the warmth from his body, but when she lifted it to her face, she could still smell his scent.

Once more the memories assailed her, memories of his hands and his lips on her body, memories that made her ache with longing. It wasn't fair! her mind screamed. Why had she fallen in love with a man who was so unworthy of her love, a man who couldn't remain faithful to her for even one day? Perversely, she refused to consider the possibility that her refusal of his proposal had freed him from any such restraints. If he had really cared for her, she reasoned, he simply wouldn't have *wanted* any other woman. She certainly didn't want any other man.

With an exasperated sigh, she threw the bandana away, or at least she tried to. Being rather flimsy, it only traveled a short distance before fluttering to the floor, where it lay like a silent accusation of her weakness. Sighing again, she suddenly realized she was sweltering under the covering Maria had thoughtfully pulled up over her before leaving. Throwing back the bedclothes with an angry jerk, she glared once more at the dark shadow of the bandana on the floor beside her bed.

She called Christian Collins some satisfactorily vile names and wished very fervently that he, too, might be lying awake in an airless room tortured by regrets. Angrily, she rose and threw open the outside window in an attempt to cool her flushed cheeks and the other parts of her that felt uncomfortably warm, but the night air seemed determined to elude her. The breeze that tossed a lone tumbleweed across the ranch yard was from the opposite direction, and not a breath of it stirred within the room. Sighing a third time, she folded her arms on the windowsill and bowed her head on them dejectedly.

On the other side of the courtyard, Kid Collins was indeed unable to sleep. After making a hopeless tangle of the bedclothes, he had finally decided that pacing was a more sensible outlet for his frustrations. He had donned a pair of jeans and now strode barefoot up and down the large master bedroom.

He tried to blame his wound, which was itching fiercely in the last stages of healing, for his sleeplessness. Unfortunately, the salve Maria had given him had eased the itching considerably, and he was still unable to rest. Every time he closed his eyes, he pictured Harlan Snyder pressing his vile mouth to Angelica's, and rage boiled up in him anew.

The worst part was that he didn't even know which of them he was angrier with. Snyder was only doing exactly what he should be expected to do if he believed Angelica was interested in marrying him. He had, in fact, played right into their hands. The Kid should be grateful for the time Snyder's delusion would buy him.

Of course, he wasn't a bit grateful, and that was the problem. When he thought of Angelica talking and laughing with that rat, the Kid wanted to shake her until her teeth rattled. Why hadn't she listened to him? He'd tried to warn her. He'd even frightened her, however briefly, in his attempt to convince her to stay away from Snyder. She had chosen to ignore his warning, though, and to place herself in danger. Now the only thing he could do was get the roundup over with as quickly as possible so Angelica could end this ridiculous game.

Suddenly, the sensation of his own helplessness overwhelmed him, and even the large room seemed to be closing in on him. Knowing only that he needed some air, he threw open the bedroom door and stalked outside.

Without planning to, he headed straight for the fountain, where he had last seen Angelica. Pausing beside it, he stood there a long moment, listening to the lazy splashing of the water and allowing the sound to soothe him. After a while he could even picture Angelica standing there beside him in the golden glow of the moonlight, her green eyes glittering with desire as he had seen them only too clearly in far too many dreams.

Angelica's head came up as her ears strained to identify the sound that had disturbed her. Anxiously, she scanned the ranch yard for any sign of activity, but nothing stirred save the lone tumbleweed that bumped futilely against the corral fence. Could the sound have come from inside the house? Was someone prowling around? Knowing Robbie's penchant for midnight strolls, Angelica decided she had better investigate.

Expecting to see a waif in a white nightshirt stealing through the shadows, Angelica threw open her bedroom door. Her surprised gasp sounded loudly in the late night stillness and startled the man beside the fountain.

"Is something wrong?" he asked with concern, taking a couple of anxious steps toward her.

"No, nothing," she managed to say, hoping her voice did not betray the shock she was still feeling. She could hardly credit the vision before her. Christian Collins looked like some sort of primitive god with the moonlight washing his golden hair to silver and bathing his bare shoulders and chest in a bronze glow. Only the small bandage low on his left side gleaming in the pale light gave silent reminder that he was not as invincible as he appeared at that moment. "I . . . I heard a noise, and I thought it might be Robbie," she explained, putting a hand over the quiver in her stomach.

The Kid nodded, although he hardly heard her explanation. She looked even more beautiful than he had imagined, with her fiery hair loose around her shoulders and thc sheer white gown hinting at the treasures beneath. His breath caught as his body hardened in response. Unconsciously, he took another step toward her.

It was only a trick of the moonlight, Angelica told herself. Why else would his eyes look so soft and vulnerable? There was nothing vulnerable about the rest of him, about his imposing height or his massive shoulders or his broad chest. If only she were closer, she would know for sure. She took a step toward him and then another. "It was awfully hot in my room," she said inanely, noticing that for some reason it was even hotter out here.

He nodded, noticing the way her bare toes curled against the coolness of the tiles. The breeze caressed her, molding the thin fabric to her breasts and thighs. Desire coiled in him tighter and tighter, until his breath came in shallow gasps.

She watched his chest rise and fall, admiring the way the golden hair grew there in swirls and then thinned out down on his belly to disappear beneath the low-slung Levis. His skin looked like satin in the moonlight, and her hands longed to reach out and test the illusion.

He knew he was going to kiss her if she stood there one more minute. He had to warn her, to send her on her way. But when he spoke, her name sounded like an endearment.

"Angelica."

She heard the summons in his voice, the need she shared, and she responded. Which of them moved first, she could not have said, but in the next instant, she was in his arms, welcoming his kiss.

His mouth was warm and blessedly familiar. She opened willingly to his invasion, knowing this was what she had hungered for. Her hands moved over him, exploring the sleek smoothness of his shoulders and back and reveling in the tensile strength she sense beneath her fingertips.

She wanted him to want her. She wanted him to love her. Her pride demanded it, and now his hands and lips revealed that he did. She shouldn't let him kiss her like this. She knew that, and she would stop him in just a minute, but first she wanted this one moment of victory.

The Kid knew he shouldn't be kissing her like this, not when they were alone in the dark, not when only one thin layer of cloth separated her from him. He should push her away and run like hell before anything else happened, before he convinced himself to carry her off to the bed that was waiting for them just a few steps away.

But he couldn't let her go, not when he remembered Snyder. Snyder had touched her and kissed her tonight. The thought made him wild with the need to stake his own claim on her lips and on her heart. She was his, whether she knew it or not, whether she wanted it or not, and he would allow no other man to have her.

"My Angel," he whispered into the hollow of her throat. Her answering cry drove him over the brink of sanity. Without another thought, he scooped her up in his arms and smothered her protests with his kiss.

Except she made no protests. Drunk with her own power, she imagined that she controlled him. He wanted her completely. She could not let him make love to her, of course, but she would have him groveling at her feet, begging for her favors, and at the last minute she would deny him.

Dimly, she heard the bedroom door slam shut behind them, and then he lowered her to the bed. She knew he would speak to her, tell her of his love. She needed that time, that break so she could regain her own control. Then she would stop him.

He could find no words to explain what was unexplainable. He had no right to even touch her, so mere words could not make *this* right. Without bothering to speak a single one, he slipped his hands beneath her gown.

Angelica gasped, but the sound was lost against his ravenous mouth. For a second she tried to struggle, tried to break free, but his hands were too compelling. They stroked and caressed until all thoughts of resistance died within her and passion was reborn in a white hot flame. The flame burned up and out of control, scorching through her like wildfire until she clung to him mindlessly, begging him with small sounds for the fulfillment only he could give.

This time she helped him discard his jeans and this time she guided him to her with knowing hands. She could not see his face in the darkness, but she heard his groan of pleasure as he sank into her welcoming depths.

"My Angel," he whispered again, as if the words were an incantation.

Angelica responded as if enchanted, giving him everything he demanded of her and more, until possession became obsession and surrender became conquest. Pleasure grew in her, swelling until she felt the bonds of her heart burst from it and her body convulsed with the explosion.

The Kid cradled her gently as the aftershocks rippled

through them both. He wanted to see her face, wanted to be certain that she understood what had happened between then, but the room was just too dark. After what seemed a long time, she moved restlessly beneath his weight, and he slid to one side, still keeping her close.

"Christian?" she asked sleepily.

"Yes," he replied, his voice hoarse with slaked passion.

"Hold me," she said, even though he already was.

In another minute they were both asleep.

Angelica awoke slowly, aware of the bright morning sunlight but lingering for a few last delicious moments in the netherworld where sweet dreams still hovered, ready to dazzle her if she surrendered to them again. Slowly, the images faded, until she had to admit she was really and truly awake and opened her eyes.

For the first few seconds, she could not recall why she felt so happy this morning, and then the memories of the night before came rushing back, flooding out her happiness and filling her with alarm.

She bolted upright and looked around, both surprised and relieved to find herself alone in the bed. "Christian?" she said, but received no answer. He was gone.

Of course he would be, she told herself, thankful that at least one of them had showed good judgment. She shuddered to think what would have happened if Maria had found them together. For another anxious moment, she wondered if he had really managed to sneak out without being seen, but then she realized Maria's reaction would have awakened her, so she knew their secret was safe.

She looked over at the other pillow, which still bore the imprint of his head. She slowly lifted it and hugged it to her, inhaling the traces of his scent from the pillowcase and reliving the events of the night before. Her memory would only conjure scattered images, impressions and sensations, but they were all wonderful, and she could still hear him telling her she was *his* Angel.

He loved her, she knew he did. No man could make love with such intensity unless his emotions were equally involved. She had to admit her experience in the matter was somewhat limited, but some sixth sense or woman's intuition told her she was right. And if he loved her, then all her concern over what his true motives might be in making love to her no longer mattered.

For the first time in many days, Angelica felt truly happy. By the time she was washed and dressed, she was actually humming. Her spirits fell a little when Maria informed her that Christian had already ridden out with the men for the day's work, but she recovered quickly. Maria and Robbie kept giving her funny looks, so she knew she must have an absolutely radiant expression on her face. That thought pleased her almost as much as the anticipation of seeing Christian again.

It was late morning and she had just finished sweeping out the entryway when she heard the riders in the yard. Peering through the peephole in the door, Angelica realized she knew none of the three men who had just ridden up.

"Hello, the house!" one of them called, giving the traditional Western greeting as he rode up closer to the door. He was a dangerous-looking fellow, tall and thin with tied-down guns that appeared to have seen a lot of service.

"What do you want?" Angelica called back.

The tall man who had spoken removed his hat when he realized he was addressing a female. His weathered face was all planes and angles with dark, deep-set eyes. "We're here to see Kid Collins, ma'am," he told her, squinting as if he were trying to see her through the small opening. "We're friends of his from the Circle M."

Relieved and delighted, Angelica threw open the huge front door and stepped out, giving the three men a welcoming smile. "Hello! I'm afraid Mr. Collins isn't here right now, but we expect him back by noon. If you're who I think you are, then you'll be staying awhile, so please, climb down and make yourselves at home," she invited.

The tall man did so, although the other two remained on their horses, as if allowing him to test the welcome before committing themselves. He walked up to her, still holding his hat. "Miss Ross, is it?" he asked politely.

Angelica didn't mean to stare; she simply couldn't help it. A dozen stories she had heard and overheard through the years came rushing back. How she could have known him, she wasn't sure, but even in range clothes, the man carried himself with a dignity that bespoke black frock coats, string ties, and conservative vests. But it was his eyes that really gave him away. She had never seen eyes so haunted.

"You're Parson Black, aren't you?" she asked before she could stop herself.

His expression darkened for a moment, as if a shadow had crossed his face, but then it was gone. He smiled, still courteous. "My friends call me Miles," he told her.

"I'm sorry," she said quickly, hoping the heat in her cheeks would convince him of how embarrassed she was at her faux pas. "I'm very pleased to meet you, Miles. I'm Angelica Ross, and I guess I'm your new boss," she announced, giving him her hand.

He shook it firmly, and she could see he had already forgiven her. She would have to remember that this was one gunfighter who did not like to be reminded of his reputation.

"It seems like lately I've made a habit of working for pretty women," Miles said with a smile.

Angelica winced inwardly, knowing he was only being kind in comparing her so favorably to the owner of the Circle M Ranch. "I've heard Rachel McKinsey—I mean, Rachel Elliot—is a real beauty," she said, hoping she didn't sound as envious as she felt. Even though she knew Rachel was married, Angelica could not forget the letter Rachel had written to Christian. She was foolish to be jealous of even his friends, but the thought that he might care for any other female, especially one much prettier than she, still disturbed her.

"Mrs. Elliot is lovely, but not as lovely as you are, Miss Ross," Miles informed her with such candor that she could only stare.

"Why, thank you," she managed at last, stunned to realize he was not simply giving her an empty compliment. He actually believed she was pretty! The very idea was so novel, she could not quite think straight for a second or two.

"And these are my two friends, Ed Harley and Dave Sanders," he said, pointing to the two men still on horseback. They murmured their greetings, and Angelica realized they were, like many cowboys, intimidated by women, which would explain their reluctance to dismount. In an effort to put them at ease, she urged them to make their way to the bunkhouse and get settled in. They seemed only too glad to do so.

As Miles was turning to follow them, Angelica responded to an impulse and said, "Why don't you come back to the house when you get unpacked and meet the rest of my family?"

His answering smile was a little surprised. "Thank you, ma'am," he said. "I think I will."

In an amazingly short time, he was back again. By

then Angelica had found Robbie and warned him against making too big a fuss over the identity of their latest visitor. The boy had heard all the same stories Angelica had heard, and he was deeply awed at the prospect of seeing the notorious Parson Black in person.

"Pleased to meet you, Mr. Blackmon," Robbie said solemnly as he shook hands with the newcomer. Only the boy's eyes gave away his excitement.

"Would you like some lemonade?" Angelica asked Miles when they were all seated in the parlor. He accepted with alacrity, rising to his feet when Maria entered the room carrying the pitcher and some glasses on a tray.

Angelica introduced them and then hid a smile as Maria sized him up in one swift glance. Apparently she approved because she gave Miles a bright smile and welcomed him warmly. When Maria had returned to the task of preparing the noon meal, Angelica poured Miles a glass of lemonade.

"Have you known Mr. Collins for a long time?" she asked, handing him the glass. The question, she judged, was innocuous enough. Miles should not suspect he was being pumped for information about the man she loved.

"Yes," he replied. "We've worked together for several years now down at the Circle M."

"You must think highly of him to have some all this way at his request," she remarked.

His eyes narrowed, and he sipped his lemonade before responding. "He's a man to ride the river with, Miss Ross. If you're worried about whether you can depend on him . . ."

"Oh, no," she hastily assured him. "I trust Mr. Collins completely. It's just that I know so little about him . . ."

Miles's frown slowly smoothed into an understanding smile. "Oh, I see," he said, and Angelica was very much afraid that he saw entirely too much. She shifted uncomfortably in her chair and glanced over at Robbie, who was watching them both with a puzzled expression.

"Angel and me want to know all about him," the boy explained when neither adult spoke. "Like about the fights he's been in and how many men he's killed and all that stuff."

"Robbie!" Angelica chastened, catching Miles's discomfort. "We most certainly do not want to know these things!"

"I do," Robbie protested.

"Well, then, son, you'd best ask Mr. Collins himself," Miles suggested gently. "But don't be too surprised if he doesn't want to talk about it."

Robbie drooped visibly under the reminder. "I already tried, and you're right, he doesn't," he confirmed.

"He says very little about himself," Angelica hastened to explain, hoping to change the subject. "I was interested in where he's from and whether he has any family, that sort of thing." She gave Robbie a sharp look that dared him to contradict her. He glared back but did not interrupt again.

Miles watched the exchange with amusement, but sobered instantly when Angelica turned to him expectantly.

"Well, I don't really know that much about him myself," Miles hedged. "His folks are dead, but of course he has a sister around these parts. Maybe you've met her," he suggested.

Angelica sighed in dismay. "I guess you haven't heard," she said and reluctantly proceeded to tell him the sad story of the Hastings family. "So after we decided that the man behind the murders was probably the same man who has been trying to get my ranch, Mr. Collins agreed to help me." she concluded.

Miles nodded grimly. "He should have told me all this. I would have brought more men with me."

"Oh, I still have two men working for me, and Mr. Collins sent another telegram, to someone called Stumpy Smith, and I believe he was going to bring a friend with him," Angelica explained.

Miles was nodding. "Old Stumpy, huh? That should liven things up a bit," he remarked, but before Angelica could ask him what he meant, they heard the front door burst open.

"Miles?"

"In here," Miles called back, rising to his feet.

Angelica rose also, her stomach fluttering at the sound of Christian's voice. She would have preferred a more private meeting, but it was too late to think of that now. He paused in the doorway, and his gaze touched her, but only for a second before skittering on to find his friend. His look was too brief for her to read his expression, and whatever emotion he might have felt upon seeing her vanished in his joy at seeing Miles.

She forgot her disappointment as she watched the two men greet each other amidst much handshaking and backslapping. Their obvious affection for each other warmed her and astonished Robbie, who apparently found it difficult to imagine two such hardened men behaving like excited children.

"I cut your sign out on the range and headed right back. How's everything at home?" Christian asked, giving Angelica an unpleasant jar. He still considered the Circle M his home, even though she had already begun to consider him an integral part of her ranch. She would have to be careful not to reveal her fantasies, at least not until Christian indicated that he shared them.

"Everyone's fine, except Colleen," Miles reported cheerfully. "She's still mad at you for leaving her. She sent you a little gift," he added with a wink. "I left it down at the bunkhouse."

Christian chuckled, and Angelica thought he looked awfully pleased at that news. Colleen? It took a minute, but Angelica finally recalled that that was the name of the girl who Rachel Elliot had reported cried for Christian daily and who expected to marry him when he returned. Jealousy bubbled up inside of Angelica, leaving a bitter taste in her mouth. How dare another woman send him a gift?

"I can't wait to see it," Christian said, making Angelica even more angry.

"Rachel sent you some things, too. We had to bring a packhorse to carry it all," Miles was saying.

"Who's Colleen and Rachel?" Robbie asked suddenly.

The two men seemed surprised at the reminder that they were not alone, and Christian stepped back, consciously schooling the delight out of his expression. "They're friends of mine from the Circle M," he explained. "I guess you've met Robbie and Miss Ross," he said to Miles, although Angelica noticed he did not look directly at her when he said her name.

"Yes, Miss Ross was just filling me in on what's been happening. I'm real sorry about your sister, Kid," Miles said, laying a comforting hand on his shoulder.

Christian's brilliant blue eyes grew bleak for an instant. "Thanks," he said.

In the face of his grief, Angelica forgot her anger. She had already instinctively taken a step toward him to offer her own comfort when his eyes changed yet again, hardening to blue flint.

"We'll find those bastards who did it, though," he said in a tone that sent chills up her spine.

Then, as suddenly as it had come on, the mood lifted. "Well," he said with only slightly forced cheerfulness, "let's go see what Colleen sent me. Robbie, would you like to come?"

Robbie replied with an enthusiastic whoop and was already out the door before Christian turned to her and added, "If Miss Ross will excuse us?"

His look was coolly impersonal, as if he were addressing his employer, as if he didn't really see *her* at all. "Yes, of course," she said, too startled to say anything else.

"It was very nice meeting you, Miss Ross," Miles said. "We're all going to do our best to get this mess straightened out."

"I know you will," she replied with an appreciative smile. Her gaze sought out Christian's again, but again he refused to meet her eyes. In another moment, they were gone, leaving her more confused than ever.

What did his detached manner mean? She could hardly believe that the man who had held her and made love to her in the dark of night could treat her so coldly in the light of day. Anyone would think they were nothing more than casual acquaintances!

At that thought, Angelica's eyes suddenly widened in understanding. Of course! How could she have been so stupid! He was trying to protect her reputation, just as he had protected her by leaving her bed before daylight this morning.

Feeling somewhat relieved, she still chafed against her desire to go after him and demand that he look at her, really *look* at her, so she could see in his eyes the love that darkness had hidden from her last night. But that could wait, she told herself sternly. Soon enough she would catch him alone where neither of them would have to pretend. She smiled at the thought as she went off to find Maria and help her prepare for the unusually large crowd who would be joining them for the noon meal.

Miles slapped the Kid on the back as they stepped outside into the blazing sunlight. Robbie was already at the bunkhouse door, waving at them to come on. "Miss Ross is quite a girl," he said as if expecting a comment in return. The Kid merely grunted, not daring to meet his friend's eyes. Miles always saw entirely too much. He didn't want Miles to guess his true relationship with Angelica.

Undaunted, Miles added, "She's about the prettiest filly I've seen in a long time, too. Why she's even prettier than you are." The Kid refused to rise to the bait and just kept walking, waving a reply to Robbie's shouted, "Hurry up!"

"Any man lucky enough to find a woman like that ought to grab her," Miles continued, impervious to the Kid's disgruntled frown. "Of course, I can see you've already staked your claim . . ."

"I have *not* staked my claim," the Kid insisted, stopping dead in his tracks and forcing Miles to do the same.

Plainly, Miles did not believe him. "She thinks you have," he corrected. "Didn't you see the way she looked at you when you came in? No, I guess you didn't," he continued, not giving the Kid time to reply. "You were too busy trying *not* to look at *her,* although why any man in his right mind would do that, I'll never know. You should have seen her eyes, though. I'm surprised your silver conchas didn't melt!"

"Miles!" the Kid tried in exasperation.

"But then, you aren't wearing your conchas, are you?" Miles continued, ignoring the Kid's outrage. "Don't worry, they're in the things that Rachel sent along. She thought you'd want your regular clothes now that you aren't keeping secrets anymore."

"Aren't you two coming?" Robbie inquired impatiently.

The Kid looked down, startled to see the boy right beside him and knowing he couldn't respond to Miles's charges in front of Angelica's brother. "Yes, we're coming," he said through gritted teeth. He would have to get Miles straightened out at the very first opportunity.

Colleen's gift was a very primitive sampler on which she had stitched his initials entwined with hers in a heart. Miles and the Kid found it very amusing, but Robbie could not see the humor.

"This is ugly," he decreed. "Even Angel can do better than this, and she hates to stitch."

"Colleen is only four years old," the Kid explained.

"Four-and-a-half," Miles corrected with mock solemnity.

This information only confused Robbie more. "Then why is she in love with you?"

"I guess she's just too young to know any better, Squirt," the Kid said with a self-mocking grin, but the boy's attention had already been distracted.

"Wow, look at this!" he exclaimed, holding up the fanciest vest he had ever seen. Glove-soft leather unfolded to reveal a profusion of intricately carved silver conchas. "I've heard about this, and I been wondering why you didn't wear it. I thought maybe it got burned up in the fire."

The Kid eyed his trademark vest skeptically. If that didn't clue people in to who he was, nothing would. He supposed he'd better start wearing it, although the idea of so blatantly advertising his profession held little appeal when he thought of the added distance it would necessarily put between him and Angelica. Still, at Robbie's urging, he reluctantly removed the plain cowhide vest he had requisitioned from Cameron Ross's wardrobe and put his own on.

"I wish I had me a vest like that," Robbie proclaimed and then discovered the curious hatband that had been packed beneath the vest. "Are these cows?" he asked, examining the carvings on the small silver conchas.

"That's right, son," Miles affirmed with a sly grin. "The Kid won that in a cow-milking contest."

The Kid made a threatening noise at Miles as he took the hatband from the boy and proceeded to put it on his hat.

Robbie's look of sorrow was comical. "You never milked no cow, did you?" he asked, loath to believe such a thing of his idol. No cowboy worth his salt would be caught dead at the business end of a heifer, and certainly no famous gunfighters would perform such a lowly task.

"Only because I had to, to save someone's life," the Kid explained. Luckily, Robbie had discovered the Kid's chaps, which also bore an interesting collection of silver ornaments, and he quickly forgot about milking cows.

Having carefully examined every item, Robbie finally lost interest in the Kid's wardrobe and wandered away, giving Miles and the Kid a chance to spend an hour catching up on what had been happening. By the time the Kid felt that Miles thoroughly understood the situation at the Diamond R, it was almost noon, and he decided he'd better take the bundle of clothes Rachel had sent him back to his room before the call came for dinner. At Robbie's insistence, he was now wearing all the accoutrements of "Kid Collins, Gunfighter." He felt oddly uncomfortable in what had for years been familiar garb. His discomfort grew when he encountered Angelica in the courtyard.

She was coming out of his room having just delivered his clean laundry and a fresh supply of towels. "Oh, hello." she said, feeling somewhat foolish for not being able to think of anything more profound to say, but since her heart had made a leap right up into her throat at the sight of him, she was doing well to utter even those few words.

"Hello," the Kid replied, uneasily aware that what

Miles had said about her was absolutely true. She was exquisitely lovely.

He looked very different, and for a moment she could not figure out why. Then she realized it was his clothes. Silver glinted everywhere, on his vest, along the sides of his chaps and even on his hat. These were the clothes Robbie had told her that Kid Collins usually wore. The thought made her frown. "You look . . . very nice," she said, knowing it was true but feeling like a liar all the same. Something within her rebelled at having him dress the part of Hired Gun.

"So do you," he said, wanting to grab her and kiss her right on the spot. Of course, that was a crazy thought, born of the same insanity that had driven him last night. Only when he'd awakened later in her bed with his arms full of her had he realized exactly how insane he had been. Even if he was in love with her, even if he wanted to make her his own, and even if she loved him in return, he had no right to take her that way, no right to betray the trust she had placed in him. God only knew what the uncertain future might bring and what tricks Snyder would pull. A man who made his living with a gun could not afford to make plans that included a woman like Angelica Ross.

Having hardly heard his compliment, Angelica continued to stare up at him, marveling that even in the light of day his eyes were as soft and vulnerable as they had been last night in the moonlight. She would have preferred to see those eyes blaze with passion. Instead he looked a little sad and not at all likely to take her in his arms. In fact, he was holding that bundle in front of him like a barricade. "Are those the clothes Mrs. Elliot sent you?" she asked.

"Yes," he replied, shifting his bundle as he resisted the urge to reach for her. Sunlight danced in her hair like tiny flames, and he knew if he so much as touched her, the fire would roar out of control and consume them both. Angelica frowned, sensing his resistance but unable to understand it. She knew so little about men and romance. Should she play coy or should she confront him and end all this uncertainty? Patience was not one of her virtues; she chose confrontation. "About last night . . ." she began, pausing only when she realized she had no idea what she wanted to say about last night.

The Kid had no such problem. "Last night should never have happened," he said, hardening himself against the pain that flickered in her emerald eyes.

"But if we care for each other . . ." she argued, knowing he was right but unwilling to accept his decree.

"Angelica," he interrupted her, making his voice hard. "I'm not some fellow you met at a church social. You hired me to fight for you. If your father was alive, he'd shoot me for what happened last night."

Angelica thought that was probably true but decided not to mention it. "My father's not alive, and I do as I please. . . ."

Her argument failed to move him. In fact, it only made him angry. "Then you'd better 'please' to watch how you act. You can get in serious trouble going to bed with strange men."

"I didn't go to bed with strange *men!*" she exclaimed in outrage.

"You said yourself you hardly know me," he reminded her ruthlessly, hating himself for hurting her but knowing he must if he were to prevent a recurrence of last night.

Angelica thought she knew him very well indeed after last night, but before she could say so, a raspy male voice called out, "Hey, Kid, where are ye?"

Christian turned toward the voice, which was coming

from inside, near the front door of the house. "Out here," he called back, a puzzled frown marring his handsome face.

A strange-looking little man came out into the courtyard from the entryway and paused until he had found his quarry. At the sight of him, Christian deposited his bundle on the nearest bench and yelled, "Stumpy!"

Crossing the courtyard in swift strides, he greeted the newcomer as effusively as he had greeted Miles. Angelica followed him at a more sedate pace, examining the man as she went. He was rightly named, she judged. He could not be much more than five feet tall, and his body was as sturdily made and as solid-looking as a tree stump. His face was literally covered with a grizzled brown beard, putting Angelica in mind of nothing so much as a cocklebur. A cocklebur with eyes, she corrected, as she watched his brown eyes dance with pleasure over the sight of Christian Collins.

"I do believe you've growed some since I seen you last," Stumpy Smith was saying.

Indeed, Christian looked to be about twice as tall as Stumpy Smith, although she knew that was simply an illusion.

"Maybe you're just drying up, Stumpy," Christian said with a grin.

"And maybe you're getting a little too big for your britches, boy," Stumpy replied with mock outrage. "Don't make no mistake. I can still whup you six ways from Sunday, and don't you forget it!"

"I won't," Christian promised with a laugh. "Where's Jack?"

Stumpy's beard seemed to droop, and Angelica realized that signaled a change in the expression of the face beneath. "I reckon you haven't heard. Jack died about two years back."

Christian's smile disappeared instantly. "Died? How?"

"Damnedest thing you ever saw," Stumpy said, driving his fist into his palm to emphasize his point. "He died of a bee sting. This little tiny bee just up and stung him, and before you know it, Jack swole up like something dead that's been left out in the sun too long. After a while, he couldn't get his breath no more, and he died."

"I'll be damned," Christian said, plainly upset.

"Can you believe it? After all those fights we were in? After all those years we followed your pappy out across the Staked Plains, chasing after the Comanche and dodging the army and never knowing if we'd get hung or shot or . . ."

Suddenly, both men seemed to notice that Angelica was standing with them, listening attentively to every word. To her disappointment, Stumpy stopped his reminiscences in midsentence. "Well, now, who's this?" he inquired, peering up at her with great interest. Suddenly, she felt very tall indeed.

Christian gave her a disgruntled frown, obviously not pleased that she had overheard the conversation. "Miss Ross, I'd like you to meet an old friend of mine, Stumpy Smith," he said quite formally. "Stumpy, this is your new boss, Miss Angelica Ross."

"Well, now, looks like things is looking up for old Stumpy," Stumpy observed, pulling off his hat as he gave Angelica an appreciative once-over. His look was remarkably free of lust, however, so she could not possibly take offense.

"I'm pleased to meet you, Mr. Smith," she said, holding out her hand.

Stumpy looked at it in astonishment for a moment, and then made a little show of wiping his own palm on his shirt before grasping her fingers gingerly. "You're not as pleased as I am, ma'am," he informed her, making her smile. Miles had been right when he predicted Stumpy Smith would liven things up around here, she observed.

"I gather that you once worked with Mr. Collins's father," she said, hoping to encourage him into some more revelations, but Christian replied first.

"They used to ride together," he explained unhelpfully, giving Stumpy a warning look which he easily interpreted.

"That's right, miss. Why, I've known this fellow here since he was knee-high to a grasshopper," Stumpy bragged, his sparkling eyes peering out at her above his beard.

Angelica smiled politely, vowing to get some more information out of Stumpy at a later time, when Christian Collins was not around. Between Stumpy and Miles, she was sure to learn everything there was to know about him sooner or later.

"Now that you're here, we can start the roundup tomorrow," the Kid said, more relieved than he cared to admit over the prospect of putting some physical distance between himself and Angelica. If she wasn't around, nothing could happen between them. He found a lot of comfort in the thought.

But Angelica was thinking, too. When the roundup started, Christian would be gone. She wouldn't get to see him for weeks, maybe even for a month, unless she did something drastic. Then she remembered what Miles had said about them needing more men. "I'm very sorry to hear about your friend Jack," she said to both men. "And that means you'll be shorthanded, doesn't it?"

Christian seemed a little surprised by the observation. "With Stumpy, we've got seven men," he said thoughtfully. "I'd like to have ten, but . . . I reckon we'll have to make do."

"Would one more man help?" she asked, hoping her

question sounded innocent.

The Kid frowned, wondering who she had in mind. "Yeah, that would help," he admitted warily. "Who were you thinking of?"

"Me," she informed him.

The Kid was speechless, but Stumpy let out a rasp of laughter. "Excuse me, miss. My eyes ain't what they used to be, but I'd bet money you ain't a man."

"No, I'm not," she agreed. "But I can ride and rope with the best of them. You know I can rope," she reminded Christian, amused to see how the reminder brought a dull red flush to his face. Whether he was just embarrassed to remember how she had sneaked up on him or if he were recalling what had immediately followed that incident, she couldn't tell, and she decided it didn't matter. She was already making her plans. She would have to take a tent, of course. Tents were considered a luxury on a roundup, but she would need some privacy and . . .

"You can't go on a roundup," Christian said.

Angelica blinked up at him in surprise. He sounded as if he were issuing an order, and one look at the expression in his eyes confirmed that opinion. "I most certainly can," she contradicted.

The Kid looked down at her, noting her defiance and deciding that arguing with her was out of the question. Stumpy or no Stumpy, once they started fighting, they were bound to end up in each other's arms. Arguing with Angelica was simply too dangerous to contemplate. "You aren't going on *my* roundup," he said.

"*Your* roundup!" she cried, but he ignored her. Turning to an amused Stumpy, he offered to escort him back to the bunkhouse. Stumpy seemed somewhat reluctant to let the little scene end, but he followed obediently when the Kid headed for the door anyway, leaving Angelica glaring after them furiously.

"I think it might be fun to have her on the roundup," Stumpy offered when they were out of her range of hearing.

The Kid's only reply was a skeptical grunt.

Chapter Seven

It certainly was nice to see so many men seated around the dining room table, Angelica reflected as she joined them for dinner. Too bad they looked so grim. Of all the males surrounding her, only Robbie seemed pleased with the current situation. The poor boy had not known so much excitement in all of his ten years.

Hank and Curly were a little overwhelmed by the combined reputations of the men with whom they would be working and so remained virtually silent. Harley and Sanders, the two men who had accompanied Miles, were by nature silent. Miles looked thoughtful and, if she was not mistaken, slightly amused, but he also had little to say. That left only Stumpy Smith and Christian Collins.

Christian appeared to be primarily interested in glaring at her from the opposite end of the table, so the burden of conversation fell on Stumpy Smith. Fortunately, it was a burden he didn't mind bearing.

When almost everyone had wiped up the last of Maria's beans with her delectable tortillas, Stumpy turned to Angelica with a mischievous gleam in his bright eyes. "Me and the boys have all talked it over, and we figure that you'd be a right smart addition to our little crew," he announced.

Christian jerked as if someone had punched him, but

Angelica pretended not to notice. She smiled beatifically at Stumpy. "Thank you, Mr. Smith," she said sweetly.

"Hank here tells me you been working cattle ever since you was old enough to sit a horse," Stumpy continued, as if he were unaware of the hornet's nest he was stirring up.

"Oh, yes, Hank was the one who taught me how to rope," she confirmed, giving Hank a fond smile that made his ears turn red. "It's been a while since I actually did it, but I'm sure if I have a good horse, I'll catch on again in no time."

Angelica glanced over at Miles, who seemed to be coughing, although when he dropped his hands from his face, he looked suspiciously cheerful. She wondered if he thought she was lying about her abilities, but she quickly discovered the true reason for his mirth. "There are some among us," Miles told her with a significant glance down the table toward Christian, "who feel it would be improper for you to help with the roundup, Miss Ross."

Angelica fought down a wave of irritation and managed to keep her voice level as she replied, "What could be more proper than the owner of the ranch going along to assist?"

"That's just what I told him," Stumpy informed her. "I said, 'She's the boss. If she wants to go, who are we to tell her she can't?' "

Which was the exact truth, Angelica thought, but luckily she saw the expression on Christian's face before she could actually say it out loud. His glare had turned murderous, although she was not sure she wanted to know whom he might be considering murdering. Still, she could not let him order her around. It *was* her ranch, whether he liked to admit it or not, and she was in charge. If she wanted to go with them, he had nothing to say in the matter.

Except that he did have something to say. "Where were you planning to sleep, Miss Ross?" he asked, his blue eyes blazing at her from across the length of the table.

She hated the heat she could feel crawling up her neck and wondered if any of the men suspected that she had once slept in Christian's arms. "I'll bring a tent, which should more than preserve my privacy."

For a few seconds she was afraid he was going to argue the point, but he didn't. Instead he pressed his mouth into a straight line and continued to glare.

In spite of all the times Angelica Ross had frustrated him, the Kid had never been quite this frustrated. He had already dismissed Angelica's suggestion as ridiculous when Stumpy had gleefully announced it to the rest of the men who were assembled in the bunkhouse. The discussion that had ensued—the Kid didn't like to call it an argument—had settled little except to isolate him as the only dissenter. Once Hank and Curly had confirmed that she was indeed capable of the work, and everyone else had begun to sense the Kid's reluctance to have her go, the matter had been settled.

It wasn't just that he had wanted to put some distance between himself and Angelica, either. There was the question of propriety. No lady should put herself in the situation of sleeping out with a bunch of men, unchaperoned and unprotected. Not that she'd really be unprotected, of course. He knew that every one of these men seated around the table would defend her to the death. Anyone who tried to get within three feet of Angelica Ross would probably get shot full of holes for his trouble.

In fact, as the other men had argued after learning of the threat of Harlan Snyder, Angelica would actually be far safer with them than at the ranch alone with only Maria and the boy for company. No, the Kid didn't need to worry about her safety, nor did he even have to worry about controlling his own desires. He would have no difficulty in resisting the temptation Angelica offered with all these watchdogs around.

But he would be damned before he'd let her work cattle like a common ranny. If she was going—and from the look in those green eyes, he knew she was, come hell or high water—then she was going on his terms.

"I don't reckon I can stop you from going, Miss Ross," he said, ignoring the look of triumph that flashed across her face. "We'll be glad for the help. I figure you can do the cooking, which would free up one of the men . . ."

He let his voice trail off in the wake of the laughter that followed his announcement. Hank and Curly were trying to choke theirs back, but Robbie was literally howling. Angelica was not so much amused as scornful.

"Angel can't cook!" Robbie announced between guffaws, earning him a dirty look from his sister, but he did not seem too disturbed by it. "She can't boil water without burning it!"

"Robbie!" she snapped in annoyance.

He gave her an innocent look. "That's what Hank said," he explained.

Angelica turned her ire on Hank, whose choking was getting worse by the minute. He gave her an apologetic shrug and with a great effort got control of his voice. "Me and Curly'll take turns with the cooking, Mr. Collins," he said at last, thus settling the issue.

The Kid felt his frustrations mounting, and once again he experienced that dreaded sense of helplessness. He knew that taking Angelica along on the roundup was just asking for trouble, but he also had no idea how to prevent her from coming. His last ploy had just failed miserably, leaving him with no other choice except to allow her to participate. He sighed wearily. "We'll leave at first light, then," he said.

Angelica glanced uneasily around the camp, feeling a little self-conscious in her jeans. All the men were still trying valiantly to pretend they weren't shocked by the sight of her in pants. That first awkward moment of silence this morning back at the ranch as they stared at the expanse of her long legs had been terrible. She knew she must look as gangly as a scarecrow in the snug-fitting denim pants and oversized shirt, but there was no question of wearing anything else on the range. Bless little Stumpy Smith, he had finally spit out a stream of tobacco juice and asked contemptuously, "Did you expect her to work cattle in a petticoat?"

That very sensible observation had ended the awkward moment, but the men were still getting used to the situation. She noticed they all made a point of looking her straight in the eye when they spoke to her, never letting their gazes drift below her shoulders.

All of them except Christian, that is. He couldn't seem to take his eyes off her pants. He wasn't admiring her figure, either, which would have made his attention acceptable. He just kept frowning that disapproving frown of his. She had a notion to go up and demand to know what he was staring at. The only reason she didn't was that she was afraid he would tell her.

"Do you need any help with that, Miss Ross?" Miles inquired from beside her. She was carrying her bedroll into the tent some of the men had set up for her.

"No, thanks," she told him with a smile. He really was a nice man. It was hard to believe he had done all the awful things she had heard. Ducking inside the tent, she dropped her bundle and then took a moment to look around at the small enclosure that would be her home for the next few weeks. Since the camp would be moving almost daily, the task of taking down and putting up the tent would become onerous, which was why they were seldom used. Unfortunately, she had little choice except to use it. Christian was already mad enough about this whole thing without her shocking everyone further by sleeping out in the open with a bunch of men.

Not that she expected any of the men to want to look at her anyway. They all conducted themselves like perfect gentlemen, and after having seen her in her jeans, they already knew what a gawky creature she was. Peeking at her while she dressed should hold little appeal for them.

Satisfied that the tent was adequate, Angelica backed out and was surprised to see Miles waiting for her to emerge. "The Kid said we're supposed to work together today," he told her. "We'll be covering the area east and southeast of the camp."

For the roundup, the men were divided into pairs, and each pair was assigned a specific area. They would ride out and drive any cattle they discovered in that area back to the base camp. There the calves were branded and saleable stock separated for holding in a herd. Each day the base camp and the growing herd would move to a new location, and the process would be repeated until the entire ranch had been covered and they had gathered a sufficient number of cattle to satisfy Angelica's government contract.

Angelica was a little disappointed to find that Christian had paired her with Miles for the first day. She had been hoping he would partner her himself. "Well, then, I'm ready whenever you are," she told Miles with as much enthusiasm as she could muster. Finding a spot and setting up the camp had taken only a few hours. They would still have time to gather a respectable number of cows and get them sorted and branded that day.

She and Miles headed to where the horse herd was being held. They had only gone a few steps when Miles said, "Cheer up, Miss Ross. Everything's going to be fine."

She looked up at him in surprise. His dark eyes, the eyes she had previously judged to be haunted, now looked only kind. Grateful for his perception, she realized she had been worrying a great deal that morning. The incident with the men staring at her jeans was nothing compared to the scene with Robbie last night.

"If they need help, I should go, too," he had argued. She was unable to convince him that a ten-year-old boy would be more a nuisance than a help.

Angelica smiled at Miles. "I really appreciate the way you and Mr. Collins handled Robbie last night," she said, remembering how the boy had gone running off to where the men had gathered in the bunkhouse to appeal to his idol.

"It wasn't me. I just backed the Kid's play," Miles demurred. "You should have heard him telling the boy how he was counting on him to take care of the ranch while we were gone, and how Robbie was the man of the family now." Miles shook his head in wonder at the recollection.

"Whatever he said, it worked," she said, instinctively searching out Christian's familiar figure as they approached the group of men waiting for their horses. Since Hank was cooking this first day, Curly had been designated horse wrangler. He had driven the herd into a makeshift rope corral and was roping the horses each of the riders designated as his choice for the day's work.

Christian, she noticed, had selected a hammerheaded roan with a mean streak a yard wide. Her impulse was to warn him, but as she opened her mouth to do so, Miles put a restraining hand on her arm. "Just watch," he cautioned her.

She did, open-mouthed, as Christian swiftly saddled and mounted the roan. The animal didn't appreciate the action and began to buck, or at least he tried to. Christian allowed him to work off a little excess energy, but then swiftly brought him under complete control. "Let's go, Stumpy," he said when the roan stood docile beneath him. Stumpy, already mounted and apparently unimpressed by the display of horsemanship, followed.

As he rode by Angelica, Stumpy leaned over and said, "Close your mouth, little girl, or you'll catch yourself a fly."

Angelica closed her mouth with a snap and then answered Stumpy's grin with one of her own. "I'll bet you a dollar Miles and I drive in more cows than you and Christian," she said.

Stumpy's grin grew puzzled. "Me and *who?*" he said, looking to Miles for interpretation.

Angelica could have bitten her tongue. She knew Kid Collins did not like being called by his "Christian" name. From the expression on Stumpy's face, he had never even heard it, but recognition was slowly dawning in those dancing brown eyes.

" 'Christian,' is it?" he asked wickedly. "You call him that to his face?" Obviously, he doubted this very much.

"Sometimes," she admitted, blushing scarlet at the thought of when those times were. "But please, don't tell him I told you," she begged, growing uneasy at the thought of how Christian would react to teasing on the subject.

"And *you'd* better not try calling him that to his face," Miles cautioned Stumpy, barely suppressing a grin of his own. "Not if you want to get any older."

Stumpy considered this a moment. "I'll take my chances," he decided at last and kicked his horse into motion. "Wait up!" he called to Christian. Angelica winced, waiting for him to shout out his news. Mercifully, he didn't.

"It's your turn," Miles informed her, gesturing toward the horses. Pulling her attention away from Christian's and Stumpy's disappearing figures, Angelica told Curly which horse she wanted and was soon riding away from the camp herself with Miles at her side.

They proved a compatible team, and by the time the sun was directly overhead, they were on their way back to camp with a respectable number of steers, cows and calves.

By then, Angelica felt comfortable enough to ask Miles one of the many questions that had been tormenting her ever since their first meeting. Shifting in her saddle so she could see him better as they rode along, she asked, "Were you really a preacher, Miles?"

He seemed a little surprised at the suddenness of her inquiry, but he replied readily enough. "Yes, I was."

She wanted to ask something else, something that would lead into a verification of the stories she had heard about him, but when she remembered his expression when she had called him Parson Black that first day, she hesitated.

As if reading her mind, he said, "You're wondering if all those stories about me are true, aren't you?"

She toyed with her reins for a moment before answering, "Some of them are pretty bad, and now that I've met you, I can't believe . . ."

"Believe," he said baldly.

She lifted her startled gaze to him. His eyes were haunted again, making his gaunt face look almost spectral.

"Those men killed my wife, Miss Ross, but worse than that, they tortured her for days before she died, using her like animals."

Angelica made a small, anguished sound at the picture he drew, and he turned away. For a minute they rode in silence, and she thought he was just staring off into the distance. Then she saw him blinking at what must have been tears. "I'm sorry, I didn't mean to . . ." she began, but he resumed his story as if he had not heard.

"I hunted them down like they were animals, too. It took me over two years to find all three of them. I killed them." He paused and turned his head back to face her. "I guess you heard what I did to them," he said hollowly.

Angelica nodded, easily reading the pain in his eyes. She could not help wondering which had hurt him more, losing his wife that way or living with the memory of what he had done to those men. "They deserved it," she said, responding to an impulse to comfort him.

He shook his head sadly. "Nobody deserves that," he replied.

"They did!" she insisted fiercely. "If someone raped me, I'd want revenge. I'd want the man who loved me to do what you did!"

Her vehemence surprised him, and he considered her words carefully. "Vengeance always seems like the proper thing until you're standing on this side of it," he concluded. "From here, things look mighty different. Revenge doesn't really right the wrong—nothing can bring my Annie back—and it takes a fearsome toll on the one getting the revenge. I turned my back on everything I believed in, on God, on love, on friends and family, everything. I got my revenge, but what do I have left? I've often wondered what might have happened if I'd simply forgiven those men."

"But you couldn't have," she argued, unwilling to let him think he had done the wrong thing. "What they did was unforgivable."

He gave her his sad smile again. "After what I've done, I'm hoping that *nothing* is truly 'unforgivable.' "

Unable to think of a reply to that, Angelica fell silent. One of their cows tried to make a break for freedom, and grateful for the distraction, she spurred her horse to head it off and drive it back to their small herd. By the time she fell in beside Miles again, his dark mood seemed to have lifted.

"I wonder if I could ask you a favor, Miss Ross," he said.

Angelica was so relieved to see that the haunted look was gone from his eyes, she would have granted him anything. "Sure," she said with a smile.

He seemed momentarily at a loss for words. "As you reminded me," he began somewhat awkwardly, "I am a minister."

She nodded encouragingly.

"I was wondering if, that is, when the time comes, when all this trouble is settled and all . . ."

She nodded again.

"If you would allow me to marry you."

Angelica gaped at him. Marry her? Was he serious? Of course he was, judging from his earnest expression. How could this have happened? They had only just met! And how could she hurt him, especially when she knew how very vulnerable he was? But she couldn't possibly marry him, not when she didn't love him and not when she *did* love his best friend. "Miles, I'm very flattered, but you can't . . . I mean, this is so sudden and . . . Miles?"

His earnest expression had changed to confusion and then disintegrated into laughter. At least, she hoped he was laughing. He was bent over his saddle horn and his shoulders were shaking. If he was crying, she would just die. "Miles?" she tried again.

He waved away her concern, and when he straightened up again, he did wipe his eyes, but he was grinning from ear to ear. "Oh, my, I made a mess of that one, didn't I?" he remarked to no one in particular.

Angelica wanted to laugh along with him, but as yet she didn't get the joke. "Did I misunderstand you?" she asked hopefully.

He nodded vigorously as he made a visible effort to regain his composure. "Let me try it again." He cleared his throat and managed to look somewhat solemn. "When you and the Kid, uh, you and Christian decide to tie the knot, I would be honored if you would allow me to perform the ceremony."

Angelica gaped again, but this time her face turned fiery red. "Miles, I, uh, I don't know where you got that idea, but . . ." she stammered.

Miles exhibited some astonishment. "Hasn't he spoken to you about it yet?" he asked, as if unable to believe such a thing.

"Well, yes, but . . ." she tried, faltering when she realized she did not want to explain the details of Christian's proposal.

Miles studied her face a moment and then nodded in understanding. "You're waiting until everything else is settled," Miles guessed.

"Sort of," she hedged, deciding that was as good an explanation as anyone needed.

"Am I right in thinking that you do plan to accept him when all this is over?" he prodded.

Angelica's face got even hotter. "Well, yes, if everything works out . . ."

Miles did not seem to notice her hesitancy. "But until then, you'd rather no one knew about it," he said with a knowing smile.

"Yes," she agreed with relief.

Miles nodded again. "But don't think it's a secret. Anyone with eyes can see how you two feel about each other." Before Angelica could begin to react to that observation, he added, "I guess Maria must know, too. That explains why she let you come out here without a fuss."

Angelica let him think that. Miles didn't have to know that Mama had kicked up quite a fuss over the news that Angelica was going on the roundup. Only by pointing out that she would be more thoroughly chaperoned in the camp than she was even in her own house had convinced her foster mother to give permission.

"Mama knew you wouldn't let anything happen to me," she told Miles.

"She was right about that," Miles confirmed. "And you will let me do your wedding, won't you?"

"Oh, yes," she agreed, having decided not to tell him how tentative her wedding plans were at the moment. "But please, don't say anything to Christian just yet. He'll be mad if he thinks I told anyone," she improvised. She couldn't let Christian think she had been making arrangements to trap him somehow.

Pleased with her promise, Miles consented to keep the secret as they rode up to the camp.

The Kid watched Angelica and Miles drive their small herd in and join it to the one already bunched near the branding fire. He was leaning against a scraggly cottonwood tree, smoking a cigarette. Stumpy hunkered nearby. He, too, was watching Angelica's approach.

"That sure is a fine-looking woman," Stumpy remarked.

The Kid decided not to reply, knowing he would only be asking for trouble if he agreed. Stumpy had been trying to get a rise out of him all day over Angelica, but the Kid had somehow managed to avoid being provoked.

Still, as much as he knew he should, he could not tear his gaze away from her.

Even in the rough range clothes with her glorious hair stuffed under a hat, she was beautiful. She rode with the same grace as she did everything else, and the sight of her tall, slender body straddling the horse caused his own body to tighten. He watched her throw back her head and laugh in response to something Miles said. He couldn't hear the sound of that laugh, but seeing her face alight with pleasure stirred something painful inside of him, something he reluctantly identified as jealousy. Why he should be jealous of Miles, he had no idea, but seeing Angelica with any other man, even one he knew he could trust, touched some possessive instinct.

"Yes, sir, a fine-looking woman," Stumpy reiterated with annoying cheerfulness. "Course, I like my women a lot shorter and a little meatier, but for a lanky fellow like you, she'd be just about right."

The Kid snorted skeptically. "You're forgetting one thing, Stumpy. She's quality. What do you reckon she'd say if she knew how my pa earned his living?"

Stumpy spat a contemptuous stream of tobacco juice. "Is that what's stuck in your craw?" he demanded, rising to his feet and planting his hands firmly on his hips in a gesture of disgust. "Hellfire, boy, you can't help who your pappy was! Do you really think she'd hold that against you?"

"I don't think she'd be too impressed," the Kid insisted.

Stumpy made a rude noise. "Then find out. Tell her and see what she says. Maybe she'll snub you and maybe she won't care. Either way, you'll be out of your misery and the rest of us won't have to watch you mooning over her like a sick . . ."

"I am not mooning over her," the Kid growled.

Stumpy muttered something incomprehensible and then waved an arm to catch Angelica's attention. Returning his wave, she turned her horse and trotted over to where they stood. The Kid waited tensely, wondering whether Stumpy had decided to take matters into his own hands, but when Angelica reined up, the old man simply said, "You owe me a dollar, little girl."

The Kid relaxed a bit as he watched their spirited argument over the definition of "cows." That morning she had said that whoever brought in the most "cows" would win their bet. Stumpy contended that although she and Miles had driven in more "cattle," he and the Kid had captured more actual "cows." Angelica protested that "cows" was a general term usually used to denote all four-footed bovines, regardless of sex.

"You old thief," she scolded in good-natured defeat, digging into her vest pocket for a silver dollar, which she tossed to him.

Stumpy cackled delightedly as he caught the coin one-handed. "I'll give you a chance to get even tomorrow," he offered generously, making her laugh.

This time the Kid easily heard the musical sound of her laughter, a sound he had never inspired, and jealousy pricked him again. Realizing he was an idiot to be standing here torturing himself, he straightened from the tree and tossed down the butt of his cigarette. "I reckon we'd better go eat before the whole afternoon is gone," he said, turning on his heel and heading for the chuck wagon.

Angelica stared after him, heedless of Stumpy's interested observation. She guessed Christian was still mad at her for coming, although it pained her to admit it. She would have thought he would be at least a little glad for her presence, even though she knew his pride had been wounded when she had pulled rank on him.

"He's a hardheaded son of a . . . gun," Stumpy observed, censoring himself at the last moment.

Angelica glanced down at the old man in surprise and instantly recognized another ally. "I'm pretty hardheaded myself," she informed him with a conspiratorial grin.

By the time Ed Harley and Dave Sanders drove in the cattle they had found, the herd numbered almost a hundred head. Many of those were unbranded calves, so the crew spent the afternoon marking those that belonged to the Diamond R. Curly provided Angelica with an expert cutting horse, one he claimed could do everything but actually drop the rope on a cow, so she worked the first turn as a roper.

Curly's opinion of the horse proved correct. All Angelica had to do was indicate which animal she wanted to separate from the rest and her mount isolated it in a matter of seconds. Then she would simply drop a loop over the chosen beast's head and drag it toward the branding fire, where one of the men would throw it to the ground and brand it.

Time passed in a blur as she worked the milling, mooing herd, surrounded by the heat and the heady aroma of a hundred bovine bodies and choked by the dust of all those churning hooves and the pungent smoke from the cow-chip fire. Even though her horse did most of the work, her arms soon began to ache from the unaccustomed task of throwing the rope and tying it securely to the saddle horn each time she captured a calf.

She was longing for a break, but when Christian called for a change in duties, Angelica found herself relieved of all duties whatsoever. "Throwing calves is too hard for a woman," Christian decreed tersely, referring to the other half of the branding process which required much more muscle than cutting and roping.

Having no argument against that statement, which was

all too true, she didn't come up with an alternative until he had already turned back to his horse. "I can do the knife work," she informed him.

By the time he swiveled around to forbid her to do such a grisly task, he found himself addressing her back. She had already shouldered a startled Ed Harley aside and braced her foot on the next calf's head, her pocket knife poised to mark its ear. The sight of her cutting the animal with such businesslike detachment shocked him so much that she had already castrated the calf before he could think to stop her.

"Angelica!" he called in dismay. "That's no job for a woman either."

She knew she should have been pleased he felt so protective of her, but she could not quite manage to dredge up that emotion after the way he had been treating her all day. "I'm not a woman," she snapped. "I'm a rancher, and I do what has to be done."

All the other men had paused in their tasks to watch the exchange. Although the milling herd still lowed and shuffled, calves were bawling, and the branding fire crackled, it seemed very quiet to Angelica as she waited for Christian's reply. His finely molded lips were pressed into a grim line, and his eyes seemed to flash blue sparks at her.

The Kid braced himself against the maddening helplessness he always felt when challenging Angelica's will. He tried to choke back the bitterness, but he couldn't stop the words. "You're the boss, Miss Ross," he said coldly. "Just don't cut your hand off."

Angelica wanted to take an inch-wide strip of hide off him with the edge of her tongue, but he was already instructing the displaced Harley to fetch some more fuel for the branding fire. Without so much as another glance at her, he mounted his own horse and proceeded to help with cutting the calves out of the herd.

Left without a victim, Angelica's fury sizzled out. With an exasperated sigh, she turned back to the chore at hand, studiously ignoring the knowing grins of the other men.

That night, immediately after supper, Angelica retired to her tent, where she scrubbed off the worst of the grime from her first day as a cowboy in the bucket of water Hank had thoughtfully heated for her. By the time she had changed into her nightdress, she was too weary to do anything except crawl into her bedroll. Every muscle was protesting at the amount of work she had performed that day, and in the few seconds before sleep claimed her, she wondered if she would even be able to crawl back out of the bedroll in the morning.

Just as she had feared, dawn came much too quickly, and she had some difficulty getting her body up and dressed. The men were all gathered around the fire devouring their bacon and biscuits when she finally left the tent. They greeted her enthusiastically, and she strained herself to match their exuberance. Christian, it appeared, had already eaten and gone about his business, since his bedroll had been tied up and deposited in the chuck wagon. As foreman of the crew, he would be scouting a site for the next camp.

"We'll see to your tent as soon as we eat, Miss Ross," Miles told her when she sank down on the ground beside him with her laden plate and steaming cup of coffee.

"Thanks," she muttered, realizing she would need all the help she could get this morning.

"Looks like you and me'll be partners today," Stumpy said from her other side.

She turned to him in sleepy-eyed surprised. "Is everybody being shifted around?" she asked, confused.

Stumpy grinned. "Yep," he informed her with obvious

delight. "But only so's you'll get a different partner every day. That way, nobody'll get too attached to you."

Angelica's confusion turned to astonishment. "Attached to me!" she echoed in disbelief.

Stumpy shrugged to indicate he didn't understand either, but his lively eyes told another story. Resigning herself to the fact that she would probably be getting no other kind except "knowing" looks from the men for the duration of the roundup, Angelica chose not to comment further on this bit of information and ate her breakfast quickly.

Revived somewhat by the coffee, she helped pack up her tent, and by the time Christian returned to guide them to the next campsite, the entire crew was ready to go.

Stumpy proved a lively companion, even if he was entirely too skillful at avoiding her inquiries into Christian's past. He certainly wasn't shy about telling her stories about every other aspect of his very eventful life, and the morning passed quickly. Before she knew it, they were riding back to the camp, and Angelica found herself in a very pleasant mood, in spite of her nagging doubts about Christian.

With new eyes, she admired the beauty of the rolling prairie, which the spring rains had recently turned into a carpet of lush green dotted with bright splashes of bluebonnet and Indian paintbrush. Above her, billowing clouds raced each other across the broad blue sky, and a pair of hawks played in carefree abandon.

She tried to recall that mood during the next two days, when she was paired with Ed Harley and Dave Sanders. Neither of them spoke more than a dozen words to her during their entire time together. She had a difficult time maintaining her cheerful demeanor through the ordeal. Christian even sent her out with Hank after that, on a day when Curly was doing the cooking. Christian rarely spoke to her except to give her reports on their progress, and even then, his blue eyes were carefully blank of any expression.

If he was still angry with her, he was hiding it well. And if he still had any feelings for her, he was concealing them completely. She might just as well have been a sixty-year-old man from the way he was treating her. In fact, when she thought about how he acted with Stumpy, she knew he treated sixty-year-old men much better. In retaliation, Angelica ignored him with equal thoroughness and lavished her attention on the other men in friendly conversation instead.

On the sixth morning, Angelica strode confidently out of her tent. Her soreness had long since faded, and her body was now accustomed to the riding and the work. The morning was bright and clear, the kind of day when the sunlight seemed to cast every object into stark relief, and her eyes grew tired trying to take in all the beauty.

Angelica felt stronger and more alive than she had in a long time, at least physically. Emotionally, she simply felt confused. The thought of seeing Christian was always enough to draw her from her blankets in the morning, but when she did see him, she was always disappointed by his failure to return her smile. Sometimes he even pretended not to see her at all.

Of course, she knew he was pretending. She had caught him watching her surreptitiously enough times to know he was as aware of her presence as she was of his. Getting him to acknowledge it was proving to be an impossible task, however.

"Well, Miles, am I riding with you today?" she asked as she joined the group around the fire to eat her breakfast.

"Not that I know of," Miles said between mouthfuls.

"I'm riding with Stumpy today."

She gave Harley and Sanders an inquiring glance, but they both shook their heads with such patent relief that Angelica almost smiled. Hank was obviously cooking, and Curly was tending the horses. A shiver of anticipation danced up her spine as she considered who her only other possible partner could be. Of course, Christian might have decided she needed a day off, although he had stopped making protective noises several days ago, having apparently accepted the fact that she was more than capable of doing the work. But if he didn't think she needed rest, that meant . . .

"You'll be riding with me today, Miss Ross," Christian said from behind her.

Angelica started a little. She hadn't realized he was even in camp, since he was usually gone at this time. As the meaning of his words sank in, she knew a quick rush of joy. They would be together, alone, out on the range today. Would he talk to her? Would he look at her and really see her? Of course he would, and she would finally get him to admit that he loved her or she would know the reason why, she decided. Carefully schooling the pleasure out of her expression, she looked over her shoulder at him. His expression was as guarded as her own, his blue eyes shuttered against revealing any emotion. "All right," she said.

Was it her imagination or did he seem to relax a little at her acquiescence? Whatever his feelings on the matter, he did not mention them. Acknowledging her agreement with a silent nod, he went over and began striking her tent.

Fighting a rising tide of excitement, Angelica gulped down the rest of her breakfast and joined the others in breaking camp. The routinely simple move seemed to take forever, but at last she and Christian were riding away. Together. Alone. At last.

"It's a pretty morning," she remarked to break the silence. When he didn't reply immediately, she couldn't help thinking about the two long days she had spent with Ed Harley and Dave Sanders, who were so terrified of her that they could hardly think straight, much less express rational thought in words.

The Kid looked around, noticing for the first time that it really was a pretty morning. "Yeah, it is," he agreed after a minute. Ever since he had decided that he could no longer avoid Angelica and that he would have to take her with him today, he had thought of little else, least of all the weather.

He let his gaze drift across the rolling prairie to admire the cloudless blue sky before allowing it to come back and rest on her. She was watching him closely. He would have to be careful, or he would betray himself. Unfortunately, he had underestimated his reaction to her. Who would think that riding beside a girl whose face had turned an unbecoming shade of pink and broken out in freckles across the nose and who was dressed in dusty range clothes that hid all but her most obvious feminine charms could be such a sensual experience?

He almost imagined he could smell her unique fragrance even above the odors of dust and horse and cow and sweat that lingered on his own clothes. It was, he recognized, a sign of his growing irrationality about anything concerning Angelica. Sometimes he even reached for her in his sleep, waking to find himself alone in a lumpy bedroll with stars winking down at him in mockery and men snoring on either side of him.

When five days of avoiding her had only aggravated his longing for her, he had decided to try a dose of her presence. Maybe they would have a terrible argument that would send her hightailing it back to the ranch. At least he told himself that was what he hoped for.

Angelica frowned when she saw how quickly he looked away after glancing at her. For the first time, she began to consider her appearance. Like the idiot that she was, she had neglected to bring a mirror with her, so she could only guess at what he had seen when he looked at her. The clothes, she knew, were not very flattering, exposing as they did her overly long legs and hiding every one of her other redeeming features. For practicality, she had been keeping her long hair braided and pinned up under her hat, and by now the sun would have wreaked havoc with her complexion. When she had dressed this morning, she hadn't known she would be spending the day with Christian, so she had not made even the smallest attempt to improve her appearance. Angelica could have groaned in frustration.

Luckily, at that moment Christian spotted a bunch of cattle off in the distance. Calling her attention to it, he spurred his horse and headed toward the animals. With little enthusiasm, Angelica followed, wishing that she had been born pretty and petite, just the way she imagined Rachel McKinsey Elliot and the mysterious Colleen were. She was certain that even sunburn and dust could not mar that kind of beauty.

To her growing annoyance, Christian treated her exactly the way he would have treated any of the men. As the sun rose higher in the sky and the day grew warmer as only an early spring day in Texas can, he looked at her less and less often, and her tolerance shrank accordingly. How had she thought to inspire a lover when she looked—and smelled—like something the cat had dragged in?

That thought was nagging at her as she rode into a clump of cottonwoods to roust out a cow and her calf. To Angelica's surprise, she discovered a shallow pool of water in the small grove. Obviously the result of a seep from an underground spring, the water fed the trees and provided refreshment to the wandering animals. When the cow and her calf had finished drinking, she sent them on their way toward where Christian was holding the rest of their gather, but instead of following them, she gazed longingly back at the water.

She hadn't had a tub bath since starting the roundup, and she had grit and sand in places she didn't even have names for. Heaven only knew how awful her hair must look, and a little cold water might do wonders for the unladylike odors she sensed must be emanating from her. Just then a trickle of sweat ran down between her breasts, and Angelica made her decision.

The Kid squinted anxiously at the grove of trees into which Angelica had disappeared. She had signaled him that she was going back in after driving out the cow and calf they had spotted, and he had assumed she was using the rare opportunity at a little privacy on the open prairie to relieve herself.

But the cow and calf she had driven out had long since joined the others he was holding, and Angelica still had not ridden out of the trees. He knew that women required a little more time for these things than men, but far more than a little time had elapsed. With a growing sense of alarm, he tried to imagine something that might have delayed her. Nothing he thought of was very reassuring. There were snakes and scorpions and all sorts of other varmints she might have run into. Then, of course, there was the spectre of Harlan Snyder and his men roaming these parts and up to no good. Could one of them been lurking in the trees, waiting for just such an opportunity? The mere thought sent his blood racing in his veins. Giving one perfunctory thought to the cattle, which seemed perfectly content to stand and graze exactly where they were for the time being, he spurred his horse in the direction of the trees.

"Angelica!" he called as he drew closer to them.

"NO! Stop!" she cried out in alarm, and his concern surged into panic.

Without a moment's hesitation, he raced into the copse of trees, gun drawn and ready for battle. To his horror, most of Angelica's clothes were lying on the ground, and she was struggling to pull her jeans up over her hips. But when he looked around for her assailants, he saw no one.

"I told you not to come in!" Angelica snapped, mortified. Of all the humiliating things to have happened, she raged silently. Without bothering to button her pants, she snatched up her shirt.

When, at last, the Kid accepted the fact that there were no assailants, he lowered his gun and looked at her again. She'd turned her back to him and was awkwardly shrugging into her shirt. It took him another few seconds before he noticed the pool of water and realized that her shirt was clinging because her skin was wet beneath it.

She'd been skinny-dipping.

The pictures that thought conjured mingled with the glimpse he'd just had of alabaster skin and rose-tipped breasts. Unwelcome desire roiled in his veins. If he'd gotten here a moment sooner . . . He closed his eyes on that vision and swallowed a groan. "I thought you were in some kind of trouble," he said hoarsely, sliding his pistol back into its holster.

"Well, I'm not!" she replied over her shoulder, thoroughly irritated. Things were going from bad to worse. First, he'd hardly looked at her or spoken to her all day. Now he'd caught her half-naked and dripping wet when all she'd wanted to do was make herself a little more attractive. She hadn't even had a chance to rinse her hair.

The Kid looked down at where she stood, still struggling with buttons on the wet fabric. If she only knew it, she was in far more trouble than she dreamed, he realized when she turned around to glare at him. The denim that clung with taunting faithfulness when it was dry was now leaving nothing to his very active imagination, and the shirt might as well be invisible.

Forcing himself to look away from where her nipples strained against the thin fabric, the Kid glanced at the pool. "That water looks good," he remarked, still a little hoarse.

Angelica swallowed an exasperated sigh. "You might as well get down and get a drink," she said ungraciously.

Knowing he'd be wiser to ride away, the Kid swung down and led his horse over anyway. He let the horse drink first and then pulled the animal back before it could overindulge. Tying his mount next to Angelica's at a low-hanging branch of a tree, he went back to the pool.

Angelica watched him kneel and pull off his leather gauntlets, the gloves she knew he wore to protect his hands. All the gunmen she had hired wore such gloves when they worked the cattle. Miles had explained to her that a callused hand could not handle a pistol deftly. Now she understood why Christian's hands were smooth.

The sight of his hands, so long and slender, as they cupped the cool water to his mouth, stirred memories of those hands moving on her naked flesh. She shivered, blaming the breeze cutting through her wet clothes. How could he have made love to her so passionately and now pretend such indifference? It simply wasn't fair, she raged silently, especially when she still longed for him with every ounce of her being.

"I'm afraid I muddied the water," she said to distract herself from her unsettling thoughts.

"That's all right," he replied, thinking how he'd drunk in places far less inviting. From the corner of his eye he could see her bare foot peeking out from under her pant leg. He remembered watching her toes on another occasion as they curled on the courtyard tiles back at the ranch. Her feet were slim and graceful, just like the rest of her. That night he had lifted her high against his chest and carried her to bed. He wanted to groan aloud when he saw her toes curl into the ragged grass.

Closing his eyes, he whipped off his hat and impulsively ducked his head in the water, hoping the drenching would wash away the images of Angelica lying beneath him that night.

He came up shaking like a dog.

"Hey!" she cried in protest. To his alarm he discovered she was now standing right beside him.

"Sorry," he muttered, trying to ignore the fresh-washed scent of her body. Why could he only smell *that* when surely her clothes must bear other, less pleasant odors? No, he realized in disgust, ducking his head wouldn't be nearly enough. Briefly, he toyed with the idea of filling his hat to deluge the part of him that was affected most by Angelica's presence.

Angelica fumed as she gazed down at him, reluctantly admiring the way the water glinted in his golden hair. He still wouldn't look at her, not for more than ten seconds at a time and then only grudgingly. Resisting with difficulty the urge to plant her foot squarely on his back and assist him in discovering the very bottom of the pool, she dropped to her knees beside him. "That looks like a good idea," she remarked with false pleasantness. It was easy to smile when she considered the expression "Go soak your head," only one of the many suggestions she would like to make to him.

Without another thought to how she might appear

before him—after all, how much worse could she possible look?—she ducked her own head into the pool.

The Kid watched, mesmerized, as she carefully gathered the length of her flame-colored hair and then spread it in the water until the whole mass floated around her head in silken splendor. The dappled sunlight danced on the surface of the water, catching the ruby highlights until they glittered like liquid fire.

Without conscious thought, he reached out to the fire, almost imagining that he could feel the heat of it warming his blood. But before he could actually touch, she came back up out of the water with a splash.

Dashing the moisture from her eyes, Angelica made a contented sound as the cool water streamed over her face and down her shoulders. There, now her hair was rinsed, and she was clean. To hell with Christian Collins and his indifference. Ignoring the dull ache that thought caused, she began to squeeze her hair dry.

Using her anger as a shield, she slanted him a cocky look that was meant to show him she cared not a bit for his opinion. She found him staring, as she had expected, but the look in his eyes shocked all the cockiness out of her. In fact, it shocked just about everything out of her.

"Christian?" she said, her voice a mere whisper.

He stared at her, taking in every detail, every bead of water that dotted the honey of her skin and every tangled strand of hair that framed her lovely face. He saw the freckles on her nose and the plaid shirt that caressed her breasts and the graceful hands now stilled as she watched him. She said his name again.

"My God, you're beautiful, Angelica," he said, overwhelmed by the simple truth of that statement.

Beautiful? Angelica stared at him in amazement. No one had ever hinted that she might be beautiful. Her own knowledge confirmed that she was not, most certainly not at this particular moment. Yet suddenly, without warning, she actually felt beautiful. Like an ugly caterpillar emerging from the cocoon to discover a complete transformation, Angelica imagined that Christian's love had somehow transformed her from the tall, gawky girl she had always been into someone he admired. That he did admire her was evident.

She could think of nothing to say. Instead, she reached out to him, needing physical contact to confirm the reality of the moment. He captured her hand and lifted it to his lips, pressing his mouth to her palm.

Her flesh was moist and sweet, hinting at the feast awaiting him if he took her in his arms. Knowing he was a fool to even think it, he pulled her closer, sliding his other hand beneath the sodden weight of her hair to grasp her neck and tip her face up to his. Her lips were cool and fresh from the water. He sipped them for a moment, tasting her and testing her response. As if surprised, she merely acquiesced at first, allowing his kiss but not returning it.

Her detachment maddened him. He pulled her to him, using his strength to mold her curves to the length of his body from knees to mouth. He could feel the chill of her dampness seeping into his own shirt, but the heat raging within him warmed that chill. Her lips parted under his, allowing him to explore the sweetness of her mouth in imitation of the union he craved.

Angelica opened to him, surrendering to the inexorable lure of his mouth and his hands. Her nerves leaped to life beneath his touch, driving away the coolness of the pool and igniting tiny flames that raced over her body, burning away all uncertainties. Nothing mattered except being close to him. When he tugged her down with him, she did not resist.

He wanted to feel her weight on him, wanted all of her

to touch all of him. His hands slipped under the edge of her shirttail, seeking out the silken flesh beneath. His questing fingers found the swollen mounds of her breasts, and he swallowed her gasp as he touched her pebbled nipples.

Angelica writhed in pleasure, twisting to accommodate him as she searched out his shirt buttons. She lifted her head for an instant, just for an instant, but he could not abide the separation. His hand came up to capture her again, and in doing so, he pulled loose the clump of hair that clung wetly to her shoulder. It swung down to slap him unceremoniously in the face.

"What the hell!" he sputtered, fighting free of the clinging strands.

Angelica jerked in reaction, and wet hair slapped her, too. Clumsily, she struggled upright as she clawed the wet mass out of her face. With both hands full of dripping hair, she peered down at him, prepared to make a flippant remark, but when she saw his expression, the words died on her lips.

"Oh, my God," he muttered. The passion was already fading from his eyes to be replaced by that shuttered blankness she hated so much. He suddenly seemed to realize that one of his hands was still under her shirt, and he hastily removed it.

"Christian," she began, wanting to somehow stop his withdrawal but unable to think of any words.

He made an attempt to get up but couldn't because Angelica was still straddling him. With a sigh of resignation, she climbed off of him, plopping down on the ground beside him. She couldn't have done otherwise, since her legs, like the rest of her, were still weak from passion.

The Kid pushed himself to a sitting position and drew several ragged breaths, trying to force his body into some semblance of calm. What was wrong with him? Every time he came within two feet of Angelica Ross, he turned into a lust-crazed animal. If he hadn't been shocked into awareness just now, he would have taken her right here on the ground. Could all those years of near celibacy have made him incapable of controlling himself?

He wanted to believe that. Unfortunately, he knew that his previous sex life, or lack of it, had nothing to do with his reaction to Angelica. He certainly had no trouble resisting other women, even when he slept in the same bed with one of them.

With unsteady hands, he smoothed his still-damp hair back from his face and hazarded a glance in her direction. She had the strangest look on her face, almost as if she were disappointed. "I'm sorry," he tried in an attempt to wipe that stricken look from her eyes.

"Sorry?" she echoed in amazement. That's what he always said. He was sorry. It shouldn't have happened. Frustration churned in her and quickly bubbled into rage over his refusal to admit his true feelings. "You're sorry? If you were really sorry, you wouldn't keep trying to make love to me every time we're alone," she accused, her voice rising with fury.

"I don't . . ." he began, but quickly realized her charge was correct. He changed tactics. "What did you expect to happen when you're running around here buck naked . . ."

"I wasn't running around! I was taking a bath and you barged right in here even though I told you not to. . . ."

"I thought somebody was attacking you!"

Angelica widened her eyes in mock amazement. "I see, and when you found out you were wrong, you decided to attack me yourself."

"I didn't attack you!"

"Well, if you weren't attacking me and you weren't making love to me, what do you call it?" she challenged, ready to choke the truth out of him if she had to. What would it take to make him admit he loved her?

"I don't call it anything," he snapped, obviously as furious as she. "But what do you expect to happen when you've been flaunting yourself all week in those pants?"

"Flaunting!" she cried, stunned at this outrageous accusation.

"Yes, *flaunting!* And *flirting,* too!"

"I was not flirting!" She was certain of that.

"I don't know what else to call it, then," he said. They were almost nose to nose, now, shouting, and he grabbed her arms as if he wanted to shake her. "You go around batting your eyes at all the men, smiling and laughing and swishing your behind like a . . ."

"I do not!" she cried, jerking free of his grasp. "You evil-minded son of a bitch!" She heard the crack of flesh against flesh even before she felt the sting of her hand slapping his face. She stared at him in mute horror for a long moment, braced for the retaliation she knew would come, but to her amazement, he didn't move. Instead of enraging him more, the slap seemed to have startled him back to sanity. His blue eyes reflected only surprise, the same surprise she felt over her rash act.

After what seemed a long time, the Kid sank back down to the ground. He felt weak, drained, and very, very stupid. What had come over him to make those ridiculous accusations when he knew perfectly well they weren't true? It was jealousy, of course, as much as he hated the thought. All week, he'd watched her befriend the other men. Each time she'd smiled at Miles, each time she'd laughed at something Stumpy said, each time she teased Harley and Sanders to make them blush, it was like a knife thrust into his vitals. He wanted her smiles and her laughter and her teasing to be for him, only for him. But of course, that could never be.

"Get the rest of your clothes on," he said without looking at her. "We've got work to do."

Work. She should have known. He always used that as an excuse to avoid her, only this time she was equally eager to end the encounter. She could still feel the sting of his unjust accusations, and heaven only knew what she might say or do if he made any more. So much for her plans to make him admit he loved her, she thought furiously.

She was still shaking, although she could not have said whether it was passion or rage making her tremble, but she managed to get to her feet and make her way over to where the rest of her clothes lay. After some fumbling, she got her socks and boots on and slipped into her vest. Her shirt was still wet, but it would dry quickly in the hot sun. Unfortunately, so would her hair. She had no comb, a fact she had failed to consider when she decided to rinse her hair. Now she realized it would dry into a tangled mess.

"So much for my beauty," she muttered bitterly as she raked her fingers through the damp tresses in a vain attempt to tame them.

"What?" the Kid said, feeling that it might now be safe to look at her.

"I said, I should have brought a comb," she replied without so much as a glance in his direction. Looking at him only reminded her of what an idiot she had been to give her heart to such a stubborn man. She snatched up her hat and jammed it on her head.

No, it still wasn't safe to look at her, he decided, watching as she stalked to where the horses were tied. No matter what she said, she really did swing that cute little bottom of hers when she walked. If he had any control over her at all, he'd forbid her ever to wear pants again. Except maybe when the two of them were alone and . . .

"Oh, hell," he growled and began to pull off his boots.

Angelica looked up in alarm. He jerked off his second boot and then began to strip off his vest. "What are you doing?" she demanded.

"I'm going to take a bath, too," he informed her through gritted teeth. "If you don't want the shock of your life, you'd better get out of here."

"Oh!" Angelica was in the saddle in record time. Her horse was reluctant to leave the cool verdancy of the trees, so she had to use her quirt. She knew it wouldn't be safe to see too much of Christian Collins right now, not when her emotions were still running so high. When she heard the splash, she kicked her horse into a gallop and headed toward where their small herd was beginning to scatter.

The Kid sat in the water until his breathing had completely returned to normal and the rest of his body was once again under his control. It seemed a long time, although he guessed it wasn't more than ten minutes. During that time, he practiced erasing images of Angelica from his mind until, at last, he thought he might be able to face her again without making a complete fool of himself.

Rising from the pool, he wiped as much water from his body as he could and then used his shirt for a towel. The shirt was quite wet when he put it back on. Maybe the cold fabric would help in quenching any fires that the sight of her was bound to start. At least he hoped it would.

She was riding slowly around the clustered cattle, keeping them together, when he rode up. She gave him a long, smoldering glance, but made no comment. Only the high color in her cheeks and the sparkle in those

ACCEPT YOUR FREE GIFT *AND EXPERIENCE MORE OF THE PASSION AND ADVENTURE YOU LIKE IN A HISTORICAL ROMANCE*

Zebra Romances are the finest novels of their kind and are written with the adult woman in mind. All of our books are written by authors who really know how to weave tales of romantic adventure in the historical settings you love.

Because our readers tell us these books sell out very fast in the stores, Zebra has made arrangements for you to receive at home the four newest titles published each month. You'll never miss a title and home delivery is so convenient. With your first shipment we'll even send you a FREE Zebra Historical Romance as our gift just for trying our home subscription service. No obligation.

BIG SAVINGS AND FREE *HOME DELIVERY*

Each month, the Zebra Home Subscription Service will send you the four newest titles as soon as they are published. (We ship these books to our subscribers even before we send them to the stores.) You may preview them *Free* for 10 days. If you like them as much as we think you will, you'll pay just $3.50 each and *save $1.80 each month* off the cover price. *AND you'll also get FREE HOME DELIVERY.* There is never a charge for shipping, handling or postage and there is no minimum you must buy. If you decide not to keep any shipment, simply return it within 10 days, no questions asked, and owe nothing.

emerald eyes betrayed the fact that she was still quite angry with him.

"Let's go," he said when he was within earshot.

Angelica watched through narrowed eyes as he choused the herd into motion again. It ought to be against the law for a man that handsome to be such a hardheaded, stubborn fool, she decided. How could he continue to resist the love that had blazed almost out of control just moments ago? Even Miles and the other men could see it. Why wouldn't *he* admit it?

And to accuse her of flirting with the other men! The idea was so preposterous that she felt her hackles rising all over again at the mere thought. He must be far gone indeed if he was jealous over her friendship with . . .

Jealous! That was it! He *was* jealous over her friendship with the other men. That explained his ridiculous accusations. If only she could get him to admit it.

Of course, Angelica had never consciously flirted with a man in her life. Not that she didn't know how, though, she thought with a small smile. In fact, if she wanted to, she could probably flirt better than any girl Christian Collins had ever known. Her smile grew as she considered the possibility of proving that to him.

Chapter Eight

Angelica bit back an anticipatory smile as she and Christian drove their cattle up to the camp. Everyone else was there ahead of them, setting the stage perfectly for the little drama she had planned.

Ed Harley and Curly were holding the cattle while the rest of the crew ate their noon meal. Stumpy and Miles were just unsaddling their horses when Angelica and Christian rode up to the improvised corral.

"Hello, gentlemen," Angelica sang out, giving them her best smile. This was going to be difficult, she realized, knowing that her hair was hanging down her back in a tangled mess and her clothes were dusty and she once again smelled of horse. Still, if flirting was what he wanted, flirting was what he would get. "Did you boys have a successful morning?"

"Yes, ma'am, we did," Miles confirmed, returning her smile with a slightly puzzled expression, as if he noticed a difference in her but could not quite figure out what is was.

"Except that Miles almost got us killed," Stumpy contradicted grumpily as Angelica swung down from her horse. "He cornered some old mossy horn back in the brush, and that critter nearly tromped us both."

"Oh, you poor darling!" she exclaimed in an excess of

sympathy, rushing to his side. "Your aren't hurt, are you?" she inquired.

Stumpy looked at her like she was crazy. "Hell, no," he said in some amazement.

"Oh, I'm so glad!" she exclaimed, batting her eyes furiously. "I just don't know what I'd do without you."

Stumpy simply stared, speechless for once. Angelica decided to switch her attention to Miles. "How naughty of you, Miles, to get yourself in a fix like that," she scolded, moving to his side and laying a hand on his shoulder. "Why, my heart's just pounding a mile a minute at the very thought of you getting hurt." She pressed her other hand to her bosom dramatically as if to still that clamoring heart and batted her eyes a few more times for good measure.

Miles's dark eyes now reflected amusement, but his tone was somber when he said, "I'm sorry to distress you, Miss Ross."

"You should be," she informed him, giving his shoulder a playful swat. "Now I'm all aflutter. Why, I feel positively faint. Oh, Mr. Sanders, I wonder if you'd help me," she called.

Dave Sanders had just wandered into earshot, having been answering a call of nature elsewhere. He immediately detoured to join the group. "What do you need?" he asked, flushing as he always did whenever he was forced to speak directly to Angelica.

"I'm feeling a little weak. I wondered if I might impose on you to unsaddle my horse for me?" She fluttered her eyelashes again.

"S-sure, miss," he said, frowning a little. "Something wrong with your eye?"

Miles coughed behind her, but she ignored him. "Oh, no," she assured Sanders with a dazzling smile. "But it's awfully sweet of you to ask."

"Yes, ma'am," he muttered, obviously confused but unwilling to make any inquiries.

Angelica turned back to Miles, not a bit surprised to find him grinning from ear to ear. "Oh, Miles, might I take your arm?"

"Of course," he said, gallantly offering it.

Angelica gave Stumpy a quick glance to see if he'd caught on yet and was pleased to note that he had. "Here, lean on me, too," he insisted, hurrying to her other side. "I'd be right proud to fetch you a plate. You just sit yourself right down, honey. Old Stumpy'll take good care of you."

Consciously swinging her hips, Angelica allowed the two men to lead her over to the campfire and fetch her dinner for her. From the corner of her eye, she saw Christian get himself a plate, but she would not spare him so much as a glance. She was too busy flirting—flirting outrageously—with her companions, who seemed only to glad to assist her in whatever game she was playing. Even Sanders was drawn into the action when she thanked him profusely for unsaddling her horse and asked him very sweetly to refill her coffee cup.

Miles and Stumpy barely had time to eat, so intent were they on telling her amusing anecdotes about their day's work. Angelica laughed loud and long at each one, taking off her hat and letting her hair blow freely around her head. The other men couldn't seem to take their eyes off it, and she suspected that maybe it didn't look quite as awful as she'd feared. From the corner of her eye, she watched Christian watching her.

The Kid watched the whole performance, growing angrier by the second. Just what did she think she was proving? That she could drive him crazy without half trying? He'd already known she could do that. She looked like some sort of sorceress, with her red hair teasing around her face and her eyes alight with a mysterious inner glow. Her *batting* eyes, he corrected, reluctantly noticing how frequently she fluttered her lashes at her appreciative audience.

Damn her! he thought furiously. He'd already admitted, at least to himself, that she hadn't really been flirting with the other men, that his accusations had been rooted in jealousy, pure and simple. Now she seemed determined to drive him to distraction in retaliation. Well, he wasn't going to sit here another minute and watch. Tearing his eyes from the little drama, he rose and dumped his half-eaten plate of beans into the wreck pan with enough force to draw a curious look from Hank, who was otherwise occupied with watching Angelica's show. The Kid had already started toward the horses when Angelica called.

"Oh, Mr. Collins?" He turned warily back, wondering what new form of torture she had thought up for him. "I'm afraid my hair is an absolute mess. I wonder if you'd be a darling and fetch my brush from my tent?"

New fury rose up in him but he swallowed the angry words he wanted to say when he saw the expectant expressions on the other men's faces. If she was baiting him, she was going to be disappointed. "Sure," he said, relieved that his voice sounded perfectly calm.

Unfortunately, he had no control over the blue fire that burned so brightly in his eyes. Angelica saw it and so did everyone else. "Maybe you boys better get going," she suggested with a strained smile when Christian had gone after her brush. She didn't think she wanted an audience for the second half of this drama.

Sanders seemed only too happy to leave. Miles and Stumpy exchanged a look of disappointment that they would not be around to see the fireworks, but they graciously withdrew. Even Hank chose this moment to go for a little walk. By the time Angelica heard Christian's footsteps, she was alone in the camp. She rose slowly to her feet so at least she would have that little advantage when they came face-to-face.

"Here," he said from behind her, forcing her to turn. He held the brush out to her, and she took it, managing a simpering smile.

"Why, thank you, Mr. Collins. You really are a dear to fetch that for me. . . ."

"Stop it, Angelica," he said, his voice hard. His eyes were even harder, and the expression in them made her stomach quiver.

Still she could not give it up quite yet. "Stop what?" she asked, tilting her head coquettishly and fluttering her lashes. Such pretenses did not come easily to her, but she had observed enough of her contemporaries carrying on flirtations to know the motions.

"Stop trying to drive me crazy!" he said, reaching out for her even though he'd sworn he wouldn't He grasped her arms and shook her once, startling that saccharine expression off her face. "You've proved your point, now cut it out."

Angelica was startled but not so surprised that she had forgotten her objective. "And what point have I proved?" she asked in challenge.

His grip tightened, but he somehow resisted the urge to shake her again. "You proved that you weren't flirting before, and you proved that I'm a jealous idiot. Aren't you satisfied yet?"

"Christian!" she cried, grabbing his vest when he would have shoved her away. "You are jealous, aren't you?" she asked, searching his beloved eyes for evidence.

His gaze held only bitterness. "Don't pretend you don't know how I feel about you, Angelica. You've been rubbing my nose in it every second since we left the ranch."

"Oh, Christian, I . . ."

"Where is everybody?" Curly wanted to know, but he stopped dead in his tracks when he saw Angelica and the Kid in a clinch. "Oh, uh, excuse me, I . . ."

They broke apart instantly. Angelica felt the heat crawling up her face, but she realized that Curly was probably the most embarrassed of the three of them.

"I . . . I'm sorry. I can come back later," he offered, backing away.

"That's all right," Christian said. "Go get your dinner. We were just leaving."

Angelica opened her mouth to contradict him, but he was already walking away, toward where the horses were being held. Her impulse was to call him back and demand that he finish their discussion and clarify his very tantalizing statement. Unfortunately, she was almost certain he would ignore such a request. With an exasperated sigh, she resisted the urge to stamp her foot in frustration.

"Is that your brush, Miss Angelica?" Curly asked timidly, pointing to the ground at her feet.

To her surprise, Angelica saw the brush that Christian had fetched her lying in the dust where she had apparently dropped it in the heat of the moment. "Yes," she said and picked it up resignedly. Briefly, she toyed with the idea of throwing it at Christian, but he was already too far away. Instead, she dragged it savagely through the tangle of her hair. The pain brought tears to her eyes, or at least, that was what she blamed them on.

The afternoon seemed unbearably long as Angelica went through the motions of helping with the branding. The sun seemed unusually hot, and the dust clung in a film to her exposed skin, making her long for the cool pool where she had bathed that morning. Christian made things hotter by issuing his orders with a tight-lipped fury that had the men muttering to themselves.

"The Kid sure is in a lather," Stumpy remarked to her at one point, while they were working on a calf. "He's as grouchy as a sore-tailed bear."

Angelica murmured a vague reply, hoping to discourage a discussion of the subject. She waited while he applied the hot iron to the calf's side, wrinkling her nose at the acrid stench of burning hide and hair and steeling herself against the plaintive bawl of the calf. Unfortunately, Stumpy was not easily discouraged.

He waited until she had marked the calf's ear and had moved to the other end of the animal. "I don't reckon he liked seeing his woman flirting with other men," he said, punctuating his remark by spitting some tobacco juice into the fire.

"I'm not his woman," Angelica informed Stumpy stiffly, straightening from her task and tossing the calf's bloody testicles vengefully into the fire after Stumpy's tobacco juice. They both sizzled in the flames, and Angelica grinned at Stumpy's disappointed look. Usually, the cowboys saved the testicles to be eaten as a delicacy, but none of them had the nerve to explain this to Angelica and ask her cooperation. For that matter, she doubted any of them had the nerve to eat the "prairie oysters" in her presence either, since she knew perfectly well they were considered a potent aid to the male sex drive.

Stumpy sighed regretfully over this latest act of sacrilege—Angelica was certain he knew that she understood her sin—and then dabbed some creosote dip on the cut and turned the bawling calf loose to find its mother. Angelica was hoping the subject was closed, but Stumpy peered up at her from over his grizzled beard and grinned. "If you ain't his woman yet, you will be," he predicted. "Kid Collins may be slow, but he ain't stupid."

Before Angelica could reply to that outlandish pronouncement, Miles dragged over another bawling calf for their attention. As the hours passed, Christian's temper seemed to cool and then to harden into a frozen implacability. Once more, he avoided her, never speaking to her unless absolutely necessary and then not looking directly at her.

As the afternoon dragged on, Angelica reflected that Stumpy was at least partially right. Christian Collins was unbearably slow. Her flirtation had been at least partially successful in that Christian had finally spoken of his feelings for her, but he seemed bound and determined to resist those feelings to the death. All that nonsense about him being a gunfighter and not the right man for her was, as far as she was concerned, completely irrelevant. But how on earth was she ever going to convince him of that, especially when he wouldn't even discuss it?

The question seemed to have no answer that Angelica could discover, even though she wrestled with it the rest of the day. By the time they were finished with the cattle, she was exhausted. After supper, she retired immediately to her tent, glad to escape from Christian's coldness and the other men's curious stares.

In spite of her fatigue, sleep eluded her for a long time, and when it finally came, it brought disturbing dreams. She was in danger, grave danger, but when she called to Christian, he turned his back on her time and again. Then, in the last dream, the sky went black and the ground began to shake. Angelica tried to run, but she fell and couldn't move. The ground shook more and more, and some terrible dark force was closing in her. She couldn't see it, but she knew it was coming, closer and closer. She opened her mouth and screamed, loud and shrill.

The noise startled her awake. The tent was dark and

for some reason, the world was still shaking. Outside, a dull roar was becoming much louder. Men began to shout, and she heard the shrill scream again, only it wasn't a scream. It was a whistle.

Someone called her name.

"Angelica!" The Kid's only thought was to get to her. Ripping aside the tent flap, he found her sitting up in her bedroll, obviously only half-awake and more than half-bewildered by the noise.

"It's a stampede," he shouted above the growing roar. "They're heading right for the camp! Come on!" He grabbed her arm, jerking her to her feet and dragging her from the tent.

Angelica came fully awake as fear surged through her. "A stampede? But how . . .?" she cried, stumbling to keep up with him and prevent her arm from being pulled from its socket.

He had no time for questions. Once again his piercing whistle rent the air, making her wince, and then she understood the reason for it. Midnight came racing up, a darker shadow against the night sky. Christian dropped her arm to catch the horse. She staggered, almost falling.

"Here, Angelica," he called when Midnight stood still. Confused, she did not respond. The pounding of hundreds of hooves was growing louder, and the ground shook as if the world would break apart. Then his hands were on her again, rough and urgent. He lifted her, throwing her onto the horse's bare back. Instinctively, she grasped the mane and clenched her knees against the animal's sides. "Ride, Angelica, as fast as you can!" he shouted, slapping Midnight's rump.

The animal bolted, nearly unseating her, but she clung frantically. As she raced away, she saw the silhouettes of other riders rushing to turn the herd and save the camp. Their voices came to her above the din, but only for a moment. Then she was gone, streaking into the night.

Her mind finally began to function, and her thoughts came in time with the jerking rhythm of the pounding hooves beneath her. Something had frightened the cattle, sending them stampeding straight for the camp. Straight for the camp and *Christian!* All the other men had been on horseback, but instead of thinking of his own safety, he had come for her first, calling his own horse to take her out of harm's way, but in doing so, he had put himself in horrible peril. A man on foot stood no chance at all against a rampaging herd of cattle. If he didn't find himself a horse before the stampede hit the camp . . .

Angelica cried out at the thought. She should go back to help him, but turning Midnight without a bridle would be impossible, she realized in near panic. It was all she could do to stay on his back.

And then the sounds behind her changed. Instead of growing fainter, the roar of the stampede increased. Dear heaven, they must have turned the herd away from the camp, but in doing so sent the churning maelstrom straight toward her!

Christian was safe, but now she and Midnight were in danger. Panic threatened to overwhelm her again until she realized that she was far enough ahead of the herd to feel reasonably secure. If she could only get Midnight to run out of the stampede's path . . .

Suddenly, Midnight did change course, turning so abruptly that he almost unseated her again. Fighting to maintain her perilous hold, she squinted into the darkness. To the right she could just barely make out the cut bank the horse had swerved to avoid. Thank heaven, she breathed, knowing that a fall like that might have broken her neck and would have surely injured Midnight.

But no sooner had she counted her blessings than she

realized with horror that she and Midnight were now trapped between the cut bank and the approaching herd. As if sensing the renewed danger, Midnight's flying legs flew even faster, but there was simply no place to go. Angelica clung with all her strength, her naked skin chafing against the animal's heaving sides as the wind caught her nightdress and sent it billowing out behind her. Praying with every breath, she buried both hands deep in the lush mane and hugged Midnight's straining neck.

The roar came closer and closer, filling the night until it swept over her like a wave as the cattle turned at the barrier, too, and caught them up in their churning mass. Clashing horns and tearing hooves and choking dust engulfed her, and still Midnight ran on and on, driven now by the impetus of the stampede. If the horse could only keep his feet, if only she could stay on his back, she would be safe.

But her knees were already slipping against his sweat-slicked sides. Her hands were already numb, and her head was fuzzy with terror. If she couldn't hold on . . .

Then Midnight stumbled, and she was flying through the air, straight toward the sea of horns and hooves.

The Kid rode wearily around the still-restless herd. One of the other men had started singing an old hymn to soothe the animals. His voice rang clearly through the darkness, and the Kid joined in, remembering the words from the days when his mother had dragged him to church three times a week

By some miracle, they had turned the herd just before it reached the camp. After letting the animals run themselves out for a few miles, the men had caught up to the head of the stampede and managed to work the cattle into a mill, circling them back onto themselves until they were so tightly packed they could no longer run. Although the cattle were still a little skittish, they were at last quiet. As soon as the sun came up, the men would ease them on back to the camp. Meanwhile, through what was left of the night, the riders would just keep circling the herd to ensure they would not run again.

As he rode, the Kid kept scanning the still-dark horizon for the sight of Angelica. He figured she would have circled back to camp, and knowing her, she would have jumped into her clothes and come hightailing it out here to help. Except that she hadn't.

Worry gnawed at him. It had only been a little more than an hour since he had put her on Midnight's back, and yet some sixth sense told him something was wrong.

"Hey Kid!"

He turned in his saddle toward Stumpy's voice, knowing even before he did that Stumpy had bad news. What he saw froze his blood. Stumpy was riding toward him, leading Midnight. The horse was favoring his right front leg, and Angelica was nowhere in sight.

Breathing a curse, he spurred his mount toward Stumpy, meeting him more than halfway. "Where is she?" he demanded as soon as he was within earshot.

Stumpy was shaking his head. "I don't have no idea. I just found Midnight limping along right over there," he explained, jerking his head in an easterly direction.

"Why in the hell didn't you go look for her?" he shouted, but he didn't wait for an answer. Spurring his horse, he took off toward the eastern horizon.

With narrowed eyes, he frantically searched every shadow on every square foot of ground in every direction. He was praying to see a slender figure in a white nightdress walking upright in search of the rest of them. Please, God, he begged, even as his heart began to shrivel within him. He could tell from the ragged ground that this was where the herd had passed.

Was it possible? Could he, in his desperation to get her to safety, have sent her right into the path of the stampede? He swore again as unspeakable visions of her beautiful body being torn to shreds beneath hundreds of deadly hooves mercilessly tormented him.

"No!" he cried aloud. He wouldn't believe that. He stood in his stirrups, straining for a glimpse of moonlight reflecting on white material. Seeing nothing, he rode on. One mile, and then two, and still nothing. "Angelica! Angelica!" Like a litany, he shouted her name over and over. Another mile and desperation became panic. He was growing hoarse, but still he called her name relentlessly. "Angelica!"

At first he could not believe it. A mirage, a trick of the moonlight. It must be, he told himself, even as he rode closer. He had almost missed it altogether, so deeply hidden was it in a shadowed depression. Closer, and the white blotch took on form and shape. Closer still and he could make out her arms and legs and the darker shadow of her hair spread out upon the grass.

"Angelica!"

She did not move as he raced toward her. Hope warred with despair. She was whole, not mangled as one who had been trampled, and yet she did not move. Dear God, just let her be alive, he prayed as he shouted her name again.

He jumped off the horse before it had even stopped, and ran to her, falling on his knees beside where she lay sprawled. His gaze swept over her, searching for some sign of life, but she was deathly still. He tried to say her name again, but his voice broke as despair claimed him.

Tentatively, knowing he might well be destroying his last feeble shred of hope, he reached out and touched her face. "Thank God," he breathed as warm flesh touched warm flesh. Swiftly, he moved his hand to her breast where he felt her heartbeat strong beneath his palm.

"Angelica! Angelica, can you hear me?" he asked urgently. Still no response. Then he noticed her face. Her hair was half covering it, but when he brushed it aside, he saw that her left cheek and eye bore the promise of the grandpappy of all shiners. Gently, he probed her scalp for evidence of more wounds but found none.

She might, he knew, have suffered a concussion from that blow to her head, but if she had been unconscious all this time, she might have much more serious injuries, too. Without hesitation, he began his examination. Starting at her shoulders, he worked down her arms. Satisfied that nothing was amiss there, he moved to her rib cage and then probed her belly and hips.

"Just what do you think you're doing?"

Had he really heard those softly spoken words, or was it only an illusion prompted by his desperation? "Angelica?" He leaned closer to her face as hope burst painfully in his chest. "Angelica, can you hear me?"

Slowly, as if it required great effort, she opened her eyes. "It's just like I said," she whispered, her voice a feeble thread of sound. "Every time we're alone, you try to make love to me."

He gaped at her, unable to quite believe his ears. She was conscious and she was complaining about . . . Suddenly he remembered where his hands were and jerked them guiltily away. "I was just trying to see if . . ." he began to defend himself, but then the truth hit him. She was *alive*. More than that, she was conscious, and she was still her irrepressible self. The relief staggered him. He sank back on his heels, closing his eyes against the unexpected weakness.

"Christian? Are you all right?" Angelica asked in alarm, managing with some difficulty to get an elbow under her in an effort to sit up. But the world started spinning, and she moaned involuntarily.

Christian's hands were there in an instant, supporting her as she struggled upright into the blessedly familiar comfort of his arms. His embrace was fiercely gentle, and to her surprise, he was trembling.

"Were you worried about me?" she asked, still somewhat dazed, although the trees and the ground had settled back down to their normal level of stability.

"Worried?" he echoed in disbelief, pushing her away a little so he could see her. "I was scared half out of my mind! I expected to find you ground to a pulp. . . ." His voice broke again at the thought of losing her. He stared down into her lovely, battered face for a long moment, searching for some clue that she understood his torment. She still looked only dazed.

"Oh, hell," he muttered, giving up the struggle. He pulled her close again and simply held her, burying his face in the cloud of her hair. For someone who had just lived through a stampede, she smelled surprisingly fresh and altogether too sexy. For a long moment, he let his hands rejoice in the feel of her vital, living body.

"How are you?" he asked when he was finally master of himself again. "Do you hurt anywhere?"

Angelica smiled slightly against his shirtfront when she heard the slight tremor in his question. He really *had* been scared to death. "I hurt *everywhere,*" she informed him, "but no place in particular. I even managed to sit up a little while ago, all by myself, but everything started spinning so I lay down again. I guess I was asleep or something until you came along and tried to take advantage of me," she added, managing to sound aggrieved.

"Dammit, I wasn't . . ." he began, pulling away again, but then he saw the faint smile playing around her lips. She was teasing him! After all she'd been through, she was still trying to give him a hard time. For a second he was stunned, but he quickly realized he should not have been. He should have known that it would take more than a stampeding herd of cattle and a near brush with death to take the fight out of his Angelica.

Love for her swelled painfully in his chest, and once again he had to close his eyes against the impact of his churning emotions. "I ought to wear you out for scaring me like that," he said when he felt he once again had control of his voice.

When his eyes opened, Angelica could easily read his anguish, but she respected his need to hide it. She gave him a little shake. "And I ought to wear *you* out for sending that stampede right after me."

"Oh, my God, was that what happened?" he asked, his eyes widening as the horror of it hit him.

She nodded. "I thought I was going to get away, even after you all turned the herd, but there was this cut bank, and when Midnight swerved to avoid it, we were trapped."

His hands tightened on her arms as he realized what must have happened next. "Did you fall?" She nodded again. "Right in front of the herd?"

"Right *in* the herd, as a matter of fact," she corrected him grimly.

He made a sound of protest. He couldn't believe it. "But you're here. You're alive. If you fell in the herd, you'd be . . ." He could not finish the sentence. The words were unspeakable.

"Oh, I fell all right," she told him solemnly, trying not to relive those moments of terror. "Or rather, Midnight fell, and I went sailing over his neck. I hit my head, and I guess I was unconscious or something. I do remember the noise and the dust and wanting to get away and not being able to move. The cattle must have run around me.

I don't know. It all seems like a bad dream." She shuddered at the memory.

His face twisted in pain as he relived his own terrible moments when he had thought her dead. The hand he raised to touch her bruised cheek was trembling. "If anything had happened to you . . ." he whispered, his voice choked with emotion.

He meant the kiss to comfort them both. His lips on hers were tender at first, but his gentleness lasted only a second. The touch and taste of her fired his blood. She was alive. They were both alive. Nothing else was more important than confirming that fact.

Angelica winced as his arms came around her. Her body was bruised and sore from the fall, but she gladly endured a little discomfort to be in Christian's arms. "You do love me, don't you?" she whispered when his mouth left hers to trail down her throat.

"Yes. God, yes," he groaned against her skin.

He loved her! No matter what he had said or done, no matter how hard he had tried to hide it, *he loved her.* Joy flooded her, singing through her veins. She breathed his name, over and over, as she matched him kiss for kiss. When he drew her down, she followed willingly, pressing him to the scarred ground with her weight.

She buried her fingers in his golden hair to hold his head still for the kisses she rained over his face. Vaguely, she realized he was not wearing a hat, that he had probably neglected to put it on before leaving the camp. Just as she had not put on any clothes that would have hindered his marauding hands from their erotic explorations.

His fingers stroked up her thighs, sliding under her nightdress to find even more sensitive spots. As his urging, she straddled him, pressing herself to the heat of his very obvious desire.

He groaned his approval as she moved against him, fueling her own fires. His confession that he returned her love magnified the pleasure she felt, giving it a dimension far beyond the physical. Still, she needed a physical affirmation of their new commitment.

"Oh, God, Angelica," he moaned when she began to struggle with the buttons of his pants. "Do you know what you're doing?"

"I think so," she murmured, wondering if she really did.

As the buttons gave beneath her fingers, though, the question ceased to matter. What she did not know, Christian taught her with loving hands, lifting her to him. Her eyes widened in wonder as he filled her. He drew in a hissing breath and groaned her name.

The wild ride through the stampede faded from memory as she rode with Christian into a magic kingdom where pleasure was life and life was precious indeed. Only the two of them existed, and they existed only to please each other. Here in the shadows, it was too dark to see his face, but she could feel the adoration in his hands as together they pursued the elusive promise of ultimate union.

Dawn's faint glow paled as the aura engulfed them. They were close, so close she felt she could have touched his very soul, and then the aura flared. Heat and light and ecstasy sealed them into one being for that precious fragment of time.

Spent, Angelica collapsed on his chest. The hammering of his heart echoed her own, and for many minutes they simply lay still, relearning how to breath and remembering how to think. His hands idly stroked her hair and her body, as if he were soothing away the last vestiges of passion to help ease her back to the real world. She made the trip reluctantly, pausing along the way to reflect on how wonderful it was to know she would never have to be alone again. She would always have Christian now, to love her and to hold her through the long hours of the night, every night.

The Kid stared unseeing at the fading stars as his hands continued to cherish Angelica. In that moment, he knew he loved her far more than he had ever thought it possible to love anyone. The depth of it staggered him. He hadn't wanted to love her at all. Ever since Lettie's death, he had closed off that part of his life, sealing it against the bitter anguish he knew love could cause, but somehow Angelica had slipped under his guard. Now she owned him, heart and soul. With that knowledge came the fearsome understanding of why he had fought so hard to keep from loving her at all: he was mortally afraid of losing her.

He had almost gone mad when he thought her dead. The fear had been even greater than the actual pain of mourning Lettie, the only other woman he had ever loved. Now he understood that his love for Lettie was but a pale shadow of his overwhelming obsession for Angelica.

Of course, Angelica was still very much alive and would stay that way even if he had to move heaven and earth to protect her. This left him with the very real—and in some ways more unbearable—possibility that she would simply cease to love him.

And she did love him, he was certain of that now. Why else would she have given herself to him the way she had? Hadn't she justified their lovemaking the other night by saying, "If we care for each other . . ."? But she wouldn't love him for long, not when she learned the truth about him. Stumpy seemed to think it wouldn't matter to her, but the Kid knew differently. He'd seen the way his mother had reacted, the way she'd never forgiven his father for being what he was. When Angelica found out, would she look at him with that same contempt? Would the light in her eyes flicker and die as the stars above him were doing?

Angelica was lost in a beautiful dream when she felt his body stiffen beneath her. "My God," he said. "The sun's coming up."

That information succeeded in startling her completely back to reality. The struggling sunlight was already invading their dark haven. "Oh!" She scrambled free of him, suddenly realizing that they were, in spite of the darkness, out in the open. If anyone else was out looking for her . . . Tugging her nightdress to a more modest position, she glanced around in alarm, but saw to her relief that they were still well hidden by the shadows and that no one else was in sight.

"You'd think one of us would have better sense," he muttered, appalled at the way he had just made love to her without any regard for the possible consequences. Sitting up and adjusting his own clothing, he, too, looked around to verify that they were still alone and unobserved.

"I guess where you're concerned, I don't have any sense at all," she replied, realizing that giving in to her impulses that way could have been foolish and even disastrous. All of a sudden, she felt very tired and even more fragile, but when her gaze came back to Christian, he was staring at her, concern warming the blue of his eyes.

"Hey, are you all right?" he asked in alarm, reaching up to graze her cheek with his fingertips. In the dim light, he could see that she was pale and the bruise on her face was growing darker by the minute.

"Yes," she lied, feeling far from all right. She supposed she had a right to feel shaken, considering she had almost been killed in a stampede and then had made love out on an open prairie.

"Are you sure?" he insisted, recalling her earlier charge that he was taking advantage of her, a charge that had proven only too true. What was wrong with him? He must have been crazy to make love to a woman who'd just been through an ordeal like that. "I didn't even think that you might be hurt someplace else besides your face."

That reminder brought her head up. "How bad is it?" she asked, gingerly exploring the bruised area with her fingers.

"Pretty bad," he told her solemnly.

"I must be a sight," she said, growing conscious of her disheveled appearance and beginning to feel unbearably awkward as dawn's golden light chased away the cloaking shadows. What had happened to the magic, the loving aura that had made everything so wonderful just a few minutes before? Now they were like two strangers. She turned away, self-conscious of her tangled hair and disfigured face.

"It's just a bruise," he assured her, seeing her embarrassment. "When I think what *could* have happened . . ."

Once more she heard a tremor in his voice. Turning back, she saw his pain and remembered how difficult it always was for him to show his true feelings. Maybe the magic wasn't completely lost after all. She managed a weak smile. "I'm sorry I frightened you. I'll try to be more careful in the future," she promised.

The Kid watched the changing emotions flicker in her emerald eyes and knew a rush of tenderness. As certain as he was that he should never have even touched Angelica Ross, he could not deny the joy loving her gave him, bittersweet though it was. But he quickly stifled that joy. He couldn't let himself get in any deeper, not when he knew the rejection that was bound to come. "We'd better get you back to camp," he said briskly, rising somewhat stiffly to his feet and then reaching down to assist her.

Angelica hesitated a moment as she tried to read his face and make some sense of his sudden change of mood. This time she had seen him putting a mask on his tender feelings. In spite of what had just happened, in spite of the fact that he had professed his love to her in the heat of passion, he wasn't quite ready to admit it in the cold light of day. She still had a few more barriers to break down.

With a sigh of resignation, she put her hands in his and allowed him to haul her to her feet. Her dirty bare feet, she suddenly realized as her toes curled in the trampled grass. His blue eyes skimmed down the length of her, making her uncomfortably aware of how disheveled her encounter with the stampede had left her. Could she really expect him to beg for her hand when she looked like a ragamuffin? she thought in a feeble attempt at comforting herself. "I guess I could stand a change of clothes," she allowed, dropping his hands and brushing ineffectually at the worst of the dirt on her nightdress.

The Kid watched her in an agony of longing. How could a woman who had passed through a stampede still look so damn beautiful? he wondered as the stiff morning breeze caught her gown and molded it provocatively to her curves.

And how could he take her back to the camp looking like that? His mind rebelled at the thought of anyone else seeing her half-clothed.

Muttering a curse, he glanced futilely around for something to cover her with. Finding nothing—he'd been in too much of a hurry last night to even tie his rain slicker on his saddle—he swiftly began to undo his shirt buttons.

Angelica stared at him in surprise. "What are you doing?"

"This is the closest thing I have to a robe," he explained tersely, jerking his shirttail free. If only he'd thought to put on a vest.

Angelica watched in fascination as he pulled his arms out of the garment. The brightening sunlight glittered off the golden hairs that swirled on his chest and gleamed off the solid muscles of his arms and shoulders. He looked even more appealing in sunlight than he did in moonlight, she thought inanely, licking suddenly dry lips, and she wanted him all over again. But she was certain he was now too much in control to betray himself again, so she regretfully resisted the urge to reach out and touch him.

"Here, put this on," he snapped, thrusting the shirt at her and turning to find his horse. The animal had stopped a short distance away and now stood quietly grazing. Glad for the excuse to put some much-needed distance between them, he went after it.

Angelica watched him go, acutely aware of every detail of his appearance. She noted with amusement the dried grass in his hair and the dirt on his pants left over from their encounter on the grass. A small, secret smile curved her lips as she noticed the same soil clinging to his shirt and gingerly shook it off. Slipping her arms into the garment, which still bore the unmistakable scent of its owner, she knew a moment of bittersweet longing. Oh, Christian, she cried silently, why can't we just love each other? Why does everything have to be so difficult?

She didn't say the words aloud, of course, because she knew that with Christian Collins, nothing would ever be easy. It had taken every bit of her ingenuity to get him to work for her in the first place. Now, in spite of his resistance, he was in love with her. All that was left was to convince him to stop fighting what was inevitable.

Lifting her chin to a more determined angle, she stalked over to where he was holding his horse. He glanced at her once, briefly, and Angelica had the feeling his eyes were drawn to her in spite of his best intentions. The knowledge gave her confidence.

"Christian," she said, drawing his instantly wary gaze again. "I think you'd better brush yourself off before we go back to camp." She smiled up at him innocently, pleased to note his flush.

He muttered something incomprehensible as he twisted to see the back of his pants and hastily began slapping the dirt out of his jeans.

"There's grass in your hair, too," she informed him sweetly before adjusting the hem of her nightdress and placing her foot in the stirrup. With as much modesty as possible, she mounted the horse.

She was settling into the saddle when he cursed again. "Dammit, Angelica, you can't sit like that," he said, making a gesture to indicate the generous expanse of bare leg exposed when she straddled the horse.

She tugged at her hem, managing to cover another half-inch of skin. "I don't have much choice," she defended herself, earning another muttered imprecation.

In a matter of seconds he was behind her on the horse. "Put your leg back over on this side," he said, grasping her right thigh in a less-than-gentlemanly grip and helping her swing it back over the horse's head in a maneuver Angelica was glad no one else witnessed.

"Christian! What are you . . . !" she began until she realized that in her new position she was being cradled against his chest. His naked chest. All other thoughts fled.

"Pull your skirt down," he commanded, dong it for her when she failed to respond quickly enough. "Hang on tight," he added, kicking the horse into motion.

Angelica only too happily obliged, slipping her arms around him enthusiastically. His breath caught, making her smile again. "I don't want you to get cold without your shirt on," she said, snuggling more comfortably against him.

He made a strangled noise in his throat but did not reply. She could feel his erratic heartbeat against her ear, and impulsively, she began to explore the muscles of his shoulder.

"Angelica," he said in warning. She ceased her exploration immediately, contenting herself with the satiny feel of his skin beneath her palms and the crinkle of chest hair beneath her cheek. Sighing, she relaxed into his embrace, closed her eyes, and inhaled deeply of his man-smell. Secure at last, the events of the night finally caught up with her, and she slept.

"Gawd almighty!"

Angelica started awake, instantly aware that her body was stiff and sore in the very oddest places, but before she could fully register that fact, someone began man-handling her.

"Is she all right, Mr. Collins?" It was Hank, and he was being far less than gentle as he helped Christian lower her from the saddle.

"Ouch," she protested groggily, but no one seemed to notice.

"She's got that nasty bump on her head, but she seems to be all right otherwise," Christian reported with annoying certainty. Angelica no longer felt at all fine. In fact, she felt positively woozy.

Strong arms took her from Hank, and she leaned her head on Christian's shoulder again. She moaned a little as her head thunked against a rather solid bone. "Sorry," he murmured as he marched somewhere with dogged determination.

"Christian, I don't feel well," she said, but he didn't seem to hear her. Maybe her voice wasn't as loud as it sounded in her own ears. Suddenly, someone blew out the sun, and the sky turned dark green. Christian set her down on her feet. Squinting, she looked around and realized he had only taken her into her tent. She felt an absurd urge to laugh.

Then Christian's hands left her and the world tilted dangerously. She cried out, but before she could fall, his hands were there again, easing her down to her blankets.

"Why didn't you tell me you were sick?" he asked, sounding alarmed.

"I did," she said, but he still didn't seem to hear.

"What am I going to do with you?" he asked in dismay, arranging the blankets around her.

"Just love me," she whispered, or thought she did before sleep claimed her again.

The Kid stared down at her pale face and drew a ragged breath. She was, without doubt, the most exasperating woman alive. First, she scared ten years off his life by nearly getting killed in a stampede, then she made love with him like the angel for which she was named, then she snuggled up to him like a temptress and slept like an angel once more.

Even with a black eye and her hair in a shambles and wearing his shirt over a tattered nightdress, she was so beautiful it made his heart ache just to look at her. With loving fingers, he brushed the wisps of hair away from her face. "Love me," she had said, as if he could help it. He only wished he didn't.

Angelica shifted in the creaky camp chair and squinted painfully up at the sun. It was almost directly overhead, and looking at it caused the throbbing behind her eyes to intensify, so she quickly looked away.

She had slept for several hours after returning to camp, and upon awakening, had washed away the worst of the remnants of the stampede with the hot water Hank brought her and had dressed in her range clothes. Unfortunately, those activities had sapped what remained of her energy. She supposed that was just as well since Christian had forbidden her under any circumstances to leave the chair he had scrounged from the chuck wagon. He was even making noises about taking her back to the ranch and leaving her there. She had no intention of going, of course, but there was no use in mentioning that to Christian, because she did not have the energy to argue with him about it quite yet. Instead, she simply sat in the chair, nursing a raging headache and wondering what her swollen face looked like.

"Won't you try to eat a little more, Miss Angelica?" Hank asked. She glanced up at where he hovered beside her like a concerned mother hen and shook her head.

"I'm not very hungry," she said, handing him the plate of beans she had barely touched. "I would like a refill on my coffee, though, if you don't mind," she added with a small smile.

He took her plate and her cup and hurried off to do her bidding. When he was gone, she turned her gaze to the men gathered for the noon meal around the campfire. On Christian's orders, everyone had taken a day off so they would not have to move the camp and disturb Angelica. The herd was grazing peacefully nearby once again, and the only evidence of the catastrophe of the night before was the ragged stretch of prairie that marked the path of the stampede.

Angelica watched for a long moment as Stumpy and Christian had a very animated conversation. Stumpy, having just ridden into camp, was quite disturbed about something, and whatever he was saying disturbed Christian, too. Angelica enjoyed the way the sunlight danced on the silver ornaments of Christian's vest. He had changed his soiled jeans for cleaner ones and had on a different shirt. Angelica had been very pleased to discover she was still wearing Christian's shirt when she awakened. In fact, she thought with a smile, she would probably continue to sleep in it until he was forced to ask for it back.

"Looks like we got some company," Miles said, rising from his place by the fire to better observe the approaching riders.

Angelica languidly turned in that direction and was startled to see Harlan Snyder and two other riders heading toward the camp. They were coming fast.

The other men put their plates aside and started to rise also, but Christian motioned them to stay where they were. Then he stepped around to the other side of the chuck wagon where he would be out of sight. He saw Angelica staring at him curiously and frowned in disapproval. "Go greet your guests," he suggested tersely.

Frowning back, Angelica pushed her reluctant body up out of the chair and began walking toward the edge of the camp. As she passed Miles, he asked, "What do you suppose they want?"

Angelica shrugged, a movement that caused an uncomfortable twinge in her shoulder, but she ignored it and concentrated on Harlan Snyder, who had left his horse a polite distance from the camp and was now hurrying toward her.

"My God, Angelica, what happened here?" he was saying, and then he looked directly at her for the first time. *"And what happened to your face?!"*

His usual smile was twisted into a look of genuine concern. Angelica was so busy with noting that fact, she failed to respond to his question.

"Darling, are you all right?" he asked anxiously, taking her by the shoulders.

Whether it was the "darling" or his hands hurting her shoulders that snapped her from her fog, she didn't bother to determine. "I'm fine," she assured him, shrugging neatly out of his grasp and rubbing her upper arms pointedly.

She tried to read the emotions flickering across his face and thought she detected guilt, although she knew she must be mistaken. Her present condition was one of the few local misfortunes for which Harlan Snyder need not feel guilty.

"You weren't . . . You didn't . . . You weren't caught in the stampede, were you?" he finally blurted.

"Yes, as a matter of fact, I was," she said, still watching him closely. The news seemed to shake him.

"Oh, my God," he said again, raising an unsteady hand to his head. "I had no idea you were even on the roundup until I went by the ranch this morning to see you. I never dreamed you'd be in the stampede. . . ." He seemed to catch himself and stopped abruptly.

"How did you know there'd been a stampede?" she asked, suddenly suspicious. How could he have known about it?

The question clearly made him uncomfortable. He glanced around uneasily, but he recovered quickly. "A blind man could see what happened here," he said quite reasonably, gesturing toward the broken landscape. "What I can't understand is how in heaven's name you got hurt."

Angelica didn't really feel like going into it, but she guessed she had no choice. Putting aside her groundless suspicions, she explained. "The cattle started running last night. They were headed right for the camp, so I jumped on a horse to ride to safety. Somehow, I ended up right in the middle of them, though, and my horse stumbled. . . ." She let her voice trail off so his imagination could fill in the rest.

His eyes widened in horror, and he reached for her again. "Angelica!" he cried in what might have passed for anguish. Angelica was too busy dodging his embrace to decide.

"Please, don't, Harlan," she pleaded, pushing him away. "I'm still a little sore from my fall."

"Oh, I'm sorry," he said, instantly contrite. "It's just . . . How did you survive? It must have been a miracle." To his credit, he really did look upset. Angelica began to wonder if he could possibly care for her as something other than owner of the Diamond R. The idea was intriguing, if a little revolting.

"I suppose you could call it a miracle," she allowed, hugging herself at the memory of that awful fall. "I've heard of it happening, though. Sometimes a running herd will part around an obstacle on the ground." Stumpy had told her that earlier when he had returned to camp and come to see how she was.

"Still, you came very close to . . ."

"Miss Ross, maybe you'd better sit down." Angelica looked up to see Miles standing beside her, looking concerned.

Snyder shot him a penetrating look, but quickly agreed that Angelica should not be standing around in the hot sun after her ordeal. Miles took her elbow and began to lead her back to her chair as Snyder trailed behind.

"Why don't you tell your men to come on in and get something to eat, Harlan," Angelica suggested as she took her seat again. "And you must be hungry, too."

"Well, yes, thank you," he said, as if such mundane things had hardly occurred to him under the circumstances. He motioned to the two men who had accompanied him to come into the camp, and they did so. Angelica did not recognize either of them, but she took note of their tied-down guns. She noticed that Miles did, also. Was Christian watching them, too?

"Perhaps you'll introduce me to your men," Angelica suggested.

"Only if you'll return the favor, my dear," he said, stretching his lips into that smile that made her skin crawl.

"Of course," she agreed, returning his smile, even though it made her cheek ache to be stretched like that.

Snyder told her the names of his two men, but neither of them meant a thing to Angelica. She nodded at the two men, who tipped their hats on their way to get filled plates from Hank. Then Snyder waited expectantly for her to return the courtesy.

"Harlan, I'd like you to meet Miles Blackmon," she said, watching Snyder's eyes narrow as he tried to place the name. "Some people call him Parson Black, but he doesn't like it much," she added, thoroughly enjoying the shock that flickered across Snyder's broad face.

Miles never batted an eye. His nod of acknowledgment was barely perceptible, and neither man offered to shake hands.

"I guess you already know Hank and Curly," Angelica continued blithely, even forgetting her headache in the novelty of seeing Harlan Snyder discomfited. "That gentleman by the fire is Stumpy Smith." Snyder's gaze reluctantly left Miles and traveled to Stumpy, who grinned impudently. Angelica knew Synder might not have recognized Stumpy's name, but his type was unmistakable. There was no kind of trouble Stumpy Smith hadn't handled in his long and checkered career.

"I have two other new men, but they're out holding the

cattle right now," Angelica continued, glancing surreptitously over toward the chuck wagon to see if Christian was prepared to make his appearance.

As if drawn by her eyes, he stepped out into the open, and once again she admired the way the sunlight glittered off his silver ornaments. He stood there for a heartbeat, his handsome face grim, his steady blue gaze riveted on Snyder.

"And, of course, my foreman, Kid Collins," Angelica concluded.

Snyder's gaze snapped toward Collins, and his surprise turned instantly to fury.

"You!" he bellowed.

As she watched Snyder's face grow purple with rage, Angelica realized that Christian had grossly understated his "run-in" with Snyder. The men were obviously blood enemies. Hate radiated from every pore in Harlan Snyder's large body, and menace echoed in every step Christian took to close the distance between them.

Gathering his composure with obvious difficulty, Snyder turned back to face Angelica. Looking up at him from her chair, she suddenly recognized the enormous physical threat he could be if all that fury were turned on her. Resisting the urge to cringe, she concentrated on keeping her expression innocent.

"Do you know who this man is?" Snyder demanded of her, making a deprecating gesture toward Christian. "Or this one? Or this one?" He indicated Miles and Stumpy. "Do you know the kind of men you've entrusted your cattle . . . and *yourself* to?"

She sensed Miles stiffening beside her and could only imagine how angry Christian would be at the implication.

"Harlan," she explained with elaborate patience, "someone has been killing people around here. Ordinary cowboys were afraid to work for me." She made a small, helpless gesture with her hands. "What else could I do?"

Snyder drew in a long breath as he scanned the trio of gunfighters once more. When his gaze returned to Angelica, he seemed to be calmer. "Perhaps we could discuss this privately," he suggested, leaning over conspiratorially.

She felt as much as heard Christian's growl of protest, but she never took her eyes from Snyder. "What is there to discuss?" she asked, wide-eyed.

Snyder's eyes cut briefly to where Christian was standing as he replied. "You were almost killed last night," he said, lowering his voice to a gentle croon. "Really, Angelica, a roundup is no place for a lady." He took in her jeans and work shirt with one disapproving look. "Let me take you back to the ranch, where you'll be safe."

Angelica frowned, mainly because she was afraid she might actually giggle in delight at the delicious opportunity Snyder had unintentionally provided her with. "I don't know," she said, pretending to consider his offer. "What do you think, Mr. Collins?" she asked, turning to where he loomed nearby. "You were insisting just a little while ago that I should go home to recover from my ordeal."

His tight-lipped glare turned even more murderous as he realized the trap she had laid for him. He wanted her to return to the ranch, but she would bet her life that he would never agree to let Snyder take her.

After a long moment during which he seemed to be gritting his teeth, Christian said, "I'm sure you'll do whatever you want to, Miss Ross."

"Absolutely right, Mr. Collins," she replied cheerfully. She turned back to Snyder. "Thank you for your concern, Harlan, but I'm afraid I must stay with my cattle."

"Angelica . . ." Snyder began in exasperation, but she silenced him with a wave of her hand.

"This is my property. I can't leave it to strangers to handle, now, can I?" she asked, knowing this was one point he could not argue, especially when he himself had just insinuated that her hired help could not be trusted.

Snyder was far from pleased, and she watched in fascination as he fought a small battle with himself for control of his temper. "I'm afraid I must insist that you come back with me," he tried.

Angelica smiled sweetly, in spite of the twinge to her injured cheek. "Harlan, may I remind you that you have no authority over me? You aren't my father or my husband or even my . . . betrothed." She lowered her lashes in maidenly shyness, grateful for the flirtation practice she had had the day before. Such an action was foreign enough to her under normal circumstances. Playing the coquette for Harlan Snyder was an absolute ordeal.

Snyder cleared his throat in reaction to her obvious hint, but he did not dare reply because of their attentive audience. "Well, then, I beg you to be more careful, my dear," he said somewhat awkwardly. "If anything should happen to you . . ."

"I promise I won't do anything so foolish as to fall in front of a stampede again," she said, batting her eyes. Considering that one of her eyes was blackened, she thought she must look ridiculous, but Snyder seemed quite affected. He even had to clear his throat again.

He straightened self-consciously and looked around at the men, who were still watching him. His gaze stopped on Christian for a long moment, and a silent message seemed to pass between them. Then he called his two men. "Let's go," he said. The pair swiftly scooped up the last of the beans on their plates and made for their horses.

Determinedly, Snyder turned back to Angelica. "Do you feel up to walking me to my horse?" he asked with his ingratiating smile.

She could feel Christian's disapproval like a palpable force. Some wicked impulse compelled her to say, "Certainly." With a smile, she rose from her chair and accepted Snyder's proffered arm.

Angelica did not dare look around. She was afraid if she caught Christian's eye, the murderous look in it would squelch any desire she had to torment him.

She and Snyder walked only a short distance, just until they were out of earshot of Angelica's men and had reached Snyder's men waiting with their horses. "Please, Angelica, won't you reconsider and let me take you back to the ranch? You look as if you'd been knocking at death's door. At the ranch, Maria would be there to take care of you, and . . ."

"Harlan!" she chastened him, not wanting to admit how tempting that sounded. She thought she might be willing to sell her soul just for the luxury of a tub bath and a feather bed, but she wasn't about to leave this roundup. "I told you, I must stay here with my cattle. You're a rancher, you can understand that."

Plainly, he did not want to. "Well, at least promise me one thing. Promise me that you'll stay away from that Collins character. He has a bad reputation with women."

This was news to Angelica. She only hoped her avid curiosity did not show on her face. "Oh? What do you mean by that?"

"Well," Snyder said, pretending reluctance to speak on the subject. "I don't want to frighten you, but he attacked a woman in town the other day."

Angelica could not help her gasp. At least it sounded genuine, although it reflected her surprise over such a whopper of a lie rather than shock at Christian's behavior.

It fooled Snyder. He nodded grimly. "It's true. The

woman works at the Dirty Dog Saloon, and he had gone with her to her house. Although I hate to brag, if I hadn't heard her screaming and burst in on them, heaven only knows what he might have done to her. As it was, she was badly injured."

Angelica felt the blood draining from her head, and she took an instinctive step back from Snyder, dropping his arm. Christian *had* been with a woman that night, she knew that for a fact. There was at least a kernel of truth to this story, but she wasn't certain she wanted to know what that kernel was. She did know she wanted to get away from Snyder as quickly as possible.

"Angelica, are you all right? I didn't mean to frighten you, only to warn you," Snyder said, reaching for her again.

She backed away another step. "I'm fine," she lied, managing a small smile. "I appreciate your concern, but don't worry about me."

"I'll be back out to see how you're doing tomorrow," he said, but Angelica was shaking her head.

"No, please, I'll be awfully busy, too busy for visitors," she said. "And I really don't like for you to see me like this," she added, indicating her work clothes.

"But you're lovely," he protested.

"Wait until the roundup is over," she said, ignoring his compliment. "Then I'll invite you over for supper so we can celebrate."

"Really, Angelica, I think it would be better . . ."

"No, Harlan, I don't want to see you again until this is all over," she insisted firmly.

"Well, all right," he agreed with obvious reluctance. "But if you need me, you know where I am."

"Yes, I do," she said, suddenly weary of this conversation and heartily sick of Harlan Snyder's company.

"Send Hank or Curly, someone you can trust," he

added.

"I will. Good-bye, Harlan," she said with finality.

Grudgingly, he bade her farewell and rode away. She waved perfunctorily before turning back to face her men. They were all watching attentively, but the only eyes she really saw were Christian's. They were like twin blue flames, and she could feel the heat of them from across the camp.

She started back toward her chair, but she was looking at Christian and not at where she was going. After only a few steps she stumbled over a rough place on the ground. She didn't fall or even come close to it, but Christian was at her side in an instant.

"Dammit, Angelica, you look like you're going to faint dead away," he said, scooping her up into his arms. "What in the hell did he say to you?"

Angelica gratefully settled against his shoulder, glad for the reassurance of his presence. "You know, for someone named Christian, your language leaves a lot to be desired," she remarked, studying the way his golden hair curled along the back of his neck beneath his hat.

His arms tightened warningly, but she only smiled. He started walking, heading toward her tent, his lips pressed tightly together as if he were fighting the urge to speak, but after several steps, he sighed in resignation. "Please, Miss Ross, ma'am, would you kindly tell me what that snake said to you?" he asked in a parody of courtesy.

"That's better," Angelica decided. Christian stooped to enter her tent and then let her feet swing to the ground.

He tried to step away, but she didn't remove her arms from around his neck. "He said," she began to explain, pulling his face close to hers, "that I should stay away from you because you had a bad reputation with women." His shock was almost comic but Angelica did not smile. "He said you'd attacked a woman in town, a woman who works in the saloon."

"That son of a . . ." the Kid began, but caught himself. There was no sense in denying it. If she didn't trust him, if she believed Snyder, all the protests in the world would not convince her. Instead, he said, "Did Snyder also tell you that he started that stampede?"

"What!" she cried, startled into dropping her arms from his neck.

Christian nodded grimly. "Stumpy found a fresh cougar skin off over where the stampede started. Somebody waved it at the herd and scared them into running."

"But we don't know it was Snyder," she argued.

Christian's eyes glinted like shards of blue ice. "You heard him say he didn't know you were on the roundup or that you'd be caught in the stampede, didn't you? You saw how upset he was. He realized he'd come awfully close to killing the golden goose."

Angelica gasped, but he didn't even pause.

"I can see you don't want to believe it. Maybe you're starting to like him. Maybe all this courting business isn't really an act anymore," he accused.

"Don't be ridiculous!" she cried in outrage.

"Just don't carry this game with Snyder too far, Angelica, not unless you want *both* your eyes blackened," he warned.

Angelica gasped again, suddenly realizing he had not denied Snyder's charge that he had attacked that woman in town. She very much wanted to hear him deny it. "And just who's going to blacken them?" she demanded. "You or Snyder?"

She instantly regretted her sarcasm. His face twisted with a fury so frightening she actually cringed. "Christian, I didn't mean . . ." she tried, but he wasn't listening. The eyes that had been so cold only seconds ago now flared dangerously, and his hands curled into fists as if he really might do her bodily harm.

"Wait and see, Angelica," he said, and then he was gone.

Chapter Nine

Angelica wasn't about to let the argument end there. She stalked after Christian, but when she got inside, she saw everyone in the camp alerted to a completely new set of visitors.

"Damn gut-eaters," Stumpy muttered, spitting a wad of tobacco juice to emphasize his disgust.

"It's Black Bear," Angelica said, recognizing the ragtag band of Comanches instantly. They were even more disreputable-looking than they had been several weeks earlier when they had brought Christian to her doorstep. The clothes some of the men wore were little more than rags.

Christian stood a few feet away, his back to her. His shoulders were still stiff with anger, but his attention was centered completely on the Comanches.

"Those are the Indians who found you and brought you to the ranch," she told him, coming up beside him.

Black Bear and his braves were approaching the camp cautiously. Apparently, they were not certain of their welcome. To reassure them, Angelica waved her arm and started forward to greet them.

An iron hand hauled her back. "What do you think you're doing?" Christian demanded.

"I was going to welcome my friends," she informed him, prying his fingers from her arm in annoyance.

"You know them critters?" Stumpy asked. He had come up on her other side.

"Yes, I've known them for a long time," she explained, still glaring up at Christian. "They are the ones who rescued Chr—Mr. Collins and brought him to my ranch."

"Well, then, I reckon we owe 'em a little hospitality," Stumpy allowed grudgingly.

"Exactly what I thought," Angelica replied, giving Christian a haughty look. She'd only taken one more step when Christian's hand pulled her up short again.

"I'll handle this," he said.

"I'm still the boss around here!" she reminded him and instantly regretted it. The anger he had displayed in her tent flared again. She felt almost scorched by the heat.

"But you are also a woman," he said through gritted teeth. "I know Comanche. If we let a woman do the talking for us, they'll think we're a bunch of milksops, and they'll steal us blind. Now stay put and keep your mouth shut."

Angelica's mouth was wide open in outrage, but she did stay put as he strode out to meet the band of Indians.

"What makes him think he knows so much about Comanche?" she grumbled aloud, irritated because she knew he was right.

" 'Cause we used to live with 'em some, off and on," Stumpy replied blandly.

Angelica's mouth dropped open again, but before she could inquire further into the matter, she heard Christian addressing Black Bear. In the Comanche language.

Most Comanche spoke Spanish, it being the trade language of the Plains, and from having overheard Christian's conversations with Maria, Angelica knew he spoke it well. To have learned the Comanche language, however, meant he must have spent considerable time with the Indians, something very few white men had done.

She listened in fascination to Christian's deep voice rumbling over the guttural sounds. He spoke formally and at length, making her realize he knew much more about the tribe than simply their language. If there was one thing Indians liked to do, it was talk, and they respected a man who knew how to observe the amenities. Black Bear and his cohorts sat completely still and expressionless in their makeshift saddles, listening appreciatively to Christian's welcoming speech.

When he had finished, Black Bear spoke at length, making gestures with his hands. When he paused, Christian asked him a question that required another lengthy answer. Christian was nodding his understanding. Something seemed to be settled between them. Then Black Bear looked over the camp, obviously sizing up the other men, who were still waiting tensely. His gaze skimmed over Angelica and then came back for a second, disbelieving look. His weathered face broke into a slow grin.

He said something that brought a burst of raucous laughter from his band and caused Christian to glance at her over his shoulder. Instinctively, she knew she was the butt of some suggestive joke and felt her face heating in response. Even Stumpy was chuckling.

"What did he say?" she hissed at Stumpy, but he was straining to hear Christian's reply.

Whatever Christian said brought down the house. The Indians cackled like geese, leaning over their horses in convulsions, and Stumpy choked on his tobacco.

"Serves you right," she whispered furiously at the old man as she thumped him on the back. "Now tell me what they said."

But Stumpy was shaking his head as he fought to regain his breath. "Not me," he told her with a grin. "I'm a gentleman."

Angelica seethed with frustration and fury. The Indians were still snickering and making remarks to each other as they pointed to her and Christian. How dare he make sport of her like that? She was his employer!

No sooner had the thought crossed her mind than Christian asked Black Bear a question that sobered the group instantly. A brief exchange followed, with Christian pointing to where the herd was being held. At last Black Bear nodded, and the small band turned their ponies in that direction. Christian headed toward the makeshift horse corral.

Livid now, Angelica hurried after him. She had to almost run to catch up, an action that rudely reminded her how stiff she still was from her encounter with the stampede. The reminder did not improve her mood.

"What were you saying to those Indians?" she demanded, grabbing his arm to stop him but not succeeding as well as he had in stopping her. He simply dragged her a few steps before halting of his own accord.

"Angelica," he said impatiently. "I have to go with Black Bear."

"Not until you tell me what you said," she informed him, clinging resolutely to his arm, even though she knew he could probably shake her off like a gnat if he chose to.

He sighed in irritation. "I told him who I was and thanked them for saving my life. I told him we'd be brothers forever, and I'd help him someday if I could." He made a frustrated gesture with his hand. "All that bull that Indians like to hear. Nothing important."

"What were they laughing about?" She tightened her grip, sensing that he would not want to answer.

The Kid looked down at the determined angle of her chin and realized she wouldn't rest until she knew. She wouldn't like it. She might even hate him for talking about her that way, but he knew that sooner or later, she was going to hate him anyway. He may as well get it over with.

"Black Bear said he could see from your face that I had a little trouble getting you to . . ." He searched frantically for an acceptable word. "To go to bed with me."

Her lovely green eyes widened and the color in her cheeks deepened. He could see her bracing herself for the rest of it. "And you said?"

He took a deep breath, hating himself, but reminding himself this was for the best. "I said it was just the opposite, that you were after me all the time, and sometimes I had to beat you to get you to leave me alone."

There, now she would despise him. He tried to pull free of her, to get away so he would no longer have to see the pain and humiliation in her eyes, but she clung more tightly.

"Is that the kind of bull the Indians like to hear, too?" she challenged, her expression defiant. Only her eyes betrayed her hurt.

"Yes, it is," he replied fiercely.

"And you know because you used to live with them," she said.

He blinked in surprise. How could she have known? This was it, the moment he had been dreading, the final blow that would kill her budding love. In a desperate effort to hide his pain, he pulled his lips back in the parody of a grin. "That's right. I used to live with them. We used to go from camp to camp, selling them guns and ammunition so they could kill innocent settlers. My father was a Comanchero."

Angelica gasped in horror. *A Comanchero!* The men who traded with the Comanches, taking cattle the Indians had stolen from white settlers in exchange for guns with which the Indians wreaked more havoc, were the most hated men on the plains. Most of them were Mexican, though, and the long-standing hatred of the Mexicans for the Texans made their treachery understandable. Only a few of the Comancheros were white men, men so low that they would turn against their own people. "Oh, Christian," she whispered. His own father! How had he borne the shame?

Her hands relaxed their grip, and the Kid pulled free at last. Her eyes were awful now, betraying every emotion churning within her. Not wanting to see her contempt, he turned and started for the corral again.

Angelica was still so stunned by his revelation that it took her a second to realize his intent. "Where are you going?" she called, running after him again.

He did not stop. "I'm going with Black Bear over to the herd to help him cut out a couple steers."

This was the last straw. "You're going to give away *my* cattle? Without even asking me?"

He stopped so abruptly that Angelica almost careened into him. His face was hard, his eyes cold. "I *am* the foreman of this crew," he reminded her. "If I don't give them some cattle, they'll steal some anyway, and if they're mad, they'll probably take the horses, too. They've got their families with them and they're starving because there aren't any buffalo left for them to hunt. Now, *Miss Ross,* do I have your permission to give them some cattle?"

"Of course," she snapped, furious that he had made her feel foolish one more. This time she let him walk away, closing her eyes so she would not have to watch him go. So many emotions churned within her that she could hardly even sort them out. Shock and horror at the kind of childhood Christian must have had mingled with fury and outrage over the way he had made sport of her. Mixed in were her feelings of confusion and anger over the knowledge that Snyder might have been responsible for the stampede, and on top of all that was Christian's cavalier attitude toward giving away her cattle. Her pride would not permit her to admit that he was right about that, no matter what her reason might dictate.

She was vaguely aware of Christian riding away a few minutes later, but still she stood where she was in a state of dazed distraction.

"Miss Ross? Are you all right?" Stumpy asked.

She was a little startled to see him. She had not heard him approach. "Yes," she said in a voice that belied her assertion.

"Come on, I'll walk you back to your tent. Maybe you oughta lay down for a while." Obediently, she fell into step beside him, aware that he was watching her closely. She looked down into his eyes, surprised to see them serious for once. Something he had said echoed in her mind, something about how he had been with Christian when he lived with the Comanches.

"Were you a Comanchero, too?" she asked, knowing few men would admit to such a thing but willing to take the risk of rebuff.

His beard quivered, telling her he was mulling over his reply. "Yes, ma'am, I was, though I hope you won't hold that against me," he said. "I could tell you that I was only a young pup and I fell in with bad companions, but that wouldn't quite be true. The truth is I was old enough to know better, though it's also true Sam Collins was about the worst companion anybody could find."

"Sam? Christian's father?" she guessed. He nodded. "But why would he take a child along with him? I mean, Christian couldn't have been more than a boy."

"He was when he started going along," Stumpy confirmed. "See, his ma died when he was still little, and his sister—Rose, you know?" She nodded. "Rose got married young. Wanted to get away from her pa, I reckon. Anyway, there was nobody left to watch after the boy, so Sam took him along with us."

"How awful," she murmured, imagining the terrible shame and danger of such a life, but Stumpy was shaking his head.

"Not for a kid. He had the time of his life. There ain't a much better life in this world than the kind a Comanche boy has, or *had,* back in the old days. He'd learn to ride and shoot and steal and fight, and he was completely free. The Comanche are great believers in freedom. They don't even have chiefs. Did you know that?"

She did, but she did not interrupt.

"A Comanche brave is his own master. He comes and goes as he pleases. He don't even have to fight in a war if he don't feel like it. In them days, that's the way we lived, too, just like Comanches." Stumpy shook his head over his memories. "I reckon that part of it kind of appealed to me, too, even though I wasn't a kid at the time."

They had reached Angelica's tent, and they stopped. Stumpy gazed out over the prairie to where the Indians were circling the herd. "At least, that's the way it used to be. Now, of course, they're all penned up on the reservation. It must be hell for those poor devils."

Angelica gazed across the prairie, too, easily picking out the rider wearing the silver conchas on his vest. Pain throbbed in her heart at the sight of him. Hell, as she well knew, could be anyplace for anyone.

When the weary roundup crew rode into the ranch yard a week later, Robbie was there to meet them. The boy was beside himself with excitement. He even forgot his dignity and hugged Angelica in his enthusiasm.

"I missed you, sweetheart," she told him quite sincerely.

"What happened to your eye?" he demanded, obviously fascinated. "It's green!"

Her hand came up self-consciously to cover the disfigurement. The swelling had gone down considerably in the past few days, but she knew it was still horribly discolored. Other places on her body certainly were. "My eyes have always been green," she maintained with a half-hearted grin.

"But now the skin's green, too," he informed her smugly. "Hey, were you in a fight?" He found the idea delightfully intriguing, but Angelica squelched it immediately.

"Of course I wasn't in a fight," she said, but before she could explain further, Miles interrupted.

"Your sister tried to stop a stampede single-handed," he reported, perfectly deadpan.

"Wow! A stampede! How did it start? What happened? Tell me!" he demanded, grabbing Miles by the arm so he could not escape.

"Yes," Maria agreed from behind Angelica. "I would like to hear this story, too."

Angelica whirled to face her foster mother's patent displeasure and earned a shocked gasp. *"Dios!* Your face! My poor little *chata,* are you hurt?" Maria grabbed Angelica's hands and examined her from head to toe as if she could see any other injuries right through Angelica's dusty range clothes.

"No, I'm fine, really," Angelica assured her. "I just had a fall and got a little bruised up, that's all."

"You fell in a stampede?" Maria asked, horrified.

"Well, yes," Angelica admitted reluctantly.

Maria murmured a fervent expletive, and turned her furious gaze on Christian, who was unsaddling his horse nearby and listening to the exchange grimly. "How could you let this happen?" she cried. "I trusted you to take care of her."

His face was an expressionless mask, but his eyes burned fiercely at the rebuke.

"It wasn't his fault, Mama," Angelica hastily explained so he would not be obliged to. "As usual, I was in the wrong place at the wrong time."

Maria dragged her gaze back to the girl. Once more she looked Angelica over, and this time her lip curled in disgust. "You, come inside with me," she commanded. "You need a bath and a dress. You have scandalized this family's name long enough." Brooking no argument, she took Angelica by the arm and led her into the house.

In point of fact, Angelica had no will to resist. She wanted—and needed—a bath in the worst way, and she was more than tired of the so-called freedom of wearing men's pants. With a great sense of relief, she put herself in Maria's capable hands.

In a surprisingly short time, Angelica was ensconced in her bedroom and luxuriating in a scented bath. While she soaked, Maria collected her discarded clothes from the bedroom floor, clucking in disapproval as she did so. *"Madre de Dios, Angelita,"* you are a disgrace to your poor mother's name, going out on the range and working like a common cowhand."

Angelica shot Maria a black look. "How do you know my mother wouldn't have done the same thing if she'd been in my place?" she demanded.

Maria made a rude noise. "Because no woman in her right mind would do what you have done. I cannot believe you thought you could win a man's heart by putting on pants and riding around the countryside, showing yourself like a *puta,* and then almost getting yourself killed." She muttered another expletive.

"But Mama, he does love me," Angelica informed her. "Regardless of what else happened, he did admit that he cares for me, and you should have seen how jealous he was when Harlan Snyder showed up. OH!" she said, sitting up quickly and sloshing water on the floor as she suddenly remembered another fact that might interest Maria. "And Snyder was the one who started the stampede in the first place."

Maria frowned. "You are sure of that?"

"Not exactly," she admitted, sliding back down into the water again, "although Christian is positive of it. There wasn't any evidence to link him with it, but we know for certain that *someone* started the stampede on purpose. Who else could it have been?"

Maria considered this information for a moment. "Tell me everything that happened," she instructed at last, laying aside the dirty clothes and taking a seat on the edge of Angelica's bed. "Start with the beginning."

The story was easy enough to tell at first. Maria smiled knowingly when Angelica described the way Christian had paired her with every one of the men except himself. She looked outraged when Angelica told how he had come upon her while she was bathing, but Angelica hastily assured her nothing had happened except that they'd quarreled again. The telling became more difficult when she got to the night of the stampede. That awful moment when she had flown from Midnight's back still haunted her dreams, and she shivered as she recounted it. Maria crossed herself and whispered a fervent prayer of thanks that her beloved child had escaped death.

"When I woke up, everything was quiet, and I realized I'd somehow survived. I wanted to go back to camp, but Midnight was gone, and I when I tried to getup, everything starting whirling around, so I just stayed put. I figured sooner or later someone would come looking for me, and when I woke up again, Christian was there. Oh Mama, he was frantic until he realized I was all right. Then he started kissing me, and that's when he told me he loved me."

Angelica hoped Maria would attribute her heightened color to embarrassment over making such an intimate revelation, or at least to the heat of the bath. She also hoped Maria would not inquire too closely into what happened next. Making a little show out of finding the bar of soap that had slipped from her grasp, Angelica lowered her eyes so Maria would not read any guilt in them.

"Everything seemed to be just fine between us," she continued, still not looking up, "but then we got back to camp, and who shows up but Harlan Snyder. By then, Christian had discovered that someone had started the stampede on purpose, so he wasn't too happy to see Snyder. Not only that, but apparently they got into some sort of a fight that day Christian went to town, and they can't stand the sight of each other. I don't know all the details, but it involved a girl who works in the saloon. . . ."

Angelica let her voice trail off as she once again experienced the pain of betrayal. Finally, she lifted her head again and met Maria's concerned gaze. "Anyway, they hate each other. Harlan warned me to be careful because Christian had a bad reputation with women, and when I told Christian that, he didn't even bother to deny it!"

Maria nodded sagely. "He made you very angry," she guessed.

"Of course I was angry! He doesn't think I believe those lies, does he?"

"Maybe he is testing you, to see how much *you* care for *him,*" Maria suggested.

Angelica sighed. "I think he knows how much I care for him. If he doesn't, he should."

Maria's face twisted into a suspicious scowl. "Why should he know?"

"I . . . because I told him," Angelica improvised, loath to admit how enthusiastically she had demonstrated her feelings to Christian on two occasions of which Maria was thus far ignorant. "And no sooner did Snyder leave than Black Bear and his band showed up," she went on, intent on distracting Maria.

"Black Bear!"

"Yes, and you should have heard the scandalous things Christian said about me!"

Maria insisted on hearing every detail, and by the time Angelica had repeated the ribald jests, she was furious once again. Maria's snickering did not help soothe her, either.

"Really, Mama, I fail to see any humor in all of this. I'm his employer, and he humiliated me in front of a bunch of Comanche Indians," Angelica pointed out indignantly.

Maria made a valiant effort to regain her composure. "I am sorry, *Angelita,* but you must admit, it is a funny story."

"I don't have to admit any such thing," Angelica insisted.

"Now let me guess, after this, you quarreled again, no?" Maria said, schooling her expression to innocence.

Angelica began to turn the bar of soap vigorously in her hands, working up a prodigious pile of lather. She refused to meet Maria's eye. "Yes," she snapped. "And we haven't spoken a civil word to each other since."

Maria made a thoughtful noise. "All this happened the day Mr. Snyder came to the house looking for you? One week ago?"

Angelica nodded stiffly, concentrating her attention on watching the billowing lather slide over her fingers and plop into the bathwater.

"That is a long time to be angry over such a little thing," Maria remarked after a long minute of silence.

Angelica smacked the soap into the water. "That's just it," she said in exasperation. "I'm not angry anymore, but he's like a stone wall. I can't seem to get through to him. Even when I try to make up, he just stares at me with those eyes of his and doesn't say a word until I'm so embarrassed I can't stand it anymore and give up."

Maria frowned. "What did you say to him when you were angry?"

"I only reminded him that it's my ranch after all, and he's just the hired . . ." The words died on her lips as she realized the impact such a statement would have on a man as proud as Christian Collins. It had seemed the appropriate thing to say at the time to a foreman who she felt was overstepping his authority. Unfortunately, Christian was much more to her than a hired hand. "I didn't mean it like that," she insisted, seeing Maria's disapproval. "Surely, he's not that sensitive! He must have known I was only . . ."

But Maria was shaking her head. "Yes, he *can* be that sensitive," she maintained. "Many things in this world are not fair. Men are strong and women are not, at least on the outside, and that is not fair, but God has made up for that. On the inside, women are strong and men are weak. A woman can bear the hardships of this world. She can hear the ugly words and forget them. She can see the betrayal and forgive it.

"But men are not like that. They are like children. When their feelings are hurt, it leaves a scar that is very slow to heal. And when someone they love hurts them, they are afraid to trust again. Perhaps you have hurt Mr.

Collins far more than you know."

Angelica's mind was racing, replaying the argument she had had with Christian. She could not even remember exactly what she had said, but his accusations echoed in her ears. He had asked if she was still only pretending to let Snyder court her. Could he really believe she would welcome the attentions of a man like that? And why shouldn't he? a voice inside her head replied, especially when she had questioned his behavior with the girl in town. Had she destroyed his trust?

"Oh, Mama," she wailed. "What have I done?"

Maria rose from her place on the bed and came to stand beside Angelica's tub. "Nothing that can't be mended, if he really does love you," she assured the girl. "And if you really love him."

Angelica's chin lifted in determination. "I do, Mama. I really do."

"Why didn't you just kill Snyder?" Robbie wanted to know when he'd heard the story of the stampede from Miles and the Kid.

"You don't just go around shooting people because you feel like it, Squirt," the Kid told him solemnly. He and Miles were unpacking their war bags in the bunkhouse. Robbie was perched on a nearby bunk.

"But Snyder deserves it," the boy insisted. "If you knew he was the one who started the stampede and almost got Angel killed . . ."

"That's just it," the Kid interrupted. "We don't know it for sure. In fact, we don't have any proof that Snyder is responsible for any of the trouble."

Robbie snorted in disgust. "I didn't think Kid Collins would need *proof.* If *I* was a gunfighter, I'd just pull out my gun and *pow,*" he said, drawing a bead on an invisible adversary with his index finger and blowing him away with an imaginary blast.

The Kid frowned, deeply disturbed. Obviously, the boy had a warped view of the way justice, even six-gun justice, was dispensed. "If I start shooting people just because I don't happen to like them, I'm no better than the Snyders of this world, Robbie," he explained, understanding only too well how easy it would be to fall into that trap. Snyder certainly needed killing, even if he *wasn't* the one who had murdered Rose and Pete. "If a man chooses to be on the side of right, then he has to follow the rules, or at least most of them."

"But you're going to get Snyder, aren't you?" the boy pressed. "That's what Angel hired you to do."

"Your sister hired me to get her cattle to market, and that's what I'm going to do," the Kid corrected patiently.

Robbie's freckled face squinched into a scowl, but after only a moment's thought, he brightened again. "Oh, I understand!" he announced. "You're just trying not to scare me! Angel does that all the time. Sometimes she forgets that I'm almost grown up, and she treats me like a baby. But you don't have to worry about me. I can take it." He grinned conspiratorially.

"Wait a minute, Squirt," the Kid began, but Miles interrupted.

"Hey, Robbie, weren't you going to help Curly with the horses?" he asked.

"Oh, yeah," the boy replied, scrambling down from the bunk. In another second, he was outside, racing for the corrals.

The Kid gave Miles a questioning look.

Miles shrugged. "There's no use trying to convince him you're not the man he thinks you are. He's got a bad case of hero worship."

"Yeah, but the hero he's worshipping doesn't exist,"

the Kid protested.

"He's going to have to find that out for himself. About all you can do is *show* him the kind of man you are. Telling him won't help at all. He's heard too many well-meaning lies."

The Kid gave a disgusted sigh, thinking how ironic it was that he was trying to convince Robbie he was good at the same time he was trying to convince Angelica he was wicked. His mother would have told him there was a moral lesson in all of this, and he was sure there was. It probably had something to do with not getting involved in other people's lives.

The mood at supper that night was rather subdued. Ever since the stampede, the men had been wary, expecting trouble at any moment, but nothing had happened. The Kid attributed the lack of trouble to the fact that Snyder knew Angelica was with them. Soon, however, they would begin the long drive north to the Indian Territory without her. They would be sitting ducks for any mischief Snyder might decide to foster.

The Kid tried to concentrate on his plans for the drive so he would not think about how delectable Angelica looked. It had been a shock to see her wearing a skirt again. He would have thought that having to look at her long, shapely legs and her round little bottom outlined in Levis every day for two weeks was the worst torture a man could endure. He had simply forgotten how sweetly feminine she was in a dress.

The green fabric matched her eyes, eyes that seemed to sparkle from some inner flame. Even her hair glowed, as if the fiery tresses really gave off heat. Only her sun-burnished cheeks and the fading bruises around her eye gave any hint of the rough life she had been living for the past fourteen days. Once again she was the lovely angel of his dreams. He swallowed down hard on the surge of desire that thought inspired.

"How soon we gonna leave?" Stumpy asked. Everyone had finished eating, the Kid noticed, but they were still sitting around as if they were waiting for a big announcement. He supposed they all wanted to know the same thing Stumpy did.

"I figured we'd go the day after tomorrow. That'll give us time to get clothes washed and lay in some supplies for the trip," he said, letting his gaze sweep over the group assembled around the table. Ed Harley and Dave Sanders were holding the cattle near the ranch, but everyone else was here.

They all seemed to be in agreement with the plan, but when he finally allowed himself to look directly at Angelica, he saw the sparkle had died in her eyes.

"Do you have to leave that soon?" she asked, obviously distressed.

"Yes," he said, knowing that if her distress was over the thought of being separated from him, he had all the more reason to get away as quickly as possible. "The sooner we get the cattle delivered, the better. There's no reason to sit around here, waiting for Snyder to think up more trouble."

Feeling somewhat chastened, Angelica nodded and dropped her eyes, hoping he could not read her pain on her face. In spite of their tender lovemaking, in spite of his avowal, she was beginning to have doubts once again. She kept remembering what Maria had told her about men being so sensitive, and again she remembered how furious he had been with her. Ever since that day, his blue eyes had been as blank and as expressionless as a pane of glass whenever he looked at her. At this point, she would even have welcomed his hatred, since that would have indicated he had some sort of feelings for her, but now she saw only indifference.

"Is there someplace in town where you could stay while we're gone?" he asked, interrupting her musing.

Somewhat surprised at the question, she glanced at Maria, who shrugged to indicate she was as puzzled by the question as Angelica was. "Why should we stay in town?" she asked.

The Kid drew in a deep breath, reminding himself to maintain his professionalism and not to betray any emotions. "Because we'll be needing every man for the drive, and we can't leave anyone here to protect you," he said, pleased to note that his voice sounded calmly reasonable.

Angelica frowned. "You don't think that Snyder would attack the ranch, do you?" she asked. "Or that he'd want to hurt me or Robbie or Maria?"

"No, I don't think he'd attack the ranch, or that he'd hurt Robbie or Maria," he said, pointedly not mentioning Angelica.

It took her only seconds to interpret his meaning. "You can't think that he'd . . ." she began, catching herself when she recalled that they had a very attentive audience.

"Yes, I can think that he'd . . ." he said sarcastically, "especially if he still believes you want to marry him."

"Mr. Collins, I think we should continue this discussion in private," Angelica said stiffly, feeling her face flame at the implication.

But, of course, a private discussion with Angelica was what he wanted to avoid at all costs, even if that meant he had to embarrass her in front of the other men. "There's nothing to discuss. It isn't safe for you to stay here without protection. So, is there someplace in town where you can stay?" He addressed this last to Maria, having decided she was the more likely person to give him a straight answer.

"Yes," Maria said, refusing to acknowledge Angelica's

outrage at being dismissed. "Mrs. Marsden owns a big house in town, and she sometimes takes in boarders. I am sure she will be glad to have us."

"Now wait just a minute," Angelica tried, but the Kid was having none of it.

"Good. Miles and I will take you all into town tomorrow and get you settled," he said.

"Wow!" Robbie said before Angelica could raise another objection. "You mean we get to stay in town the whole time you're gone?"

"That's right, Squirt," the Kid assured him, ignoring the fact that Angelica was giving him a look that could have raised blisters on a rock. "And I'm counting on you to look after your sister and make sure she doesn't get into any trouble."

Robbie grinned beatifically at Angelica's outraged gasp. "You can count on me," he assured his idol. "I'll get me a gun, and if Snyder comes around I'll fill him full of lead. . . ."

"Robbie!"

Angelica and Christian reprimanded him in unison, shocking him into bewildered silence. Her eyes met Christian's across the length of the table, and for that one second, Angelica thought she caught a glimpse of the warmth she had believed permanently extinguished. She was so startled, she forgot for a moment what had prompted it.

But the Kid wasn't so hampered. "No, you are not going to get a gun, and you are not going to shoot anyone," he informed Robbie so sternly that the boy flushed.

"Y—yes, sir," he mumbled, doubly humiliated because the reprimand came from Kid Collins.

"Don't worry, Robbie," Miles said in at attempt to smooth things over. "You won't need a gun to keep Snyder in line. All you have to do is be there, and he won't dare do anything to Angelica."

Robbie looked up at Miles suspiciously, but Miles's sober expression quickly convinced him that Miles was sincere. "Do you really thing so?" he asked eagerly.

"Of course I do," Miles assured him.

"And I do, too," the Kid hastened to add. "I know I can count on you, or I wouldn't have given you this job."

Slightly mollified, Robbie accepted his charge with good grace, flashing Angelica a superior look, which she did not notice. She was still staring at Christian, trying to find the hidden meaning in what had just happened.

The Kid rose from the table, signaling to everyone that the discussion was over. Maria told the men to bring her their soiled clothes, and she would wash them in the morning. With that settled, they quickly left to take advantage of the offer, with Robbie following closely behind. In a matter of minutes, Maria and Angelica were alone in the room.

"He sures takes a lot upon himself, doesn't he?" Angelica remarked, not certain whether she should be furious or happy over this latest turn of events. If Christian had been offended by her reminders that she was still his boss, he certainly wasn't letting it affect his behavior. On the other hand, she couldn't like the high-handed way he ordered her around.

Maria grinned knowingly. "He will be a good husband to you, Angelica. He does not bend to your will." Before Angelica could find her tongue, she added, "And he will be a good influence on Robbie. The boy needs a man to guide him."

Angelica had no argument with that statement, but she didn't think she needed a man to guide *her* quite so stringently. "I don't see why we have to leave the ranch.

It might not be a good idea. Snyder could send his men over to burn down the house, for heaven's sake!" she contended.

Maria gave her a skeptical look. "Not if you make him think you are still interested in him. He will want this house for himself. He will dream of carrying his new bride into the master bedroom and . . ."

"Mama!" Angelica cried, completely revolted. She shuddered at the picture Maria had painted.

Maria's eyebrows rose. "If you think that will be so awful, you should be glad your man has thought to send you to town."

"My *man?*"

Maria ignored the outburst. "Snyder may decide he can't wait until the wedding. If you are here with only me and Robbie to protect you, he might force you to . . ."

"Stop!" Angelica begged, shuddering again. "All right, all right, I'll admit he was right if you'll stop talking about Snyder. Just the thought of him touching me . . ." Angelica swallowed hard, feeling as if her dinner might be trying to come back up.

Maria nodded her approval, and then she grinned slyly. "Now, if you want to get back at Mr. Collins, all you have to do is follow his orders meekly, and do not complain about anything he wants you to do to protect yourself. That will make him worry about what you are up to."

Angelica smiled in spite of herself. It was, she had to admit, a very good idea.

"I didn't know who he was! I swear! He never told me his name or anything," Sunny insisted, cowering on her bed.

Snyder glared down at her, curling his hands into fists as if he would like to do more than just slap her a few times, but he managed to restrain himself. There was little point in beating her when he was already convinced she was telling the truth. He turned to Jake Evans, who was standing by the door and watching the proceedings with little interest.

"We should've known he was somebody," Snyder said. "Espccially after the way he buffaloed Kennedy." The memory of having one of his best men stuffed, unconscious, into a rain barrel still rankled. The poor fellow had been so humiliated, he'd left town immediately and hadn't been seen since.

"Maybe," Jake allowed, "but did you ever know one of them hotshot gunslingers to keep it a secret? Besides, he disappeared. We figured he was long gone."

Snyder nodded, retaining the hold on his temper with difficulty. He had spent the last week tracking down information on the men who were working for Angelica. He had already known a little about Collins and Parson Black, and what he had subsequently learned had borne out those rumors. It would have been difficult for Angelica to find two tougher hombres, but she had come close in Stumpy Smith. The man had most recently been a buffalo hunter, but before that his cxpcrience involved selling guns to the Indians and other unsavory activities.

What Snyder could not figure out was how a sweet, innocent girl like Angelica Ross had happened across a gang like that. It was something he intended to question her about at the first opportunity.

Not that it really mattered, of course. He fully intended to convince her to fire the lot of them as soon as the roundup was over. His men could take over their duties, even if Angelica continued to play coy about setting a wedding date. In any case, Snyder did not intend to let her play coy for long, and if she tried, he would simply take her to bed, with or without her consent. After that, a lady like Angelica would feel she *must* marry him.

He glanced down at Sunny, who was still cowering on the bed. "Get up and get back to work," he told her gruffly, disgusted by the way she cringed. Angelica Ross would never cower. No, she would fight and hiss and scratch and bite. The thought excited him so much that he almost called Sunny back, but she was already outside, running toward the back door of the saloon in her hurry to escape.

He swore softly. "Let's go to the ranch," he said. "I want to be there when the boys get back with their report." He had assigned two men to the task of watching Angelica's roundup so he would know the minute she returned home. He would give her twenty-four hours to contact him. If she failed to do so, he would simply appear on her doorstep, ready to take her in hand. She would require quite a bit of handling, he was sure, but the prospect was not at all daunting.

And if Collins or any of the rest of them gave him trouble, he would be ready. "When did Rivers say he'd be here?"

"He didn't say, but he was going to leave Dodge right away. I expect he'll show up here any time now," Jake reported blandly.

"Good," Snyder said, rubbing his well-manicured hands in anticipation. Tom Rivers was rapidly gaining a reputation as one of the fastest guns in the West. If anyone would be a match for Kid Collins and his crew, Rivers was the man. He had certainly jumped at the opportunity to prove he was.

Sunny paused inside the back entrance to the saloon to catch her breath. She could hear Snyder and Evans talking as they left her house, and she waited tensely until she was certain they were well and truly gone. Absently, she rubbed the cheek that was still stinging from where Snyder had slapped her. He was certainly upset with her. Luckily, he believed her or she knew she would not have gotten off so easily.

When he had come into the saloon a few minutes earlier and insisted that she go outside with him, she had been certain he was going to hurt her badly. Even Otis had been reluctant to let her go, especially when Snyder refused to pay, declaring that he only wanted to talk to her for a minute.

Sunny had been dreading this confrontation ever since she learned the identity of the handsome stranger who had rescued her. The rumor had passed through Snyder's crew like lightning and been carried to town only slightly less quickly. Sunny had been praying that Collins would return to town to check on her as he had promised before Snyder got around to confronting her. Even Snyder wouldn't dare bother her if he knew she was Kid Collins's girl.

Now it was too late for that, and of course, she wasn't Collins's girl, at least not yet. But she would be, just as soon as Collins showed up again. She would see to it, and then Harlan Snyder would never hurt her again.

The afternoon shadows were growing long when the Diamond R group rode into town the next day. Angelica was driving the spring wagon, and Maria rode beside her on the seat. In the back was all their luggage. Robbie, taking his role as Angelica's protector very seriously, escorted them on his pony, as did Miles and Christian.

From time to time on the long trip out from the ranch, Angelica would glance over at where Christian rode nearby and catch him giving her a puzzled look. She would simply smile sweetly and return her attention to her driving. Maria had been right. Angelica's docility was driving him crazy.

Angelica pulled the wagon up outside the Mercantile and waited patiently for Christian to dismount and tie his horse so he could come around and help her down. Anticipation tingled along her nerve endings, but she schooled her expression to indifference as he came up beside the wagon and reached for her.

His hands were strong at her waist, but he refused to meet her gaze when her face passed only inches from his. The moment her feet touched the ground, he released her, pulling away as if touching her had burned him.

She let her hands linger just an instant on his shoulders, but he stiffened beneath her fingers, so she let him go. As irritated as his resistance made her, she reminded herself that he wouldn't be fighting so hard if he weren't still strongly attracted to her. Hadn't he chosen to sleep out in the bunkhouse last night with the other men instead of taking his customary room in the house? Obviously, he did not even trust himself under the same roof with her.

The thought made her smile as she turned and started up the steps to the raised sidewalk in front of the store.

"Angelica!" Kate Marsden hurried out from behind the counter to embrace her friend. "I haven't seen you in a month of Sundays!"

"It has been a while," Angelica agreed when Kate finally let her go.

"And I've been hearing all sorts of stories about you, too," Kate began, but stopped short when she saw Christian entering the store. "Hello, again, Mr. Collins," she said with a knowing grin. "You must think I'm a ninny for not recognizing you when you were in here before."

"Oh, no, ma'am," he assured her. "I was trying to keep it quiet back then."

Kate shook her head in wonder at her own denseness. "Well, I wish you'd set me straight," she scolded. "I can keep a secret, and I would've worried a lot less about Angelica if I'd known a man of your caliber was working for her."

The Kid frowned. He wasn't certain exactly what Mrs. Marsden meant by "a man of your caliber," so he decided not to inquire.

"I guess this means that you've finished the roundup," Kate said without pausing for breath.

Angelica nodded. "Yes, my men are taking the cattle north tomorrow, which is why I'm here. It seems that with all the trouble around here lately, Mr. Collins thinks it might not be safe for me to stay out at the ranch with just Robbie and Maria."

"He's absolutely right, too," Kate said, flashing him an approving look. "You *are* going to stay with me, aren't you?"

"We were hoping you'd offer," Angelica admitted with a smile. "We'll pay for our keep, of course."

"Don't be silly." Kate dismissed the offer with a wave of her hand. "It's not often I get so much company. I'm starved for a little female companionship. Maria!" she exclaimed, bustling over to greet the Mexican woman as she came through the front door.

Robbie arrived on Maria's heels, full of requests for rock candy and licorice whips, and for a few moments, confusion reigned. When Robbie had been pacified with a few treats from the candy jars sitting on the glass counter, Kate noticed another newcomer.

"And who's this?" she asked with great interest, gazing up at Miles's very superior height.

"That's Miles Blackmon, Kate," Angelica said. "He's a

good friend of Mr. Collins's, and now he's a good friend of mine. Miles, this is Mrs. Marsden."

"Pleased to meet you, ma'am," Miles said, tipping his hat and shifting uncomfortably under her continued scrutiny. He was accustomed to being stared at, but not by tiny little ladies in widow's weeds. They usually crossed the street to avoid him.

"I've heard a lot about you, Mr. Blackmon," she said at last. "And I must admit, I'm impressed."

He stared down at her in surprise, and when her small round face lit up with an incandescent smile, he grew positively bewildered.

"Kate is the Marsden behind 'Marsden's Corners,' " Angelica explained in an attempt to ease Miles's acute embarrassment. She knew he hated being stared at, but of course, that wouldn't bother Kate any if she felt like staring. There wasn't much that could discourage Kate.

"Now *I'm* impressed," Miles said perfunctorily, still ill at ease.

"Don't be," Kate informed him. "It was actually my husband who founded the town. We just had a trading post here at first, and the town grew up around it. My husband was a man of vision. Unfortunately, he didn't live to see his dream fulfilled."

"I'm sorry to hear that," he said.

Kate seemed to weigh his statement. "Yes," she concluded thoughtfully. "I guess you would be. You know what it's like to be the one left behind, don't you?"

Angelica's mouth dropped open in stunned surprise. She had never heard Kate speak so freely of her husband and certainly never to a total stranger. Of course, she was correct in assuming Miles would understand the depth of her loss, but what had ever possessed her to mention it? Angelica watched in amazement as Kate and Miles seemed to come to some sort of silent understanding.

She had a feeling that a lot was happening between them without a single word being spoken. Maybe, she thought irrelevantly, she ought to try that method on Christian, considering how much trouble she always caused when she tried to talk things out with him.

"Well, I guess you boys need some supplies for your trip, don't you?" Kate inquired, emerging from the spell that had momentarily held her gaze on Miles.

"Yes, ma'am," Christian said. "Ang—Miss Ross has the list."

Kate's brown eyes darted to Christian and then to Angelica, narrowing speculatively. Angelica gave her a guileless smile, knowing she would have to answer some questions later about her relationship with the handsome Mr. Collins. Angelica reflected that she wouldn't mind doing so. At this point, she could use a fresh perspective on the situation. Maria was becoming tiresomely maternal about the whole thing.

When Kate had filed their order and the men had loaded the supplies onto a packhorse, Kate sent her guests over to her house to get settled in before supper. Christian and Miles carried the luggage up to the guest rooms on the second floor of Kate's massive home and then prepared to leave.

To Angelica's disgust, she realized that Christian intended to simply bid her a terse good-bye and be on his way, much as Miles would have done. She had no such intention. "Would you step into the parlor with me a moment, Mr. Collins?" she asked. "There's something I'd like to discuss with you before you leave."

She could almost see his guard go up, but he followed her into the large room. He stiffened visibly when she slid the pocket doors shut behind them.

Angelica turned to face him. He was standing in the middle of the room, his hands clenched into fists at his sides, his silver conchas glittering brightly in the late afternoon sunlight that filled the room. The brim of his Stetson threw his eyes into shadow, but she could feel the intensity of his gaze like a warm hand reaching out to her.

Now that they were alone, she was no longer certain what she wanted to say to him. She had wanted to tell him of her love, had wanted to beg him to be careful on the long, dangerous journey ahead. She wanted to tell him a thousand things, but for some mysterious reason, none of them seemed important any longer.

"Oh, Christian," she whispered, the words throbbing with all the longing she felt for him. As if of their own accord, her arms lifted to him.

He murmured something incoherent as the last of his resistance crumbled. In the next second, she was in his arms. His mouth ravished hers as his hands explored the remembered delights of her body. She grew pliant beneath his touch as her blood thickened to liquid flame and melted her very bones.

Her eager hands brushed his hat away so they could explore the silky thickness of his hair and hold him fast against her lips. His hands molded her to his solid length, capturing her in the cradle of his thighs and holding her there against his surging desire.

Desperation fueled the fires that blazed between them, and they clung for long minutes until both of them were weak and trembling. He lifted his mouth from hers, gasping for breath, and rested his forehead against hers so as not to break the contact.

"Oh, Christian, I love you!" she breathed against his heated skin. She felt the shock of her words vibrate through him, and he pushed himself away.

"Don't say that!" he commanded. His breath still came in ragged gasps, but his eyes reflected a new kind of desperation.

"I have to say it, because it's true," she insisted, clutching at him. "And you love me, too. I know you do!"

He shook his head. "No, you mustn't think that. It isn't true," he insisted, but she knew he was lying.

"How can you say that after all that's happened?" she demanded.

He looked down at her lovely face, and his heart ached at the pain he saw reflected there. But he had to cause her pain now to protect her against the greater anguish loving him would cause her. "Angelica, listen to me," he said, grasping her shoulders in a grip that made her wince. "I'm no good for you. You know what I am, *who* I am and who my father was, how he made his living and how I make mine. A man like me isn't good enough to wipe your boots on."

"That's ridiculous!" she cried, but he silenced her with a little shake.

"It's not ridiculous. It's true, and don't forget about the job you hired me to do. There's no guarantee I'll even make it back here alive, and if I do, there's a dozen men just waiting for the chance to make a name for themselves by killing me. You're too young to be a widow, Angelica."

"What about your responsibility to me?" she asked, grasping at straws now. "You made love to me! What if I have a baby?"

Plainly, this was a possibility he had never considered. "Are you . . . ?" he asked, shaken.

She wanted to lie, wanted to tie him to her in some way he could not break, but faced with the opportunity, she found herself unable to do so. "No," she admitted reluctantly.

His shoulders sagged with relief as he expelled the breath he had been holding. "Good," he decreed. "Then this is the time to end it, before you get hurt any more."

Angelica didn't think she *could* hurt any more. "I don't want it to end," she insisted, throwing her arms around his neck and holding him fast. "You'll be back, I know you will, and I'll be waiting for you. I don't care who you are or who your father was. As long as we love each other, everything will work out. Promise me that when you come back we'll . . ."

She stopped when she sensed his continued resistance, and his hands came up to gently remove her arms from around his neck. "That's just it, Angelica. I can't even promise that I'll be back at all." His eyes were bleak with a despair she did not even want to understand, but before she could mount an argument against it, he was gone, scooping up his hat and leaving the room in a motion so quick she didn't even have time to react.

"Christian!" she called, but he was gone, outside and down the front steps to where Miles was waiting with their horses.

Tears stung her eyes as she watched him ruffle Robbie's hair and bid the boy a careless good-bye as if he had not just shattered her heart into a million pieces. He raised his hand in silent salute to where she stood in the front doorway and rode away.

With difficulty, she resisted the urge to run after him, to call him back and demand he listen to reason. There was no use in that, she knew, at least not now, so she chose to preserve what was left of her pride. All she could do now was prove him wrong. When he came back—and she was certain he would—she would confront him. The past did not matter to her, so why should it matter to him? Together they could overcome the past the same way they were going to overcome Snyder. And when everything was settled, Christian need no longer make his living with his gun, either. There were answers to his arguments. While he was gone, she would find them. When he returned, she would be ready, she vowed as she watched him and Miles ride away.

The Kid stared resolutely ahead, resisting with difficulty the urge to turn back for one last look at her. "I need a drink," he announced as they walked their horses around the corner and back onto the main street.

"You look like you do," Miles remarked blandly. "That can't have been easy."

"*What* can't have been easy?" the Kid asked suspiciously.

"Saying good-bye to her," Miles said, clearly puzzled at the Kid's obtuseness.

"Oh, yeah," he agreed, realizing that he hadn't even actually said good-bye.

They tied their horses outside the Dirty Dog Saloon and headed inside.

"Does this place ever heat up?" Miles inquired, surveying the nearly deserted street.

The Kid bit back a grin. "It *is* heated up," he replied, making Miles chuckle.

"Kid!" Sunny cried, rushing to meet him the instant he stepped through the swinging doors. She wrapped her arms around him and planted a kiss right on his mouth.

"Friend of yours?" Miles inquired from behind him.

Thoroughly embarrassed, the Kid pulled gingerly out of Sunny's embrace. "Sunny, I'd like you to meet a friend of mine, Miles Blackmon. Miles, this is Sunny Day."

"Oh!" Sunny squealed. "You're the one they call Parson Black, aren't you?"

"Yes, I am," Miles admitted reluctantly.

Sunny's eyes grew wide. "Oh, my," she said, looking Miles over from head to foot and obviously trying to reconcile the legends she had heard with the man before her. "You're the one who killed the men who raped your wife. Did you really cut off their . . ."

"Sunny," the Kid quickly interrupted her. "Miles doesn't like to talk about his reputation."

She frowned in disappointment. "Oh, I understand," she assured them, plainly not understanding at all. She turned her attention back to the Kid. "I been wondering where you were. You promised to come and check on me," she reminded him with a hint of reprimand.

"I'm sorry," he said, realizing he had, indeed, broken a promise to her. "I got a job, and I've been kind of busy."

"I know," she informed him proudly. "You're working for that Ross girl, but I heard she's going to marry Harlan Snyder," she added, leaning close and lowering her voice so the handful of patrons standing at the bar could not overhear. "He won't want you hanging around, so you're going to be out of a job again soon. I warned you, but that's all right," she concluded, brightening again. "Now we can go to New Orleans!"

Miles coughed behind him, but the Kid ignored it. "I won't be going anywhere as exciting as New Orleans for a while," he told her with a placating grin. "Come on, I'll buy you a drink. A *real* drink," he added for Otis's benefit as they approached the bar.

Grudgingly, the heavyset bartender poured three glasses of his best whiskey. The two men toasted Sunny, and then the Kid explained to her that they would be leaving in the morning on a trail drive.

"Tomorrow!" she exclaimed, suddenly panicked. "How long will you be gone?"

The Kid shrugged. "A month or so, I figure."

With obvious effort, she regained her poise. "Oh, well, in that case, I've got a little going-away present for you. It's out in my cabin."

She smiled in what she imagined was a seductive manner and pressed her body suggestively against his. Unfortunately, the memory of Angelica's body was still too fresh, and he instinctively pulled away.

Instantly, he knew he had made a serious mistake. The hurt in her eyes tore at his heart, reminding him as it did of the hurt he had seen in Angelica's only minutes ago. In an attempt to smooth things over, he tried to make light of his refusal. "I really appreciate the offer, Sunny, but I'm not the man for you. You'd be a fool to waste your time on a drifter like me."

"I like drifters," she insisted, but he could see the hope dying in her eyes and turning to resentment at his rejection. What hopes she could have pinned on him, he could not imagine. As hurt as she was, this was probably for the best, too, he told himself. There was no use in poor little Sunny waiting breathlessly for his return when she would never mean anything to him.

"Well, wish me luck," he asked with false heartiness.

"Luck," she replied with a smile just as false. "And you, too," she added to Miles.

As she watched them leave, her smile faded and her pale blue eyes narrowed down to hate-filled slits. "Damn you," she whispered to Collins's back. She'd built all her plans around him, and he'd treated her like dirt. He'd lied about coming back to see her, and now he was leaving her to Snyder's mercy. "You'll be sorry for this, Kid Collins," she promised fervently as he disappeared from sight.

Chapter Ten

Angelica muttered an imprecation when she read the note that one of Harland Snyder's cowboys had just delivered to her. Luckily, she had gone into the parlor and closed the door before reading it so the cowboy could not see her initial reaction and report on it later.

"What does he say?" Maria asked, looking up from her knitting. Until the messenger had interrupted them, she and Angelica had been enjoying the leisure of their first morning in town.

"He says he will be delighted to call on me at Mrs. Marsden's house this afternoon. I didn't think I could feel any more miserable, but Harlan Snyder has managed to prove me wrong." Angelica crumpled the note in disgust. "Maybe I'll tell him I have a headache."

But Maria was shaking her head. "You must meet with him. You must reassure him so he will not attack your cattle drive."

"Or my *men,*" Angelica added with a shudder. She had only been separated from Christian for one night, and already she missed him terribly. Right now, she would even be glad to see him scowling at her or pretending not to know she existed. Anything was preferable to this abominable loneliness.

"It is a hard thing for a woman to pretend to care for

a man she despises, but I think you have a good reason," Maria said.

Angelica sighed again. "Yes, I have a very good reason," she agreed. "I just don't know how I'm going to convince Snyder that my cattle and my men must arrive at Camp Hope safely."

Maria grinned. "I think I have an idea about that," she said provocatively.

"Really?" Angelica asked skeptically, but at Maria's confident nod, Angelica's hopes lifted. "Then I'll be right back to hear it," she said, hurrying to slide open the parlor doors. The waiting cowboy immediately rose from the bench where he had been sitting in the hallway.

Angelica gave him a brilliant smile. "Please tell Mr. Snyder I will be happy to receive him this afternoon."

"Yes, ma'am," the young man said, obviously uncomfortable with his role as go-between. "Thank you, ma'am."

She did not even wait to see him leave. If Maria had an idea on how to ensure Christian's safety, she wanted to hear it right away.

Angelica smiled at Snyder across the remnants of their picnic. "More chicken, Harlan?" she asked. Sometimes she even amazed herself with her ability to hide her true feelings. In the few short days since her men had left, she had become a brilliant actress.

"Yes, I'll take a drumstick," he replied, holding out his plate. He was half reclining on the blanket across from her. He had removed his suit coat because of the heat, and Angelica found the sight of his thick arms straining against the fine linen of his shirt very disconcerting. Once again she was reminded of the physical threat he could pose to her.

She pulled a chicken leg from the picnic basked Maria had packed for them earlier and leaned over to place it on his plate, but instead of accepting it, he withdrew the plate. To Angelica's dismay, he grasped her wrist to steady it and simply took a bite right out of the chicken.

"Harlan!" she chastened him for the intimacy of the act. His eyes danced wickedly as he chewed the meat with sensual slowness, still grasping her wrist. Angelica fought down the wave of revulsion she felt, reminding herself that this was for Christian. She pulled on her arm, trying to break his grip, but he clung tenaciously.

He swallowed and then pulled his lips back in that feral grin of his. "You should be pleased to have me eating out of your hand, Angelica," he said, setting his plate down on the blanket. He purposefully removed the chicken leg from her fingers and dropped it on the plate. His face was so close, she could feel his hot breath on her hand, and she gasped when his tongue flicked out and captured a crumb of chicken coating that was clinging to her finger.

"Did I frighten you?" he asked with feigned regret. He was feeling the delicate skin of her wrist for her pulse. His grin broadened when he discovered her heart was racing. Obviously, he found the thought that she might fear him exciting. His small brown eyes glittered, and a faint sheen of perspiration appeared on his forehead.

Angelica swallowed against the nausea that threatened and twisted her arm again. This time she succeeded in breaking his grip. "Of course you didn't frighten me," she said, but even she could hear the breathlessness in her voice. She hoped he couldn't guess how much revulsion was mixed in with her fear.

"You don't have to be afraid, my dear," he assured her, pushing up to a sitting position so he could loom over her. "I respect your innocence. I'll be very gentle. . . ."

"Maria!" Angelica called, scrambling quickly to her feet. "I think we'd better be getting on back now." Maria turned from where she had been observing Robbie fishing in the nearby creek and waved an acknowledgment.

When Angelica returned her gaze to Snyder, she caught a glimpse of his annoyance, but only a glimpse. He covered it quickly and resumed his ingratiating smile. He, too, was rising so he could once more loom over her and remind her of his physical superiority.

"I can't wait until we're married, Angelica," he whispered, undaunted by her obvious attempt to avoid the discussion.

His hand sneaked up to stroke her arm, a touch she unconsciously cringed from, but instead of annoying him again, her reaction only seemed to arouse him more. To her alarm, she realized that her reluctance pleased him in some unnatural way.

Memories of Christian's warnings echoed in her head, and she remembered that Snyder had accused Christian of beating a woman in town. Instinctively, she knew the crime had been Snyder's and she shuddered slightly.

Snyder smiled with satisfaction. "It's so difficult to wait, especially when there's really no reason for it. What's to stop us from getting married right away?"

"We've never really discussed marriage," Angelica pointed out to him primly, wishing he wouldn't insist on standing so close to her.

His eyes gleamed knowingly. "Then let's discuss it now," he suggested.

Angelica glanced nervously over to where Maria and Robbie had finally finished gathering up Robbie's fishing gear. Unfortunately, they were still out of earshot, so she could not use them as an excuse for changing the subject. "Harlan," she began, trying to sound reasonable, "I simply can't expect a man of your position to marry a woman whose ranch is on the verge of ruin."

"I wouldn't mind," he insisted, but she cut him off.

"*I* would mind. I have my pride. If I can't bring a suitable dowry, then I simply won't marry at all," she concluded, glad to note that she sounded as determined as she felt.

"Angelica," he tried again. This time is voice fairly dripped with condescension, as if he were addressing a simpleminded child. "You can't be serious. . . ."

She wasn't interested in hearing him, however. "I am perfectly serious. And if, for some reason, my cattle don't get through and I am ruined, then I'm afraid I'll simply have to go into a convent," she informed him, revealing Maria's brainstorm.

"A convent!" he fairly shouted.

Angelica nodded regretfully. "I couldn't possibly be a burden to anyone, and the church would gladly take my worthless ranch. They could use it as a mission—"

"The church! Angelica, don't be ridiculous," he tried, getting control of his temper with difficulty. "What about your brother? The ranch is his heritage, too."

Angelica was hard pressed not to smile at Snyder's phony concern for Robbie's future. She managed a melodramatic sigh. "A bankrupt ranch is hardly a heritage, Harlan," she pointed out. "I would have to send Robbie back East where we have some family. In a way, it would be better for him. He could get an education and . . ."

"But there's no reason why you couldn't marry," he pointed out, beginning to sound almost frantic. Angelica could tell he was seeing all his plans going up in smoke right before his eyes. He was not about to let her turn her property into a mission. Even Harlan Snyder would not attempt to steal from the Catholic Church.

She gave him a sad smile and patted his arm comfortingly. "You're right, of course," she agreed. "I might change my mind about the convent, but I could never saddle my husband with the Diamond R unless it was a financial success. I think I would still sign it over to the church. That's the only way my conscience would be clear. So you see why it's important for my cattle to be delivered to Camp Hope. If I don't fulfill my contract . . ." She let the sentence hang ominously.

Snyder looked almost alarmed, although he was making a visible effort to remain calm. "Perhaps we'd better be getting back to town now," he said, just as Maria and Robbie strolled up. "I've just remembered some very pressing business."

Angelica felt an answering prickle of alarm. Was it too late? Had he already set a plan in motion for Christian's destruction?

The Kid leaned low over Midnight's neck as the horse's pounding hooves carried him beside the herd of stampeding cattle and into the night. Wind and rain slashed his face and tore at his clothes as if they would strip him naked with their force, but he hardly noticed. His ears were straining for the faint sound of gunfire above the rumble of the herd and the roar of the storm.

The pops were faint, hardly more than echoes, but he pulled on the reins, directing Midnight toward the sound. The lightning flashed, illuminating the prairie for a heartbeat with the glow of day. In that instant, he saw every detail of the herd as it raced along. He caught a glimpse of a rider up ahead, his gun raised and spitting fire, and then darkness descended again.

The Kid reached for his own Colt, pulling it from his holster and lifting it in defiance of the wind and rain that tried to snatch it from him. His finger squeezed the trigger and the gun bucked in his hand. Once, twice, again, until it clicked empty. The acrid scent of gun smoke whipped by and was gone, swept away on the relentless wind. All around him guns spoke to the night. Men shouted, horses ran, and a body could tell neither friend nor foe in the darkness.

Then he sensed the change: the cattle were slowing. When next the lightning flashed, he saw the head of the heard turned back on itself in a mill. The cows bawled their protest. They wanted to continue their fight from the storm, but they could no longer run in the ever-tightening mass of the herd.

The Kid rammed his gun back into its holster. Hundreds of horns clashed, sending showers of sparks into the supercharged air but he watched unseeing. Instead, he concentrated on the mill, closing it until the herd ground to a halt, ending the murderous stampede.

When next the sky was lit up, he saw some familiar figures nearby. The men were still but alert in their saddles, ready to stop another run before it started. He reined up beside the one closest to him just as the roll of thunder died away.

"Nice night for a ride, ain't it?" he remarked above the constant din of the rain.

Stumpy shouted back a rather obscene reply. The old man was reloading his gun as he sat his horse. "Damn thing misfired three times," he reported in irritation.

The Kid smiled his sympathy, although he knew Stumpy could not see in the darkness. "It's the dampness," he replied, ducking his head and sending down a cascade of water from his hat brim.

Stumpy cackled appreciatively. "It felt awful good to shoot at something, though," he said. "Even if it was just the stars." It was common practice to use gunfire to frighten the herd into changing direction.

"I know what you mean," the Kid replied, pulling out

his own gun for reloading. As he stuffed shells into it, he reflected on his own frustration. They had been on the trail for two weeks now, expecting trouble at every turn. All the men shared the uneasy feeling that Snyder's men were planning something and would strike at any moment. "You reckon we'll find a fresh cougar skin back where all this started?" he asked hopefully.

"Hell, no," Stumpy replied, his disgust evident. "I seen what started this. It was lightning. It come down not two feet from where they was bedded down."

The Kid swore. It was just as he'd suspected, and yet the part of him that was itching for a fight had hoped for a more mysterious explanation. He knew he was crazy. He knew he should have been glad the trip had been uneventful thus far. Still . . . "Why doesn't he just hit us and get it over with?" he muttered aloud. The wind stole his words and carried them away into the darkness.

Harlan Snyder burst into the nearly empty saloon, marched over to where Sunny was sitting at a table with two cowboys, grabbed her arm and jerked her to her feet.

"Come on," he said, fairly dragging the girl toward the back door. The two cowboys made a move as if to protest such rough treatment, but a look from Snyder silenced them.

As he passed the bar, Snyder reached into his vest pocket and pulled out two silver dollars, which he slapped down for Otis. "We won't be long," he said to the rotund bartender.

Otis frowned but did not reply.

"Hey, what's your hurry?" Sunny asked with a forced laugh. "We got all night."

Snyder tossed her a contemptuous look. "You think I'd waste the whole night with the likes of you?"

Sunny flushed, but she bit her tongue to keep from reminding him that he'd only felt that way for the last several weeks, just since Angelica Ross had come to stay in town. There was no use in antagonizing him further, though, as she knew from experience. When they reached her house, he slammed the door shut behind them and shoved her toward the bed. She tumbled down on it in a heap.

"Do you want me to . . ." she began, but he was already unbuttoning his pants.

"I don't have time," he replied. With a rough jerk, he threw her skirt over her head. His weight bore her down into the mattress, and she cried out in pain when he thrust into her. His movements were swift and urgent, but mercifully, he was quick. In only a few short minutes, he shuddered out his release with a guttural moan and then withdrew.

With hands that shook, Sunny pulled her skirt back down to cover herself. She watched him adjust his clothes. "Are you having dinner with Angelica Ross this afternoon?" she could not help asking.

For an instant, his eyes flashed with anger, but apparently he decided her question sprang from some sort of jealousy. "Yes, I am, as a matter of fact," he told her smugly.

Sunny tried to hold back the words, but they broke free as if of their own accord. "Does she know you ease yourself with me because she won't spread her legs for you?"

"Damn you," he gritted just as his hand delivered a resounding smack to her face. "That'll teach you to talk back to your betters." Giving his coat a final tug, he turned on his heel and left. He hadn't been in the room more than five minutes.

Sunny lifted a hand to her tingling cheek and smiled ruefully. It could have been worse. At least he hadn't marked her. In fact, it had actually been worth it to see the shock on his face. Sunny supposed he thought of her as something less than human, someone lacking normal human feelings. Someone to whom his abuse would not matter.

But she did have normal human feelings, and she was heartily sick of his abuse. Things had been bad enough before, when he had only hurt her physically. Now, for the past several weeks, he had only come for a humiliatingly quick release either right before or immediately after he spent time with Angelica Ross. The girl must be leading him a merry chase, Sunny thought with bitter envy, wondering what it would be like to be able to say no to a man like Harlan Snyder.

Slowly, she rose from the bed, moving cautiously lest she discover he had hurt her with his roughness. When she experienced no unusual discomfort, she went over to the washstand to scrub away the residue of Harlan Snyder. When she was finished, she made a few repairs to her hair, using the foggy mirror hanging on the wall.

Squinting at her reflection, she frowned at what she saw: a plain girl in whom hope had been all but extinguished. What about her dream of going to New Orleans? What about her plans for a better life? She thought briefly of Kid Collins. She had hoped he would be her protector, but he had failed her. Now she was alone again, defenseless against Snyder and his humiliations. With a defeated sigh, she returned to the saloon.

The two cowboys were gone. The room was empty except for Otis. "You all right?" he asked.

"Sure," she replied, knowing he was only wondering if she would be available to work the rest of the day. Even her own brother didn't care that Snyder had robbed her of what little self-respect she had left.

She went to one of the tables where a worn deck of cards lay. Sitting down, she dealt herself a game of solitaire. She was still at it several hours later when the saloon doors swished open. She jumped, automatically on guard in case Snyder was returning for another session after his visit with Miss Ross. But it wasn't Snyder.

The man was a stranger, small and lean but dressed to the nines. His black broadcloth suit was a little dusty from a long ride, but it fit him perfectly, indicating that it had been tailor-made for him. His vest was brocade, with gold threads glittering through it and a heavy gold watch chain stretched across it. His boots were hand tooled and almost new, and his Stetson was spotlessly white with a snakeskin hatband.

Aside from the clothes, the man himself wasn't much to look at. His face was ordinary, his brown hair lank, and his eyes small and somewhat beady. What drew Sunny's attention were his hands. They were long and slender and had the well-tended look of a professional gunfighter's. They went perfectly with the silver-mounted, ivory-handled pistols that hung on his hips.

Laying her cards aside, she rose from the table. "Howdy, stranger," she said, smiling pleasantly. "Buy a lady a drink?"

He grinned, making her realize he wasn't even as old as she had first thought. She judged him to be about twenty-two or twenty-three. "Sure, honey, step right up," he invited with a smile that revealed less-than-perfect teeth.

She joined him at the bar. He didn't seem to notice when Otis filled her glass from a different bottle, but that was all right because he was looking at her the whole time. He apparently liked what he saw.

He downed his whiskey in one gulp, but Sunny just sipped on her cold tea and pretended it was too strong for her. "You're new around here, aren't you?" she asked, having already decided he must be Harlan Snyder's latest addition.

"That's right. I'm going to work for Harlan Snyder," he announced proudly, confirming her suspicions. "You know him?"

"Everybody knows him," she replied with an inward wince and quickly changed the subject. "I reckon that means you'll be around for a while," she added, letting him see how much the idea pleased her.

"I reckon it does," he allowed. "Say, what do they call you, honey?"

She told him her name, making him grin again, and then asked, "What do they call you, stranger?"

He almost seemed to preen. "Tom Rivers, at your service."

Sunny had never heard of Tom Rivers, but it was easy to see he thought everyone had, so she played along. "Not *the* Tom Rivers?" she asked, feigning awe.

"I don't know of no others," he said, tucking a thumb into his vest pocket in a pose she suspected he practiced in front of a mirror.

"Are the stories they tell about you true, about how you've killed seven men and all that?" she improvised.

"Oh, not seven," he assured her modestly. "At least not yet, but I've done my share to decrease Dodge City's undesirable population."

"Oooo," she cooed, and managed to look wistful. "I don't reckon you'd like to tell me all about it, would you?"

Just as she'd suspected, he would like nothing better. After ordering a bottle, he escorted her to a table and began to regale her with tales of how he had made Wyatt

Earp and Bat Masterson quake in their boots like frightened schoolboys.

She drank his whiskey and listened, ignoring Otis's disapproving glances. He didn't like for her to drink. He said it wasn't ladylike, a condemnation Sunny found hilarious, considering her occupation. She quickly realized Tom Rivers was a braggart who had an inclination to stretch the truth, but she also realized there was enough truth in his stories to prove he was a dangerous man. He had that reckless conviction that he was invincible and enough pride to compel him to fight even when retreat might be the wiser choice.

In less than an hour, she had even managed to wheedle out of him his purpose for being here. "I'm supposed to kill Kid Collins," he confided when half the whiskey was gone.

Sunny's eyes widened in surprise. She knew a moment of distress. Kid Collins had once been kind to her, after all. But she was too practical to let that influence her decision. She had to look after herself, and Kid Collins had made it clear he wasn't going to help her do that. If Snyder had hired Tom Rivers to fight Collins, then Rivers must be just as good with a gun, maybe better. That meant Rivers would be an even better protector than Collins. Besides, Rivers was here, and heaven only knew where Collins was or when he would be back.

Sunny laid a hand on Rivers's arm and said, "If anyone can get Collins, I'll bet you're the man."

The brocade vest seemed to swell as he acknowledged her compliment. She managed another wistful sigh. "I'll bet a fellow like you has lots of girls."

"I've had my share," he boasted. "Women just naturally follow after a man like me."

Sunny smiled. She doubted that. The man who really did have lots of women didn't need to brag about it.

"Would you like one more?" she asked, letting her hand slide up and down his arm.

He almost tipped his chair over in his haste to get up, and Otis had to holler after him to get him to pay in advance. Sunny slipped her arm around his waist as they walked out to her cabin, and she mulled over her plans. She'd have to be careful with him. Men who were so eager often were unable to perform at all when confronted with a genuine naked woman. If Rivers were embarrassed, he wouldn't come back to her, and she wanted him to come back, again and again.

In fact, she wanted Tom Rivers to inform Otis that she was officially "retired," that she would sleep with no one but Tom from now on, not even Harlan Snyder. That might take a day or two to accomplish, but Sunny was confident she could accomplish it. She could see that Tom Rivers was going to be an easy man to manage.

"Have you ever been to New Orleans?" she asked as they entered her house.

Angelica smiled politely at the story Harlan Snyder had just told her and tried not to look at the parlor clock again. If she stared at it too pointedly, he would know how desperate she was for his visit to end. She didn't mind too much when he took her someplace, on a buggy ride or a picnic, but just sitting here making conversation with him was an ordeal. He always wanted to hint at subjects she did not dare discuss.

Of course, she realized that he brought them up on purpose, to upset her. The more nervous she was, the better he seemed to like it. She had begun to understand that he enjoyed her uncertainty, that he gained some sort of satisfaction from it. Consequently, she no longer tried to hide the way her hands trembled when he came too close or the way she quaked when he hinted at the pleasures awaiting them after their marriage.

Nevertheless, she had begun to sense a fine tension in him, as if time were running out. Before, he had always laughed off her coy rejections, but for the last week or so, he hadn't been quite so cheerful.

"What do you hear from your men?" Snyder asked when he grew tired of waiting for her to contribute to the conversation. All this formal courting was beginning to wear on him, especially now that Sunny was no longer available.

"Uh, not a thing," she admitted reluctantly, hoping he would not guess at how apprehensive she was over the prolonged silence. "But you know what they say, no news is good news," she added with forced brightness.

Snyder frowned, thinking of how his plans had gone awry. He had originally wanted to ambush Collins and his crew and steal the cattle. He would have had the money from the cattle, and a penniless Angelica would have been forced to marry him, giving him the ranch and the girl both. If only Angelica wasn't such a stubborn little baggage, he'd be done with the whole business by now, and Angelica would be his wife. Reminding himself that his waiting was almost over in any case, he managed to smile again. "I wish you had let me send some of my men along on the drive. That crew of yours is a very untrustworthy lot," he said.

He was giving her that condescending smile that made her want to gnash her teeth. "I trust them completely," Angelica insisted, trying not to sound as irritated as she felt.

His smile never wavered. "You're such an innocent, Angelica. I'll never understand why you hired a man with Collins's reputation in the first place. You probably trust everyone."

No, not everyone, she denied silently. "Oh, I admit that I'm not very knowledgeable about some things," she said instead, lowering her eyes with maidenly modesty.

"And that's why you need a man to take care of you," he replied, as if on cue.

Angelica was thoroughly sick of discussing this subject. "Please, Harlan, I've asked you not to even mention that until I know my cattle have been delivered to the reservation," she chided him gently.

"But what if your cattle don't get delivered at all?" he insisted, dropping his pretense at pleasantness. "That's what I've been trying to get you to realize, Angelica. It pains me to say this, but it's been five weeks since those men took your cattle. That's more than enough time for them to get there and bring the money back. I think it's time that I sent—"

"Harlan!" she interrupted, speaking more sharply than she had intended and startling him a bit. With a concentrated effort, she got her voice back under control. "I've asked you not to interfere in my business dealings, haven't I? I'm afraid my wishes in the matter have not changed. If you were to send some men out to check up on my crew, I would have to consider it a violation of trust. I would hate to think I couldn't trust *you,* Harlan."

He was quite plainly displeased at her ultimatum, but mercifully, he did not press, although she knew he would not let the matter drop. Tomorrow, they would have to go through all of this again. Unable to resist the temptation a moment longer, she glanced at the clock, wishing there was some way to make the hands move faster so she could send Snyder on his way.

The Kid was mad. For over five weeks, he'd been expecting a fight. Every minute of every day, he'd been on his mettle, ready to face whatever challenge Snyder sent. Unfortunately, no challenges had come.

Even the drive itself, normally a situation fraught with potential dangers, had been relatively uneventful except for that one awful storm. Stumpy had been right, too. The stampede had been simply an act of God and nothing more. Day after day, they had trudged along, slogging through mud or choking on dust and waiting for the crisis that never came. By the time they'd delivered the cattle to Camp Hope, the tension was almost unbearable. The whole crew was as sour tempered as a herd of turpentined bears, and the Kid was the worst of the lot. He was wound tighter than an eight-day clock and spoiling for trouble.

They'd made the trip back in record time. As soon as they had hit Marsden's Corners, the rest of the men stopped at the Dirty Dog Saloon for a celebratory drink, but in response to a compelling need to see Angelica, the Kid headed straight for Kate Marden's house. His boots stirred up belligerent puffs of dust as he marched across the main street and down the side street toward Kate's front walk.

He tried to tell himself that this was business, that he was just eager to report the success of his trip and turn over the contents of the heavy money belt he had carried back from Indian Territory. The sooner he did so, the sooner he could set to work tracking down his sister's killers. When he had settled all that, he could finally break his ties to Angelica Ross and his life would return to normal.

The problem was, he couldn't quite recall just what "normal" was, and even his vague recollections of it were singularly unattractive. Did he want to return to the Circle M ranch, where, friendship aside, he'd still be only one of Cole Elliot's hired men? Did he want to watch Cole and Rachel exchanging intimate smiles while he lived out his life alone, spending his nights in a narrow bunk surrounded by men equally lonely?

The answer, of course, was no. He wanted the kind of life Cole had. He wanted a home, and he wanted a woman, his own woman, a woman with long red hair and eyes the color of spring grass. Longing swelled in him, searing in its intensity, as he envisioned what it would be like to have Angelica as his wife, to possess her, body and soul, and to know he owned the fierce loyalty that she would only give to the man she loved.

But could he ever be that man? She did love him, that much he knew, but did he dare accept her love when he knew the pain he might bring her in the future? What if he accepted it only to die the way most men of his stamp did, in a blaze of gunfire at the hand of some worthless drifter out to make a name for himself? Losing him to death would break her heart, as he knew only too well from his own experience, but the shame of a death like that would break her pride, too. And what if they had a child on whom the taint of his father's death would fall? The Kid also understood what it was like to bear the sins of a father.

Knowing all that, knowing the inevitable end to his imagined idyll, he could not let her love him. He would have to destroy her love now to spare her the greater pain that would come later. The mere thought of turning her against him sent an agony of despair coursing through him, but he gritted his teeth against it, vowing that he would not do what his father had done and leave behind him a family to suffer for his wrongs. With this thought firmly planted in his mind, he turned in at Kate Marsden's gate.

The windows of the big gray house were shuttered

against the afternoon heat, but he heard the music of Angelica's laughter drifting out as he bounded up the steps to the open front door. The sound caught him unawares, touching him in an unprotected spot and stirring all the tender emotions he had thought were so firmly under control.

"Angelica," he whispered. Before he could stop it, a need that transcended physical desire swept away all his good intentions. Only at the last second and by the merest chance did he remember to stop at the doorway and knock instead of charging inside to claim her.

Angelica responded to the sound even before she consciously heard it. *His* footsteps on the porch. Every nerve in her body prickled to attention. She had already risen from her seat when the knock sounded. "I'll see who's there," she told Snyder as calmly as she could. The stiff smile she had been wearing for his benefit suddenly became one of genuine joy as she turned toward the parlor doors. With difficulty, she kept her step sedate, but the hands that slid the doors open were trembling in anticipation.

Her breath caught painfully at the first glimpse of him standing there on the threshold. Swiftly, before Snyder could see who was there, she slid the doors shut behind her. Only then did she dare to breathe his name. "Christian!"

At that one word, the last of his carefully constructed defenses crumbled, leaving him exposed and vulnerable and totally unable to resist the joy that lit her face. He opened his arms and filled them with her. She was soft and fresh and more infinitely precious than he had remembered. Like a man starved, he devoured the honey of her mouth, a sweetness she offered up with an eagerness that fired his blood.

Angelica clung to him with all her strength, scarcely

able to believe that he was really here, at last. Yet his presence flooded her senses with whatever proof she might have needed. His mouth on hers tasted blessedly familiar. His scent, mingled with the smells of outdoors and horses, evoked memories of the last time they had made love, out on the open prairie with only darkness as a cover. His breath rasped in his chest, and she could almost hear his heart pounding in time with hers. His body beneath her searching hands was solid and strong, not the stuff of dreams at all.

When at last he broke their kiss, she opened her eyes to confirm what she had only half believed before. "You're home!" she cried. It was as much a prayer of thanks as a declaration.

His lips twitched into a tiny smile, but before he could reply, Harlan Snyder's voice boomed rudely. "Angelica? Who was at the door?"

Christian's eyes widened in surprise, but there was no time to explain. Hastily, she pulled out of his embrace, freeing herself just as the parlor doors slid open again. "Is anything wrong . . . ?" His question died on a growl of displeasure when he caught sight of Christian. The two men glared at each other across the width of the hallway.

"Why, no, nothing's wrong at all," Angelica assured him in a voice that was slightly breathless. She wondered if she looked as thoroughly kissed as she felt. "In fact, everything is perfectly right. Mr. Collins had just returned. You see, Harlan, you were worried for nothing."

She could feel Christian's displeasure bearing down on her like a palpable force, but she could not look at him for fear of betraying herself to Snyder. If the rancher had not already sensed her feelings for Christian, it would be a miracle.

"I'm very glad for you, Angelica," Snyder was saying,

looking anything but glad. After a few seconds, he forced his gaze to move from Christian to her, during which time she had managed to compose herself a little more. He smiled that smile she hated. "Now that you know your herd has been safely delivered, you'll be able to think about other things. *Personal* things."

Angelica almost winced, but before she could respond, he added, "I'll come by tonight to take you to supper so we can discuss the matter in private. Shall we say about eight?"

Christian did not move a muscle, but Angelica could sense the magnitude of his growing wrath. Inanely, she wondered why she could not smell sulfur in the confines of the hall. Still she dared not look at him. "Oh, I'm afraid I couldn't, not tonight," she replied, frantically searching for a legitimate-sounding reason. "You see, I promised my men a celebration when they got back, and it looks like tonight is the night. I can't disappoint them, now can I? Especially after they served me so loyally." Angelica smiled sweetly and struck her best "modest maiden" pose.

Snyder's smile sloughed instantly into a frown, but before he could protest, she said, "I'd ask you to join us, but I wanted it to be a private party, with just my family and my men. You understand, don't you, Harlan?"

"Yes, of course," he ground out ungraciously.

"I knew you would," Angelica said innocently. "And I know you'll excuse us now, too, so I can get Mr. Collins's report as soon as possible."

Snyder's face grew red as he shifted his gaze back to Christian again, but he could not very well refuse her request. "Of course," he said again. "I'll . . . I'll call on you tomorrow."

"That would be lovely," she lied, still smiling.

He waited another moment, as if debating something

with himself. Angelica wondered if he had guessed the truth about her feelings for Christian, but he did not look jealous, merely annoyed at having his plans thwarted. She hoped that was all it was, at least for now. Things would be terribly unpleasant when he discovered her duplicity. After another moment's thought, he seemed to surrender to the inevitable and headed for the door, taking his bowler hat from the hat tree on the way.

"Good afternoon, Angelica," he said, turning back to face her when he had placed the hat on his head.

"Good afternoon, Harlan," she replied with just the slightest excess of enthusiasm.

Another long moment of waiting while he and Christian glared at each other again, and he was gone.

Only then did Angelica trust herself to look at Christian. His eyes were fierce, as she had expected, but to her surprise his anger was directed at her. "Just what in the hell has been going on here?" he demanded.

"What?" she asked stupidly, unable to reconcile this furious stranger with the man who had just kissed her.

"Didn't I tell you to stay away from him while I was gone? And here I find you all alone with him in a room with the door closed. . . ." His furious gesture toward the door in question froze in midair when he caught sight of Maria standing there.

"She wasn't completely alone with him," Maria reported with a grin as she stepped out of the parlor and into the hallway. "I think maybe she would like to be alone with you, though, so I will go and find Robbie. He will want to know you are back, too. Welcome home, Señor Collins," she added before heading toward the back door of the house.

"Oh, uh, thanks," he replied, lowering his arm self-consciously to his side.

Angelica studied him closely, noting how reluctantly he

returned his gaze to her. His fury had cooled considerably. "Were you jealous?" she asked, delighted at the prospect.

Jealous? Of course he was jealous, puredee green with it, but he wasn't about to say so. Kissing her had been bad enough. Now that he had control of himself again, he was going to maintain that control. "Do you really want a report, or was that a windy, too, like the story about the celebration dinner?" he asked with what he hoped sounded like disgust.

Angelica laughed delightedly. He really was jealous! "Of course I want a report," she assured him.

There it was, the gentle music of her laughter, but he reminded himself that a few brief moments ago she had been laughing for Harlan Snyder. The memory galled him, but still he allowed her to take him by the arm and draw him into the parlor. "Now sit down right here and tell me everything," she commanded.

He sat down on the sofa as she instructed. "Take off your hat and stay awhile," she remarked impudently, reminding him that in all the excitement, he had neglected to remove his Stetson. He did so immediately, setting it on a nearby table as she sank down beside him in a swoosh of skirts and petticoats. "Now tell me everything," she said, laying her hand along the back of the sofa and leaning so close that he could smell the fresh scent of her hair.

Resolving to ignore her nearness and the effect it was having on him, he concentrated on telling her every detail of the trip. In less than five minutes, he was finished. Only then did he trust himself to look directly at her again. Her eyes were the color of rain-washed leaves, and her smile was soft. He swallowed to keep the huskiness from his voice and said, "I have the money right here." He patted his middle where the money belt was strapped beneath his clothes.

Her smile grew wicked. "I noticed," she informed him.

The urge to kiss that grin off her lovely mouth was almost irresistible. He jumped to his feet. "I'll keep it until you can put it in the safe back at the ranch," he said.

"That will be fine," she agreed, rising more slowly. "How much of a bonus did you give the men?"

"I didn't pay them at all. I figured you'd want to do that yourself," he replied, taking a step backward to put some space between them. He thought if he just couldn't smell her quite so clearly, he might be able to resist the desire to take her in his arms.

"That was very thoughtful of you," she said, closing the space between them. "And I really do want to treat all the men to supper tonight. Tell them we'll meet down at the restaurant at eight o'clock. We should have the place to ourselves by then, and I'll arrange for a special meal."

"They'll like that," he said, backing up again and thinking that if Harlan Snyder dared to show up, he would receive a warm welcome indeed. Angelica followed him intently, once more closing the space he had made. If he didn't think of something to wipe that adoring look off her face, he'd be wrestling her down onto the sofa in another minute. Suddenly, inspiration struck. "You never did say what Snyder was going here," he said accusingly.

Angelica blinked in surprise at the abrupt shift in subject. "Oh, just the same thing he's done every day," she replied flippantly, wanting to dismiss the subject.

Her remark had the opposite effect. *"Every* day?" Christian demanded, his eyes hardening to blue flint. "Has he been here every day since I've been gone?"

Angelica hesitated. Making Christian jealous was one thing, but she sensed that his outrage went deeper than that. "Well, not every single day. I told him people would talk if he came by too often."

"How often did he come by?"

Angelica almost imagined she could smell sulfur once again. She gave him a placating smile. "Maria said that I had to see him a few times a week so he would think I was still interested. I told him I couldn't make any wedding plans until I knew my cattle had arrived safely. That was so he wouldn't do anything to stop you from getting through. . . ."

Her voice trailed off when she saw the tremor go through him. He was holding his temper by the sheerest force of will. "Damn it to hell, Angelica, I told you to stay away from the man," he said, his voice dangerously low. "Didn't Maria tell you what he did?"

This time it was Angelica who backed up a step. "I've been very careful," she assured him. "Whenever we went out anyplace, I . . ."

"You went *out* with him, too?" he roared.

Angelica flinched, but she stood her ground. "Just a few times. We had a couple of picnics and . . ."

"Picnics! What in the hell is wrong with you?" he shouted, planting his hands on his hips in a very threatening manner. "Don't you have the sense God gave a ripe gourd?"

"There is nothing whatsoever wrong with me, Mr. Collins," she informed him as her own temper rose. "I have perfectly good sense, and I'll have you know that Maria and Robbie were with us on those picnics and on every other outing, and whenever Snyder came to call, either Maria or Robbie or both of them stayed with us the entire time. *And* I think you have a lot of brass hollering at me when I'm your boss and all I was doing was trying to protect you!"

Her reminder hit him like a slap in the face. That was

it, the real problem. Her being with Snyder was only part of it. The reason behind her sham courtship was what stuck in his craw. He couldn't stand the idea that she was putting herself in danger to protect him. It went against every instinct he possessed and every code he knew.

The fury strangled in his throat as that old sense of helplessness overwhelmed him. He couldn't claim Angelica, he couldn't control her, and he couldn't even protect her. As strong as his need to see her had been, his need to escape from the frustration of her presence was even stronger

"You've heard my report," he said tersely. "I'll be on my way."

"Christian!" she cried, grabbing his arm, but he shook her off effortlessly and kept going. He pushed the parlor doors aside with a crash, and he was in the hallway when she caught up with him again. "Christian, wait! We need to talk!" Again she tried to stop him, but he shook her off like a minor annoyance and went out the front door.

Angelica stared helplessly after him, silently cursing herself for her blunder. Hadn't she sworn never to pull rank on him again? Hadn't she vowed that things would be different when he came back? But here she was doing the same old things and causing the same old problems. If only Snyder hadn't been here when he came home. If only she could have kissed Christian a few more times before they started talking. If only she would learn to mind her tongue!

"Christian! Don't forget to tell the other men about supper tonight!" she called as he strode, hatless, out onto the dusty street. If he heard her, he gave no indication.

Angelica muttered a curse at his departing back.

The men were already assembled when Angelica made

her grand entrance into Marsden's Corners's modest eatery. From their surprised gasps, she knew they approved of her new gown. Even Christian's mouth dropped open, although he very quickly resumed the fierce scowl of disapproval he would continue to wear all through the evening.

Angelica had designed the gown with Christian in mind, and she noticed that in spite of his apparent disapproval, he could not seem to keep his eyes off of it. Or, rather, off of the parts of her it didn't quite cover. She had to admit the neckline was rather low, baring a generous expanse of shoulder and bosom. Luckily, the suntan she had acquired on the roundup had faded so that her face and neck did not contrast too vividly with the whiteness of her shoulders.

The dress itself was moss green taffeta starting with a form-fitting bodice that made the most of her less-than-ample breasts and accentuated her narrow waist. The rest of it, yards and yards of it, were swathed up into a bell-shaped skirt in front and a tidy but elaborate bustle in the back. As Stumpy so gallantly put it, "Miss Angelica, you look as pretty as a red heifer in a flower bed." The others concurred, with even the usually reticent Harley and Sanders vigorously nodding their agreement.

Kate Marsden, who Angelica had insisted must join them, came in behind her. She introduced her friend to all the men she had not yet met. Only then did Angelica have a chance to look around the room. She had requested a special meal, and she was pleased to note that the proprietors of the small restaurant, the Wallaces, had complied. Mrs. Wallace had even procured some tablecloths to cover the scarred wood of the table. It added just the right festive touch.

"Let's see now, where shall everyone sit?" she asked aloud, considering the rows of benches along either side of the table and the chairs at either end. After a few moments of thought, she began to give her instructions. With what she hoped was discretion, she managed to place Miles next to Kate Marsden. The rest of the table was easy to arrange once she decided to seat herself at one end and Christian at the other, where he would have an unobstructed view of her but would not be able to get into an argument with her. Robbie went beside Stumpy so the old man could entertain the boy with tall tales. Harley and Sanders were together, of course, and she put them on the opposite side of the table from where Kate and Maria sat on either side of Miles. Hank and Curly deserved the places of honor on her right and left as her senior cowhands, and the table was filled.

Everyone except Robbie, who was not allowed to partake, enjoyed the wine Kate had brought from her cellar, especially when Angelica proposed a toast to her loyal crew. When they had drunk, all eyes went expectantly to Christian, who was compelled by protocol to return her tribute. Rising slowly with what might have been reluctance, he lifted his glass and said, "To our very lovely Boss Lady."

Angelica, it seemed, was the only one who noticed the slight bitterness of his tone. The men enthusiastically echoed his compliment, but Angelica was glad she did not have to drink, because suddenly there was a large lump in her throat. Oh, Christian, she cried silently, I wanted everything to be different when you got back, but things are worse than ever.

The Wallaces began to serve the meal, proving that they had taken Angelica's instructions seriously. In addition to the standard beef, they brought out steaming bowls of fresh vegetables, new peas, stewed tomatoes, and succotash with early corn. Then came mashed potatoes and golden brown biscuits, followed by cake and two kinds of pie. Conversation centered around the abundance and variety of food. Everyone seemed to be having a wonderful time except Christian, who remained virtually silent unless answering direct questions from those seated around him.

His eyes were eloquent, however, sending Angelica the message that he was vitally aware of her no matter how detached his manner appeared. As the evening wore on, she began to think about the future and what it might hold. Now that her cattle had been delivered safely, Christian's job, and the others' as well, was ostensibly over. No one had mentioned that fact, however, because the spectre of Harlan Snyder still hovered. Until they knew what his next move might be, Angelica's ranch could not yet be considered safe.

Until such time as it could be, Christian would remain in her employ, but when she pictured that, she frowned. He would be working for her, and if she knew anything at all about the man, he would be staying as far away from her as possible. Opportunities for them to be alone, for her to overcome his mysterious reluctance to acknowledge his love for her, would be few and far between.

She could simply wait and watch for the right chance, but that chance might never come. Besides, waiting was not something she did well. No, if she wanted a chance, she would have to make it herself. As she considered her options, a plan began to form in her mind. It was daring and reckless and probably a little foolish, but if it worked, it would be well worth the risk.

By the time dessert had been served, her plan was all but perfect. The only problem she could foresee was getting by Maria, but Maria played right into her hands.

"Robbie, I think we should be going back to Kate's now," the Mexican woman said, having noticed the boy yawning prodigiously.

Robbie put up a token protest, but even he realized the game was up. After bidding everyone good night, he and Maria left.

As an extra treat for the men, Angelica produced a box of the finest cigars Kate's store could boast and induced the men to try them after she and Kate had assured everyone that the smoke would not bother them in the least. This bought her the time she needed. When the cigars were gone, she judged that Robbie and Maria would have long since turned in. Now she had to deal with Kate, of course, but from the way her friend was conversing with Miles, she judged that would not be too difficult.

"I think it's time Kate and I were getting on home," Angelica announced. "I know you gentlemen would like to retire to the saloon where you can finish up this celebration in style. Please, enjoy a round of drinks on your Boss Lady, and take tomorrow off. I won't expect to see any of you at the ranch until suppertime or later."

The men greeted this offer with a murmur of gratitude. Angelica and Kate were almost to the door when Miles, bless his heart, said, "Would you ladies like me to walk back with you to the house?"

Angelica noticed how pleased Kate seemed at the offer and realized this was going to be even easier than she had hoped. "Oh, thank you, Miles, but would you mind escorting Mrs. Marsden alone? I'd like to speak to Mr. Collins in private for a moment."

From the corner of her eye, she saw Christian's head come up, and she could almost feel his instant wariness from across the room. She concentrated her attention on Miles, who was accepting her charge with surprising eagerness. In a moment, all the others were gone, leaving her alone with Christian in the restaurant.

"What did you want to talk about?" he asked, maintaining his distance. His voice was perfectly modulated to express only a courteous interest, but she could see the suspicion in his azure eyes.

She ignored it. "About the size of the bonus I should give the men. Do you think one hundred dollars is enough?"

Plainly, he did. "If you can afford it," he allowed.

"Oh, I'm feeling very rich right now, and I wouldn't be if it weren't for my men," she replied cheerfully.

He said nothing, since no response was necessary. A few moments of silence stretched between them. He was still standing several yards away. He shifted his weight from one foot to the other and asked, "Was there something else?"

She could almost see him trying to figure out what she was up to. Meanwhile, she was listening for the sound of Miles's and Kate's voices to fade, indicating they had a fairly good head start. "No, that's all," she demurred when she could no longer hear her friends.

Neither of them moved for several more heartbeats. She was hoping he would offer, but she was forced to ask, "Would you mind walking me back to Kate's?"

The Kid drew a long breath and let it out slowly as the trap closed around him. He had that old feeling of powerlessness again, but this time he surrendered to it, knowing that his will to resist any scheme she was cooking up would vanish the moment he got within an arm's length of her anyway.

Certain he was being infinitely foolish, certain he was dooming them both to an anguish far greater than any joy could justify, still he went to her and offered his arm. Without warning, the words "Like a lamb to the slaughter" came to his mind. He smiled grimly, and he could see she was a little surprised. She even hesitated a second before taking his arm, as if she were suddenly afraid he might have a plan of his own. Then her reckless confidence took over once again, and with a toss of her head, she slipped her hand into the crook of his elbow.

Angelica looked up at him out of the corner of her eye. He was being awfully docile, and the aura of wariness had vanished. Was it possible? Could he have surrendered so easily? She would soon find out, she realized as they walked outside, crossed the short distance to the corner and turned onto Kate's street.

Her house, sitting between two smaller edifices in which the town's other merchants lived, was lighted only by a lamp in the front hall that Kate had apparently just lit. Angelica noted with satisfaction that both Robbie's and Maria's windows were dark.

In the evening stillness, Kate's voice came to them clearly as she spoke to Miles on the porch.

"Do you dance, Mr. Blackmon?"

Miles chuckled. "I haven't in many years."

Angelica could just barely make out their silhouettes in the shadows of the porch. "They make a nice couple, don't they?" she whispered.

The Kid glanced down at her in surprise, and then looked back at the figures on the porch, the tall, lanky one and the shorter, softly rounded one. This time he saw them with new eyes. Miles? With a woman? In all the years the Kid had known him, Miles had never so much as looked at a woman. Having lost Lettie himself, the Kid had understood Miles's reluctance to get involved again. Could it be that they had *both* succumbed at last?

"I was thinking about having a dance here in town," Kate was saying. "Mrs. Wallace and I have been talking about it for months now."

"That sounds like a fine idea," Miles replied.

Angelica and Christian were at the front walk. "A dance! How lovely," Angelica exclaimed as they moved out of the darkness into the dim circle of light coming from the front doorway.

"You'll have to help me, of course," Kate said.

Angelica laughed. "You know I'd love to." Christian stopped when they reached the bottom of the porch steps. Apparently, he thought his duty was done, and she would now release him. Instead, she smiled up at Kate. "Would you mind if we borrowed your buggy, Kate? It's still early, and Christian and I would like to go for a ride."

Christian's arm tensed beneath her fingers, but she knew he was too much of a gentleman to contradict her in front of their friends.

"Well, certainly," Kate agreed quickly, although Angelica could almost see her thinking that it really wasn't early at all but actually quite late for a young lady to go riding with a gentleman. Fortunately, Kate had no idea of her real plans, or she would never have consented to let her use the buggy at all.

Angelica turned to Christian, expecting to see rebellion etched on his fine features. Instead she saw what she thought was resignation, but that might only have been because the light was so bad. "I'll wait here for you to get back with the buggy," she told him, assured of his compliance. "I want to get my wrap." She gave his arm a small squeeze before letting him go, and mounted the steps without looking back. She smiled sweetly at Miles and Kate and wished them good night, ignoring their knowing looks.

The Kid watched her go, admiring the picture she made in that fancy green dress. She was a piece of work, all right. So she wanted to go for a buggy ride. She'd want to talk, of course, but he could handle that, even if she started in about how she loved him again. He'd have his hands full with driving so there would be no temptation to take her in his arms, and if things did get that far, a buggy was much too cramped for them to go any further. Just to be on the safe side, he'd leave the top of the buggy down, though. Nothing untoward could happen in an open vehicle.

Miles cleared his throat rather loudly. "Weren't you going to go get the buggy?" he asked, startling the Kid out of his reverie.

"Oh, yeah," he said, chagrined that he had been caught mooning after Angelica. "Good night, folks," he called back over his shoulder as he hurried toward the livery stable.

Angelica slipped silently into the room she shared with Maria and fumbled in her dresser drawer until she found the shawl she was looking for.

Maria stirred, causing Angelica to freeze in place. "Angelica, is that you?" Maria asked sleepily.

"Yes, Mama. I'm sorry I woke you. I was just getting a wrap. Christian and I are going to sit on the porch for a while," she lied.

Maria mumbled something unintelligible in agreement and rolled over to a more comfortable position. In a few moments Angelica heard her breathing settle back down to the regularity of sleep. Satisfied that Maria was not a threat, Angelica moved to the bedroom door and listened until she heard Kate climb the stairs and enter her own bedroom.

Only then, when she knew she would not have to answer any more questions, did she venture back out. Down in the parlor, she went straight to Kate's desk and scribbled a note of explanation. There would be hell to pay when Maria read it, but Angelica would be many miles away by then. She hoped.

Propping the note up on the hall table, she blew out the lamp and went out on the front porch to wait for Christian. She was not a moment too soon. The minute she stepped outside, she heard the rattle of the buggy and the clopping of the horse on the deserted street. Anticipation tingled over her, making her shiver. She hugged the paisley shawl more tightly around her bare shoulders and hurried down the steps.

Christian was just climbing out of the buggy when she reached him. "It's a lovely night for a ride, isn't it?" she remarked, smiling when she noticed he had left the buggy top down. She knew he thought she had planned this ride so they could be alone for a little spooning. It was a logical assumption, but Angelica's plan did not include anything so obvious.

She allowed him to help her into the buggy and busied herself with adjusting her skirts as he climbed up beside her. He was reaching for the reins when she spoke. "Christian?" she said, her voice soft with affection.

A million stars twinkled overhead, but they did not illuminate his face. Anxiously, she tried to read his expression as he turned toward her, but the night was simply too dark. Then she heard the rasp of his breath as he struggled against the temptation to touch her. It was a battle she wanted him to lose. "I love you," she whispered, reaching out to stroke his cheek.

In the next instant, his arms were around her, his mouth on hers, forcing her lips apart as he crushed her to him. His kiss was the same as it had been this afternoon, desperate and wonderful. Angelica gave herself up to his dominance even as she clung to him with equal urgency. Mouths fused, hands explored, bodies strained together, frustrated by the barrier of clothes and the narrowness of the wagon seat.

After long, breathless minutes, he pulled slightly away.

They were both gasping by then. "We can't do this here," he murmured, his warm breath caressing her face. "Someone will see us."

"We can go out to the ranch," she murmured in reply. "No one will see us there." She felt his surprise—or perhaps it was shock—and his instinctive resistance to the idea, so she hurried to explain. "If we go out there now, we can be alone together all night."

All night. The words seemed to echo in his head, conjuring visions he knew he should not be seeing. "Angelica," he protested, knowing that she was offering far more than a night of lovemaking. Her invitation was for a commitment, but it was a commitment Kid Collins could not make. "Your reputation would be ruined," he argued in an attempt to dissuade her. "When people found out . . ."

"No one will find out!" she insisted. "I left a note for Mama. I told her to tell everyone we went out to the ranch at first light. No one else will know we really left tonight except Miles and Kate, and they won't tell."

He felt his resolve slipping. She was right, they might well be able to protect her good name, but he reminded himself that he had an even better reason for refusing to go with her. "Are you forgetting what I told you before I left on the trail drive? Nothing has changed. I'm still a gunfighter and . . ."

"I don't care about that!" she cried, clutching his shirt with both hands as she felt the momentum slipping away from her.

". . . and I was a Comanchero . . ."

"You were just a child! You had no choice! Oh, Christian, don't you see? If those things don't matter to me, they shouldn't matter to you, either. We love each other. Are you going to let things that aren't really important keep us apart? You also said you couldn't make any promises because you couldn't guarantee that you'd come back from the trail drive alive. Well, here you are, alive and well. We've been apart too long already. I don't want us to be apart any longer."

He stared down at her. In the shadows all he could see clearly were her eyes. They gleamed up at him, filled with the love he knew she felt for him, mirroring the love he felt for her. Was she right? Was he a fool to let his past destroy his one opportunity for happiness? For the first time, he began to see things from her point of view. If she didn't care about his past, if none of that mattered to her, then he really was a fool to let it stand between him and the woman he loved, to let it keep him from the life he longed for with every fiber of his being.

Suddenly, the strongest sensation engulfed him. So long had it been since he had allowed himself to feel hope, at first he did not recognize the emotion surging through him. Was it possible? Could Kid Collins really have a future with Angelica Ross? To live with her, to laugh with her, to love with her, for the rest of his life? The image shimmered tantalizingly close. It was all within his reach. He had only to take the precious gift she was offering.

"I . . ." He had to clear the hoarseness out of his throat. "I don't want us to be apart anymore, either." He wanted them to be together, forever. Cupping her face in his hands, he pressed one brief kiss to her mouth. Then, releasing her, he reached for the reins again. When he slapped the horse into motion, he knew exactly where he was going.

Angelica grabbed onto the seat as the buggy jerked forward, hardly able to believe she had convinced him so easily. Apprehensively, she stared up at him in the darkness, trying to read his mood. He was going, but suddenly he seemed like a stranger, an angry stranger. Her nervousness prickled into fear. "Christian?" she whispered, as if she could call him back from wherever he had gone.

He glanced down at her, startled by her tentative tone. She was clutching her shawl around her as if for protection, and although it was too dark to really read her expression, her eyes were glittering suspiciously. He realized he had frightened her with his abruptness. Quickly, he shifted the reins to his left hand and curved his right arm around behind her. "Come here," he commanded softly, giving her a gentle nudge.

With a grateful sigh, she eagerly complied. He tightened his arm, pulling her closer still until nothing separated them but the layers of their clothing. The sweet fragrance of her hair rose around him in an invisible cloud, clogging his senses until the world now hidden by the night no longer existed. They were the only two people in the world, and they were riding to their destiny.

Chapter Eleven

"Angelica, wake up. We're here." The whispered words tickled her ear, sending delicious shivers down her spine. She roused slightly, snuggling more closely into the solid warmth beside her.

"Oh, no, you don't," Christian chuckled, gently pushing her upright. His lips brushed her temple, his breath stirring the tendrils of hair the night wind had pulled loose from her chignon during the long ride out from the ranch. "When you set out to seduce a man, you aren't supposed to fall asleep."

His smile was a caress against her cheek. She nuzzled him, reveling in the prickle of his whiskers as the meaning of his words gradually sank into her sleep-fogged brain. "Seduce!" she exclaimed, coming instantly awake. Blinking away her fog, she glanced quickly around and discovered they were inside a barn, a very familiar barn. Her gaze came back to his face, which she could barely make out in the dark shadows. "I don't remember trying to seduce you," she lied.

He made a disgusted noise in his throat. "That's probably because as soon as you talked me into bringing you out here, you curled up on my shoulder and fell asleep."

"Talked you into it!" she cried in mock outrage. "That's not the way I remember it."

"I thought you didn't remember it at all," he challenged. She could hear the laughter in his voice, and her own lips twitched in response. His hands were moving sensuously up and down her arms, sending a heated glow over her body.

"It's coming back to me now," she informed him, reaching out to do some stroking of her own. Beneath her palms, his heartbeat quickened, and she let her hands splay across his chest, as if she were measuring its breadth. "As I recall, I merely asked you to drive me out to the ranch . . ."

"So we could be alone," he reminded her provocatively. His hands began to move more urgently against the bare flesh of her arms where her shawl had fallen away.

She smiled at the huskiness in his voice, feeling a new sense of power. She let her hands slide up until she, too, encountered bare flesh. Her fingers skimmed his throat and then his face before delving into the thick softness of his hair. He needed no further encouragement. His mouth came down to hers, open and demanding a response she eagerly gave.

For a long moment, the night closed in about them, shutting out all sense of time and place. Angelica forgot everything except the reality of his lips on hers and his body straining to get closer. Then the whole world lurched, jarring them rudely apart.

Christian muttered an expletive. "Stay right here," he commanded, giving her arm one last squeeze before moving hastily away.

The buggy jounced as he jumped out, and she heard the horse stamp impatiently in the darkness. She muttered an expletive of her own when she realized the source of the interruption. Their whole world had not lurched, only the buggy. The horse was still hitched and was apparently anxious to be free. Romance would have to wait a few more minutes while Christian took care of the animal.

The horse was not the only impatient one, she noted with a smile as she heard Christian murmuring imprecations and thumping around in search of a lantern. After several loud bumps, she finally saw the flare of a match, and in another second he held a lighted lantern aloft triumphantly.

Instantly, his gaze sought hers. For just one second, she thought she caught a glimpse of uncertainty, as if he were concerned that their brief separation might have destroyed the mood. She reassured him with a smile, openly admiring the way the lantern light turned his hair to gold and reflected off his finely molded features. "Ahem," she cleared her throat meaningfully. "I'd appreciate it if you'd hurry."

His eyes glinted wickedly as his beautiful mouth stretched into a grin. "Yes, ma'am," he replied. In record time, he unhitched the horse and hurriedly rubbed him down with an old feed sack. Fascinated, Angelica watched his hands moving confidently over the animal, and she shivered slightly with anticipation. Soon those hands would be moving on her body. Desire coiled within her, tightening all her secret places. She pulled her shawl more closely about her and shifted restlessly on the seat.

In another minute, Christian had turned the animal loose in the corral outside and returned for her. He hesitated beside the buggy, wiping his hands on his pant legs as he looked up at her. In the flickering lantern light, his eyes were unreadable. For a second, he looked like a stranger again, and doubts began to gather, hovering just out of sight in the darkness. They had been separated for so many weeks. Would things still be the same between them? Then he breathed her name. When he reached for her, his hands were not quite steady.

Her momentary uncertainties vanished, driven away by the knowledge that he, too, had uncertainties. "Oh, Christian," she whispered, going eagerly into his arms.

He lifted her from the buggy with loving care, and when her feet touched the ground, he did not let her go. His arms slipped around her, and once more, his mouth found hers. This time, his kiss conveyed far more than passion and desire. His lips claimed hers with a possessiveness he had never shown before, and she gloried in it.

The kiss went on and on as each wordlessly told the other of feelings that transcended speech. When at last he lifted his head, they were both weak and breathless. "I think . . . we'd better . . . go in the house," he rasped.

She nodded, not trusting her voice. He tucked her firmly against his side with one arm and snatched up the lantern with his free hand. As one, they left the barn and moved toward the house.

The swinging lantern cast eerie shadows across the empty ranch yard, and somewhere far away a lone coyote howled, but in the circle of Christian's arm, Angelica was immune to the desolate air of the dark ranch buildings. Even the forbidding aspect of the house with its shuttered windows held no fear for her. Nothing could touch her now that she had Christian back again.

The unlocked front door swung open silently beneath her touch, and the cool, musty air from the long-closed house engulfed her. The lantern cast strange shadows here, too, but she saw only the shadows of desire in Christian's eyes.

By unspoken consent, they hurried through the entryway, out into the courtyard. There, the fragrance of a thousand flowers swirled around them and the fountain trickled faintly in the darkness, but they took no time to search out these familiar sights. Instead, they hurried toward her bedroom.

His arm fell away from her as she opened the door and stepped inside. Everything here was exactly as she had left it, exactly as it had always been, except that now Christian was with her. She turned to find him watching her from the doorway. His eyes were eloquent as he let his gaze skim over her. They spoke of his love and his admiration and his desire.

She tilted her head coquettishly and gave him an impudent grin. "Won't you come in, Mr. Collins? And please, close the door behind you."

Slowly, carefully, he set the lantern down on the table just inside the doorway and reached blindly for the door, never taking his gaze from hers. His deliberate movements made her shiver at his silent message. This was not a night for haste.

With care equal to his, she let the paisley shawl slide from her shoulders and slither to the floor. She heard his breath lodge in his throat for a second before he released it on a shaky sigh. He reached up and removed his Stetson. Glancing around for a place to put it, he sent it sailing toward a chair in the corner. It fell short, clumping to the floor. Neither of them noticed.

"This time I want to see you," he said, staring at the swell of flesh above the neckline of her gown. "*All* of you."

Angelica felt desire coiling tighter and tighter inside of her. "I want to see you, too," she said, her voice strangely breathless. Suddenly, her bodice seemed much too tight as her nipples hardened and strained for freedom. "You'll have to help me, though. I can't get out of this dress by myself." Eager to be rid of the restraining garment, she turned, offering him her back.

The Kid stared down at the wispy, flame-colored curls hugging the alabaster skin of her neck. He swallowed against a suddenly dry mouth and reached for her.

"The hooks are kind of tricky," she warned, but her tone was more enticing than distracting.

He grasped the stiff material, feeling for the first fastening. The fabric was warm from her skin, and her fragrance, sweet and earthy, drifted up in invisible torment. His hands began to shake. "I've never done this before," he confessed, feeling the need to explain his clumsiness and not wanting her to know that her nearness was causing him to tremble like a willow leaf in the wind.

Angelica caught her breath at the huskiness of his voice. "I'm glad to hear it," she replied with an unsteady laugh. His fingers brushed the bare skin above her gown, sending more delicious shivers racing over her body. The first hook gave, releasing the strain on her breasts. Instinctively, she lifted her hands to catch the gaping bodice.

At that moment, he let out the breath he had been holding. It gusted over her like an invisible caress, stroking the tendrils of hair that had come loose from her chignon and gliding down her shoulders, which hunched in reaction. The gown slid a notch lower as the second hook gave beneath his fingers.

Now he had the knack. In seconds she was free. "There," he said to tell her he was finished. His voice was hoarse. She whirled to face him, catching a glimpse of naked longing before he had time to compose himself. She wanted to see that look again, wanted him unable to control his feelings.

Slowly, deliberately, she let the bodice drop and shimmied her arms free. Her wispy chemise was all that covered her breasts above her corset, and she gloried in the way his eyes were drawn there inexorably. Once he had said she was beautiful. Tonight, seeing his undisguised admiration, she finally felt beautiful.

She tried a small smile and lifted her hands to his chest, slipping them inside his vest this time so she could feel the heat and the strength of his body through the fabric of his shirt. His heart thudded unsteadily beneath her palm in an echo of her own. "I guess I should return the favor," she said, working one of his shirt buttons free.

His breath jerked to a halt and then came back with a rasp. "If you like," he said. She paused, looking up to study his eyes. They were the color of a stormy sky.

"I like," she replied, smiling again when she felt a small tremor go through him. As she fumbled with the rest of his buttons, he quickly disposed of his vest, letting it fall to the floor behind him.

With eager hands, she spread the shirt wide to expose the furred expanse of his chest. He shrugged out of the garment, tossing it aside. For several heartbeats he simply stood there so she could marvel at how imperfectly she had remembered his blatant masculinity.

"I'm getting ahead of you," he pointed out, distracting her from her admiration of his bared shoulders.

She glanced down at herself and then back up to catch his perplexed expression. Plainly, he did not know how to proceed with undressing her now that he had taken care of the only obvious fastening to her clothes. With a knowing smile, she reached back and untied her petticoats. In a few seconds, they swooped to the floor, carrying her gown with them and leaving her standing in her chemise and corset.

"You ought to be able to figure it out from he—" Her sentence ended in a squeal of delight as he scooped her out of the birrowing pile and lifted her high against his chest.

She wrapped her arms around his neck, burying her

face in the warmth of his shoulder and inhaling his scent. He sank down on the bed with her, laying her flat and looming over her for a moment that stretched into eternity. His eyes were so full of love, she thought her heart might burst in her chest. In vain, she sought the words to tell him what she was feeling. At last, knowing mere speech could never convey her love, she reached up and drew his face to her.

His kiss was fiercely gentle, devouring yet careful, lest he harm her with his urgency. She tolerated that briefly before pulling him closer still with an urgency of her own. His restraint crumbled. No longer gentle, no longer careful, he plundered her mouth until she was breathless and panting. Then he moved on, sampling every inch of flesh exposed to him. First her face, then her throat, down and down until the barrier of her chemise stopped him.

With hands made clumsy by haste, he tugged at the material but found it anchored in the iron grip of her corset. The fastening of that contraption baffled him completely, and he drew back with a muttered curse.

"I'll do that," she offered breathlessly. While he watched in fascination, she released the front clasps of her corset and wrestled it out from under her.

She expected him to come back to her then, but instead he simply let his gaze run over her. It skimmed her breasts, down past where her thin chemise caressed her hips and thighs, and on to her long legs, still encased in shoes and stockings. Slowly, deliberately, he took one of her ankles and stroked his way up past the lower edge of her chemise until he found her garter. Tingles danced up her thighs and settled in her loins as he leisurely peeled her stocking down and then pulled off her green satin pump. By the time he had removed the second one, she was fairly writhing with the need to be touched.

"Christian," she whispered, desire strangling her voice. "I think . . . you'd better put out the light now."

But he was shaking his head. "I said I wanted to see you this time, Angelica."

Something about the way he said "this time"—as if this were a special time—excited her even more. This time was indeed different from all the other times they had made love. This time was forever. Then his hands were working the buttons of her chemise, and such distinctions ceased to matter.

No longer patient, he stripped the garment down her arms, down and down, until she lay completely exposed beneath his heated gaze. She opened her mouth to protest, but she had no time. Her mouth stayed open in wonder as she watched his eyes fill with awe.

"My God, you're even more beautiful than I'd imagined," he said after what seemed a long time.

The instinctive urge to cover herself fled before such a tribute. Angelica lay still, mesmerized by his adoration. "I said I wanted to see you, too," she reminded him when she finally found her voice.

Something flickered in his eyes, something warm and wonderful. Slowly, he rose from the bed and began to remove the rest of his clothes. She looked away when he stripped off the gun belt and let it fall, not wanting to think about what it stood for. Only when the rustle of cloth ceased did she dare look back.

He stood before her completely naked, proud and bold and thoroughly aroused. His body looked like bronze in the flickering lamplight, and the air seemed to crackle with the tension that stretched between them. With a cry of need she lifted her arms to him.

He came immediately, covering her, enfolding her, possessing her. His mouth was hot and hungry, but he found a banquet awaiting him. She offered herself with abandon, willing and even eager to be consumed.

Angelica felt as if a thousand tiny flames burned beneath her skin, heating her, scorching her, and turning her blood to liquid fire. Christian's hands and lips were everywhere, but instead of smothering the flames, he fanned them, until her whole body ignited.

For the first time they were completely free. No clothing restricted them, no fear of discovery haunted them, no doubts about the future clouded their happiness. Tonight they could touch and explore. Tonight they could linger and love, secure in the knowledge of each other's love. Hands stroked silken flesh, lips suckled greedily, legs tangled into love knots, and in the silence of the night, heart spoke to heart.

"Christian!" she cried, not knowing how to tell him of her need.

He responded, understanding her nevertheless. They communed without words, through touch and taste and scent, telling each other of emotions for which words did not exist.

Angelica watched his face as he filled her, once again seeing her own wonder reflected in his eyes. Joining their bodies was only a symbol of the love that had already joined their hearts, a love that pulsed through her now in joyous waves. She whispered it to him in disjointed phrases that he echoed back to her as together they soared into the sweet oblivion of fulfillment.

For a long time afterward, they clung to each other, futilely resisting the inevitable return to reality. Kisses, caresses, and softly spoken words slowed their descent, but long before either of them was ready, they found themselves firmly back in the real world.

The lantern cast shadows in the corners of the room and across their damp bodies. Self-conscious of the nudity she had rejoiced in only moments ago, Angelica turned in Christian's embrace, shielding herself against him. Misinterpreting her intent, he murmured his approval, settling her more comfortably upon his shoulder. His fingers toyed with the remnants of her chignon, absently pulling loose the few remaining pins so the heavy mass of her hair could fall free.

She, in turn, raked her fingers through the golden curls on his chest, giving the process her entire attention so she would not have to meet his eyes as she said, "Christian, I love you."

Steeled for the protest she had learned to expect, she waited apprehensively as he drew a deep breath and let it out with a long sigh. "I love you, too, Angelica, more than I ever thought it was possible to love anyone."

"Oh!" was all she could think to say as she lifted her head so she could see his face. "Oh, Christian!" His image blurred.

"Are you crying?" he asked in alarm. "Did I hurt you?"

"No," she assured him, hastily wiping the moisture from her eyes. "You've made me so happy!"

"People don't cry when they're happy, Angelica," he informed her with a frown. Gently, he eased her away from him while his concerned gaze swept over her, looking for possible injuries.

"Women cry when they're happy," she contradicted him. "At least, I do, and . . . stop that! You're embarrassing me." She snatched the edge of the coverlet and tried to pull it over to shield herself from him, but he caught her hand.

"Is that true?" he demanded.

"Of course it's true. I'm not used to having men stare at me that way," she assured him vehemently, fighting for possession of the quilt.

"No, I mean is it true that women cry when they're

happy?" he insisted.

"Yes, it is," she said, "But I promise not to cry if you'll give me this cover, even though it will make me very happy."

His frown twitched into a grin. "But that would make me very unhappy," he said, prying her fingers loose from the fabric. "I'm afraid you'll have to get used to having at least one man stare at you, because I intend to do it a lot." Effortlessly, he pinned her hands to her sides and looked his fill. She felt her cheeks growing hot, but whether her reaction was embarrassment or pleasure, she did not bother to decide.

His grin grew positively wicked. "You know, I've spent a lot of time wondering if your hair was red *all over,*" he said with a meaningful downward glance.

Angelica felt her blush spreading rampantly. "Christian!"

"I tried to tell you I wasn't fit company for a lady," he reminded her playfully, "but you wouldn't take no for an answer, so now you have to pay the price." His hands released hers and slid to stroke more sensitive spots.

Angelica gasped, but after a few seconds, she decided she would not mind at all paying whatever price he demanded. She might even have told him so if she had been capable of speech at that moment. Instead she showed him, using hands and lips to bring him to the same level of mindlessness to which he was bringing her.

The torment continued for what seemed an eternity, neither of them willing to bring on the climax that would end this bliss. But even pleasure has its limits, and at last they reached them, dissolving into the maelstrom of passion until all differences between them disappeared, and they became truly one.

* * *

"Christian?" Angelica emerged from sleep to find the bed beside her empty in the early dawn light.

"Shhh," he said, hurrying to her side. He was half-dressed. She rubbed the sleep from her eyes, or tried to. Her body did not want to come fully awake. "Go back to sleep. It's early yet," he urged, gently brushing the hair from her face.

"Don't leave me," she said, irritated to hear how child-like she sounded. After last night, she had never felt more like a woman.

His chuckle was a comforting sound. "I'm not going far, just out to the bunkhouse. I don't want anyone to find me in your bed. That would be a little much even for Miles to overlook, and Maria would probably shoot me."

"Oh," she said, too groggy to express her real feelings on the matter. Already her eyes were drooping shut again. "I wanted to make love with you again." Her voice was little more than a whisper.

His lips brushed hers in the lightest of kisses. "Don't worry. We'll have all the time in the world for that once we're married."

Married. The word settled into her consciousness, becoming part of the beautiful dream that was just beginning. She never heard him leave.

Much later she awoke with a start, instantly alert and aware. She was alone, as she had known she would be. Dimly, she remembered that sometime in the dawn hours, Christian had stolen from her bed and left her room. Looking around, she saw that he had taken with him every trace that he had ever been there.

Well, not *every* trace, she conceded with a rueful smile as she stretched experimentally and found that her body ached in several new and very interesting places. Memories of the night before flickered across her mind with tantalizing clarity. Christian's face alight with desire, his eyes smoldering with want, his body taut with longing. Christian's face content, his eyes warmly satisfied, his body replete from loving her. He had called her his angel and cried aloud with joy at the pleasure she gave him.

With a satisfied sigh, Angelica curled up into a more comfortable position, drawing his pillow to her so she could have something soft to hold that smelled of him. Christian loved her. He had told her so, and he had spoken of marriage, or at least she thought he had, during that fuzzy time when she had awakened to find him leaving her room. Even if that had only been part of her dream, though, she knew he would speak of it soon. They belonged to each other now in every way but one. It was the next logical step.

She toyed with that idea for a few moments until her thoughts led naturally to Maria and what her foster mother would say when she heard of the impending marriage. Thoughts of Maria jarred her back to the present and a much more immediate problem. *Maria would be here soon!*

Angelica bolted upright, alarmed to see that the sun was well up. Maria would have read her note by now and would be on her way to the ranch with blood in her eye. Wedding or not, Angelica's *mamacita* would be furious over her conduct of the night before. With a groan, Angelica rolled out of bed, praying that she could get dressed and have the bed made, at least, before the hour of reckoning arrived.

By the time Maria's wagon rattled into the yard, Angelica had managed to pull herself together. She was dressed, quite primly, in a sprigged muslin gown which she had found hanging in her wardrobe. She had made the bed and removed all traces of the little drama that had been played out in her bedroom the night before.

She had hoped to seek out Christian for a good-morning kiss before having to deal with Maria, but she had run out of time. Instead, she went outside and waved a welcome, a stiff little smile pasted on her lips as Maria reined in the horses.

Maria was fit to be tied. Her wide mouth was pressed into a grim line, and her black eyes flashed fire. Angelica winced a little in anticipation of the scene to come, but managed to greet Miles and her brother, who had accompanied Maria, with a semblance of calm. Robbie hopped off his pony and ran over to where she stood by the front door.

"How come you didn't wait for us?" he demanded. "Maria said you left before daylight."

Angelica glanced up to where Miles was dismounting. His eyebrows were raised expectantly, and she thought his lips were twitching with amusement. She brought her gaze quickly back to Robbie. "I woke up early and couldn't go back to sleep, so I figured I'd just come on home," she lied, wondering how on earth she could expect him to believe such a whopper. "I found Mr. Collins at the livery stable, and he was kind enough to drive me out."

Robbie's expression was perplexed but not disbelieving. Obviously, he had heard enough adult explanations that made little sense to predispose him to believe her. "You could have waited," he insisted.

Angelica nodded. "I will next time," she promised, sure that next time there would be no need to sneak away to be alone with Christian. She lifted her gaze to Miles, who was helping Maria down from the wagon seat. "Where are the rest of the men?" she inquired with forced cheerfulness.

"They took you at your word," Miles reported, returning her smile with a knowing one of his own. "They're sleeping it off at the livery. They were all so drunk last night that I doubt they even heard the Kid come back after your buggy ride."

"Oh," she said, not knowing what else to say. Maria was glaring daggers at her. Angelica knew her foster mother would not say a word in front of Miles and Robbie, but as soon as they were alone, she would scorch her ears.

"Where is Mr. Collins?" Maria inquired grimly.

"Here I am," he called, emerging from the barn. He was smiling, but even from across the yard, Angelica could sense his wariness. "Morning, everybody," he said, striding toward them. "You folks must've got an early start, too."

"We did," Robbie informed him, racing across the yard to meet him. "Maria woke everybody up when she read Angel's note. She was mad as a wet hen."

Christian stopped, and his gaze went to Maria's. He was close now. No more than ten feet from where she stood. His smile vanished. "She was right to be mad," he told Robbie, although his eyes never left Maria. "We should have waited, but if she's going to be mad, she can be mad at me. I should have refused to bring Angelica out here without a proper chaperone."

Angelica started to protest, but Maria cut her off. "I *am* mad at you, Señor Collins, but I know where the real blame lies." Her dark eyes shifted to Angelica. "Will you come inside with me, *Angelita?* I would like to talk to you."

Without waiting for a reply, she took Angelica's arm and started for the house. Knowing it was foolish to resist, Angelica went meekly along.

"Maria!" Christian called, plainly intending to stop her, but Angelica gestured for him to stay where he was.

"It's all right, really," she told him confidently, touched

by his desire to protect her but knowing she did not need any protection. She had endured enough of Maria's diatribes to know she would survive. This one would be the easiest of all because Angelica had the perfect response. She would save it until the very last, however.

Maria was already muttering imprecations under her breath by the time they reached the courtyard. When the bedroom door closed behind them, she burst into a full-scale attack.

"Madre de Dios! What is in your head? Is this what I have raised you to be, a *puta?"* Maria spat out the word, making Angelica wince, but she refused to be ashamed. Keeping her head high, Angelica stood dumbly before Maria's outrage. The tirade was a confusing mixture of Spanish and English, but Angelica understood every ugly word. Although she winced several more times, she still managed to maintain her dignity.

At long last Maria's fury began to cool, and the flood of angry words slowed and finally stopped. "Do you have nothing to say?" Maria demanded after a long moment of silence.

Angelica studied her shoes for a second or two before lifting her eyes to Maria again. "I'm sorry, Mama. You're absolutely right, I should have used better judgment and not come out here last night."

Maria's mouth dropped open in astonishment at this uncharacteristic show of humility, but before she could speak, Angelica continued. "I took a terrible risk, a risk I probably shouldn't have taken, but I'm not sorry I did it, Mama. Christian and I are going to be married."

"Married?" Maria echoed, still stunned. "You are sure?"

Angelica nodded. "He told me he loves me."

Maria frowned. "You have set a date?"

"Not yet," Angelica admitted reluctantly. She didn't

want to explain that she and Christian had not yet actually discussed the matter. "But we will, soon. Now that my cattle have been delivered, there's no reason to wait."

"Harlan Snyder may give you a good reason to wait," Maria said. "What do you think he will do when he finds out we have tricked him?"

The first shiver of unease slithered over Angelica as she considered the possible answers to this question. Suddenly, she recalled that Christian still had not found his sister's murderers, either. Things were actually very far from being settled, and probably always would be as long as Snyder was around. "Christian can take care of Snyder," Angelica said, with more assurance than she actually possessed.

Maria clasped her hands prayerfully in front of her. "I hope you are right, *Angelita.*"

Out in the yard, the Kid helped Miles unload the wagon. They had given Robbie his own bag to carry in, and now they stood alone. The Kid could not keep his gaze from straying toward the house, where he knew Angelica was incurring Maria's wrath.

"Don't worry about her. She can take care of herself," Miles said, giving the Kid a friendly slap on the back.

The Kid managed a weak smile. "Oh, I know she can. It's just that she shouldn't have to, at least not on my account." His gaze drifted over to the house again, and his smile faded as he considered the many problems they still had to overcome, Maria's disapproval being the least of them.

"It was a pretty daring thing to do, carrying the girl off right under everybody's nose like that," Miles observed with amusement. "I don't think I've ever seen a woman as mad as Maria was this morning. Of course, when she finds out you plan to marry Angelica, everything will be fine." Miles waited, and when the Kid did not reply, he asked, "You *are* planning to marry her, aren't you?"

"What? Oh, sure," the Kid replied, forcing his attention back to Miles and frowning his irritation that Miles had felt it necessary to ask. "I just don't know how long it'll be before it's safe to even have a wedding." He'd been thinking about the situation all morning, ever since he'd left Angelica's bed. The things that had seemed so simple last night looked far more complicated in the light of day. He still had to deal with Snyder and find the mysterious Ace, the only man he knew for certain had been a party to Rose and Pete's murders.

"That reminds me," Miles said, changing the subject with obvious reluctance. "I hate to bring this up right now, but I don't reckon there'll ever be a good time to mention it. Snyder's hired himself a shootist. Name's Tom Rivers."

"Rivers?" the Kid repeated thoughtfully, searching his memory. "Do we know him?"

Miles shook his head. "He's from Dodge. Spent some time as a deputy there, I hear."

The Kid grunted his understanding. Everyone knew the cattle-town lawmen were nothing more than hired killers who made their living by pistol-whipping Texas cowboys too drunk to defend themselves and then hauling them off to jail for fifty percent of the fine. The lawmen were usually Yankees in the bargain, too. Texans held no affection for such men.

"Did you talk to him?" the Kid asked.

"No, I didn't see him. Seems like he sticks pretty close to Snyder. The bartender told me about him. I got the feeling it was more in the nature of a warning, though."

The Kid nodded. One more obstacle to add to his list. He shifted his shoulders in unconscious protest at the invisible burdens resting there. How long before thus ugly mess would finally be settled so he and Angelica could live together in peace? Suddenly, he felt very impatient. Reaching into the back of the wagon, he grabbed one end of Angelica's trunk. "Let's take this inside and see what's going on," he suggested.

Angelica was coming out of her bedroom when they arrived, each carrying one end of her trunk. She was smiling, and her eyes lit up like green flames when she saw Christian. "I was wondering where you got off to," she said, stepping out of the way so they could carry her trunk into her room. "Put it over there," she instructed, pointing toward the empty corner.

They did her bidding, and when they straightened from their task, both men looked around. "Where's Maria?" the Kid asked.

"She went to see about getting a meal started," Angelica reported, thoroughly enjoying his concern. His blue gaze was studying her for any signs of distress from her encounter with Maria.

After a long moment, Miles cleared his throat, making them aware that they had been staring at each other rather raptly. "If you'll excuse me," he said with a grin. He started for the door, but Angelica was blocking his way, and she did not move. She wasn't about to let him get away so easily, not when he looked so smug.

"How's Kate?" she asked innocently.

"Kate?" he replied as if he'd never heard the name before.

"Yes, Kate," she repeated patiently. "You remember, Mrs. Marsden. You saw her this morning, didn't you?"

"Uh, yes, I did," he said. His smugness was gone.

"Did she say any more about the dance she's planning?" she inquired guilelessly, but Miles wasn't fooled. Unless she was mistaken, he was actually turning red.

"She said she's having it next Saturday. She'd like you

to come in a few days early and help her get ready," he reported stiffly.

Angelica considered this a moment. "Maybe she'd like you to come in a few days early, too," she suggested. Now he really was red, no question. "That is, if Christian can spare you."

For once, Miles seemed at a loss for words. He glanced helplessly at Christian, but found him thoroughly enjoying his friend's discomfort. "I'm sure we can spare him," Christian said.

Miles shifted his gaze back to Angelica. "Well, then, I guess I'll go see about the rest of the luggage," he said. This time Angelica stepped out of his way—it was either that or be run over. When he was gone, she turned to Christian, who returned her conspiratorial grin.

"Good morning," she whispered.

"Good morning," he whispered back. For a long moment they simply stared at each other, savoring the delicious knowledge of each other's love.

"I don't think you kissed me yet today," she informed him.

He frowned at her in mock consternation. "You're not one of those women who nags a man to death, are you?"

"I most certainly am. Now get yourself over here right now and—*omph.*" He smothered the rest of her command with his mouth, pulling her close in an embrace that was at once demanding and gentle. She went to him willingly, holding him to her with all her strength. The kiss was sweet and long, but not long enough. When he finally pulled away, she made a small sound of protest.

"No," he said, holding her firmly away from him. "First tell me what Maria said."

Seeing he was implacable, she sighed in defeat. "I don't think you want to know *exactly* what she said. Basically, she was furious and told me I shouldn't have come out here with you alone and things like that. She calmed down when I told her that . . ." She stopped, not wanting to admit she had stretched the truth a bit and committed him to marriage before he had mentioned it himself.

"You told her what?" he insisted.

"Well, after what happened, she'd naturally assume that . . . I mean, the proper thing would be to . . ." She shrugged in dismay.

His lips twitched suspiciously. "You told her we were getting married?" he guessed.

She nodded reluctantly.

He heaved a mock sigh of relief. "I was getting a little worried about you, Miss Ross. After all, you've ruined my reputation, but you haven't said a thing about making an honest man out of me—ouch!"

Angelica punched his shoulder again for good measure. "This isn't funny," she insisted.

He sobered instantly. "No, you're right. It isn't funny at all," he conceded. He lifted his hands to tenderly cup her outraged face. "If my life had followed its normal plan, I never would have known you or anyone like you, Angelica. I still don't have a right to you, and God knows, I've never done anything to deserve you, *but,*" he went on when she would have contradicted him, "I'm not going to let that stop me. Angelica, will you marry me?"

"I . . . Yes! Oh, yes!" she cried, throwing her arms around his neck and pulling his mouth down to hers.

"Most people wait until *after* the wedding to have their honeymoon," Maria informed them caustically.

Angelica and Christian broke apart guiltily and turned to face her. She was standing in the doorway, her arms folded belligerently across her ample bosom. Angelica felt Christian stiffen beside her.

"You're right, Maria," he said. "I've taken advantage

of my position here, and I'm sorry for that, sorrier than you'll ever know, but I'm going to make it up to Angelica. I know I don't deserve her, and I'm not the kind of man you would have picked for her, but . . ."

"You are right," she interrupted. "You are not good enough for my *Angelita.*"

"Mama!" Angelica protested.

Maria ignored her. "But no other man would ever be good enough for her, either. And you are wrong when you say you are not the man I would choose for her. I chose you the first day you came here. Sometimes I think perhaps I made a mistake, but then you change my mind again."

He stared at her in astonishment. "And how are you feeling about me this morning?" he wanted to know.

She shrugged eloquently. "Like I should take a stick to you, to *both* of you," she amended, giving Angelica a sharp look. "But I know you love my Angelica and she loves you. I think you will make each other very happy."

With a grateful cry, Angelica went to her. The two women embraced tearfully while Christian looked on. "Thank you, Mama," Angelica whispered before she pulled away. "I guess this means we have your blessing," she said aloud.

"You have my prayers," Maria corrected her. "You will need them, no?" she asked, turning back to Christian.

He frowned at her question. "Yes, I'm afraid we will. It seems that Snyder's getting ready to stir up some more trouble, so we'll have to put off our wedding plans for a while."

Maria nodded grimly, but Angelica refused to be discouraged. "But only for a little while," she insisted.

"And until then," Maria informed them, "no more sneaking away into the night. He," she gestured to Christian, "will sleep in the bunkhouse, and he will court you properly, with a chaperone."

"Of course, Mama," Angelica agreed meekly, but when she looked at Christian, her eyes were bright with mischief.

He bit back a smile of his own. "Of course, Maria," he confirmed.

Unfortunately, they quickly discovered that Maria had meant every word of her caution. She never allowed them more than a few brief minutes alone for some hurried good-night kisses. Their frustration grew with each day that passed. Being together without really being together was difficult enough, but waiting for Snyder to make his next move was driving everyone insane.

For some reason, Snyder chose not to call on Angelica out at the ranch, making it impossible for her to tell him she did not intend to marry him and thereby possibly jog him into action. It went against her nature to take the initiative and actually invite him over, since the very last thing in the world she wanted was to see him again. Consequently, she found herself stuck in a limbo of waiting.

Then Kate sent a note out, begging for her presence and her help with the upcoming dance. Angelica saw it as the answer to her prayers, until Maria informed her she could only go if Christian remained at the ranch. After a long and fervent discussion, conducted under Maria's watchful eye, Angelica and Christian finally decided that a short separation might well be for the best, considering the current state of their emotions.

Reluctantly, tearfully, she allowed Miles to take her back to Kate's.

"Well, what do you think?" Kate asked, turning slowly so Angelica, who was entering her bedroom, could see her gown from every angle. They had both just finished dressing for the dance, which would be starting as soon as they made their appearance.

"It's beautiful!" Angelica exclaimed, admiring the way the rich burgundy fabric enhanced Kate's dark hair and fair skin. "I'm so happy to see you out of mourning."

Kate shrugged self-consciously. "It's been over two years now. I guess it's past time."

"Of course, you never really had a good reason for coming out of mourning before," Angelica remarked slyly, coming closer to make an unnecessary adjustment to Kate's bustle.

Kate's dark eyes glinted mischievously. "What makes you think I have one now?" she asked, straightening the modestly low neckline of her dress and smoothing the crepon fabric of her skirt.

Angelica made a rude noise. "Oh, probably the way you've been pumping me for weeks for information about a certain member of my crew," she said, stepping back to admire Kate's dress once again. "And the way you've found little jobs to keep him occupied here in town for the past few days so he couldn't go back to the ranch."

To Angelica's delight, Kate actually blushed. "Have I been that obvious?" she asked in some distress.

"Only to me," she assured her friend. "He doesn't have a clue . . . yet. You *are* planning to give him one tonight, though, aren't you?"

Kate sighed with determination. "I'm certainly going to try, although he's awfully difficult to flirt with. He seems almost oblivious to my 'charms.' "

"He isn't," Angelica assured her. "Believe me, he's only being cautious. I told you about his wife. My guess is that he's afraid of ever loving anyone like that again. He just needs a little more time to get used to the idea."

"I hope you're right," Kate said with another sigh. "And what about you? You look like you're ready to knock some poor cowboy's eyes out."

"What? This old thing?" Angelica said with a self-mocking gesture toward her fabulous green taffeta gown. She had chosen to wear it again not only because it was the most beautiful dress she had ever owned but because she wanted to remind Christian of the night he had helped her take it off. Since leaving the ranch, she had seen him for only a few minutes, when he delivered Maria and Robbie to Kate's house this afternoon. His kiss of greeting had been short and desperate. Angelica had a sneaking suspicion that he might, with the proper encouragement, be ready to forget his plan for postponing their marriage. She certainly was.

Kate gave her a wink. "If you don't have every man at the dance panting after you, I'll eat my hat."

"You aren't wearing a hat," Angelica pointed out.

"So much the better," Kate replied with a grin. "Shall we go? Everyone will be waiting." Maria and Robbie had already gone on ahead.

The two women went downstairs and out of the house. Arm in arm, they made their way down the street toward the vacant lot where local handymen had constructed a wooden dance floor, a bandstand and a brush arbor. At the sight of them, the large crowd already assembled in the twilight gave a cheer, and the band struck up a rousing chorus of "Dixie."

The Kid knew the instant Angelica stepped out of Kate's house. Some sixth sense warned him, drawing his attention like a lodestone. She looked like a queen with her flaming hair piled high on her head and that beautiful gown hugging every precious curve of her body. As she and Kate moved down the street toward the crowd, graceful as two brightly colored swans, he remembered how Angelica had looked that night in her bed with no covering at all. Longing stirred in him, a longing that was only part physical desire.

He wanted her, but more than that, he wanted to claim her as his own. He wanted to tell all these people she belonged to him, but of course, he could not do that, not quite yet. First he had to deal with a certain little problem. Instinctively, he tore his gaze from Angelica to search out the source of danger.

Angelica was searching the crowd, too. Her eager gaze skimmed over Maria, who was clad in her usual gray, over Robbie, who was dancing a furious jig with several of the town boys, over Miles and the rest of her men, who were gathered near the whiskey barrel, until she finally found Christian. He was standing a little apart from the others, tense and watchful, as if he expected trouble. In what she knew intuitively was an unconscious gesture, his hand moved to the grip of his gun as he caught sight of something in the crowd that made him frown.

Her gaze shifted automatically to see what had disturbed him, and her heart plummeted when she saw Harlan Snyder bearing down on her.

"I'm going to claim the first dance," he said brazenly, taking her hand and slipping it into the crook of his arm as he led her to the dance floor.

Angelica managed a polite smile and carefully avoided looking at Christian again. His glare would have turned murderous by now, or she'd missed her guess. She had come to accept the fact that Christian was insanely jealous of her attentions to Harlan Snyder, even though he knew perfectly well he had nothing to be jealous of, and even though he knew perfectly well the reasons behind her charade.

Of course, the reasons were no longer valid. Her cattle

had been delivered, and Christian was safely back. She no longer needed to keep up the pretense of a courtship with Harlan Snyder.

Snyder took her in his arms as the band launched enthusiastically into the "Tennessee Waltz." The smile she gave him now was one of relief as she realized the time had finally come when she could gracefully end the ordeal of his attentions once and for all. He wouldn't dare cause a scene in such a public place. All she had to do was tell him she had no intention of marrying him, and she would be free of him.

"You're very lovely tonight, my dear," he said, his eyes gleaming appreciatively.

"Thank you," she replied perfunctorily. From the corner of her eye she caught sight of Christian moving toward them. Snyder seemed unaware of his approach, but still he moved her effortlessly to the opposite side of the dance floor. She followed obediently, reluctant to allow a confrontation between the two men if she could possibly prevent it. Vaguely, she noted that Snyder was a wonderful dancer. If only he wouldn't keep trying to hold her too close.

"I've missed you this week," he said with apparent sincerity.

She could not respond in kind, so she simply said, "You know I've been busy helping Mrs. Marsden prepare for this. I explained the first time you called." That, as she recalled, had been an awkward moment. Having learned she was in town again, he had immediately come to see her. Kate had rushed to her rescue by spreading out drawings of the bandstand design and seeking his approval on every little detail of the construction until, in self-defense, he had left.

He sent his compliments daily, leaving his card along with a request for her company. Angelica had kept herself unavailable by working in Kate's store during the day and on the dance preparations by night. She had been avoiding the inevitable moment when she must tell him that she had no intention of marrying him. Now she could not understand what had made her hesitate. The sooner he got the news, the sooner this would all be over.

"It seems that everyone within a hundred miles is here tonight," he said, glancing around at the assembly. Wagons and buckboards full of families and men on horseback were still arriving. Angelica thought he might be correct in his assumption. Before she could say so, however, he added, "This would be the perfect opportunity for us to announce our engagement."

Angelica's jaw dropped in horror. His beady eyes were lit with confidence and a smugness that told her he would not be denied. Suddenly, she realized she had been a fool to believe he would take her refusal with equanimity, even in a public place. A cold lump of dread formed in the pit of her stomach as she frantically tried to form a reply. Before she could, Stumpy cut in on them.

" 'Scuse me, but you can't expect to hog this pretty lady all night, now can you?" Stumpy inquired with a tobacco-stained grin.

Snyder plainly would have liked to argue with him, but Angelica had already gratefully shifted into Stumpy's embrace. With a triumphant smirk, the old man whirled away with her.

"Thanks for the rescue," she said with relief, smiling down at him. The top of his head barely cleared the end of her nose.

He shrugged, adroitly sidestepping another couple who seemed determined to careen into them. Vaguely, Angelica noted that Stumpy was a remarkably skilled dancer, too. Now where on earth could he have developed that ability? Before she could inquire, he said, "I saw the Kid watching you two and figured I'd better break things up before there was any gunplay."

A shiver of apprehension ran up her spine. "Oh, dear," she murmured, glancing anxiously around to see if she could spot Christian in the crowd. He was nowhere to be seen.

Stumpy grinned. "Don't get yourself in a lather, honey. I was just joshin' about the gunplay, although I don't reckon 'Christian' likes watching you dance with that sidewinder any more than I do."

"I certainly hope not," she informed him acerbically. "But you can inform Mr. Collins that unless he's prepared to ask me for a dance himself, he's got no business standing over there fuming over my choice of partners."

Stumpy cackled his approval. "I'd like nothing better," he said. "It's too bad I ain't a foot taller and twenty years younger, or I'd invite you for a walk in the moonlight. That ought to really get his dander up."

Angelica threw back her head and laughed aloud at the picture of Stumpy trying to make Christian jealous. When she had regained her composure, she gave him an inviting smile and said, "It might be worth a try anyway. I declare, Mr. Smith, I've rarely ever danced with a man so light on his feet. Why, it's enough to turn a girl's head!"

"I can turn more than your head," he replied with a twinkle and whirled her around until she was dizzy and breathless and laughing with delight.

Almost before she realized it, the dance was over, and the fiddler, a cowboy from an area ranch, was announcing a reel. Before she could even try to locate Christian again, Mr. Wallace, who owned the restaurant, claimed her for that one. At the end of the reel, a neighboring rancher who had been a friend of her father's claimed her for a waltz. One dance flowed into another for the next hour, and after each one Angelica was surrounded by potential partners. With some judicious maneuvering, she managed to avoid Harlan Snyder and the conversation she knew he would insist upon, but never once did Christian even attempt to partner her. By the time the sun had set and the stars were twinkling brightly in the night sky, Angelica was quite annoyed with him.

Meanwhile, back in town, three people loitered in the otherwise deserted saloon. Here the music was a faint echo to which Sunny unconsciously tapped her foot. Otis stood behind the bar, methodically polishing glasses that did not need polishing. Tom Rivers drained his glass of whiskey and wiped his mouth with the back of his hand.

"I gotta go now, honey," he told Sunny with real regret. "It's business."

Sunny sighed and leaned back against the bar, resting her elbows on the scarred wood. "I know," she replied. The sound of other people having a good time always depressed her. Tonight was particularly bad because she was probably the only person in Marsden's Corners who would not be welcome at the party. Even Otis, as a town merchant, could attend, although folks would probably frown on his asking any of the respectable ladies to dance. But Sunny couldn't go, oh no. She sighed again.

"You understand, don't you?" Tom said, lifting her chin with one finger until her gaze met his.

She managed a small smile. She had grown surprisingly fond of him in the few short weeks he had been in town. Of course, as she reflected often, it was easy to like someone who adored you. Apparently, she was the only girl who had ever given Tom Rivers more than a passing glance, and as her reward she had earned his undying devotion.

And his protection. She would never forget the look on Harlan Snyder's face the day he had plunked his two silver dollars down on the bar, and Otis had simply said, "Sunny ain't working no more."

Snyder's sharp gaze had gone to where Tom, who had come into the saloon with him, was greeting Sunny. She had slipped her arms around the gunman and given him a long, lingering kiss that left no doubt as to their relationship. "What's this?" Snyder had asked with feigned good nature.

Tom turned with a cocky grin. "It's what it looks like, boss," he replied, pulling Sunny close to his side. His *left* side so his right hand would be free. "Sunny is my girl now."

Snyder's displeasure was obvious, but she could feel the tension in Tom, too, a tension that teetered precariously on the brink of violence. She saw something in his face in that moment, a fierce recklessness, that spoke eloquently of how willingly—and how carelessly—he would answer a challenge, even from the man who was currently paying him. Snyder, apparently, had seen it too. He backed off, figuratively if not literally.

"Well, now, isn't that sweet," he had said in a tone only faintly contemptuous. "Let me buy you kids a drink then." Not even Tom could take offense at that. They had drunk to Sunny's health, and Sunny had ignored the warning gleam in Snyder's eye.

Since that day Snyder had not come near her. Sometimes Sunny wondered how he managed to cope with the pressures of Miss Angelica Ross without her help, but she considered the matter with malicious glee. The rest of the time, she concentrated on keeping Tom Rivers happy, a remarkably easy chore.

Sunny smiled at Tom. "You go on now, but don't you dare have a good time," she warned him playfully.

He bent down and gave her a short kiss. "I told you, this is business," he said, his face grave. "Snyder wants me to keep an eye on Collins tonight." Suddenly he grinned. "Hey, maybe tonight's the night, honey. Snyder promised me a cool thousand when Collins is dead. Then we can head out for New Orleans and good times."

Sunny's smile wavered just a bit at the thought of Collins lying dead, but she forced herself to think of New Orleans. A girl in her position could not afford to be sentimental. She reminded herself sternly that Collins meant nothing to her, less than nothing, while Tom Rivers was everything.

"Be careful, darlin'," she said as he headed for the door. He didn't seem to hear her.

Angelica plopped down on the bench next to Kate in an unladylike heap. With practiced ease, she flipped open her ivory fan and flapped it enthusiastically in an effort to cool away the effects of too much dancing, unbelievably grateful that the band was taking a break. Kate smiled with understanding. "Have you missed a single dance?" she asked.

Angelica groaned dramatically. "Not a one, and my poor feet are about to fall off. Robbie!" she called as the boy raced by in the company of his friends. "Fetch me some punch, will you, please?"

Robbie's groan of dismay sounded surprisingly like Angelica's, but Miles rescued him. "I'll get you some, Miss Ross," he offered as he appeared at their side and handed Kate a glass.

"Thanks, Mr. Blackmon," Robbie called over his shoulder as he and the other boys ducked into the crowd and out of sight.

"Thanks, Mr. Blackmon," Angelica echoed with a grateful smile.

To her surprise, he sketched what might have been a

courtly bow before going back into the fray for her punch. "Well, my goodness," she murmured, giving Kate a suspicious look. "Where did that come from?"

Kate shrugged, looking a little smug, Angelica thought. "I think it was in him all the time. He's just been hiding it."

"But now he's not hiding it anymore," Angelica surmised astutely, studying the way Kate's gaze seemed drawn to thc tall man threading his way through the dancers to the refreshment table. She sighed. "Well, at least one of us is having a successful evening."

Kate's expressive glance came back to Angelica. "He hasn't even asked you to dance, has he?" she asked sympathetically.

Angelica shook her head, trying to appear unconcerned, but the vigorous motion of her fan gave her away.

"Maybe he's just trying to protect you from gossip," Kate suggested.

Angelica raised her eyebrows at such a feeble excuse. "People would hardly gossip because he asked me to dance. Half the men here have danced with me already."

Kate laid a hand on her arm. "Yes, but they didn't look at you the way he looks at you."

"How does he look at me?" Angelica inquired, her interest piqued.

Kate considered a moment. "As if you were a pool of water, and he was dying of thirst," she finally decided.

"Kate!" Angelica protested, feeling a warm flush of pleasure neverthless.

"Well, he does," Kate insisted, still much too smug for Angelica's liking. Unfortunately, Miles chose that moment to reappear with her punch, ending all possibility of further discussion of the topic.

On the other side of the dance floor, over by the

whiskey barrel, Harlan Snyder watched the two women talking. His eyes were narrowed as he puffed thoughtfully on his expensive cigar.

"There's not much left to do now, is there, boss?" Jake Evans inquired from beside him.

"No, Jake, there isn't," he replied. "We've cleaned out all the squatters. We've made sure that Miss Ross's herd got through all right." His voice held only the slightest hint of irony, but Jake slanted him an understanding grin. "Now all that's left is to tie up the Diamond R ranch and its pretty mistress."

Jake's grin faded, but Snyder didn't notice. He was too busy watching Angelica. "A woman is a lot like a horse, Jake. She can be pretty and spirited, but she's no good to a man until she's broke to the saddle. Angelica Ross is a thoroughbred. She'll need more breaking than most." His thoughts ran momentarily to the insipid Sunny Day, who had broken at a touch. Angelica would not be like that. She was a fighter. The image heated his blood.

He would strip her naked, and the fear she had tried so hard to hide from him would be exposed along with her velvet flesh. She would tremble in his arms, expecting gentleness, but he would give her none. Then she would struggle, scratching and clawing and biting until she was exhausted by his superior strength. When she had nothing left with which to fight, when she lay limp and panting in his arms, he would take her, bursting the barrier of her innocence and conquering her once and for all.

"Boss?"

Snyder started at Jake's voice, suddenly aware that he was sweating beneath the fine linen of his shirt and the expertly cut broadcloth of his suit. His face must have reflected the intensity of his emotions. Jake was looking at him peculiarly. "I think I'll ask Miss Ross to dance," he said, tossing down his cigar and grinding it out with his heel. "But first, where's Rivers?"

Kate glanced up from where she still sat. "Uh-oh, look who's coming," she murmured to Angelica.

Angelica looked, too, and once again her heart plummeted when she saw Harlan Snyder heading her way. She could tell from the determined set of his jaw that this time he would not be put off. This time she would have to tell him and be done with it. Reminding herself how relieved she would be to have it over with, she lifted her chin, prepared to match his determination with her own.

On the other side of the dance floor, Stumpy scowled up at the Kid in disgust. "Ain't you even going to ask her to dance once?"

The Kid tore his gaze from where Angelica was sitting talking to Kate Marsden, and glanced down at Stumpy. He grinned apologetically. "I can't keep an eye on Snyder if I'm dancing," he pointed out. "And I still haven't seen that hired gunnie of his."

"Oh, that's him, standing over under the cottonwood," Stumpy informed him. "Short fella, fancy rig."

The Kid's eyes narrowed as he studied what he could see of Tom Rivers in the flickering light of the lanterns surrounding the dance floor. "He doesn't look like much from here," the Kid concluded.

Stumpy made a derisive noise. "Don't let looks fool you. It's them little fellas you gotta watch out for. They're mean."

The Kid looked down at Stumpy again and gave him another apologetic grin. "Sorry, I forgot there for a minute," he said.

Muttering something about ungrateful children, Stumpy started to walk away, but a movement from under the cottonwood tree stopped him. "Look out, he's coming this way," he warned, stepping off to one side, where he could watch the Kid's back if necessary.

The Kid tensed, every nerve in his body coming instantly to attention as he watched Tom Rivers's seemingly casual approach. The little gunfighter strutted like he was cock of the walk. Well, maybe he was, back in Dodge City, but this wasn't Dodge City, the Kid thought. His lips stretched into an anticipatory grin.

Harlan Snyder smiled down at Angelica. The band was striking up another waltz after their break. "May I have the pleasure?" he inquired.

Vaguely conscious that Miles had risen to his feet as if to provide her with some protection, she returned Snyder's smile and gave him her hand. "Of course," she said, flipping her fan shut and rising to her feet. Once on the floor, he took her in his arms, pulling her close even though she tried to resist.

"We were having a very interesting conversation when we were interrupted," he reminded her.

"Yes, we were, and there's something I have to tell you. . . ."

"Not here," he said, cutting her off. "It's too public. Let's go where no one will bother us."

To her surprise, she discovered that he had already maneuvered her to the far end of the floor. Now he led her to where a large weeping willow tree stood, not far from the dance floor but deep in the shadows. As apprehension prickled down her spine, she reminded herself that they were still within a stone's throw of a hundred people. What could he possibly do? Besides, Christian would be watching. Christian was always watching.

Christian let his right hand drop casually to his side as Tom Rivers approached. The man was smiling, but his coat was open, pushed back from his guns. Closer and closer he came, until the Kid could smell the sickly sweet scent of Rivers's fancy hair tonic.

At last Rivers stopped, planting his feet firmly in the trampled grass. "Hey," he said with what might have passed for casual interest. "Are you the one they call Kid Collins?"

Chapter Twelve

Snyder held the willow branches back so Angelica could enter the dark sanctuary beneath the tree. She hesitated, instinct warning her that she should not go with him, but he would not tolerate her qualms and pulled in with him. The branches fell back into place with a whisper of sound, effectively hiding the two people behind them.

Alarmed, Angelica tried to free herself from Snyder's grasp, but he yanked her arm until she stumbled into his arms. He smothered her startled gasp with his mouth, crushing her lips beneath his while his hands pressed her intimately against him.

Revolted, she struggled, fighting frantically to free her mouth and her body. Then, suddenly, he released her, quickly and completely, so that she staggered backward. His breath ragged, he said, "Please forgive me, my dear, but it's been so long, I couldn't help myself."

It was too dark to see his expression, but he didn't sound one bit sorry, Angelica noted as she scrubbed the taste of him from her mouth with the back of her hand. At least he didn't seem disposed to attack her again. Although she was trembling in reaction, she felt her initial panic receding. Still, she backed up another step, ready to flee in case he made another threatening move.

She would simply tell him quickly and get this thing over with.

"Harlan, I . . ."

"I'm tired of waiting, Angelica," he said, ignoring her attempt to speak. "I've been patient with you, more than patient."

"Yes, you have . . ."

"I want to announce our engagement tonight and have the wedding as quickly as possible. You need a man to take care of you, Angelica. The sooner we're married, the better." He straightened to his full height, tucking his thumbs into his vest pockets as if he were quite satisfied with the way things were going and quite confident of her reply.

Angelica's breath was still unsteady from her shock over his assault, so her voice quivered slightly when she said, "Harlan, I can't marry you."

She felt as much as heard his startled reaction to this, but it passed quickly. Plainly, he thought she was just being coy. "Don't be silly, my dear," he said patiently. "Of course you can marry me, and you will. There's no reason why . . ."

"Yes, there is a reason why," she interrupted him. "I'm going to marry someone else."

"*What?*" The word was vicious, torn from his throat. His body loomed up before her, a darker shape among the dark shadows. His hands came out to her. She tried to run, but he was too fast. She opened her mouth to scream, but rough fingers clamped over it, smothering the sound.

The Kid nodded at the little gunman. "Yeah, that's right. I'm Collins," he said. "Who wants to know?"

Rivers's grin widened. "My name is Rivers, Tom Rivers, from up Dodge City way."

The Kid was vaguely aware that all other conversation around him had ceased. The eerie quiet was spreading over the crowd like a vapor as the whispered word went from person to person and everyone looked to see the two known men facing off. Then he heard a child's voice piping. "A gunfight! A gunfight!"

Robbie! Robbie was coming to see, coming to watch him shoot this man down. And Angelica was here, too. For a second he could picture her beautiful face twisted in horror at the sight of him taking a man's life, and his insides wrenched in agony. But only for a second. Rivers was still speaking.

"Folks around these parts aren't very friendly to strangers are they?"

"I don't know about that," the Kid replied, his voice surprisingly cool considering the way adrenaline was pulsing through his veins, jangling every nerve into awareness so that he saw each tiny detail of Rivers's appearance with crystal clarity. "I'm new in these parts myself, and folks've been mighty friendly to me."

The whispers had reached the band. The music squawked to a discordant stop, making the ensuing silence sound thunderous to the Kid's oversensitive ears. Running feet clattered across the wooden dance floor as people scrambled either to safety or to get a better view. Where was Angelica? Would she have sense enough to get Robbie away?

Rivers's grin faded. "Are you saying that I'm not the kind of man folks like to be friendly to?"

Here it was, the forced insult, the flimsy, trumped-up excuse that would mean life or death for someone. The Kid had played this scene before. His mouth was cottony. He could see the beads of sweat forming on Rivers's forehead and smell the stench of fear radiating from him. Neither of them wanted this. Neither of them wanted to die. Suddenly, the senselessness of it struck him. Why should he pick up the gauntlet Rivers had thrown? Why should he kill a man he didn't even know?

From some distant time and place, his mother's voice came to him, quoting scripture as she had so many times. "A soft answer turneth away wrath." Would it work? Was he brave enough to risk it? Then he heard the echo of Robbie's voice, asking him how many men he'd killed, as if that were something to brag about. A soft answer, that's all he needed to keep from adding one more to this list and show Robbie what a real man was made of. He had opened his mouth to speak it when he heard the scream.

Angelica! Instinctively, he turned, forgetting his own danger, knowing only that he had to get to her. The dance floor was deserted. On the other side, far distant, he caught a glimpse of green skirts beneath willow branches. Everyone else was looking, too, but no one else moved. He started running.

"Look out!" Robbie's voice, and then the explosion of a gunshot, but the Kid didn't stop. If he was hit, he knew he wouldn't feel it right away. He'd get to her first.

The branches shook and a figure in green burst through. "Christian!" she cried as another gunshot thundered in the night. Still he did not stop, did not look back. She was running toward him, her skirts flying around her legs, her eyes wide with terror.

Then he realized that if Rivers were shooting at him, he might hit her instead. "Get down!" he cried, catching her when she would have thrown herself into his arms. Shielding her with his own body, he forced her to the ground, crouching over her, and then he spun around, drawing his gun as he turned.

The scene before him was branded forever in his memory. Rivers lay in a crumpled heap, his smoking gun still clasped tightly in his hand. Behind him stood Miles, his pistol drawn, too, and giving off its own gray cloud. Nearby, Stumpy held Robbie immobile. The boy's face was awful with fear and shock. The few spectators who had not run for cover seemed frozen in place. That same look of stunned surprise was on all their faces.

"Christian! Are you hit? He said they were going to kill you!" Heedless of any danger, Angelica scrambled upright behind him, her hands moving over his back in search of wounds.

Was he hit? If so, he felt nothing. Still keeping his gun at the ready, he rose slowly from his half-kneeling position. Only when he had scanned the crowd again was he satisfied that all imminent danger was past. With his left arm, he reached down and helped Angelica to her feet.

"You shot him in the back, Mr. Blackmon!" Robbie cried, his disbelief obvious.

A murmur started among the spectators, and those who had run away began to drift back to see what had happened. Angelica and Christian moved cautiously forward until they were close to where the body lay. Christian kept his gun drawn.

"What's going on here?" Snyder's voice rose above the murmur as he shoved his way through the mass of people gathering to look at the body. He had circled around in the darkness and was coming from a completely different direction from the tree where he had held Angelica captive. Angelica realized he had done so in order to create an alibi for himself in case she made any accusations. "It's Rivers!" he said in apparent surprise. "And he's been shot in the back. Who did this?"

"It was Blackmon, boss," Jake Evans said, pointing at Miles, who still held his own gun ready in case any more of Snyder's men wanted to get in on the action. "See, his gun's still smoking. He shot Rivers down in cold blood."

The crowd gasped almost as one. Compelled to defend himself, Miles said, "He was going to shoot the Kid in the back. There was nothing else I could do."

"Is that true?" Snyder demanded of the witnesses. "Mr. Wallace, is that what you saw?"

The restaurant owner gave Miles a dismayed glance. "I didn't see anything. Everything happened so fast. First Collins and this fella was talking, and then we heard Miss Ross scream. Collins took off after her, and I was watching him. I never saw what Rivers did."

"Did anyone else see what happened?" Snyder demanded. He waited, but the other witnesses shrugged and shook their heads.

"I guess we was all watching Collins and Miss Ross," someone said.

"I saw it," Jake Evans said with an evil smile. "Blackmon pulls out his gun and shoots Rivers down in cold blood, just like I said. Rivers tries to fight back. He got his gun out and got off one shot, but he was already falling."

"That's not true!" Robbie screamed, breaking free of Stumpy's grip at last and running up to Snyder. "I saw the whole thing! Rivers was going to shoot Mr. Collins in the back, like Mr. Blackmon said. Mr. Blackmon shot him first. Rivers's gun went off, but it just hit up some dust."

Snyder smiled benignly. "Mr. Collins and Mr. Blackmon are good friends of yours, aren't they?" he asked Robbie.

"Yes, sir, they are," Robbie confirmed proudly.

"Well, then," Snyder said, addressing the crowd, "we have the word of a grown man." He gestured toward Jake Evans. "And the word of a boy who is a good friend of the guilty party. I guess I don't have to tell you who to believe."

"Just a minute, Snyder." The Kid's voice rang like steel, silencing the murmuring crowd. "You have Miles Blackmon's word, too, and that's good enough for me."

"The word of a hired killer?" Snyder asked with disdain.

Angelica opened her mouth to protest but caught herself just in time. She wanted to demand to know how a man who had been manhandling a lady only moments ago dared to question anyone else's veracity, but she knew that do so would be folly. Even if Snyder admitted to having been with her under the willow tree, even if he acknowledge having been the one to make her scream, how could she explain the fact that she had gone off with him alone in the first place?

Everyone knew that Snyder had been courting her. If she had foolishly led him on, if she had brazenly snuck away from the dance with him, then most people would believe she had only gotten what she deserved. To accuse him would do him no harm at all and would cause her reputation irreparable damage. With difficulty, she swallowed her angry words of repudiation, even though they were as bitter as gall.

"Tom! Tom, where are you? What happened?" A small, frantic figure clad in a garish red dress burst into the clear space around Rivers's body. *"Tom!"* Sunny screamed when she saw his body lying still on the ground.

Heedless of all the others, she threw herself down beside him, calling his name in desperation. Her hands touched his face tenderly as she begged him to speak to her. His staring eyes didn't blink.

Although Angelica had never seen her before, she knew instinctively this must be the girl who worked in the saloon, the girl with whom Christian had once spent the night. Angelica would have expected to hate her on sight, but the girl's frail body bent over the dead gunman looked so tragic that Angelica could feel only pity, pity and empathy. If Miles had not been fast enough, Angelica might now be kneeling beside Christian's lifeless form.

Without conscious thought, Angelica moved to the girl's side. "It's no use," she said softly. "He's dead. I'm sorry." She laid a comforting hand on he girl's thin shoulder, but Sunny started as if she had been bitten by a rattler.

"You!" she snarled, shaking off the hand and glaring at Angelica with hate-filled eyes. "And *you!*" Sunny pointed an accusing finger at Christian as she lunged to her feet. "You killed him! You murderer!"

Suddenly realizing that his gun was still drawn, the Kid hastily stuffed it back in its holster. "I didn't kill him, Sunny," he said.

Sunny's fury faltered a moment. "But he was supposed to . . ." She turned in confusion to Snyder. "He was supposed to kill Collins. . . ."

Snyder stared at her in horror for one split second before recovering himself. "It was Blackmon who killed him," he said, turning her to face Miles, who also quickly resheathed his gun.

"He was trying to shoot the Kid in the back," Miles tried to explain, but Sunny wasn't listening.

"Murderer!" she screamed, lunging at him.

Sunny raised her fists and beat ineffectually against Miles's chest. He stood stoically under her blows, making no move to defend himself, an anguished expression twisting his weathered face. Although Angelica knew the tiny girl could not possibly hurt the giant man physically, the knowledge of the emotional pain he was suffering tore at Angelica's heart. She raced to help him, grabbing the hysterical girl and pulling her free, surprised to find Kate helping. It took the two of them to subdue her. After a few moments of struggle, however, Sunny surrendered to her grief, falling into Kate's arms and sobbing on her shoulder.

"You see what this man has done?" Snyder was saying. The crowd was grumbling now, plainly disturbed by Sunny's outburst. "He's a killer, we all know that. We can all see what he's done. The evidence is here before us. Do we need to wait for a trial?"

"NO!" The shout came from only a few voices, probably Snyder's own men, but others soon picked it up.

"I say, see justice done here and now! I say, we get a rope!"

The cheer that rose spontaneously ended abruptly at the sound of a gunshot.

"Nobody move!" the Kid commanded, leveling his pistol at Snyder. As if by prior arrangement, every one of the Diamond R crew drew his gun and held it on Snyder and his men. "There's not going to be a rope and there's not going to be a hanging. If you want this settled, we'll send for the county sheriff and let him handle it."

"How do we know Blackmon will still be here when the sheriff finally comes?" Snyder sneered.

The Kid glared at Snyder and then at Snyder's men, who were watching him with hostility. "I know he *won't* be here if your men have anything to say about it. Miles, I think you'd better go into hiding for a while."

Miles glanced around at the surly faces surrounding him and nodded.

"You head out right now, and I'll keep these fellows occupied for an hour or so," the Kid told him.

"Right," Miles said, but before he left, he glanced over at Sunny again. She was still sobbing on Kate's shoulder. "I'm really sorry, miss, but I didn't have any choice."

If she heard him, she gave no indication. He turned and slipped away into the night.

Angelica met Kate's agonized gaze for a moment before turning back to where Robbie still stood, looking lost and alone, all but forgotten by everyone else. His eyes were slightly glazed, as if he could not quite believe what had happened. She went to him, enfolding him in an embrace he would have shunned at any other time.

"Why didn't they believe me?" he asked so poignantly it brought tears to Angelica's eyes.

"They did believe you, Robbie," she assured him. "Your story just wasn't the one they wanted to hear."

"You're going to be sorry you ever crossed me, Angelica," Snyder said so softly only she and Robbie could hear. Angelica lifted her gaze to the rancher. His expression was murderous. Robbie stiffened her arms, but she tightened her hold on him and refused to drop her eyes, staring Snyder down until he was forced to look away.

Occupied with more pressing matters, the Kid missed this exchange. He had caught sight of Otis hovering on the edge of the crowd and called him to come and take Rivers's body away, assigning two townsmen to help. Then he dispersed his own men to guard the perimeter of the area so none of Snyder's men could sneak away to follow Miles.

"All right, everybody," the Kid called when Rivers's body was out of sight. "This is a party. How about a little music? Nobody is going anywhere for at least an hour. We might as well make use of the time."

The next hour was the longest Angelica ever lived through. The band valiantly continued to play, but no one felt like dancing. The guests stood or sat in groups, talking in hushed tones about what had happened and what was going to happen now. Snyder and his men gathered at the far end of the dance floor. They did not talk, but no one doubted what they intended to do as soon as Christian called off his guards.

Kate and Angelica sat on one of the benches with a shaken and subdued Robbie between them while Maria paced nearby, wringing her hands. After what seemed an eternity, Christian told everyone they could return to their homes. Snyder and his men were the first to leave. As a body, they headed first to their horses and then to the livery stable where Miles had stabled his own mount. They were hoping to pick up his trail from there.

In a matter of minutes, the dance area was deserted except for the Diamond R crew. Christian walked over to where the women sat. "I'm sorry I ruined your party, Mrs. Marsden," he said.

Kate gave him a wan smile. "It wasn't your fault and you know it."

The Kid nodded his acknowledgment of her exoneration, but he knew she was wrong. While he had not actually started the fight, there would not have been one if he had not been Kid Collins. Because of who he was, trouble followed him like a plague. For one brief moment when he had been facing Tom Rivers, he had entertained a fantasy of being able to change the preordained course of his life by simply walking away from the fight. Now he realized that was impossible, no matter how much he might want to change.

He turned to Angelica. Her eyes were filled with love, but they were also shadowed by the pain of the events she had witnessed tonight. He shared that pain, but he could not give in to it, not now. He had too many responsibilities. "Maybe you'd better stay at Kate's tonight," he told her.

"Where are you going to be?" she asked.

"The men and I will go back to the ranch. I think Miles might go there for supplies, and he might leave some word about where he plans to hole up. Anyway, I figure that's the first place Snyder will go when he loses Mile's trail. I want to be there when he shows up so he doesn't tear the place apart."

"Then I'm going with you," Angelica said, rising to her feet.

"Wait a minute," Christian tried, but Angelica did not plan to be deterred.

"Mama, what about you?" she asked. Maria nodded.

"I want to go home, too, Angel," Robbie said, clasping her hand.

"Good, then it's settled," Angelica said, turning back to Christian in silent challenge.

"It's late," he tried. "You'll all be exhausted by the time we get back there."

"We want to go home, Christian," she said, laying an entreating hand on his arm.

He looked down into the depths of her green eyes and knew he could deny her nothing. "Let's get going then," he said. "Stumpy, will you get the wagon and bring it around to Mrs. Marsden's?"

Maria came over and drew Robbie up off the bench. "Come, little one. You can help me and Mrs. Marsden get our things together," she said, thoughtfully allowing Angelica a few moments alone with Christian.

When Kate and Maria had taken Robbie away, Angelica and Christian were alone beside the deserted dance floor. She slipped her arms around his waist and held him close. He pulled her to him with the strength of a man who had come very close to death that night and needed to renew his bond with life.

"He was going to kill you," she said, still not willing to accept the cruel reality of it.

"But he didn't, that's all that matters," he replied, thinking how many times in his life he had missed death by a hairbreadth. By now his luck must be running pretty low, but he wouldn't allow himself to dwell on that. "I never did find out why you screamed."

She pulled away so she could see his face. "Oh, darling, it was so awful. He told me you were going to be killed. He said that any minute I'd hear the gunshot and . . ."

"Who told you that?" he demanded.

"Snyder," she said, realizing she needed to start from the beginning. "He asked me to dance, and I realized I'd better tell him I didn't intend to marry him and get it over with. When I started to, he said he wanted to talk more privately, and he took me over to the willow tree."

"Angelica!" he said in exasperation. "I've told you a dozen times to stay away from that snake. . . ."

"It was only a few feet from the dance floor," she defended herself. "And I knew you'd see us go. You'd been watching me like a hawk all evening," she reminded him.

He frowned. "Except for that moment. He must have planned to have Rivers distract me. Go on, what happened then?"

She decided it would be in her best interest to skip the part where Snyder kissed her. "I told him I couldn't marry him because I was going to marry someone else. He was furious, of course, and I tried to get away, but he grabbed me and held me. He demanded to know who his rival was, so I told him." She shuddered at the memory of Snyder's reaction to that. She knew she would have bruises tomorrow from Snyder's violent grip. "That was when he told me I wouldn't be able to marry you because in a few seconds you'd be dead. I knew I had to warn you, so I started fighting him. Then I screamed, figuring he'd let me go rather than cause a scene. I was right."

The Kid pulled her close again, pressing his lips to the throbbing pulse at her temple. It had been a hell of a night for all of them, and it wasn't over yet. "Come on, let's go. I want to get out to the ranch before Snyder does."

Reluctantly, she released him, although he kept possession of her hand as they walked the short distance to Kate's house. Maria and Kate, with Robbie's halfhearted help, had already gathered all their belongings. By the time Stumpy brought the wagon, they were ready to go. Angelica and Maria embraced Kate, apologizing to her for all the trouble. Once again, she reminded them that she held Harlan Snyder completely responsible for everything and sent them on their way with the assurance that she bore them no ill will.

Kate stood on her porch and waved until they disappeared into the darkness. Then she went back in the house and closed the door, sinking against it wearily for a few moments while she gathered the strength to climb the stairs to her lonely room.

Every time she closed her eyes, she could see the haunted expression in Miles's eyes when that girl had called him a murderer. She hadn't seen that expression for a long while now, not since the first time she'd met him. In some secret part of her heart, she had entertained the hope that she would be able to keep it away forever.

Now it was back, and Miles was riding for his life, alone in the darkness. She sighed in despair and headed for the stairs. In her bedroom, she lighted the bedside lamp and slowly began to undress. With a heavy heart, she stepped out of the beautiful red gown that had been meant to turn Miles Blackmon's head. How foolish it all seemed now, she thought as she pulled open the heavy door to her wardrobe.

She screamed before she could stop herself and found the long barrel of a Colt .45 pointing at her. Behind it was Miles Blackmon's face. He looked as startled as she felt.

"I'm sorry, ma'am. I never meant to scare you like that. I was planning to warn you I was here, but I've been sitting here so long, I must've dropped off and . . ." He was thinking how odd it was for him to have fallen asleep, considering there was a lynch mob looking for him and he was folded up practically double in Kate Marsden's cabinet. Ordinarily, he slept poorly even in the comfort of his own bed. Then he realized he was still holding the gun on her and quickly lowered it.

"I'm sorry I screamed," she replied, drawing a deep breath to help her regain her composure and then managing a small smile. "It's just so seldom I find a man in my wardrobe."

He smiled back sheepishly. "I figured it would be more dignified than crawling under the bed," he explained.

"Of course," she replied wryly, fingering the gown she still held.

Suddenly, they both realized that she was standing there in her petticoats. He looked quickly away while she hastily pulled her dress close to shield her bosom. An awkward moment passed, and then Kate said, "If you'll hand me my robe . . . It's hanging behind your head. . . ."

Miles had to juggle his gun and twist around to an uncomfortable angle, but he managed to get the robe. He handed it to her while keeping his eyes discreetly averted.

Kate stepped over to her bed and laid her dress down. Slipping on her robe, she belted it before hurrying back to the wardrobe. "All right now, let's see if we can get you out of there."

Miles insisted he could manage by himself, but then he discovered that one of his legs had gone to sleep, so he needed Kate's help after all. Leaning on her with obvious reluctance, he limped over to her bed and sat down gratefully on the edge next to where she had laid her dress. He glanced at it in renewed embarrassment. "I never should have come here," he said, briskly rubbing his leg back to life. "It was a stupid thing to do, and . . ."

"Why *did* you come here?" she asked with interest.

"What?" he replied, as if he hadn't understood her question, his hands stilled in their task.

"I was wondering why you chose to hide in my house, of all places. I'm quite flattered, but I expected you to be ten miles away from here by now."

"Well," he hesitated, trying to put his reasons into words she would understand. He was having some difficulty, since he didn't really understand the reasons himself. "I figured everybody would expect me to run off someplace, so I decided I'd hide here in town until they took off after me. Then I'd be behind them."

Kate nodded. "Sounds like a good idea, but that still doesn't explain why you were tucked in my wardrobe when there must be a hundred places in town where you could hide."

Miles opened his mouth to explain, but nothing came out. How could he say that he'd chosen her house because he knew here he would fee safe? It didn't make any sense at all. "I guess I . . ." he began, but a noise outside distracted him.

Kate heard it, too. Motioning for him to stay back from the window, she went and pulled it open. In the darkness she could just barely make out a body of men coming up her front walk. Someone pounded on her front door. Behind her, Miles came to his feet, and she heard the whisper of a sound as he drew his gun.

"Who's out there?" she called sharply.

"It's Harlan Snyder and some of my men, Mrs. Marsden," he replied from the front porch.

"It's late for a visit, Mr. Snyder. I've already retired," she informed him.

"We're looking for Blackmon, ma'am. We think he may be hiding someplace in town.

An icy chill shivered up Kate's spine. So much for Miles's plan. "Just a minute," she said, and stepped back, sliding the window shut.

When she turned to face him, Miles was heading for the door. "Don't! They'll kill you!" she whispered fiercely, rushing to intercept him. "Just stay right here. I'll get rid of them."

"I can't let you take that chance. If they find me here, your good name will be ruined," he reminded her.

She sniffed contemptuously. "You let me worry about my good name. And what makes you think I'll let them find you, anyway? Just keep the door closed and don't make a sound."

Not having much other choice, Miles stood there dumbly as she hastened out and down the stairs. Someone was pounding again. Kate decided she was annoyed. She threw open the door and gave Harlan Snyder the brunt of her irritation.

"Heavenly days, Mr. Snyder, I'm surprised at you for bothering a respectable woman in the middle of the night on such a fool's errand," she said, stopping him in his tracks when he would have forced his way past her. "Of all the harebrained ideas! Any idiot knows that Mr. Blackmon is a hundred miles away from here by now."

"I'm afraid not, Mrs. Marsden," he informed her with an ingratiating smile. "You see, we found his horse still at the livery, so we know he's hiding nearby."

Kate rolled her eyes in disgust. "I don't suppose it occurred to you that he might have taken someone else's horse to throw you off the trail, now did it?"

Snyder glanced at Jake Evans and the other men gathered on her front porch. Jake shrugged as if the idea had possibilities he might not have considered. Snyder, however, was not about to back down in front of a woman.

"Still, there is every chance that he is here in town. Certainly, you won't object if we make certain he isn't using your house as a refuge." He started forward, confident of her cooperation, but she stopped him with a palm to his chest.

"I most certainly do object. I don't want a bunch of cowboys tromping dust and dirt all over my house," she informed him in outrage. By now she had realized he was determined to search her house, with or without her permission. "I will," she compromised, "allow you and one other gentleman to come in. The rest must remain on the porch."

Snyder made an exasperated noise. "Very well, Mrs. Marsden. Jake, come with me. The rest of you take a look around outside."

"Wipe your feet first," she instructed them sternly before stepping aside to allow the two men to enter. She closed the door on the others. "There's a lamp on the table there you can use, but be careful and don't break anything."

As Snyder lit the lamp, Kate wrapped her robe more tightly around her and took a deep breath to calm her jangling nerves. She wasn't certain how long she could cover her fear with outrage. She only hoped it would be long enough to save Miles from discovery.

Snyder and his foreman made short work of their search. Kate followed them from room to room as they explored the entire lower floor. When they were finished, she planted herself at the bottom of the stairs, blocking their way to the upper floors. "I hope you gentlemen are satisfied that no fugitives have sought refuge in my home. Now I'll thank you to be on your way—"

"I'm afraid we'll have to check around upstairs, too, Mrs. Marsden. It's for your own safety," Snyder added.

Kate made a disgusted noise. "It was my understanding that Parson Black made his reputation by avenging a woman's honor, Mr. Snyder, not destroying it. I seriously doubt *I* have anything to fear from him."

From the corner of her eye, she caught a glimpse of Jake Evans's uncomfortable expression. Plainly, he had no stomach for this. She knew he was one of those men who stood in awe of real ladies, and she guessed he would not approve of this invasion of her privacy. Perhaps she could use this knowledge for her benefit. She gave him an appealing glance, but before she could do more, Snyder said, "You'll pardon me if I seem overly cautious, Mrs. Marsden, but I did notice you danced with Blackmon rather frequently this evening. If I can be forgiven for saying so, you might have some tender feelings for Blackmon which would compel you to hide him from justice."

Kate felt her face growing red and hoped they would put it down to anger. She certainly was furious enough. "As you point out, Mr. Blackmon was rather attentive to me, but that was *before* he killed a man at my party. Whatever 'tender' feelings I may have had for him are quite gone now, I assure you. However," she added, silently praying her bluff would work, "if you doubt my word, I must insist that you search my bedrooms, too."

In a huff, she started up the stairs. To her dismay, Snyder started after her.

"Boss," Evans protested, "if he was up there, do you think she'd invite you to look?" To Kate's relief, Snyder hesitated halfway up the steps.

She kept going. Reaching the landing, she turned and glared down at them disdainfully. "Quite right, Mr. Evans, but Mr. Snyder has made it perfectly clear he thinks I am a liar and the kind of woman who would allow a murderer to hide in her home. I insist on being vindicated."

She stomped determinedly over to the first door at the top of the stairs, one they could both clearly see from where they stood, and threw it open. "Perhaps you think I have granted him the use of one of my guest rooms," she said sarcastically.

"Boss, let's get out of here," Evans said, his distaste evident.

"Or perhaps," Kate continued, pretending not to notice how uncomfortable Harlan Snyder was growing, "you think I have hidden him in my own room!" She marched across the hall to her bedroom door and threw it open, knowing they could not see inside from where they were. "Mr. Evans, would you like to come up and look under my bed, just to make certain?"

"Boss." Jake's voice was insistent now. "We're wasting time. She's probably right about him using another horse. I still think our best bet is to start at the Diamond R. If he's running, he'd go there first."

Kate crossed her arms belligerently while Snyder debated the issue with himself. After a few seconds, which seemed much longer to Kate, Snyder turned abruptly and started back down the stairs.

Fighting the urge to sigh with relief, Kate followed him. He was going out the front door when she reached the bottom of the staircase. He had the grace to turn back and make her a small bow. "Please accept my apologies, Mrs. Marsden. Under the circumstances, I felt I had a right to be suspicious of you."

Kate humphed a disgusted reply.

"For your protection, I'll leave one of my men to guard your house . . . from the outside," he added.

"I'm sure I'll sleep much more soundly knowing that, Mr. Snyder," she replied scornfully.

He bowed again to acknowledge her thrust, and then he was gone. Jake Evans set the lamp he had been using in the search on the hallway table and tipped his hat. "I'm right sorry about all this, ma'am," he said before following Snyder out.

No sooner had the door closed behind them than Kate was there, turning the key in the lock. Her hand, she was surprised to note, was trembling. Only now did she allow herself that sigh of relief. Resisting the urge to call out to Miles that they were gone, she forced herself to blow out the lamp and walk sedately back upstairs. She didn't know where the guard was posted, and if he was on the porch, she did not want him to hear her running.

The house was dark now except for the small circle of light coming from her partially open bedroom door. "Miles?" she called softly as she stepped into the room. There was no sign of him. Then she heard a faint scraping sound beside her, and he slipped from behind the door.

"They're gone," she reported, laying a hand on her heart, which was only now beginning to beat normally again.

"I know," he said. He still held his gun, and when he saw her looking at it, he stuffed it back in its holster. He looked relieved but wary, as if he still faced some danger. "You were magnificent. Even I didn't believe I was here."

She smiled in spite of herself. "I had a few bad moments. I thought Snyder was actually going to call my bluff and follow me upstairs."

But Miles was shaking his head. "Nobody would believe you'd hide a murderer."

It was the bitterness in his voice that alerted her to what was really wrong. His wariness was not for any imagined danger but for her. Something had happened while she was gone to cause an awkwardness between them, and now she knew what it was. "I wouldn't hide a murderer," she said, knowing he'd heard the lies she'd had to tell Snyder and been hurt by them. "But I did hide you."

He seemed a little surprised at her statement. "As you said, I ruined your party. You saw me kill a man tonight," he pointed out.

"Kill, yes, but only to protect your friend."

"Rivers wasn't the first man I've killed, either," he said, as if determined to convince her. "And surely you've heard the stories about me . . ."

"Miles!" she protested. "If you're trying to convince me of what a bad man you are, you're wasting your time. I've already made up my mind about you."

"Have you?" he asked defensively. "And what have you decided about me?" For just one instant his mask slipped, and she saw the vulnerability beneath it, a vulnerability she understood only too well. The knowledge gave her the confidence she needed.

"I have decided," she said, managing a semblance of nonchalance, "that in spite of your reputation, you are really a warm, sensitive man."

While he digested that, something he was obviously having a difficult time doing, she reached out and closed the bedroom door behind her with a decisive click.

"I have also decided," she continued, walking purposefully over to the bed and picking up her discarded gown, "that you are a man worth risking my reputation to save."

Without even glancing over to see what his reaction to

that was, she went to her wardrobe and hung up her gown. Closing the cabinet door, she turned once more to face him. He looked absolutely bewildered. "And in addition, I have decided to keep you here, *right* here, until the sheriff comes to straighten this mess out." She punctuated her statement by pointing, so he would have no doubt that she meant this exact room.

"I . . . I guess I don't have any choice about accepting your hospitality, Mrs. Marsden," he began.

"Please," she interrupted. "I believe that when a gentleman falls asleep in a lady's wardrobe, it is henceforth permissible for him to address her by her given name."

He shifted uncomfortably under this reminder of his inexcusable invasion of her home. "As I was saying, *Kate,* I've forced you into offering me the use of your home, but I have no intention of forcing you out of your own room. I can take one of the guest rooms."

He had already started for the door when she said, "I didn't say I was going to leave my room. I thought we could share."

He stopped dead in his tracks. "Share?" he asked incredulously.

"Yes, share. We can share the room, and," she paused for effect, "we can share the bed."

She could actually see the shock going through his body. "Kate, have you lost your senses?" he demanded.

She pretended to consider this. "I don't think so, although I suppose I am a little bold. There's probably a better way of doing this, but I've never seduced a man before, so I have no idea how to do it any differently."

"Seduce? Kate, are you forgetting that I have a lynch mob on my trail? I'm the very last man a woman like you should get involved with," he argued.

She was upsetting him, and she was sorry for that, but there was no help for it. She had known before she started that he would be reluctant. That was one of the reasons she loved him. She sighed. "You're probably right about that. I should have chosen some nice, respectable, dull fellow to fall in love with, I suppose, but it's too late now."

"Love? You're in love with me, Kate?" he asked, still incredulous, but she could see the deep pleasure the thought gave him.

She sighed again. "I'm afraid so, and I must warn you that I have every intention of forcing you to marry me after things have settled down. I've been looking for you for a long time now. I'm not about to let you get away."

"Kate, I . . . I don't know what to say." He made a helpless gesture with his large hands, hands Kate was wishing would reach for her, but of course, he was too much of a gentleman to make the first move.

"You could say you love me," she said with a self-mocking grin, "but I know it's a little early for that. I was hoping, in time, you'd come to, and things would follow their natural course. This trouble has sort of rushed things a bit, but I promise I'll make it very easy for you to love me, and maybe in time . . ."

"I don't need any time, Kate," he said. Now it was her turn to be surprised. "I guess I've loved you from that very first day I saw you at the store, when you looked into my eyes and saw things in me I'd hidden from every other living soul." He paused, obviously searching for the right words to explain the unexplainable. "You scared me at first, but the next time I saw you, you were so friendly, I forgot to be afraid anymore."

They stared at each other across the room for a long moment, silently acknowledging the implications of the confessions each had made. The silence grew strained and then awkward. Kate fiddled self-consciously with the tie belt of her robe. "I'd feel a lot less foolish if you'd come over here and kiss me," she said at last.

"I thought you'd never ask," he murmured, closing the gap between them in two long strides and taking her in his arms.

His kiss was gentle and tentative at first, but her eager response made him bold. He pulled her closer, aware that she was on tiptoe to reach him. She parted her lips, and he deepened the kiss. He wanted her closer. He wanted to feel her against his heart, but she was just too small. At last, he broke the kiss, wrapping his arms around her and pressing her head to his chest.

After a minute, Kate pulled away and grinned up at him. "I think we'd have an easier time if we were lying down." She studied his expression and asked with some concern, "Have I shocked you again?"

He drew a deep breath and let it out in a long sigh. "Yes," he informed her, scooping her up effortlessly in his arms and heading for her bed, "but I think I'm getting used to it."

Angelica glanced over at Christian sitting beside her on the wagon seat. His hands guided the reins with a careless competence, but his eyes were never still. He kept searching the darkness, as if he could see past the circle of light from the lantern they carried to guide their way. She knew he couldn't, of course. Still, she kept searching the darkness, too, even though she knew her own men rode out there alongside them for protection.

She also knew that neither of them was really concerned for their own safety so much as for Miles's. Where was he? Was he safe? Would they be able to keep him safe? The questions tumbled over one another in her mind, but she found no answers.

"Mr. Collins?" It was Robbie's voice. He and Maria

were sitting in the wagon bed. He had been lying with his head in Maria's lap, and Angelica had thought he was asleep.

Christian half turned in the seat, still keeping his gaze alert for potential danger. "What is it, Squirt?"

"I don't understand what happened tonight. I mean, why didn't *you* just shoot Rivers when you had the chance? Then it would've been a fair fight, and . . ."

"Robbie," Angelica interrupted, seeing the spasm of pain that twisted Christian's face, but Christian refused to allow her to protect him.

"Just because a man calls you out is no reason to kill him, Squirt," he tried to explain. "I never set eyes on Rivers before, and I didn't have anything against him."

"But he was a dirty, no-good backshooter," Robbie insisted. "He *needed* killing!"

The Kid winced inwardly at the excuse he himself had used more than once to justify taking a man's life. "I don't reckon I'm fit to judge who should live and who should die, Robbie. No man is."

"But . . ."

"Robbie," Angelica said sharply. "Mr. Collins doesn't want to talk just now. He's got a lot on his mind."

"Try to go to sleep, little one," Maria urged, gently pressing the boy's head back down to rest comfortably on her lap. "It is a long ride yet."

Even in the flickering shadows, Angelica could see Robbie's dissatisfied frown. It distressed her almost as much as Christian's tortured expression. Obviously, Christian's concern covered more than just Miles's safety. He was carrying the guilt for Rivers's death, too, and for much more, for secret hurts she could only guess at. Instinctively, she laid a hand on his arm, silently telling him of her desire to comfort him. To her dismay, he did not even seem to notice.

"Miles," Kate whispered, shaking him gently. He was instantly awake. With one swift glance, he took in the bed, the room, the sunlight brightening the curtained window, and the fact that she was already up and dressed. She watched his eyes cloud as the memories of last night, both good and bad, crowded in on him. The gaze he lifted to her was wary once more.

"Why didn't you wake me up?" he asked, struggling to sit up and self-consciously adjusting the sheet over his naked chest.

"I just did," she reminded him.

"I mean earlier," he said, making a gesture at her dress, indicating he knew she must have been up for some time.

"I didn't see any point in it. You can't stir from this room until the sheriff gets here anyway, and you were sleeping so soundly, I didn't have the heart to disturb you," she said, giving him a small smile.

Miles frowned. He was sleeping soundly? He *never* slept soundly, not for more than an hour or two. Then the dreams would start or else he'd be afraid they would and he'd automatically wake up again. He hadn't dreamed at all last night, though. After he and Kate had made love, he had clung to her like a drowning man clings to his only hope of rescue, and for the first time in almost twenty years, he had surrendered fearlessly to sleep.

"You're quite a woman, Kate," he said, his eyes seeing past her austere black dress to the woman he know knew intimately. He remembered how it had been between them last night and the way he had felt afterward, peaceful as he'd never hoped to feel again. He would have been hard pressed to choose which was better, the loving itself or the contentment that came afterward. He supposed his thoughts must show on his face, because her cheeks grew pink.

"I made you some breakfast," Kate said, pointing to the tray she had set on the bedside table and feeling unaccountably embarrassed under his unblinking gaze. After the shameless way she had behaved last night, she supposed she had no excuse for blushing. Still, it felt good. She felt like a girl again.

"You don't have to wait on me," he protested, glancing over at the tray and trying to remember if anyone had ever served him breakfast in bed.

Kate smiled, glad for such a mundane topic to discuss. "I'm not waiting on you," she informed him, "so don't go getting any ideas. It's just that Snyder left one of his men here last night, and he's still poking around outside. I've got all the windows shuttered and the drapes and curtains drawn, but I think you'd best just stay put. If you were to make a noise, he might decide to come investigate."

Miles nodded, his eyes clouding again, this time with anger. "I should've lit out last night. I don't have any right to involve you in all this. . . ."

"Miles Blackmon!" she scolded, deciding to silence him in the most effective way. She caught his face with her hands and pressed her mouth to his for a long moment. When she drew away, he pulled her back for another kiss. When this one was over, the bleak expression was gone from his eyes.

"You should've woke me up *before* you got dressed," he said with a teasing grin.

"Next time I will," she promised, grinning back as she straightened from where she was sprawled half across his lap. Standing up, she adjusted her dress and patted her hair to make sure there was no visible damage. Thank goodness the warm glow that was spilling from her overflowing heart did not show, or everyone who saw her would know she was keeping a man in her bedroom.

"Now I'm going to the store, but on the way, I'm going to stop at the telegraph office and make sure somebody remembered to wire the sheriff. I'll be back at noon to fix you a meal, and," she added with a twinkle, rubbing her abraded cheek, "I'll bring you some shaving gear. That's a fierce set of whiskers you have there, Mr. Blackmon." With another quick kiss, she left him.

When she was gone, he lay there for a long time, reflecting on his good fortune and what he might have done to deserve it.

It was two days later when the sheriff finally arrived in Marsden's Corners. He'd brought the circuit judge with him since Kate had suggested in her wire that he would want to hold an inquest. Kate arranged for the sheriff to meet the fugitive at her home so he could take Miles into protective custody. Everything went more smoothly than even Kate could have wanted. By the time Snyder got word, the inquest had been scheduled and the Diamond R crew was already in town to assist the sheriff in protecting Miles.

"I'll never forgive you for not letting us know Miles was with you," Angelica said to Kate, a grateful smile softening her threat. They were sitting in the front row of the makeshift courtroom. The judge had appropriated the Wallaces' restaurant for the occasion. He sat at the front of the room behind a small table, pounding his gavel for attention. Angelica leaned closer to Kate and whispered, "Christian and the men have been riding all over the countryside looking for him. We were all worried sick."

"It just wasn't safe," Kate explained. "Snyder had someone watching me all the time, and I didn't know who to trust with the message."

The two women fell silent as Snyder and several of his men entered the restaurant and made their way to an empty bench on the opposite side of the room. Angelica watched them, remembering the ugly scene several days ago when Snyder and his crew had ridden into her ranch yard looking for Miles. She had been willing to allow Snyder to search the house just to get rid of him, but Christian wouldn't hear of it. He and her other men had driven Snyder off with drawn guns and threats to shoot them for trespassing.

As she had watched Snyder and Christian go head to head, she was reminded of two wild range bulls clashing ferociously. Wild animals would fight to the death, and she had instinctively known that Snyder and Christian would, too, if the need arose. The knowledge had chilled her then, and even now it sent a shiver over her.

She glanced apprehensively over her shoulder to catch a glimpse of Christian. He was standing in one of the rear corners, while Stumpy occupied the other; they commanded strategically important positions in case any trouble broke out. She shivered again.

The room was filling up quickly with townspeople, and the judge gave up his pounding for a few more minutes until everyone had settled in a seat. "All right, folks, I reckon we'll get started," the judge said at last. He was a short, round man with wire-rimmed spectacles and a shock of white hair, both of which made him look wise. Angelica prayed he was. "This isn't a trial, just a hearing. We want to get at the truth about how this fellow Tom Rivers got himself killed and decide whether a crime has been committed or not. I'll start off by calling Miles Blackmon to the stand."

Miles took the chair to the judge's right, and at the judge's request began to explain in his own words exactly what happened. He was grim and tight-lipped at first, but then Kate caught his eye and smiled bravely. He relaxed almost visibly, at least to Angelica's eye, and the story flowed out of him. When he was finished, a murmur went through the room, but the judge banged everyone to quiet and called Kid Collins to testify.

Angelica locked her hands together in her lap to keep them from trembling as Christian made the long, slow walk to the front of the room and took the chair Miles had vacated.

"Would you tell us, please, Mr. Collins, what you and Rivers were talking about right before the shooting," the judge asked.

Angelica tried to catch his eye, but he deliberately avoided looking in her direction. Instead he watched Snyder and his crew as he recounted his brief conversation with the dead man. "And then I heard Miss Ross scream. I figured she was in some kind of danger, so I left Rivers and took off to find her," he concluded. "I heard two shots behind me, and when I looked back, Rivers was down."

The judge thought this over for a minute. "You say you'd never met Rivers before that night?"

"No, never saw him before in my life," the Kid replied, thinking again how crazy it would have been to take the life of a man he didn't even know. The thought had become like a lead weight he carried around in his heart, a wearisome burden that he could never quite shake.

"If you didn't know Rivers, then we must assume he didn't know you, either," the judge concluded aloud. "Why then do you think he might have tried to kill you as Mr. Blackmon claims?"

The Kid shifted uneasily in his chair, knowing the havoc he would wreak with his next remark. "Because somebody paid him to do it," he said.

The crowd's murmur broke into a roar, and Harlan Snyder lunged to his feet. "Your Honor, I object!" he cried.

The judge was pounding again. "You can't object, Mr. Snyder. You aren't a lawyer, and like I said, this isn't a trial. We're just trying to get at the truth." When the room was quiet again, he turned back to Christian and said, "What makes you think he was paid to kill you?"

Christian's face hardened, and Angelica held her breath, wondering what he would say. "Because," he said after what seemed a long silence, "he came up and purposely started to pick a fight. First he asked me who I was, like he wanted to make sure he had the right man. Then he twisted what I said into an insult so he could take offense. No reasonable man does that unless he's looking for a fight."

"You believe that someone paid him to do it, but perhaps he just wanted to make himself a reputation by being the one to kill Kid Collins," the judge suggested mildly.

The Kid felt the question like a kick in the gut. He'd been wrestling with that thought ever since he'd seen Rivers lying dead, ever since he'd realized that Rivers had wanted more than just whatever money Snyder had offered him. Rivers had also wanted the reputation he would gain by being the one to kill Kid Collins. Tom Rivers was dead now, but there were plenty more like him out there. They would never let him rest. "I reckon that was part of it," he allowed to the judge.

The judge nodded slowly, considering. "He couldn't make much of a reputation by shooting you in the back, though, could he? How do you explain that?"

The Kid shrugged, not wanting to speak ill of the dead but having no other choice. "He panicked. He was sweating and I could smell the fear on him. When I turned away from him, he saw his chance going, too, so he . . ."

"Your Honor!" Snyder protested again, rising to his feet. "That is just his opinion. Rivers isn't here to speak for himself."

"It's a lucky thing he has you, then, isn't it?" the judge asked with a chilly little smile while he banged his gavel for order once again. Snyder sat down angrily as the judge thanked Christian and dismissed him. Next he called Angelica to the stand.

"Why did you scream, Miss Ross?" he asked, getting right to the point.

Angelica allowed herself one glance at Christian, who had resumed his position at the rear of the room. His sky blue eyes were riveted on Snyder, though, so she could not draw any courage there. Taking a deep breath to still any quivering that nerves might cause in her voice, she said, "Someone told me that Mr. Collins was going to be in a gunfight. I was trying to stop it," she said.

"Mr. Collins is your foreman, is that correct?" the judge asked, letting his wise eyes stray toward Christian and then back to Angelica.

"Yes, that is correct," she replied, meeting his gaze unflinchingly.

"Who told you about the gunfight?" the judge inquired.

"I believe it was Mr. Snyder," she said, not looking at Snyder but sensing his surprise that she had not told the rest of it. Christian, however, had insisted on discretion, knowing that it would serve no useful purpose to admit she had been off under the willow tree alone with Snyder. She still dared not accuse Snyder of attacking her for fear of ruining her own reputation. In any case, only the bare facts would help Miles, so she stuck to them.

"I see," the judge was saying. "And did you see the

actual shooting?"

"No, I did not. I was on the other side of the grounds. As I was running towards the dance floor, I heard two shots, and then Mr. Collins knocked me down so I wouldn't be hit. I did not see who fired the shots."

Next the judge called Robbie to the stand. He hesitated, giving Angelica an apprehensive glance, but she patted his shoulder and whispered a few words of encouragement to him. Taking a deep breath, he rose and made his way to the empty witness chair with his small head held high. Maria reached over and gave Angelica's hand a reassuring squeeze, which she returned.

Once he got started, Robbie told his story with increasing confidence. The judge was patient with the boy but showed him no more consideration that he had shown Angelica. Still, there were some in the audience who were inclined to disbelief.

"Your Honor, the boy worships Collins and Blackmon," Snyder called out when Robbie had finished his story.

Robbie bristled visibly. "I don't hold with backshooters, though, friends or not," he piped. "I wouldn't stick up for Mr. Blackmon unless he'd shot fair and square."

The judge banged his gavel again, rubbing his mustache to hide a smile. Then he told Robbie he could step down. The judge called several other people who had been present, but no one else could confirm or deny Miles's story since they had all been watching Angelica and Christian at the crucial moment. At last the judge called Jake Evans.

Evans was plainly ill at ease in the formal setting with all eyes fastened on him. He rubbed his palms along the thighs of his jeans as if to dry them.

"Mr. Evans, would you tell us, please, who fired the first shot that night?"

Evans squirmed, looking around, first at Snyder and then the various members of the Diamond R crew who were scattered about the room. "It's kind of hard to remember," he hedged. "But if it's a matter of who fired the first shot, I'd have to say Blackmon. Even the boy said that," he pointed out.

"All right then," the judge agreed, "did you see Rivers pull his gun and aim it at Collins?"

Evans glanced at Snyder again. The rancher was glaring, his arms crossed forbiddingly. Evans straightened in the chair as if in silent rebellion. "I didn't actually see that part. I was watching Collins. When I heard Blackmon's shot, I looked back and Rivers was falling. His gun went off and hit the dirt."

"When you looked back, Rivers's gun was already in his hand? You didn't see him draw?" the judge insisted.

"That's right," Evans said, although he clearly would have liked to say otherwise.

"I see," said the judge, and Angelica was certain that he did. After dismissing Evans, he asked if anyone else had anything to add. When no one did, he said, "After considering all the evidence, it appears to me that we have an unfortunate case of justifiable homicide. In plain talk, that means that Blackmon shot Rivers to keep Rivers from shooting Collins. Mr. Blackmon, you're a free man."

A cheer arose from the Diamond R crew, and many of the townspeople who had been convinced of Miles's innocence by the testimony joined in. Only Snyder's crew remained silent, rising and stalking from the room as a group. Angelica hugged Kate and Robbie and Maria, all at once. Then she looked around to see Miles being congratulated by everyone near him, but when she tried to find Christian, he was nowhere in sight. She finally located him out on the sidewalk, still keeping an eye on

Snyder and his men, who had gathered in the street.

"Let's get out of this town," she heard Snyder say.

"What about Rivers?" Evans asked. "Are you gonna take him out to the ranch for burying?"

"Hell no," Snyder scoffed. "Although I suppose it would be un-Christian to leave him to the county. Ace," he said, calling to one of his men, "go tell the undertaker to charge off the coffin and burial plot to me. Nothing fancy, though."

Angelica watched the cowboy heading over to the barbershop since the barber doubled as undertaker. Snyder led the rest of his men toward the livery and their horses. When Angelica turned back to Christian, she caught the strangest expression on his face.

"Christian?" she said, reaching out a tentative hand to him. His eyes were awful, as if they were seeing something unspeakable, something invisible to everyone else.

The bulk of the crowd was coming out of the restaurant now with Miles in the lead. "Come on, everybody," Stumpy was yelling, "this fellow looks like he needs a drink. Kid, you gonna join us?"

Christian shook himself slightly, as if emerging from a bad dream. "What? Oh, yeah, go ahead. I'll catch you up," he instructed. The jovial group moved across the street to the Dirty Dog.

"Christian, what is it?" Angelica asked, gripping his arm anxiously. For a moment there he'd looked so far away, and for days, ever since the dance, he had been so distant, as if something was eating at him. That was understandable, what with Miles being in trouble and all, but now he should have been happy. Instead, his mood seemed more troubled than ever.

"It's nothing," he said. "Go on over to Kate's. I'll bring Miles by before he gets too drunk to be respectable," he said with a perfunctory smile that did not quite reach his eyes. With that, he bounded off the sidewalk and hurried to catch up with the celebrants.

"What is wrong?" Maria asked when she and Kate came out with Robbie a moment later.

"I don't know," Angelica said, watching Christian disappear into the saloon. She did know she was very frightened all of a sudden, more frightened than she had been in a long time.

Over at the saloon, Miles ordered up a round of drinks on him, and everyone drank to his health, everyone, that is, except Sunny, who watched the proceedings from a corner table through red-rimmed eyes. Miles had seen her, however, and as soon as he could, he broke free of his well-wishers and made his way over to her.

She lifted her gaze to him, and her pale blue eyes sparked with hate. He did not flinch. "It was just like I said, miss. He was gonna shoot the Kid in the back. There was nothing else I could do. I'm real sorry."

"Sorry?" she hissed back at him. "What good does that do me? We was gonna go away together, him and me, to New Orleans. I'd never have to whore again, he said. Now what have I got?"

Miles had no answer. "I'm sorry," he repeated, knowing how small it sounded to her.

"I'm sorry, too," the Kid said, coming up beside him. "If you still want to go to New Orleans, maybe we can help," he tried.

"Damn you! Damn you to hell!" she cried. "Get away from me, the both of you." Pushing out of her chair, she fled for the back door of the saloon.

The disturbance caused an uncomfortable hush to fall over the crowd, but the Kid diplomatically called for another round of drinks, and soon the party was going again. When it was in full force, the Kid motioned Miles outside. They slipped discreetly out the door, and the Kid led Miles around to the back of the saloon, past Sunny's cabin, all the way to the edge of the lot, where the outhouse stood and where they would not be overheard.

"I finally found Ace," the Kid said.

"Ace?" Miles searched his memory in vain.

"You remember, I told you. That day they burned my sister's cabin, right before I got away, I heard one of the attackers call another one Ace. Today, just now out in the street, I heard Snyder call one of his gunnies by that name," the Kid explained.

Miles frowned. "Are you sure? You were shot up pretty bad when the Indians took you to Angelica's place. Maybe you only dreamed it."

"I wasn't shot when I heard the name Ace," the Kid insisted. "I'll remember that until the day I die."

"Well, then, maybe we oughta talk this over with the sheriff," Miles suggested.

"Not until I've had a chance to talk to this Ace myself, in private," the Kid said, his eyes glittering dangerously.

"Be careful," Miles warned. "We'd have a tough time explaining another killing."

"I said I just wanted to talk," the Kid repeated. "I'm as interested in getting the man behind the killings as I am in getting the men who actually killed my sister and brother-in-law. But for now, we've got some celebrating to do, and I promised I'd take you over to Kate's before you got too drunk."

"Let's go, then," Miles said.

For a several minutes after they left, the area was still. Then, once she was sure they were gone, Sunny slipped from behind the bushes where she had taken refuge when she'd heard them approaching. At the time, she had simply wanted to escape their notice. Now she realized that hiding had been the best thing she had ever done because she had learned that Kid Collins was the man who had escaped the fire, the man who had run to the Indians, the man Snyder and his men had been wondering about for months. They thought he was dead, or at least they were hoping he was.

Imagine how surprised they would be to discover that he was not only alive but was a very dangerous enemy who could link them to murder. Sunny wondered idly how much money she could extort from Harlan Snyder for this piece of information. Would it be enough to go to New Orleans?

Chapter Thirteen

Angelica found Christian standing out in the shadows of Kate's big front porch. Inside the house there was a party. It was much more sedate than the one still perking at the saloon, but the mood was no less joyous. The guests included the judge and the sheriff as well as many of the townspeople. Kate and Miles had not yet said a word about their relationship, but no one doubted for a moment that Kate had finally decided to end her widowhood.

Angelica had tried all evening to share the festive mood, but whenever her gaze strayed to Christian, she felt the same shiver of apprehension that had first come over her in the courtroom. When she had seen him slip out just now, she had followed, hoping to learn the reason for the haunted expression he had worn ever since the inquest.

"Christian, is something wrong?" she asked, coming up beside him and slipping her arm through his in a gesture of intimacy.

He took one last drag on his cigarette and tossed it away before replying. "I'm just worried about what Snyder's going to do next," he lied, resisting the almost overwhelming urge to pull her close. Her fragrance enveloped him in an invisible cloud, tempting him, drawing him, but he stood where he was, unmoving. Soon he would bloody his hands once again. Those hands had no right to touch Angelica Ross.

"There really isn't anything Snyder *can* do, is there?" she asked. "I mean, we have the law on our side now, and . . ."

"Snyder has never been too particular about following the law," he pointed out. "Besides, the law only works if you get caught. Snyder's never been known to do his dirty work himself."

"What are you going to do?" she asked, knowing already she would not like the answer.

"I'm going to try to catch Snyder red-handed," he replied.

"No!" she cried, certain that he would not be content simply to sit around and wait. No doubt he had some plan for provoking Snyder to action.

She saw the white slash of his teeth as he smiled away her protest. "Don't get yourself in a tizzy," he said. "All I'm gonna do is a little spying." His voice was reassuring, but it was too dark to see his eyes. Instinct told her not to believe him, but she didn't think she had a choice.

"You'll be careful, won't you? If anything happened to you, I don't know what I'd do."

Her words stung him, wiping the smile from his face. He hated the way the thought of losing him hurt her, but he knew beyond doubt that she was bound to lose him eventually, one way or another. It was written in the book for a man like him. He should tell her that, he should try to make her understand how crazy it was to love him, and somehow, he should try to make her stop.

But he couldn't, not just yet, anyway. Instead, he reached for her, pulling her close for his kiss. Her mouth was sweet and yielding, her hands eager as she clung to him. When the kiss was over, he held her to his heart for a long moment, imprinting the feel of her against him for the lonely days ahead.

"I want you and Robbie and Maria to stay here at Kate's while I'm gone," he said into the softness of her hair. "I'll leave Miles with you for protection."

"That will make Kate happy, at least," she murmured into his shirtfront.

"I'll take Stumpy with me, and the rest of the men will go back to watch the ranch. Then I won't have to worry about anyone or anything except Snyder."

She nodded her understanding, knowing it would be senseless to argue. She did not want to spoil this night, in any case. Giving him one last squeeze, she released him. "Come back inside now and enjoy the party," she urged, covering her misgivings with a smile. Tomorrow was soon enough to start being afraid again. Tonight, while he was here and still safe, she would somehow forget her fears and simply enjoy his company.

"This better be good," Snyder informed Sunny as he followed her into her cabin and closed the door behind them. When one of his cowboys had first brought him her message late this morning, his impulse had been to ignore it. After thinking things over, however, he had realized that Sunny now had a grudge against Kid Collins, too. Her hint that she possessed information about the Kid that Snyder would find interesting was too provocative to pass up.

"It's good," she assured him, "but before I tell you, we've got to settle our terms."

"Terms?" he asked disdainfully. "These are my terms, honey: you tell me or I'll beat the sh—"

"No!" she interrupted him, no longer afraid of him. "You can beat me to death if you want to, but I'll never tell you what I know. Otis saw you come in here, so if you really do kill me, you'll swing for it. If you only hurt me, I'll go to the sheriff. I think he'll be real interested to find out who burned that squatters' cabin and what happened to the people in it."

Snyder's eyes narrowed as he studied her defiant face. Something had happened to Sunny, something that had changed her from a meek little mouse into a tigress. He felt a small stirring of excitement at the thought of conquering that tigress, but he repressed it. There would be time for that later, after he learned Sunny's secret.

"All right," he conceded. "What are *your* terms?"

"I want a hundred dollars, cash, right now, and then I'll tell you something that will save your neck." She crossed her arms confidently over her middle.

Snyder grinned slowly as he took in her determined stance. "What'll you do with a hundred dollars?" he asked with casual interest.

"I'll go to New Orleans, so you'll never have to worry that I'll tell what I know about you."

He nodded, realizing she had thought this thing through rather thoroughly. Maybe she was smarter than he'd given her credit for being. One thing was certain: having lost Rivers's protection, she felt she no longer had anything else to lose. For some reason, Snyder believed she wasn't bluffing about standing up to a beating. Besides, he didn't want to waste any more time. Giving her the money was easy enough. He could always take it back after he'd heard her story.

With a conciliatory smile, he reached into his vest pocket and counted out five double eagles. "Here you go," he said, offering them to her.

Her eyes grew wide for a moment before she snatched them from his palm. Clutching them to her bosom, she said, "You remember when that squatters' cabin burned, one of them got away?"

Snyder nodded patiently. "The Comanche got him."

"No," she contradicted him smugly. "The Comanche took him to Angelica Ross. It was Collins."

"Collins?" he echoed incredulously. "Where did you hear a fool thing like that?"

"From him," she replied. "I overheard him and Blackmon talking about it. He said the squatters were his sister and her husband. The Indians took him to Miss Ross's ranch after he got shot. But there's more," she added, her smugness growing. "He knows that your man Ace was one of them that attacked the cabin."

Snyder snorted in disbelief. "If he knows that, why hasn't he gone to the law?"

"He just found out yesterday that Ace works for you."

Snyder's face twisted into a worried scowl. "Then he probably told the sheriff last night while they were all cozied up at Mrs. Marsden's house. . . ."

"No, he told Blackmon he wasn't going to the law just yet, not until he'd talked to Ace himself and gotten something on you," she explained, backing up a step as Snyder's scowl grew more fierce.

But he was no longer thinking of her. His mind was on other things. "Then there's still time," he muttered.

"Did you bring Ace with you like I told you?" she asked.

He nodded vaguely. "Stay here," he commanded as he left to find Ace in the saloon.

As soon as he was gone, Sunny went to the loose floorboard under the stove where she hid her valuables and cached her money. There, she thought, even if he does beat me up later, I'll still have the money.

She went to her window and looked out. Snyder, Jake

Evans and the man called Ace had come out the back door of the saloon. They stood in the alley, talking. Sunny watched, wishing she could hear what they were planning. Suddenly, she saw a movement out of the corner of her eye and a stray dog came streaking down the alley followed by a running boy carrying a bunch of tin cans on a string.

Snyder caught the boy's arm. For a moment Sunny thought he was just going to chasten the child and send him on his way, but then she recognized the boy. It was Robbie Ross. Snyder clamped a hand over the boy's mouth and sent Jake to see if any other children were behind him. To Sunny's horror, Snyder hefted Robbie under one arm, keeping his other hand firmly over the squirming boy's mouth, and carried him to her cabin.

"What are you doing?" she demanded when he brought the child inside.

"Getting some bait," Snyder replied cryptically.

"Now where could that boy have gotten to?" Angelica muttered in irritation as she scanned the empty street once more. "Robbie!" she called for the tenth time in as many minutes.

"Maybe he is with the Wallace boy," Maria suggested, coming out onto the porch to help Angelica look.

Angelica made an impatient noise. "Well, he's going to miss his supper if we don't find him pretty soon."

"I will go to the Wallace's house to see if he is there," Maria offered. "Why don't you go over to town and look?"

"All right," Angelica replied, still straining for a glimpse of the small redheaded figure. "That boy." She was still muttering imprecations when she ran into the

Wallace boy and two others with whom Robbie had been playing earlier in the day.

"We seen him going after Ol' Blue a while ago," one of the boys explained, naming the town's resident stray dog. "He was gonna tie some cans to his tail. They ran down the alley behind the saloon, and we didn't see him no more. We figured Blue bit him, and he went running home 'cause he didn't want us to see him crying."

Now Angelica was really getting angry. After thanking the boys and sending them home for their own suppers, she went after Robbie, ready to blister his ears when she found him. The alley behind the saloon was deserted and dreary, as she had expected. Trash and broken bottles sat in piles, and the stench of whiskey tinged the dusty air.

She didn't think to feel alarmed until she saw the tin cans and the tangle of string lying discarded on the ground. How many times had she scolded Robbie for tricks like that? she wondered, kicking the cans out of the way in disgust. He probably really had gotten bitten, and now was afraid to face her. Where could he be hiding, though?

As she looked around, she caught sight of a woman's face at the window of the ramshackle cabin on the other side of the alley. Although she knew Sunny Day would have no reason to be friendly to her, perhaps the girl had seen Robbie. It was worth a try, she reasoned as she walked over to the cabin.

Stumpy peered through the spyglass one last time before passing it to the Kid. "I'm getting too old for all this skulking around," he complained, shifting his butt to a more comfortable position on the hard ground.

"I recollect a time when you could keep ten skinners

busy shooting buffalo from a single stand. You oughta have all the practice you need sitting still," the Kid replied, using the glass to examine every square foot of Harlan Snyder's ranch. There were about half a dozen men around the place, but none of them was the elusive Ace.

"What happens if you can't find this Ace fellow?" Stumpy inquired, brushing absently at the gnats circling his face. The two men were sitting behind a clump of bushes on a small rise overlooking Snyder's ranch buildings.

The Kid heaved a long-suffering sigh. "I reckon I'll have to go back to town and start over. I hate to ask about him, because he's sure to get wind of it, but right now I can't think of any other way to find him except wearing out the seat of my pants sitting on this hill."

"We can wait till supper, anyways," Stumpy said. "If he's around, he'll come in then for sure."

The Kid glanced up at the sun and judged he could be patient a while longer.

"Now they are both gone," Maria told Kate in disgust as she entered the steamy kitchen where Kate was preparing the evening meal.

Kate looked up from rolling biscuits on the table and gave her a puzzled smile. "You mean you've lost Angelica, too?"

Maria nodded, stepping out of the doorway to make way for Miles, who was carrying in a load of firewood.

"They can't have gone far," Miles pointed out. "This town isn't that big." He dropped the logs into the woodbox and straightened again, frowning as he considered various possibilities. "Where all have you looked?"

"Every place except the saloon and that whore's house," Maria reported, sinking down into one of the kitchen chairs wearily.

Kate was shaking her head. "They probably stopped off to visit somebody, and you just missed them. It can happen, even in a town as small as Marsden's Corners," she added, arching her eyebrows at Miles in response to his implied criticism of the size of her town.

"Kate's right," Miles agreed, ignoring her disapproval. "You ladies sit tight. I'll take another look around. I'll even check the saloon," he added with a wink as he ducked out the door.

"Don't check it too long," Kate warned as he bounded down the back steps.

Of course, Miles did not imagine for one minute that he would find Robbie and Angelica in the Dirty Dog Saloon, but he did stick his head in to ask if anyone had seen them. The place was empty except for Otis and Sunny. Otis shook his head at the question, and when Miles let his gaze stray to Sunny, she looked quickly away.

Once again, Miles felt the pang of guilt for what Sunny had suffered. He thought about her dream of going to New Orleans, a dream that had died with Tom Rivers. Not for the first time, Miles wished he knew a way to make things up to her. She didn't seem inclined to even glance his way, but he ignored his common sense and impulsively entered the saloon, determined to at least make her listen to his apology this time.

She was sitting at one of the tables, a deadlocked game of solitaire spread out before her. The eyes she lifted to him were wary and afraid. Her hands clenched on the tabletop, and her narrow shoulders stiffened defensively. Hoping to put her at ease, he reached up and pulled off his hat, but to his dismay, the sudden motion made her flinch.

"I know it doesn't change much, miss, but I do want you to know how sorry I am about what happened," he said.

Miles watched her tongue come out and lick the tiny beads of sweat from her upper lip. It was a warm day, but she seemed a little warmer than even the weather would have made her. Dark circles of moisture had formed under her arms, and stray tendrils of hair clung damply to her neck. Did his presence make her that uncomfortable? He swore silently at the thought, wishing once again that he knew of a way to wipe that tortured look from her eyes. If only he could help her somehow . . .

The idea came from nowhere, and when it did, he felt like a fool for not having thought of it sooner. "I know that Rivers was going to take you to New Orleans," he said, fishing in his pocket. Her wary expression vanished behind her astonishment as she watched him pulling the gold coins from his vest. He laid them down in front of her. It was the bonus Angelica Ross had given him. He didn't need it. He had money put aside from many such bonuses. "This isn't much, I know, but it'll buy your way to New Orleans."

Sunny stared down at the five gold coins. A hundred dollars, the same amount that Snyder had given her except this man asked for nothing in return. While it was true that he probably owed her that and more for having killed Rivers, experience had taught her not to expect men to feel any obligation to her. Her gaze flew to Blackmon's face. His eyes were sad, but more than that, they were kind. He was giving her the money out of kindness. When had someone last been kind to her? Tom had been generous and protective and even loving in his own way, but kindness was not in his nature.

Collins's face swam before her for a moment, his face the way it had looked that day he had saved her from Snyder. He'd been kind to her, too, never even asking for repayment for the favor. Guilt twisted her stomach. How could she be a party to a plan that would hurt him now?

"Miss?" Blackmon's eyes narrowed in concern as he sensed her distress.

Sunny swallowed the lump of fear that had seemed permanently lodged in her throat ever since Snyder had carried the Ross boy into her house. She knew if she betrayed Snyder, he would kill her, and yet she also knew she could not let Snyder get away with what he had planned. If only she could put Blackmon and Collins on Snyder's trail without actually admitting what she knew. Then she remembered something Blackmon would consider important enough to pursue.

"Are you still looking for that Ace fellow?" she blurted.

"Ace?" he repeated, wondering how on earth she could know about his interest in the man.

"Yes, I . . . I overheard you and the Kid talking yesterday out behind the saloon."

"You couldn't have . . ." he began, but she interrupted him.

"I was hiding in the bushes. I thought you were looking for me again, and I didn't want you to see me. I heard what you said, and I know where Ace is." Her small hands were twisting nervously, but he put that down to her fear of him.

He wanted to ask her why she was willing to help him after what he had done, but decided it was probably rude to question her motives, especially when she was so obviously sincere. Instead he asked, "Where is he?"

She drew a deep breath to steady her voice. "Ace works out at one of the line shacks, the one on Deep Creek," she said, naming the place she had overheard Snyder mention as his destination. "Do you know where it is?"

Miles nodded. "Does he have a partner?"

"He usually works alone, I think, but I'm not sure," she added guiltily, hoping Blackmon would have sense enough to be prepared for more than one man. It was the only warning she could give him. "Will you go out there right away?" she asked anxiously. "If he finds out you're looking for him, he'll hightail it out of there."

Miles frowned thoughtfully. "As soon as I find the Kid, we'll go after him . . . and you know we don't aim to do him harm," he reminded her.

She nodded, knowing he would change his mind when he discovered what new mischief Ace was involved with. "Good luck," she whispered.

"Thanks, miss, and good luck to you, too," he said as he hurried out of the saloon and down the street to Kate's house.

Kate tried to convince him to wait until the Kid got back, but Miles knew the Kid was in a hurry to get this settled. Besides, night would be the perfect time to catch this Ace fellow unawares, and Miles figured he had just enough time before dark to find the Kid and get out to the line shack. Kate threw some food into a sack for him to carry along. He remembered to apologize for not finding Angelica and Robbie just as he was leaving.

"That's all right," Kate told him. "They'll be along in a minute, I'm sure. You be careful, and don't take any chances."

He gave her a quick kiss. "I'll be as careful as a cat in

a roomful of rocking chairs," he promised with a grin. "I've got too much to live for now."

Smiling back in spite of her fears, Kate waved him good-bye. When he was out of sight, she turned to Maria. "Well, I reckon it's my turn to go looking for our little lost lambs."

Maria shook her head. "We will let them go hungry if they do not show up soon."

Angelica cringed inwardly when she saw Harlan Snyder's familiar figure astride a horse and waiting for them up ahead. She was sitting stiffly beside Jake Evans on the wagon seat as she had been ever since they had left Marsden's Corners over an hour ago. Robbie lay on the wagon bed behind her, covered by a tarp. With him was that awful man Ace, who was holding a gun to the boy's head to ensure her cooperation. Having her ride on the seat in plain sight had been Snyder's idea, so if anyone in town had seen her leaving, they would have thought she was going of her own free will.

Evans pulled the wagon to a halt. "You can come out now, Ace," he called over his shoulder as Snyder rode closer, leading a second horse.

Apprehension roiled in Angelica's stomach when she saw the calculating gleam in Snyder's eye. He looked her over with a proprietary air that made the turmoil in her stomach want to rise higher. Resolutely, she fought back the wave of nausea and turned to see Robbie emerging from beneath the tarp.

"Robbie, are you all right?" she asked anxiously.

He nodded, never taking his eyes off his captor, who still held a gun on him. The boy's face was pale, making his freckles stand out like dark splotches on his skin, but otherwise he looked little the worse for wear. He was bound and gagged and his hazel eyes were huge in his small face, full of fear and impotent fury. She understood his feelings only too well.

Snyder reined up beside the wagon. "Ace, I think you'd better tie Miss Ross up now that we're clear of town. We don't want her getting any silly ideas about escaping."

Jake Evans scowled as Ace produced a length of rope from the back of the wagon and reached up to pull Angelica's arms behind her. "I don't cotton much to this, Boss," he said. "There's no call to tie her up. She'll behave as long as we've got the boy, now won't you, miss?" he appealed to Angelica.

"Oh, yes," she agreed, knowing that her only hope lay in remaining free. "You have my word that I won't try anything."

Ace paused in his task, glancing at Snyder for his decision. The rancher gave a disbelieving snort. "Tie her up and be quick about it," he said. "One thing you have to learn about women, Jake, and that's that their word isn't worth a plugged nickel."

Ace grinned evilly and grabbed Angelica's arms again. This time he was none too gentle. She wanted to struggle, wanted to fight and try to make a break for it, but she couldn't, not with Robbie lying helpless in the wagon. Instead she fought back with words, the only weapons left her.

"Where are you taking us, Snyder, and what do you plan to do with us?" she demanded, wincing in spite of herself as Ace drew the ropes tight around her wrists.

Snyder's grin was as evil as Ace's. "We're just going over the hill a little ways to one of my line shacks. When we have you all settled, we're going to send word to your 'foreman' about where he can find you and wait for him to show up. Until then, you're going to be my guests. That's all. Nothing to worry your pretty head about."

Angelica stared at him in horror. All the nebulous fears she had harbored for herself and her brother since the moment she had seen Ace holding a pistol to Robbie's head coalesced. Now she knew the greatest danger was not to herself and the boy at all, but rather to Christian, who would, no doubt, be riding into a carefully laid trap. Would he suspect? Would he be ready for it?

Common sense told her he would, and yet what could he do to defend himself if he feared for her and Robbie's safety? She opened her mouth to try another argument, but Ace stuffed a gag into it. She did struggle then, but it was too late. In another moment, Ace had dragged her roughly over the seat and into the back of the wagon, where she lay, as helpless now as Robbie.

"Thank you, Ace," Snyder said, ignoring Evans's murmur of disapproval. "I'd say your job here is done now, and you can be on your way. You'll want to be clean out of the state when Collins comes looking for you."

The gunman hardly seemed to hear Snyder. He was busy positioning Angelica on the wagon bed beside her brother. Angelica fought him as best she could, cringing from his grasp, but her struggles only seemed to encourage him. His wandering hands played insolently over her breasts while he grinned at her helplessness.

Fury boiled up inside of her, and she squirmed violently in frustration and revulsion. Her muffled protest alerted Jake Evans, who slapped the gunman's hands away from her.

"You son of a bitch," Evans said, giving Ace a shove. Ace growled a reply and seemed about to retaliate when

Snyder called out to him.

"I'll thank you not to manhandle my future wife, Ace," he said coolly. The gunman paused, apparently considering the implied warning. Then, reluctantly, he began to climb down out of the wagon, keeping his eye on Jake Evans as he did so.

Snyder watched with mild amusement. "I'm sorry you won't be able to go back to the ranch and retrieve the rest of your belongings, but I've included a little bonus in with your pay so you can replace your things later," he informed Ace.

With one last glance at Evans, Ace turned and mounted the spare horse.

Snyder gave Evans a nod. "You can go ahead to the cabin. I'll catch up in a few minutes."

Evans grunted his reply and slapped the horses into motion. Angelica gave Robbie what she hoped was a reassuring look as they began to roll. Inside, her nerves were taut with fear. How long would it be until Christian came, and what would happen to them in the meantime? Angelica reminded herself of what Kate had told her about Jake Evans. The man might have few redeeming qualities, but he would tolerate no disrespect to a lady. She had already seen evidence of that. As long as Evans was around, she need not fear for her virtue. That left only her and Robbie's physical safety and the showdown that was coming between Christian and Snyder. Which, she decided grimly, was more than enough to worry about.

Snyder reached into his coat pocket and pulled out a small leather sack, which he tossed to Ace. "Payment for a job well done," he said with a small smile. They had waited until the wagon was out of sight and then ridden back off the road a ways, out of sight of anyone who might happen by.

Ace quickly pulled the drawstring loose and emptied the coins into his palm to count them.

"It's getting awfully warm, isn't it?" Snyder remarked to no one in particular as he began to shrug out of his suit coat.

Ace didn't glance up from his task until he had finished. Plainly, he was pleased with the total. "That's damn generous of you, Mr. Snyder," he said, dumping the coins back into the sack and pulling the string tight again. "I never expected . . ."

Something slammed into his chest, cutting off his words. The accompanying explosion was strangely muffled, so that at first he did not recognize it for what it was. By the time Ace saw the smoke curling from the bundle Snyder had made of his coat, he was sliding helplessly from his saddle.

"What the hell . . . ?" No one answered his question. When his body thumped to the ground, he lay still, staring up at the sky.

Snyder waited for any sign of movement. When there was none, he carefully unwrapped his coat and shook it out, regretting that the material would now smell of gunsmoke. But there was no help for it, he reminded himself, replacing his gun in its holster.

Calmly, as if he were simply retrieving a dropped item, he swung down from his saddle and scooped up the small sack of coins that had been jarred loose from Ace's lifeless hand. Snyder slipped his coat on again and dropped the pouch back into his pocket. Without so much as a second glance at the body on the ground, Snyder remounted and caught up the reins of the other horse. When he reached the road again, he gave the second horse a slap, sending it off to find its way back to his ranch. Kicking his own horse into a gallop, he hurried to catch up with the wagon.

Angelica tensed when she heard the approaching hoofbeats. Snyder was back with them, and she knew she and Robbie were in far more danger while he was near.

"Hold up there, Jake," she heard him call. Evans pulled the wagon to a stop, and from where she lay, she saw Snyder ride up beside them. He spared her a glance, but she could not read his expression. "There's been a slight change in plans," he said to Evans. "I want you to take my horse and the boy and ride back to the ranch. Wait for me there."

Angelica felt her heart rising up in her throat. She wasn't sure which she feared more: being separated from Robbie or being left alone with Snyder.

"What about the girl?" she heard Evans ask, echoing her own concern.

"She'll stay with me for a while," Snyder replied. His tone did not invite discussion.

"I don't like it, Boss," Evans said anyway. "She ain't done nothing. . . ."

"She's done plenty," Snyder snapped. "And don't forget, you're in this as deep as I am."

"But kidnapping women and children . . . I never thought it'd go this far," Evans complained.

"Well, it has, and we've got to see it through," Snyder informed him. "Just remember, once Collins is out of the way and I've taken the fair Angelica as my bride, no one will dare touch us. Now get the boy and be on your way. You want to get back to the ranch before dark."

Angelica and Robbie felt the wagon tip as Evans climbed down. The boy's eyes widened in renewed fear, and Angelica easily read his terror at being separated from her. She shared his fears, but could not let him see that she did. Instead, she tried to silently convey some bit of reassurance in the few moments they had before Evans reached into the back of the wagon and dragged Robbie away.

To the boy's credit, he tried to fight, but he was no match for the much larger man, especially since both his arms and legs were bound. The last anguished look he cast her before Evans carried him away tore her heart. Tears stung her eyes, but she blinked them back. They were a luxury she could not afford just now.

She heard a murmured conversation between Snyder and Evans. Robbie was grunting as if he were still fighting, but then she heard a slap and the grunting stopped abruptly. Frantic, she tried to struggle upright for one more look at her brother, but the wagon tilted again, knocking her back down as Snyder climbed up into the driver's seat. She felt his eyes on her as she tried to get back up, but she refused to look at him. Then she heard him chuckle. The sound sent chills racing over her.

"You're all mine, now, Angelica," he said softly. "In a little while, you'll know exactly what that means."

Before she could even begin to absorb the meaning of his words, she heard the horse carrying Jake Evans and her brother ride away. Snyder chuckled again and slapped his own team into motion. Angelica fell back, helpless against the jouncing of the wagon. Once more tears threatened as she knew the terror of being under Snyder's complete control, and once more she blinked them back. She forced herself to concentrate on Robbie and her prayers for his safety so she wouldn't begin to imagine what Harlan Snyder had in store for her.

By the time the wagon halted again, Angelica's wrists were raw from struggling against her bonds, and still the ropes held fast. From where she lay she could see the roof of a small cabin and knew they had reached the line shack Snyder had spoken of earlier. He was going to take her inside now. She had no illusions about what would happen then. Once more she felt the icy fingers of fear clawing up her spine, and her body trembled.

Snyder swung his legs over the seat and came down on the wagon bed beside her. Something of her fear must have shown on her face, because he studied her for a long moment with apparent satisfaction.

"I've waited a long time for this, Angelica," he told her, his gaze malevolent. "I treated you like a lady because I thought you were one. Now I know better, and I won't make the same mistake twice." He reached out, and his beefy hand closed determinedly over her breast, squeezing cruelly. She cried out in pain beneath her gag, and her body recoiled from his hated touch, but she could not escape him. Terror scorched through her, searing away hope and leaving only bleak despair.

"When I'm finished with you, you won't have any choice but to marry me," he informed her confidently. "Breaking you will be a job, Angelica, but it's one I've been anticipating with great pleasure."

Angelica heard his voice only faintly as her fear choked her, cutting off her air and slowing the blood in her veins to a trickle, until she thought she might actually pass out. Even if she had been free to scream, there was no one near to hear her voice. Even if she could have run, he would have easily caught her. Bound and gagged as she was, she didn't have those options. She couldn't even spit out the venomous words that had lodged in a lump in her throat.

He grinned down at her as if he understood her frustration completely and reveled in it. "Come, my dear. Let's get started, shall we?" he asked mockingly.

Snyder moved to the rear of the wagon and climbed down. Angelica's panicked mind was racing as she desperately searched for a way of escape. Even delay was no use since no one knew where she was so the possibility of rescue was nonexistent. Still, she instinctively kicked at him when he tried to grasp her ankles and haul her out of the wagon.

He dodged, but she managed to make contact with his shoulder. His grunt told her she had done a little damage, but the hands that reached for her a second time were quick and wary and successful. He pulled, dragging her unceremoniously to the tailgate and over the edge despite her resistance. She made a desperate attempt to keep her skirt from riding up to her waist, an attempt that made him laugh wickedly.

"Your modesty is commendable, my dear, but wholly misplaced, I assure you. Before I'm finished, you will have no secrets from me." Angelica shuddered in horror as he pulled her over the edge and set her feet on the ground. "Won't you come in?" he asked sarcastically, shoving her toward the cabin.

She staggered, knowing that no matter how futile it was, she would run as soon as she regained her balance. But Snyder caught her, his hands crushing the delicate skin of her upper arms as he propelled her through the doorway into the cramped interior of the line shack. The room was musty and dark in the twilight. She heard the frantic scurrying of mice as they ran for cover. Their panic echoed her own.

Two bunks were built into two corners of the single room. Snyder threw her down on one. She bounded back up immediately, responding to the instinctive need to get away, but her face met the rock hardness of his fist. Pain exploded inside her head, and she went flopping back momentarily stunned.

As her head cleared, she was vaguely aware that he had lit a lamp somewhere nearby. The flickering flame cast strange shadows everywhere and turned Snyder's already frightening expression into a mask of evil. He was bending over her, untying her hands and removing her gag. "I promised Jake that I wouldn't mistreat you," he explained quite casually. "He's such a gentleman. Of course, I assume he expected me to control my baser urges, too, or he never would have left you with me. I confess, I gave him every reason to believe I would, but I consider this merely a prelude to our honeymoon."

"You pig!" she rasped when the gag had slipped from her face.

He laughed as if she had told him a joke. "I've always admired your spirit. That's why I'm untying you. I'm actually looking forward to your struggles. It adds to the thrill of the ultimate victory."

Angelica stared up at him incredulously. He wanted her to fight him! Fury surged through her, blocking out some of the fear. Well, if he wanted a fight, he would certainly get one. What he didn't realize, however, was that Angelica would die before submitting to him. If she could win no other way, she would still rob him of his "ultimate victory."

When her wrists were free, he stepped back as if to admire his handiwork. Angelica immediately began to flex her fingers in an attempt to get the feeling back. It was an excruciating process as her stiff joints protested the movement.

At the same time she was working on her hands, she was looking around the room, searching for potential weapons and potential avenues of escape. Except for the door and one tiny window on the opposite wall, there were no other exits. If she wanted to get away, she would have to get to the door. He had left the horses hitched to the wagon. If she were quick enough, if she could incapacitate him somehow . . . if, if, if . . .

"Go ahead and try it," he said smugly, seeing her measuring the distance from the bed to the door. "I enjoy the chase almost as much as the capture."

Angelica glanced at him and froze in horror as she saw him removing his suit coat. He laid it carefully on the other bunk and began to unbutton his vest.

Oh, dear heaven! her heart cried in anguish. Her body reacted instinctively, surging up off the bed and toward the door. She was outside when he caught her. His arm came around her waist, jerking her off her feet. She flailed wildly, scratching and clawing at his restraining hands, kicking frantically. He tightened his arm, driving the breath from her lungs. Dark spots danced before her eyes, but still she fought until his arm tightened again, threatening this time to crush her ribs. His other hand grabbed a fistful of hair and yanked her head back to an impossible angle until she cried out.

"I told you I'd enjoy this," he reminded her as he half carried, half dragged her back into the cabin. This time he threw her to the floor. She landed on the packed earth with a thud that jarred a grunt from her. Lying there in a heap, she gasped desperately for breath as Snyder nonchalantly removed his vest and started on his shirt.

Breathing in labored gasps against the pain of her bruised ribs, Angelica cast about for a weapon. The only thing she saw was a cast-iron spider skillet sitting beside the crude stick-and-mud fireplace. Driven as much by instinct as by conscious thought, she scrambled to the fireplace. With hands still cramped, she snatched up the lid to the large frying pan. Putting her weight to it, she threw herself around and let it fly.

"What the . . . ?" Snyder's question ended in a howl of outrage as the lid struck his leg just above the knee and clattered to the floor, barely missing his foot.

Angelica wanted to run again, but she knew he wasn't disabled by the blow. She had to do him more damage than that if she hoped to get away. Grabbing the spider's handle with both hands, she heaved it up as she lunged to her feet.

But he was hurtling toward her like a man possessed, his eyes blazing. Before she could swing the pan, he was on her. His hand went up and came smashing down against her face. The pan crashed to the floor, but he wouldn't let her fall. He held her upright for the next blow and the next.

As he rode, the Kid glanced uneasily at the setting sun. Soon it would be too dark to see, and he wanted to arrive at the line shack in time to get the lay of the land before confronting Ace.

"How much further is it?" he called to Miles.

"A couple more miles," Miles called back.

"I'm getting too old for this," Stumpy grumbled, bringing up the rear of their party.

The Kid squinted into the sun again, trying to judge how much daylight he had left. Enough, perhaps, if they hurried. When he brought his gaze back to the road, he noticed something he had missed before.

"Is that buzzards?" he asked Miles, pointing to the dark shapes circling slowly in the sky up ahead.

"Looks like," Miles replied. "Think we ought to take a look?"

A premonition prickled the hairs on the back of the

Kid's neck. "Yeah, I think we better." The nagging uneasiness he had felt for the past several hours settled into a definite foreboding. Something up ahead was dead, and he knew he would not be pleased to discover what it was.

When they arrived at the area where the birds of prey circled, they split up to search the brush. The search did not take long.

"Over here! It's a man," Miles shouted.

Following the sound of his friend's voice, the Kid rode into a small clearing. Miles was squatting next to a sprawled body.

"Who is it?" Stumpy demanded as he rode up from the opposite direction.

"I'll bet it's our friend Ace, isn't it?" Miles asked grimly. The Kid nodded reluctantly when he'd taken a good look at the man's face. "But he's not quite dead yet," Miles reported. "Stumpy, toss me that canteen."

The Kid swung swiftly from his saddle, bringing along his own canteen, even though it was almost empty. Miles was pulling the cork from Stumpy's canteen when the Kid reached them. The man on the ground gave no indication that he was alive, and from the amount of blood soaking his clothes and the ground around him, the Kid very much doubted he could be. When the Kid came closer, however, he heard the whispered demand for water coming from the barely moving lips.

Miles tilted the canteen carefully, allowing only a few drops to fall on the man's parched tongue. Ace's glazed eyes instantly focused. "Water!" he said more forcefully.

"Just a little, now. Take it easy," Miles said, giving the man a bit more. "Who did this to you?" he asked.

Ace mouthed the moisture for long seconds before replying. "Snyder," he said at last.

"Snyder!" the Kid echoed incredulously. "Why?"

Ace did not reply, or perhaps he simply *could* not reply. Stumpy had dismounted and now stood with them. "Snyder must've found out we was looking for this fella," the old man theorized. "He didn't want to take a chance that we'd get him to talk."

"How did he find out, though?" the Kid demanded, looking down at the wounded man and wishing futilely that he knew of some way to stop the flow of life's blood from the only man who could lead him to those responsible for his sister's death.

Miles looked up from where he still crouched beside the wounded man. "Sunny knew. She must've told him. That would explain why she was so nervous with me," he said, feeling foolish for not having figured it out sooner.

"Yeah, that's it," Ace murmured, his voice little more than a raspy whisper.

"Son of a bitch," the Kid said, a helpless rage building in him. Now how would he ever implicate Snyder in Rose's murder?

Ace was still struggling to speak, and Miles leaned closer to catch the words, which were growing even fainter. "Get Snyder," he was saying, and then he said something the Kid didn't catch.

"Oh, my God!" Miles groaned. "Where are they?"

"Line shack," Ace said.

"Who?" the Kid and Stumpy demanded in unison.

"Snyder has Angelica and Robbie," Miles replied, turning anguished eyes to the Kid.

The impact of Miles's words was like a body blow. The Kid stared back dumbly, unable to speak or even to think as images too horrible to imagine swam before his eyes. His Angelica at the mercy of Harlan Snyder. The rage he had felt seconds ago boiled into a maelstrom of fury. He heard Miles as if from a great distance.

"Damn!" Miles said, slapping his leg in disgust at his own stupidity. "Robbie and Angelica had both disappeared right before supper. Kate sent me out to look for them, and that's when I ran into Sunny. She told me about Ace. . . ." He paused as the last pieces of the puzzle came together. "She must have known Snyder had them, and this was her way of getting us out here without implicating herself," he concluded. Then he saw that the Kid was already mounting his horse. "Wait! We can't just go off half-cocked!" he shouted, running to stop the Kid.

"He's got Angelica," the Kid replied, shaking off Miles's restraining hand. "God only knows how long he's had her and what he's done already." His voice cracked, and he drew in a long hissing breath to settle his fury back into something manageable.

"You can't just go riding up to the cabin. That's a sure way to get them both killed and yourself, too," Miles pointed out. "We need a plan."

"A plan?" the Kid repeated incredulously. "We don't have time to make a plan when Angelica is . . ." The words died in his throat as he gestured off toward where the line shack lay and noticed the dark stain rising against the twilight sky. "What's that?" he asked even as he identified what could only be smoke. "The cabin's on fire!"

In an instant he was on his horse and galloping away. Miles was halfway into his own saddle when he remembered the wounded man. No matter what he'd done, it wasn't decent to leave him to die alone.

As if he had read Miles's thoughts, Stumpy said, "He's gone." The old man leaned over and closed the gunman's eyes. "Let's go," he told Miles when he was finished.

Angelica jerked violently aside to avoid Snyder's next slap. Slipping from his grasp, she fell to the floor again. Her ears ringing from the force of his blows, she rose painfully to all fours and shook her head to clear it. Then she saw the spider. Lying on its side now, it was right in front of her. She could touch it if she reached out her hand.

For a second she hesitated, wondering if she could strike a telling blow this time. Then a kick sent her sprawling facedown on the packed earth floor again. Now the spider was literally under her nose. Without another thought, she reached for it.

Snyder was laughing, amused at her humiliation, at her vulnerability, but he would not be laughing long, she vowed. A rough hand came down and captured a fistful of her dress to haul her upright. He didn't seem to notice she now possessed a weapon. She remained limp until she was on her feet again, and then she came alive in his hands. This time she swung low, aiming for his most vulnerable spot.

She connected. His agonized groan filled the small cabin, and he slumped to the floor. Without waiting to see how much damage she had done, Angelica raced for safety. Snyder's bulk blocked the way, but she hopped over his body without hesitation. She had just cleared his body when something grabbed her ankle and sent her careening into the rickety table that held the lamp and onto the floor again. Vaguely, she was aware that the table had tipped over and the lamp had smashed to the floor, but she couldn't worry over that. Instead, she used all her strength to fight against whatever held her ankle in a viselike grip.

She struggled up, pulling and thrashing furiously against the restriction, but it would not let go. Suddenly, the room lit up as if the sun had broken through a cloud bank. The fire from the broken lamp had chased the spilled coal oil to the bunk where she had lain just moments ago. The straw mattress had burst into flames.

In the brilliant light, she caught sight of Snyder's face twisted in agony but grim with determination nevertheless. It was his hand holding her fast, a hand now possessed of superhuman strength. With a panicked cry, she reached down to pry his fingers loose, but his other hand snatched at her wrist.

"Harlan, let me go! We'll burn to death! Let's get out of here!" she cried, near hysteria as she struggled futilely with his tenacious fingers. The flames had traveled up the wall and now crackled in the rafters. The shack was as dry as tinder. A few more moments were all they had.

Then she heard the horses, running horses, and someone calling her name. Smoke stung her eyes, but she squinted toward the door. "Here! I'm here!" she shouted, prying frantically at Snyder's hands, but still he did not release her. Smoke swirled around her, and the beams above her head creaked ominously.

The Kid raced into the small clearing where the isolated line shack stood. "Robbie! Angelica!" he shouted over and over. Flames danced through holes in the dilapidated roof, and smoke filled the evening sky, swirling through the treetops and obscuring what little light remained. "Angelica!"

Terror twisted inside of him as the scene from his worst nightmares replayed itself before him. In his dreams it was Rose inside the burning house, Rose whom he could not reach in time, but reality was even worse. Rose, at least, had died before the flames touched her, but where were Angelica and the boy? "ROBBIE! ANGELICA!"

Smoke billowed out the door, and a shadowy figure hovered in the opening. "The boy's gone, Collins," Snyder's voice called out. "I sent him to my ranch, but Angelica's in here with me."

"Then let her come out, for God's sake. I won't shoot!" he called back.

"She's tied up. If you let me come out and give me your horse, you can come in and get her. Otherwise, I'll let her burn!"

Snyder's voice was hoarse, as if he were in pain, but the Kid too no time to analyze it. Instead he was straining to catch a glimpse of Angelica through the smoke.

"Is it a deal?" Snyder asked.

"It's a deal. Come on out!"

"Get down off your horse, throw your gun down, and walk away first," Snyder commanded.

Even through the smoke, the Kid could see the pistol in Snyder's hand. Without his own gun, the Kid would be at Snyder's mercy, a quality which Snyder did not possess. It was easy to figure that as soon as the Kid threw down his gun, Snyder would shoot. Only a fool would give him a chance like that, especially when the Kid's death would guarantee Angelica's.

"All right, Snyder," he said, kneeing Midnight around so he could keep the horse between them as he dismounted. Swiftly, he swung down from the saddle. As soon as his feet hit the ground, he reached into his holster and drew out the pistol, flinging it over Midnight's back so Snyder could easily see it from where he stood.

In the distance, he could hear running hooves. Miles

and Stumpy would be here in a minute, but a minute might be too late. The beams of the cabin groaned ominously as the flames burst through the roof in yet another spot. In one swift movement, the Kid threw himself to the ground and rolled clear of Midnight. When he came up, he held his other pistol, but Snyder had not noticed. The rancher was running for Midnight, an awkward, shambling run, and firing as he ran.

One shot, then two. The first whizzed past the Kid's ear and the second kicked up dust beside him. The Kid took careful aim and fired. Snyder's third shot went wild as the bullet entered his brain and he fell backward.

Before Snyder hit the ground, the Kid was up and running. "Angelica!" Twenty feet, then ten to the door, but the groan of the cabin became a roar as the center beam gave way, crashing inward and sending smoke and flame belching from the door.

"Kid, no!" Miles's voice came to him through the smoke as he fought his way toward the cabin, oblivious to the fire and heat. Before he could get there, strong arms caught him and dragged him back. He fought, calling her name, but Miles and Stumpy held him fast.

"It's too late, boy," Stumpy kept saying, over and over. "Can't you see that!"

"No! NO!" the Kid shouted, shaking his fist in fury at the powers that be for allowing such an outrage. It couldn't be too late. If he'd only had a minute, just one more minute, he would have gotten her out. Failing that he would have died with her. Nothing, not even the roaring flames, could be worse than the agony twisting his guts. How could he live knowing he might have saved her? And did he even want to?

Miles and Stumpy dragged him clear of the fire and smoke. Vaguely, he noted Snyder's body as he passed.

The small black hole on his forehead hardly seemed capable of stilling so massive a man, but the look of eternal surprise etched on his features said otherwise.

By the time they reached clean air, all three men were coughing and choking. After a few minutes, when they had recovered, they simply stood numbly, watching the flames devour what remained of the line shack. The sparks that flew upward burned brightly for a few seconds before dying out. For those few seconds they were the color of Angelica's hair.

The Kid closed his eyes, shutting out the sight. He wanted to cry, wanted to break down in complete surrender to this unspeakable grief, but the pain ran too deep even for tears to wash away. As long as he lived, he would carry this agony. Time would dull it, as he knew from experience, but nothing could ever erase it. He had loved the most beautiful woman alive, and he had let her die.

"Angelica," he said aloud. He opened his eyes, and he thought he actually saw her, coming to him through the smoke, her hair the color of the flames that had taken her from him.

Chapter Fourteen

The Kid blinked, but the apparition did not disappear. Instead it came closer and closer still, and then she was there, in his arms, soft and warm and *alive*.

"Oh, Christian," she was saying, "thank God you're all right! I was so scared when they told me you were here and I heard the gunshots. I couldn't have lived if anything had happened to you!" She hugged him fiercely and then lifted her face so she could see his.

He stared down at her in disbelief, still not quite able to accept the fact that she was real. The irony of her statement made the whole thing that much more unbelievable. "Angelica," he said, speaking slowly so as not to frighten her away if she were indeed a vision. "How did you get out of the cabin?"

"Black Bear got me out," she said, glancing over her shoulder to see the Indian emerging from the smoke fog. He rode his scruffy mustang proudly, as if he had just conquered a horde of enemies. Black Bear lifted his hand in greeting, and to the Kid's astonishment, he grinned like a mischievous schoolboy.

"Black Bear? But how . . . ?" The Kid's mind was reeling. "Snyder said you were inside the shack, tied up. He said if I gave him my horse and let him get away, I could get you out. He came out shooting, and by the time I got to the shack, the roof had collapsed and . . ."

He couldn't speak of the rest of it, but he didn't need to. She saw the horror of it in his eyes, and she understood it only too well. "Oh, my darling," she said, letting the tears she had been fighting fall freely now. "I wasn't in there at all. Black Bear had gotten me out before you arrived. You see, one of his braves was hunting, and he saw Snyder and his men tying me up and putting me in the wagon. He rode for help, and the Indians tracked us here."

"Then they set the fire after you were free?" he asked, certain he had the truth of it at last.

"No. You see, Snyder and I were fighting, and . . ." She felt him stiffen as he pulled back and noticed her bruised face for the first time. "Nothing happened," she assured him hastily. "He was going to rape me, but it never came to that. I hit him with a cast-iron spider so he couldn't have done anything anyway." She paused, too embarrassed to dwell on that detail.

The Kid nodded his understanding. That explained Snyder's odd, shambling run as he left the cabin. "Go on. You were fighting with Snyder, and . . ."

"And we knocked over the table where the lamp was. It broke and set the place on fire. I tried to get out, but Snyder grabbed me and wouldn't let go. I think he wanted me to burn alive." She shuddered at the memory, and he pulled her closer, instinctively offering comfort. "Just when I thought I'd never get away, Black Bear showed up. He was calling me, except he was calling me Burns-like-embers. I was half-hysterical by then, but I still recognized my Indian name and answered him. He came charging into the cabin and got me out."

Angelica would never forget the sight of the Indian appearing in the doorway like some avenging angel. He had kicked Snyder aside and dragged her outside. By the time Snyder had drawn his gun and started shooting at them, they were riding at a dead run to safety. "We didn't get very far away before one of Black Bear's men intercepted us to tell me that you had just ridden up and were calling for me. We started back right away, and then we heard the shots. . . ."

She shuddered, remembering all the things she had imagined on the interminable ride back. "Thank God nothing happened to you," she whispered.

"Thank God nothing happened to you, either," he replied, pulling her close again.

Over her head, he saw Black Bear still grinning. "I owe you another life, my friend," he said in Comanche.

The Indian proudly nodded his agreement. Then the Kid became aware that Stumpy and Miles had come close. Stumpy was blowing his nose suspiciously, and even Miles's eyes seemed moist.

"We're real glad you're all right, miss," Stumpy said when he had composed himself.

Angelica released her death grip on Christian a bit and smiled at the old man. "Thank you, Stumpy," she said with a small smile.

"You gave us quite a scare, young lady," Miles told her with mock sternness.

"I know," she admitted, her smile growing. "I'll try my best not to let it happen again."

Miles nodded his understanding. "I guess Robbie got away when you did," he added, having almost forgotten about the boy in all the excitement.

Angelica's smile vanished. "No, he's not here at all. Snyder sent him back to his ranch with that man, Jake Evans." She turned back to Christian. "We have to go after him."

Christian exchanged a look with Miles before replying. "We will, but first we need to get you back to town. I don't think Robbie's in any danger, not with Snyder out of the way. Evans will simply hold him until he gets some more instructions from Snyder, and that isn't going to happen," he explained grimly, looking off over her shoulder.

Angelica followed his gaze to where the rancher's body lay. She shuddered again, recalling only too vividly the way she had fought for her life such a short time ago. It was hard to believe that one small bullet had been able to stop so evil a force as Harlan Snyder. They would probably never know the full extent of the suffering he had caused, but they could take comfort in knowing it was over now.

Stumpy cleared his throat to draw everyone's attention back to more practical matters. "I reckon we'd better get on back to town right quick now. What do you want to do with the bodies?"

"Bod*ies?*" Angelica echoed, puzzled.

"Snyder killed that man Ace back up the road a ways," the Kid informed her.

"Why?" she asked, unable to believe yet another tragedy. Although she could not feel sorry for the man, his murder made no sense.

The Kid shrugged. "Snyder must've figured it was safer to have him out of the way. Anyhow, Stumpy is right, we'd better be going. I guess we should take the bodies, too. We can pack them in the wagon."

Black Bear and his braves helped load Snyder and Ace into the wagon. Angelica did not want to ride with the bodies, but now that the excitement was over, she was beginning to feel the effects of the beating Snyder had given her. Seeing her growing discomfort, Christian took her up in front of him on his own horse so he could cradle her against the worst of the jarring she must endure on the long ride back to town.

Everyone kept assuring Angelica that Robbie was perfectly safe, so by the time she and Christian had put a little distance between themselves and the wagon with its unfortunate burden, Angelica's mind, at least, was calm. If her body ached, she could bear it, knowing how much worse she might have been hurt. She clung to Christian, grateful that his mere presence had the power to allay even her nagging worries about her brother and make her fccl really safe at last.

"I'm so glad you weren't hurt," she told him again when they had ridden for a while.

The Kid kissed her forehead in response, unable yet to speak his gratitude at having her with him once again. "What I can't figure is how Snyder thought he'd get away with kidnapping you. Didn't he know that he'd lose the respect of every decent person alive by doing that?"

"I doubt he'd thought that far ahead," Angelica explained from the comfort of his shoulder. "His plan was to kill *you*. He was only using me and Robbie as a lure to draw you into a trap. He seemed to think all his problems would be over if you were out of the way."

The Kid went cold at her words. Her association with him was what had put her in danger! All the reasons why they should not be together came rushing back to him. He wasn't good enough for her. He was a killer. He would only bring her shame. Now he had yet another to add to the list: his love put her in danger, too.

Angelica Ross was the most precious person in the world to him. Only now when he had so recently suffered the agonies of losing her did he realize exactly how precious she was. How could he possibly stay with her when he knew the full extent of evil he would bring to her life?

The answer, of course, was that he couldn't.

Before he could more than form that thought, he was

distracted by a group of riders approaching at a gallop. He was reaching for his gun when he recognized some of the men from town. They had recognized him and Angelica, too, and were calling and waving furiously.

"You're brother's safe, Miss Angelica!" one man called, managing to make himself heard above the others.

Angelica gave a joyous cry as the riders reined up around them. "What happened? Where is he?" she demanded.

"That fellow Evans turned him loose right outside of town," another man explained. "The boy went running over to Mrs. Marsden's house and told her and Maria the whole story. Seems like Snyder ordered Evans to take the boy back to his ranch, but Evans started having second thoughts. He told Robbie to get up a posse and go rescue you, so that's what we done," he added, making a gesture to include the entire group.

"Thank heaven he's safe," Angelica breathed, weak with relief.

"What happened to Evans?" Christian wanted to know.

"We figured he either went back to Snyder's ranch or lit out completely. You reckon we oughta go find out?"

The Kid nodded. Behind them, Miles and the wagon were catching up. He turned in the saddle. "Robbie's been found," he informed his friends. "Seems like Evans had an attack of conscience and took him to town. Miles, will you take Angelica back? I want to join these fellows for a look-see at Snyder's, though I have a feeling the place'll be deserted by the time we get there."

Angelica gave him a worried look as he passed her a gently as possible into Miles's arms, but he reassured her with a few words, promising to return as soon as possible.

Keeping that promise was easier than he had imagined. As predicted, Snyder's ranch was deserted. Apparently, Evans had returned to warn the other men that Snyder had finally gone too far.

When the Kid returned to town late that night, he found that an exhausted Robbie and Angelica had been put to bed by Kate and Maria. After a happy reunion, the two former captives were sleeping soundly. Knowing Angelica was in capable hands, the Kid joined the rest of his men, who had been summoned from the ranch too late to join the posse, and they all bedded down at the livery stable.

The Kid knew he should have had no trouble sleeping after the long hours he had spent in the saddle that day, but each time he closed his eyes, he saw the flames from the burning cabin blazing into the color of Angelica's hair. Once again, he experienced the throbbing ache of loss as he relived those awful moments when he had thought her dead. Was putting her in that kind of danger worse than leaving her completely? Unfortunately, he did not know.

Angelica awoke the next morning stiff, sore, and black and blue, but she was too grateful to be alive to spend much time on regrets. Kate provided her with a steamy bath that helped restore her somewhat. By the time Christian came to call on her, she was feeling almost human again.

The Kid couldn't quite believe how beautiful she looked in the morning light. Her green eyes literally sparkled with hope and joy, but the dark bruises that stained her face were grim reminders of the ordeal she had gone through less than twenty-four hours ago.

She came to his arms as naturally as if she had always

belonged there, and he enfolded her in his embrace, unable to deny her the comfort she needed. But even as he pulled her close, he felt the heavy burden of duty. He couldn't allow her to be hurt again, not like that and certainly not because of him. His own pain made him rough, and the kiss he gave her verged on desperation.

When she pulled away, her eyes were puzzled, but there was no time for questions. Robbie had descended on them.

"Angel said you killed Snyder. Tell me how it happened!" he begged, pulling the Kid into the parlor. "Tell me everything!"

The boy had obviously recovered completely from his kidnapping and now considered the whole episode an adventure. The Kid could not make such a transition so quickly. "He was shooting at me. I didn't have any choice," he hedged, finding he had no patience for the subject, especially not when he still carried the taste of Angelica on his lips.

"Did you think we burned up in the cabin?" Robbie asked, drawing the Kid down on the sofa next to him.

A remnant of the rage the Kid had felt surged to life momentarily as he saw again the scene that had haunted his dreams the night before. "Snyder told me you were gone, but I did think Angelica was inside, yes," he replied reluctantly.

"Robbie," Angelica cautioned, taking a seat nearby. "I don't think Mr. Collins wants to discuss this."

"But I missed the good part!" Robbie protested. Then he turned back to the Kid. "Did you really shoot Snyder right between the eyes?"

Angelica saw Christian wince at the question. "Robbie, that's enough!" she told him sharply. She knew how much Christian hated killing, and she wouldn't allow even her beloved brother to torment him about it. "Mr.

Collins did what had to be done. I told you the whole story. Now leave the poor man alone."

Robbie's freckled face screwed up in humiliation at the rebuke. He turned humble eyes to his idol. "I'm sorry, Mr. Collins," he said meekly.

"That's all right, son," the Kid assured him, laying a hand on the boy's thin shoulder. "I'm still feeling a little shaky from yesterday, that's all. Maybe I'll tell you about it later."

The promise pacified the boy somewhat even as the admission of shakiness astonished him. "All right," he agreed reluctantly.

The Kid took pity on him then. "Now tell me all about what happened to you. I never did hear how you got away from Jake Evans."

Robbie's eyes lit up again, and his dejected expression evaporated into a grin. "Well, it was like this," he began, eagerly explaining how he and Jake had found Ace's horse with blood on its saddle. "I didn't know what that meant then, but he must've, because that's when he told me he was going to take me to town and let me go. I begged him to go back for Angelica, but I guess he didn't want to face down Snyder after what he did to Ace."

"I guess not," the Kid agreed solemnly, a little amazed at Robbie's perception.

Angelica had heard enough rehashing of the previous day's adventures. "How soon can we go home, Christian?" she wanted to know.

He looked up, a little startled at the sudden change in topic. "You can go right now if you want to," he replied, unconsciously changing her "we" to "you" as he mentally began the process of separating himself from Angelica and the Diamond R. It was going to be an agonizing process, he knew, much like cutting out his heart with a dull knife, but it was something that must be done if he was to protect Angelica from all the evil he was destined to bring into her life if he stayed.

Angelica did not seem to notice his verbal distancing, however. Her smile was radiant.

"Let's go, then," she said, thinking how happy she would be when her life returned to normal. Now, however, "normal" included Christian. They would be married as soon as possible since there was no longer any reason to wait. They would be together forever with no threats or dangers to mar their happiness. She wondered idly how long it would take before such bliss erased all memory of Harlan Snyder from her mind. "Robbie, go tell Maria to start packing. I want to go *home!*"

The packing took longer than expected, so it was late afternoon before the caravan of horses and wagons returned to the Diamond R. All day long, Angelica had been fighting a feeling of uneasiness. It had started with Christian's strange kiss that morning, and he had been awfully reticent ever since. She tried to put it down to some mysterious aftereffect from the day before. She, herself, still felt unsettled and jumpy. If Christian seemed unusually subdued, he was probably only suffering from the same malady. Once they were back in familiar surroundings, she was certain things would return to normal.

To Angelica's dismay, however, supper that evening was a surprisingly quiet event, when it should have been a joyous celebration. For the first time in longer than she cared to remember, she felt truly safe. That fact alone should have made her happy, she reasoned, but reason played no part in the mood of the people gathered around the Diamond R dining room table. They were acting as if they were attending a wake.

Perhaps they were only being considerate, she reasoned. Perhaps they were experiencing the same letdown she was after the weeks of vigilance. She glanced down the long table to where Christian sat opposite her, hoping to see at least a trace of the happiness she wanted so desperately to feel. Instead his eyes were guarded, as if he had some secret he must conceal from her

Angelica tried to dismiss the notion as fanciful, but instead she felt a slight panic at the thought. Christian had said nothing, done nothing to indicate he had changed his mind about the promises he had made to her. Why then was she beginning to believe that he had?

In silent panic, she replayed all their conversations since the moment she had rushed into his arms outside the burning cabin. What had he said or done to make her doubt him? Nothing, she had to confess, and yet she was growing more certain with every passing moment that something was terribly wrong between them.

She glanced around the table again. The others were settling back in their chairs, having finished their meals. In a few moments the men would leave, moving outside for a smoke. After that, they would leave for good. Not tonight, of course but in a day or two, they would pack up and head out. Harley and Sanders would return to the Circle M, Miles would be moving into town as soon as he and Kate could be married, and Stumpy would head for parts unknown.

And what about Christian? What would he do? Instinct told Angelica *she* must do something, say something to stop this exodus, to keep things just as they were, just as they had been, in order to prevent Christian from making the move she somehow sensed he planned to make.

Rising from her chair with an air of purpose that drew every eye, she cleared her throat importantly. "I know none of you wants to hear a speech, but I do want to tell you how much I appreciate everything you've done for me and Robbie and for the Diamond R," she began, improvising as she went. "I've grown awfully used to having you around, so I want you all to know that you'll always have a place here, not only in my heart but on my ranch." She paused a moment, searching for the proper words while her audience waited in fascinated silence.

"What I'm trying to say is that all of you will have a job here at the Diamond R for as long as you want it." She was vaguely aware of the murmurs of surprise but she went doggedly on. "Now I know some of you have other plans that will still keep you close," she said, giving Miles a small smile, "but I truly hope the rest of you will choose to stay on here."

She hoped her desperation did not show in her voice or her face. She was beginning to feel like the boy in the fairy tale with his finger in the dike. For some reason she felt that if she let even one of these men get away, she would lose Christian. It was irrational, she knew, but she also knew it was true.

"That's a right generous offer, Miss Ross," Stumpy said as she sank back into her chair. "Especially for an old codger like me who ain't got too many good years left. I'm right grateful."

"I'm grateful to you, too, Stumpy," Angelica reminded him. A silence fell then as everyone waited for someone else to speak. Angelica watched Christian's face, but he was keeping his expression carefully blank. After what seemed like a long time, he said, "Like Stumpy says, your offer is mighty generous. I reckon some of us won't be able to take you up on it, though."

His words cut into her like the sharp edge of a knife, robbing her of thought and speech for a moment. As if in a dream, she watched him rise from his chair and leave the room. She sensed the wave of sympathy that rose up around her, but she could not respond to it, not yet. The pain was still too great.

Tactfully, the others began to leave, too. She heard Robbie's voice ask, "What's going on?," and Stumpy murmured a reply as he led the boy from the room. At last only she and Maria remained.

"What did he mean, Mama?" she asked, hoping with the last shred of her faith that she had misunderstood.

"I think you know what he meant, *Angelita.* I warned you that this might happen," Maria reminded her with profound regret.

"No!" Angelica protested, lunging to her feet. "You warned me that he might not love me, but he *does* love me, I know he does!"

"Then why would he leave you?" Maria asked, her dark eyes full of the pain she felt for Angelica's loss.

"I don't know," Angelica admitted as anger flooded out her own pain, "but I'm going to find out." With that she shoved aside her chair and stormed out of the room in search of Christian Collins.

She found him in the courtyard, standing by the fountain. His back was to her, and although he must have heard her shoes clicking angrily against the tiles, he did not turn to face her, but continued to stare at the trickling water.

Angelica's step slowed as she drew near and saw the implacable set of his shoulders. The fury that had carried her here cooled in the wake of an icy fear that gripped her heart as she stopped beside him. His face was an expressionless mask. "Christian?" she whispered, not knowing what else to say.

She watched his eyes close for an instant, as if hearing his name had caused him a spasm of physical pain. "I always used to hate that name," he said, still not looking at her. He continued to stare at the water. "My mother was real religious, and she named me when my pa was off on a trip one time. I always thought she did it to make him mad. It worked, too. He never called me by that name, not as long as he lived. He always called me Kid."

"Oh," Angelica said, aware of how ridiculous it was to discuss his name when they had so many more important things to discuss. "I always thought that . . ."

"You always thought that I earned the name, like Billy the Kid," he finished for her.

"Yes," she said, wondering if she should grab his arm and force him to look at her. Then, at last, he turned toward her, but his eyes were so bleak, so hopeless that her heart convulsed in agony.

"It was like fate, Angelica. I already had the name, so I had to earn the reputation to go with it. Kid Collins, Gunfighter. It was easy, too easy. It started in a saloon in Fort Worth. Some tinhorn gambler tried to cheat me, and when I called him on it, he drew. We both emptied our guns. When the smoke cleared, he was dead and I didn't have a mark on me. I never even knew his name."

"Christian, don't," she begged him, reaching out to comfort him, but he shook off her hand.

"You have to hear this, Angelica. You have to understand. The next time it was a man who insulted me, or at least I thought he did. I can't even remember now what he said or didn't say that made me think I had to kill him. It was senseless and stupid, but I was just a kid, and I thought I had to defend my honor." He made a derisive noise in his throat. *Honor.*" He spat out the word as if it left a vile taste in his mouth. "After that . . ."

"No!" she cried, clutching at him as tears blurred her vision. "I don't want to hear this. I told you before, none of it matters anymore! You aren't like that now. You're a grown man now who doesn't need to prove anything . . . ."

"That's where you're wrong," he told her, rigid and unresponsive under her hands. "I thought that, too, at first. I loved you so much, I wanted to believe it was true, but then Rivers came along and brought it all back. He reminded me of who I really am."

"But Snyder hired him to kill you. That's the only reason . . ."

"No, it's not the *only* reason. You heard the judge that day at the trial. He hit it right on the head. Rivers had been paid to kill me, but he took the job because he wanted to be the man to kill Kid Collins."

"But Rivers is dead," she argued. "He can't hurt us anymore."

"You don't understand. There's a hundred more just like Rivers out there, waiting for their chance. One of them'll be along, sooner or later. Maybe next week, maybe next year, but he'll be here. Then I'll have to kill him or be killed by him."

"You don't have to fight!" she insisted. "You can walk away . . ."

"Like I did with Rivers?" He looked down into her eyes, eyes so full of love and pain he could hardly bear it. For her love, he might even be willing to play the coward and turn away from a fight, but what good would that do when there were men like Rivers willing to shoot him in the back? He had to face it: there was simply no escape from who and what he was.

"Angelica," he said, resisting with difficulty the urge to take her in his arms. "I can't drag you into this. You've already been hurt enough. I can't let you get hurt any more."

"*You* can't let me!" she repeated in outrage, giving him

a shake. "And how do you propose to stop me? For your information, I'm already in this up to my eyebrows, and the only way you can hurt me any more is by walking out of my life!"

"You don't know what your life would be like if I stayed with you," he told her, knowing he had to make her understand even though he felt as if his own heart were being torn from his chest. "People whispering behind their hands, pointing at you because your husband is a killer. Your kids not being able to go to school because the other kids spit on them and call them ugly names. Even in church, they pretend you aren't there and walk right by without speaking."

His eyes stared past her into a distant time. She knew he was telling her of things he himself had suffered, but he was wrong and she had to make him understand. "Christian, I'm not your mother, and you aren't a Comanchero. Nobody is Marsden's Corners is going to snub me because my husband killed a snake like Harlan Snyder or even a little worm like Tom Rivers."

Something flickered in his eyes, something cold and cynical that made her draw back as his lips stretched into a mirthless smile. "Maybe you're right," he allowed. "Maybe we can live happily ever after, at least until the next two-bit gunnie rides into town and makes you a widow."

Her heart felt like stone inside her chest, cold and dead. He was right, of course, that danger would always exist. It would hang over them like the executioner's ax, ready to strike when they least expected it. The very thought of losing him that way was like a wrenching agony, and yet the thought of never having him at all was even worse. Could she make him believe that?

"Christian," she tried, grabbing him again as if she could get through to him with physical force. "What if I told you I was sick, very sick? What if I told you that in six months I'd be dead? Would you leave me?"

"No," he said with a frown. "Of course not."

"You'd stay with me, wouldn't you?" she asked eagerly. "You'd cherish every day we had together, even though it might be the last, wouldn't you? In fact, that would make each minute of our time together that much more precious, wouldn't it?"

He nodded, his eyes still wary, not quite understanding.

"Don't you see? You're telling me that you might die—*might* die, mind you—and so you're going to leave me now and cheat me out of whatever time we might have had together."

"Dying of a sickness and getting killed in a gunfight are two different things."

"Only in your mind," she countered. She was fighting for her future now, and nothing would stop her. "You're afraid you might shame me somehow, make my life hard after you're gone, but what do you think my life will be like if you leave me now?"

"You'd have the ranch and Robbie and . . ." he faltered, hearing how empty it sounded and knowing how empty his own world would be without her. The idea took hold in his mind. Was it possible that leaving her would be more cruel than staying with her? Could she love him that much?

She saw the question on his face. "I love you, you idiot. What more do I have to do to prove it to you? I'm going to say this one last time and then never again: I don't care who you are or what you've done or who your family was. None of that matters to us. I love you, and I want to be your wife for as long as we both shall live, whether that's a long time or a short time. There aren't any guarantees in this world. We have to take whatever little bit of happiness comes our way and hold on tight. So if you try to leave me, I swear I'll follow you. I'll follow you to the ends of the earth. You'll never get away from me, Christian Collins!"

She was right, he knew she was. He felt his resistance cracking like a shell that had been covering him. Little by little, as if he were emerging from that shell, his spirit worked free from the restraints of his old fears. Looking down into her face, at the spirit and determination that had won his admiration even before she had won his love, he realized that she really wasn't like his mother at all. She would never hang her head, never let people shame her. Nothing and no one could ever hurt her unless he left her alone. He was the only person in the world who could cause her the kind of suffering he most feared for her. The irony was that he would have caused it with his misguided effort to protect her. She had called him an idiot, and she was right about that, too.

"Angelica," he said, lifting a hand to brush one fiery curl away from her cheek. "I can't understand why you love me so much, but," he continued when she would have interrupted him, "since you do, I'm going to grab it and hang on tight."

It took a second for his words to register, but when they did, Angelica gave a joyous cry and flung herself at him. He crushed her to him, finding her mouth with his in a kiss that went on and on until both of them were weak and breathless. Desire flared as eager hands encountered the frustrating barrier of clothing, and bodies pressed close but not close enough.

At last Angelica broke free, backing away but with the glint of mischief in her glorious green eyes. At first he did not understand her intent, but he followed her nevertheless, drawn inexorably. Then she whispered, "Just like the first time," and turned and ran, straight toward her bedroom.

He hesitated only an instant. She was closing the door as he reached it, but she was laughing, that joyous, unrestrained laughter that he loved so well but heard so seldom. When he reached the door, she was already on the bed. He pushed the door shut, and in another instant, he was there beside her, catching her laughter with his kiss, drinking it in as if it were a lifegiving elixir.

Seeking hidden treasures, they torc away each other's clothes with hands made clumsy by haste, until at last they lay heart to heart as God had made them. He hesitated when he saw her bruises, silent reminders of her ordeal with Snyder.

"I don't want to hurt you." he said, needing her more than he would have thought possible but loving her too much to cause her pain.

Angelica only smiled. "You'll never hurt me," she replied, sliding her arms around his neck. She welcomed him to her, certain that their love could withstand any trial that might come. He came to her with a promise of forever, as long as that might be.

Hands worshipped, lips adored, and desire blazed into white-hot passion as their bodies melded into one. Love words breathed in fever kisses told of hopes and dreams fulfilled. With fear's bonds finally broken, they loved with abandon, giving until there was nothing left to give.

A long time later, Christian asked, "Am I too heavy?" He had slid to one side, but their bodies were still joined below, neither of them wanting to break the physical contact that symbolized their commitment.

"Yes, you weigh a ton," she informed him impishly, "but don't you dare move!"

He smiled, rising up on one elbow so he could study her beloved face. The bruises were still there, but when he looked into her eyes, he could forget all the ugliness that had gone before and all his worries for the future. His fingers brushed damp curls away, and he frowned in mock concern. "Uh-oh," he teased. "I reckon we'd better send for a preacher first thing in the morning."

She lifted her eyebrows in surprise. "And why should we do that?" she inquired.

"Because," he said, suppressing a grin, "Anybody who takes one look at that satisfied expression on your face will know exactly what we've been up to, and I, for one, don't want to get lynched by that bunch of protective cowboys that work for you."

Angelica pretended to consider. "You're absolutely right," she replied, surprising him. "One look at *your* satisfied expression, and they'll know *exactly* who to hang!"

Before he could pretent to be outraged, however, she continued. "But you don't have to send for a preacher."

He frowned again. "And why not?" he asked skeptically.

"Because we already have a preacher right here," she said. His frown did not clear, and she realized he did not have a clue. "I believe some people call him Parson Black," she added.

"Miles?" he asked incredulously. His astonishment made her laugh.

"Yes, Miles," she replied. "I promised him he could marry us."

"And when was this?" he asked suspiciously, wondering at what point Miles had broached the subject with her.

"Oh," she said, pretending to search her memory. "I believe it was while we were doing the roundup. It was the funniest thing . . ."

"The roundup! You mean you'd already decided way back them?" he demanded.

"Oh, no," she assured him outrageously. "I decided the very first day you got here, when I saw that beautiful body of yours buck naked. . . ."

"What!"

"Oh, yes," she confirmed smugly. "I sneaked a peek in spite of Maria's efforts to shield me from the awful truth. Have I shocked you?" she asked with feigned concern.

His reply was an incoherent growl as he levered himself over her again. "Angelica Ross, you are by far the most exasperating woman alive," he declared.

"Don't you approve?" she asked innocently, wrapping her legs around his as she felt him quicken inside of her.

"I'm thinking it over," he replied as his mouth closed over hers.

Epilogue

In the end, all of Angelica's "hired guns" decided to stay in Marsden's Corners, although Stumpy was the only one who took Angelica up on her offer to stay at the ranch. The old man lived out his remaining years as one of the Diamond R's most loyal hands.

Harley and Sanders decided to try their hand at ranching themselves. The two went into partnership and settled on a portion of what had once been Snyder's extensive holdings. Angelica protested, pointing out that their ranch was much too small to support one family, much less *two* families, and if the men ever married, they would regret their decision.

Christian explained to her that there was absolutely no possibility that either Harley or Sanders would ever wish to marry. Although Angelica found it difficult to believe the two men actually preferred each other's company to that of a woman, she finally came to accept it.

Miles married Kate Marsden, of course. To everyone's surprise, he took to storekeeping with a natural flair and became somewhat of a leader in the community. When the railroad came to West Texas, he managed to win a spur line for Marsden's Corners, ensuring the town's future prosperity. In later years, he established the first bank in town. It went down in history as the only bank in Texas that was never robbed—at least not in Miles's lifetime. When the Baptists got around to building a church nearby, Miles Blackmon became the first deacon. Only then did Kate declare him officially civilized.

Christian married Angelica in a lavish ceremony attended by everyone within a hundred miles, and shortly thereafter, Kid Collins died.

It happened one lazy summer afternoon. Stumpy was relaxing in the Dirty Dog Saloon when a stranger wandered in. Stumpy knew him for a gunfighter the moment he set eyes on him, but the old man kept his opinions to himself, pretending a great interest in the beer Otis had set before him.

The stranger ordered a beer of his own. When he'd downed about half of it, he looked up at Otis and said, "Say, isn't this the town where Kid Collins settled?"

Otis had never openly taken sides in the previous conflict, but when it was over, he had expressed his own relief over Snyder's death, as did the rest of the townsfolk. He looked upon the people of the Diamond R as valuable customers, too valuable to offend. Otis's small eyes grew even smaller as he glanced at Stumpy for a cue as to what he should say. The stranger's gaze followed the bartender's, and Stumpy looked up at the young man with interest.

"That's right, sonny," the old man replied, enjoying the annoyance that flickered across the young man's face. "Kid Collins did settle here a while ago, but he's gone now."

The young man frowned. "You mean he left?"

"Not exactly," Stumpy hedged, looking to Otis for inspiration, but the portly bartender just shrugged helplessly. "See, it's like this, he . . . he died," Stumpy improvised.

"Died? Did somebody gun him down? I hadn't heard . . ."

"Oh, no, nothing like that," Stumpy assured the stranger. "You might say he did himself in."

"Suicide?" The young man was aghast.

Otis went into a coughing fit, but Stumpy ignored him, warming to the story now that it had sprung full-blown into his head. "You could call it that, I reckon," Stumpy allowed, "although most folks around here don't like to say the word. The poor fella just couldn't take it no more, being such a famous gunslinger and all. Somebody tried to backshoot him, and he never quite got over it. He couldn't stand the strain of waiting for it to happen again, I guess." Stumpy shook his head sadly and took another sip of his beer.

"I'll be damned," the young man muttered, draining his glass. "Poor bastard."

Otis had recovered and now managed to present a semblance of calm. "Another beer?" he inquired.

The young man looked down at the empty glass for a long moment and then shook his head. "No, thanks. I reckon I'll be on my way. No reason to stay around here now anyhow."

With that, he turned on his heel and strode out of the saloon. Stumpy did not dare meet Otis's eye until he had heard the stranger's horse ride away.

"I'll be damned," Otis said, cocking Stumpy a wry look.

Stumpy shrugged in a parody of Otis's previous action. "It's pretty much true, ain't it?" he argued. "Kid Collins is deader than a doornail."

"He is now," Otis agreed.

That evening Stumpy and Otis gleefully told the story of how Stumpy had hornswoggled the would-be gunfighter. Soon the tale achieved mythic proportions, and every man in the county wished for the opportunity to best Stumpy as a liar. From time to time they found a chance to do so. Word traveled fast in the West, but still there were some who had not heard of Kid Collins's "demise." When they reached Marsden's Corners, however, they heard the ever more lavishly embellished story of how Kid Collins had done himself in. Even Kate Marsden Blackmon once had an opportunity to regale a visitor with the details.

Consequently, a generation of children grew up in Marsden's Corners who were ignorant of Christian "Kid" Collins's true history. One of these children was playing on the sidewalk on an autumn morning when a stranger asked if he knew where Kid Collins lived.

The boy squinted off into the distance as he tried to place the name, and he caught sight of Mr. Collins coming across the street carrying his young son on his shoulders. Little Cameron was a kid, wasn't he? the boy reasoned. His last name was Collins, too. "There he is," the boy informed the stranger, pointing at the three-year-old.

The young man turned to see a prosperous-looking rancher dressed in what was probably his "town" suit. The redheaded child that straddled his shoulders was pounding the daylights out of what had once been a very attractive Stetson, but the rancher seemed only amused at the child's antics.

"Are you Collins?" the stranger asked doubtfully. God Almighty, the fellow wasn't even packing a gun! He couldn't possibly be Kid Collins.

"Yeah, that's right," Christian assured him, swinging his son down and settling the boy on his hip. The child grinned at the stranger, who stared back as if he had never seen a young boy before. "But if you're looking for work, I've got a full crew right now. You might try the H & S outfit. I think they could use somebody," Christian suggested.

The stranger blinked, looking at the man and then the boy and then back at the man again. Somebody had made a serious mistake, and he was beginning to think he might be the one. "Yeah, uh, thanks," he muttered.

"There's Papa," he heard a woman's voice call, and the rancher turned toward the sound. "Go show him what you got," the woman urged a little girl with long blond curls. The woman was tall, and she had the reddest hair he had ever seen.

The little girl came skipping across the street toward them. "Look, Papa! Mama bought me a new dress," she told the rancher, holding out her skirt for him to admire.

"Rose, I was talking to the gentleman. It's rude to interrupt," the rancher chastened her gently.

She grinned up at the stranger and said, " 'Scuse me," very prettily. She dropped him a curtsey. That was the last straw. Nothing in his experience had prepared him for a scene like this, when he was really looking for a fight.

"I, uh, I guess I'll be going," the stranger stammered, backing away.

Christian watched in amazement as the man fairly ran down the street toward where his horse was tied. In another minute he was galloping away.

"Who was that?" Angelica inquired as she joined the rest of her family.

Christian did not answer her for a long moment. He was staring at the cloud of dust the stranger's horse had left behind as if it held some secret message.

"Christian, is something wrong?" she asked when he did not respond.

"That, my dear Angelica, was a gunfighter," he said at last.

"What!" she cried, turning back for another look, even though the man had long since disappeared from sight.

"Hey, Tommy," Christian called to the boy playing marbles nearby. "I saw you talking to that fellow. What was he saying?"

The boy shrugged. "He asked me if I knew where Kid Collins lived, so I pointed out Cam to him."

Christian nodded. His son Cameron was squirming, so he set the boy on his feet. The child was off in an instant to examine Tommy's marbles.

"Papa, don't you like my new dress?" Rose asked impatiently.

Christian glanced down at the child, whose beauty never ceased to amaze him. "It's real pretty," he said. "Makes you look like a grown-up lady. And since you're so grown-up, why don't you go buy a stick of candy for yourself and your brother," he added, handing her a penny.

With a hasty "Thank you, Papa," the girl was off. When they stood alone, Angelica turned worried eyes to him. "A gunfighter! What happened?"

"Nothing," he replied in amazement. "I didn't even realize it until he took off. How could I have been so stupid?" he asked of no one in particular. "All the signs were there, the fancy clothes, the tied-down guns, the wary eyes . . ." His voice trailed off as his gaze wandered again to the rapidly settling dust cloud that was all that remained of the gunfighter. "I didn't even realize it," he repeated incredulously.

"He didn't call you out? He didn't try to pick a fight?" Angelica insisted.

Christian shook his head, still staring off into the distance.

"Christian, don't you see what this means?" Angelica demanded, forcing his attention back to her.

"I'm not sure that I do," he admitted with a self-mocking grin.

"It means that Kid Collins really *is* dead!" Seeing his skepticism, she took his arm, needing to convey the importance of her discovery. "Think about it. You didn't recognize him. That means that you've finally been able to wipe that portion of your life out of existence. You don't even think that way anymore. And *he* didn't recognize *you!*"

"He probably never saw me before," Christian argued.

"No, I mean he could tell by looking at you that you weren't the man he was after. You just aren't Kid Collins anymore!"

"Who am I then?" he asked as understanding gradually dawned.

"You," she told him smugly, "are a very civilized, very straitlaced, and probably very boring husband, father and rancher.

"Boring!" he protested as she slipped her arm through his and directed him back to the store into which their daughter had disappeared.

"Well, maybe not boring," she allowed. "If you were, I probably wouldn't be expecting another child. . . ."

"Angelica! When did you find out?"

Rose appeared in the doorway of the store and called, "Cam, I've got a peppermint stick for you!"

The small boy tore across the deserted street, almost knocking his mother down in his rush.

"Cam, be careful!" Christian yelled at his oblivious son. "Are you all right?" he asked Angelica solicitously.

"Good heavens, yes," she replied, rolling her eyes. "You aren't going to go crazy on me again like you did the other two times, are you? I promise, I won't break."

"I'll try to behave myself," he promised, but he took her arm and conducted her to the sidewalk with a caution that belied his words. At her chastening look, he shrugged apologetically. "I can't help it. I just can't stand the thought of anything happening to you."

"Nothing is going to happen to me as long as you're with me," she said. As always, whenever she spoke of their future together, a shadow clouded his eyes, but this time Angelica knew his fears—those for himself at least—were groundless. She gave his arm a reassuring squeeze. "When are you going to believe that it's all over?"

His face reflected his initial confusion, but slowly his expression cleared. "Kid Collins really is dead, isn't he?" he asked, as if that were the most amazing thought he had ever had.

"Yes," she confirmed, "and Christian Collins is alive and very well. Now take me inside. I think our third child would like to have a peppermint stick, too."

Author's Note

As soon as my friends read my third book, TEXAS TRIUMPH, they wanted to know, "What happened to Miles and the Kid?" That was where the idea for this book came from. I hope everyone who asked that question is satisfied with the answer. If you missed TEXAS TRIUMPH, be sure to ask your bookstore owner to order a copy for you; you can also get one directly from Zebra Books.

I love to hear from my readers. Please write to me in care of Zebra Books, 475 Park Avenue South, New York, NY 10016, and let me know how you like this book.